P9-CBG-325

An Accurate Watch

An Accurate Watch

DAVID W. DOYLE

William Morrow and Company, Inc.

New York

Recognizing the importance of preserving what has been written, it is the policy of William Morrow and Company, Inc., and its imprints and affiliates to have the books it publishes printed on acid-free paper, and we exert our best efforts to that end.

Library of Congress Cataloging-in-Publication Data

Doyle, David W.
An accurate watch / David W. Doyle.
p. cm.
ISBN 0-688-09054-0
I. Title.
PS3554.097434A65 1990
813'.54—dc20 89-48816
CIP

Printed in the United States of America

First Edition

1 2 3 4 5 6 7 8 9 10

BOOK DESIGN BY CLAUDIA CARLSON

To my dear wife, Hope,
who saved my life and otherwise made
this book possible

Preface

The words *working case officer* are used in the CIA to describe the members of a small band of truly professional craftsmen—perhaps only a few hundred—in the U.S. clandestine services (CS). The CS is the so-called cloak-and-dagger part of the CIA. Its members include the men and women who elect to spend most of their careers overseas, carrying out the business of spotting, assessing, developing, recruiting, and managing espionage and/or covert-action agents.

The working case officer in the CIA may be at any level of seniority, from the newest graduate of the career-trainee program to be bloodied in the field up to the director of central intelligence (DCI) himself. True working case officers use the title with pride; they value it and do not relinqush it no matter how far they rise in the Agency.

The working case officer will serve anywhere. He will work seven days a week, all day and all night if necessary. He is never really on vacation, and never entirely free of risk.

The title of this book comes from a saying in the U.S. clandestine services: A good field case officer always has *an accurate watch, a pocket full of change,* and *an empty bladder*. He needs an accurate watch to get to meetings on time, meetings where lives may be at stake and seconds count. He needs a pocket full of change so that, for example, he can quickly hop on a bus, buy a newspaper, or make a telephone call without having to change paper money into coins. An empty bladder is vital if you're on a stakeout and can't move, or if you're being surveilled and don't care to have your track disturbed by your own body's needs.

The working case officer bases his efforts on those of his agents—men and women of all nationalities, ages, and skills who are the secret, covert agents of the CIA. If his agents are valid, they are always at the risk of losing something they value—most often their own lives, their freedom, or their possessions. If they are not valid, if they in fact work for another service or for themselves, then they are a risk to, and at risk from, the agency they are deceiving. It is a prime function of the case officer to verify the accuracy and reliability of his agents and of the information they give him or the functions they perform for him.

The working case officer, serving as his country's first point of intelligence collection and filtration, must be ruthlessly honest with himself. He must constantly force himself to question the information he receives and the sources from which it comes, no matter how reliable his agents have been in the past. The truth, the most important criterion of good intelligence, eclipses perishability as a gauge of value.

In the 1960s and 1970s, a generation of case officers in the CS were plagued by stories of a mole, whose existence was loudly asserted by a number of competent officers. A number of other officers just as loudly proclaimed that there was no mole. Many took sides, and vitriol was hurled with consummate skill. One very senior officer even had the gall to tell his officers that there "definitely was no KGB mole in the CIA"—an astonishing statement coming from on high.

Thus the mole, whether or not he existed, caused great damage as the debate surged back and forth, costing careers, ruining morale, and shredding reputations. Good operators and operations were choked and poor ones rewarded. The debate spilled into the public domain through the media and the Congress of the United States.

I do not know whether or not there was a KGB mole in the

Soviet division of the CS at any time in the history of the agency. This book is a fictional account, set in 1972–73, of such a mole—what kind of person he might have been, what damage he might have done, and how he might have been trapped and turned around.

Mark Cameron did not exist. Neither villain nor hero, he is an amalgam of many former working case officers. While this tale is fiction, everything in it could happen to any case officer in any country's service, and the essence of espionage—as seen from the viewpoint of the working case officer—is accurately presented. This is the daily life of professionals such as Mark Cameron and Pyotr Petrov, stripped of the romance and mystique that grace the pages of spy thrillers.

It is hoped this story will entertain many former intelligence officers as they see something of themselves in it. Moscow Center will see ghosts and hear creakings that may, or may not, have existed. Young case officers, who need all the compassion and understanding their countrymen can offer, may learn and be encouraged as they laugh at the old guard. It is even possible that the KGB's unwitting helpers in the Western media, political life, and academia may dimly glimpse that their principal enemy was, all along, not the CIA but the greedy, shallow, arrogant, ethics-free, eternally wrong communist bureaucrat and his shield and sword: the KGB and its assigns and satellites.

Intelligence agencies normally use a twenty-four-hour clock. Thus 2400 is midnight, 1200 is midday, 1500 is 3 P.M. and 0300 is 3 A.M. I've used the twenty-four-hour clock for section headings and—for contrast—the twelve-hour clock in the text itself.

For those who aren't familiar with the shorthand or jargon of espionage, there is a glossary at the end of the book; it is intended to define some of the more commonly used intelligence terms. Like most glossaries, it is incomplete and subject to criticism.

For those professionals who may claim that the fictional events I've described are farfetched, I invite you to query your colleagues who served in Africa. They will tell you stories that top mine in the realm of the fantastic, both as regards Africa and as regards what can happen to KGB officers who are stationed there.

—DAVID W. DOYLE

Honolulu

And ye shall know the truth,
and the truth shall make you free.

—JOHN 8:32

*(carved in marble in the entrance lobby
of CIA Headquarters,
Langley, Virginia)*

PART I
August–December 1972
The Scent

Tokyo: The Rumanian Embassy—
0315 hours, 22 August

The entry team, its work complete, cleaned up the walls, floor, and window seats of the Rumanian ambassador's study. There was no trace of the twin binaural microphones they had buried in the wall behind the spot where the ambassador's desk would be placed in the new embassy building.

The plaster had been patched and repainted with odorless matching paint. On the floor no scraps of wood, plaster dust, or tiny wire clippings were left. On the exposed woodwork, no scratches.

Mark Cameron, senior CIA case officer and entry-team leader, made the final inspection with Korekiyo Takahashi. Known as the Cat, Takahashi was a highly experienced audio technician, one of the very best. The other team members waited silently as Mark and the Cat checked where work had been done.

Mark briefly shone his flashlight on his own smiling face as he gave the team thumbs-up and signaled them to start down the long hall for the front door. In five minutes they would be safely outside the embassy compound. There was only the garden to cross. The night watchman had been drugged. His watchdog was fast asleep also, thanks to tranquilized hamburger meat. Over the wall, and it was done. Project GOLD was going to be a solid twenty-four-carat success.

Langley, Virginia: CIA headquarters—
1700 hours, 21 August

The DCI (director of central intelligence) looked at the cable from Tokyo with disbelief. He read it again, now standing at the window. His pipe had gone out; he ignored it. There was no doubt: a routine operation had become a disaster; an officer was dead.

SECRET IMMEDIATE
TOKYO TO HQS 0556 HRS 22 AUG
GOLD

REGRET ADVISE ENTRY TEAM JUMPED BY NIGHT WATCHMAN AND DOG DESPITE DRUG INTAKE. DOG KILLED TECH OFFICER KOREKIYO TAKAHASHI. REST OF TEAM EXITED UNHARMED. NIGHT WATCHMAN BEATEN UNCONSCIOUS, PROBABLY DID NOT REPEAT NOT IDENTIFY TEAM EXCEPT POSSIBLY TAKAHASHI. WATCHMAN ARRIVED AFTER AUDIO GEAR INSTALLED, SITE CLEANED UP. CIRCUMSTANCES SHOULD PERSUADE RUMANIANS THIS WAS LOCAL BURGLARY ATTEMPT.

MARK CAMERON WILL DEPART STATION 1200 HRS 22 AUG ACCOMPANYING WIDOW AND BODY. STOPOVER HONOLULU TO OFFER PROFOUND REGRETS PARENTS AND ATTEND TAKAHASHI FUNERAL. ETA DCA 1939 HRS 23 AUG, WILL REPORT HQS 0830 HRS 24 AUG. FULL REPORT FOLLOWS ASAP. END.

The DCI shook his head. He buzzed his secretary.

"Please get me the DDO, Jane."

Frank Wales, the deputy director for operations, head of the U.S. clandestine services, came on the line.

"You see this Tokyo cable yet, Frank?"

"Yes, Mr. Director. I'm stunned. I've started a crash investigation already, here and in Tokyo. Cameron's coming right home, we'll get details then." Frank Wales was being formal with his old friend, but the DCI was persistent in his anger.

"Any theories? The cable tells us almost nothing."

"Not really, sir. Obviously, the drugs and girl didn't work on the watchman, or the hamburgers on the dog. God knows why. I'll keep you fully informed, of course."

"I want to talk to Cameron first, Frank. As soon as he gets here. Before he sees anyone else. Just the two of us. See to it." His usually mild voice was thick with anger.

"Yes, sir." There was no use arguing with the old man when he was in this mood. "I'll have him in your office first thing."

"Okay, Frank. By the way, the watchman was Japanese. Any chance the drug we used doesn't work on Orientals?"

"Not very likely, but I'll find out, sir. That still wouldn't explain the dog not being tranquilized."

"Someone reading your mail in Tokyo, Frank? Any clues?"

"No, sir. For that matter it could be that kind of thing anywhere along the line. Even here."

"Useless speculation, Frank. I'll dig it out of Cameron. Get his butt up here ASAP. Understood?" He hung up, sorry he was taking it out on his subordinate, knowing it was only a measure of his belief that something was dreadfully wrong.

Honolulu, Hawaii: Punchbowl—1000 hours, 22 August

The hot, dry wind in the shallow crater of Punchbowl Cemetery made the sound of "Taps" seem thin and far away, a lonely, sad cry for Korekiyo Takahashi and for all the others under the neat rows of white crosses. Mark watched in sympathy as Linda Takahashi struggled to control her sorrow.

Linda's slender height and blonde hair were in sharp contrast to the Cat's two short, brown-skinned parents, standing on each side of her. When the honor-guard officer handed her the folded flag, Linda lost the struggle, and Mariko Takahashi joined her in tears. The women bowed, arms around each other's shoulders. The Cat's father, "Mits" Takahashi, glanced at them but made no sign. He stared at the flag high above the cemetery. He was having his own struggle, but his Japanese code forbade visible emotion and he was outwardly impassive.

They were all relieved when the brief ceremony was over

and they could go home. The Takahashi house was at the end of Manoa Valley, where the hills slope up steeply to the Lyon Arboretum and beyond to the sharp crest of the Koolau range. An older house, with a small but well-tended Japanese garden and an aura of peace and quiet comfort. It, too, was in sharp contrast to the mourning of this day.

Mark was grateful when Mits Takahashi suggested that they take a drive. "To get away from here for a bit, go and see some of the places Korekiyo liked, where we had fun."

They spent the rest of the time until Mark's flight visiting some of the most beautiful scenery in the world: the blue-green ocean from the dark green pineapple fields above Haleiwa, the water bright blue inside the reef; diminutive Waimea Bay with the papaya tree growing from the roof gutter of the little church; fabled Kahana Bay, scene of so many tropical movies; the unique sight of the conical island known as Chinaman's Hat, just offshore near Kaneohe Bay; the glorious view from the Pali lookout; another from Makapuu; then Sandy Beach, where Linda and Mark body-surfed for an hour.

Mits and Mariko sat on the sand, watching the surfers. "You brought Korekiyo here first when he was tiny, remember?"

"Yes," said Mits. "He was never afraid of the sea."

"Or anything much else. I'll miss him always."

"What do you think of this man Cameron?"

"Nice manners, for a Haole. Good-looking, tall. Maybe six feet. Strange, those green eyes. They don't seem to go with brown hair. I wonder how old he is . . . he looks thirty-five, but he could be ten years older. Hard to tell with Caucasians."

"No, I mean what's inside him? Why did he put Korekiyo into that place?" Mark had told them, without details, and sworn them to silence.

"I don't know," said Mariko. "He went in too, you know. He took the same risks."

At Honolulu Airport, seeing Mark off, Mits said: "I'm a chemical engineer, Mr. Cameron. I don't know much about your business. Korekiyo said almost nothing. Why do you do it, if the risks are so high?"

"They aren't usually, sir. Besides, we have to know what the other side is thinking and doing, or we're blind. It's that simple." He changed the subject: "Linda will stay with you a few days?"

"Forever, if she wants. She's all we've got now, with both boys gone."

"Both?"

"Korekiyo's brother was shot down in Vietnam two years ago. In 1970. Didn't he tell you?"

"No, and we were very good friends."

"That's like him." Mits turned to the women. "We'd better let Mr. Cameron go. They've called his flight."

"See you in Washington," said Linda when they got to the security gate. "Don't blame yourself, Mark."

Georgetown, D.C.: a private house—
1930 hours, 23 August

The DCI came late to the cocktail party, a bright, noisy Georgetown affair. Even the president was there, and he motioned to the DCI to step out onto the veranda for a private chat. The Secret Service men stayed inside, peering anxiously out of the windows at their charge, a shadowy form in the dusk.

"Alden," the president asked. "You have a man in Kitty Bangi, don't you?" He couldn't pronounce the African name of the capital of Bwagania, and made it sound vaguely rude.

"Of course, Mr. President. With everything in such a mess there, we wouldn't miss a thing like that." The DCI silently chided himself for not having sent a man there yet, *and* for lying about it. He made a mental note to get a man to Gitabwanga in a few days. Meanwhile, the White House could go on thinking the DCI was on top of his job.

The president nodded, pleased. They chatted for a few minutes about Africa, its tribal wars, insurrections, famine, disease, and how the Soviets and their clients were trying to get a foothold. Decolonization had brought more problems than it had solved.

"No surprises, Alden. We want to know what happens in

places like Kitty Bangi before it happens. Keep the lid on and don't let the commies grab it. I'm counting on you, Alden." He smiled at the DCI and went back into the house.

The DCI stayed outside despite the muggy August heat. The president's request would enable him to get more money from Congress for operations in Africa. That was a plus. Then he ran through a mental list of possible station chiefs. He needed an experienced case officer with fluent French. A man able to take central Africa as a challenge, not exile.

Langley, Virginia: CIA headquarters—0830 hours, 24 August

Mark Cameron reported to Jack Mason, Russia division chief, as tired as he'd ever been. The Cat had been a close friend, his death a shocking blow, and passing through eleven time zones on his way to headquarters, he'd thought about little else, blaming himself and scanning all the options to try to piece together what had gone wrong. Was it an agent gone sour? Tokyo station penetrated? Or was someone reading the communications between headquarters and Tokyo?

The secretary showed him in to Mason at once. The division chief never gave him a chance to speak.

"The director wants to see you pronto, before you talk to anyone. Just you and him. Get up there right now."

"Yes, sir. You're not coming?" They hadn't even shaken hands, he realized. It was going to be rough.

"No, Mark. Not invited. Nor's the DDO. Nor the chief of the Pacific division or the technical people. You're going to be dissected alone. Quite alone." He gestured upward. The DCI's office was on the top floor.

"He's blaming me, then?"

"He's looking for someone to pin it on. You're the obvious one, but maybe you can turn him around. Let me know what happens. I'll help if I can." Jack Mason felt protective toward all his officers, especially the good ones. Mark was as good as they come, but in this business you only got one really big mistake.

Langley, Virginia: the DCI's office— 0840 hours, 24 August

Jane, the director's executive secretary, was utterly discreet, utterly unflappable, never at a loss for appropriate words or actions. Her manner oozed the impression that she was at the heart of things, the director's most important confidante. Slowly, she reacted to Mark's standing in front of her desk, looking over the top of the document she was reading—top secret, of course, nothing else in *this* office, her look seemed to imply—and smiling in recognition. Then she went back to the document. Mark suspected he would be kept waiting. Last time, he'd walked out of the director's office with a medal. This time, he could be getting forty-eight hours' notice.

Five minutes later, a tiny light blinked on Jane's desk. She nodded toward the door and Mark walked past her into the sanctum, to where the director sat in a huge armchair next to a coffee table. There was an air of green baize, glistening brass, oiled leather, guns and hunting dogs. Those and the scent of pipe tobacco always surrounded the DCI.

He waved Mark to a straight-backed chair facing him. Waved with his pipe, then took a minute to light it. Several matches, some hissing and bubbling, and it was done. Throughout it he looked at Mark. Quite a neutral look, Mark thought.

The director, always confident of his own ability, said: "I'm starting this with an open slate, Cameron. One of our best technical officers is dead. Killed, on your operation. It should not have been. But you can be sure I've an open mind. No prejudgments. I want to hear your story. Then I'll make up my mind. Cables and dispatches never give me enough."

"I'm grateful for the chance to tell you, sir."

The DCI nodded, looking benign. He knew his words would be repeated in the corridors.

"Yes," he said. "I'll be completely fair."

He tapped the file in his lap. "I've read all this. All the key cables, field dispatches, and headquarters documents from the outset of this GOLD operation. 'An empty embassy, duck soup,' you said. But it was anything but that. The operation was your concept, eh?"

"Yes, sir." Mark looked for a sign to continue. The DCI waved his pipe, started lighting it again.

As he began the story, Mark could see the Rumanian embassy looming dark and enormous above the wall of the compound. Blackened faces of the entry team as they huddled against the wall, trying to keep the worst of the rain from running inside their clothes as they waited for the signal to go over the wall.

"I considered the target worth the risks and effort, sir. The new Rumanian ambassador to Tokyo is a top Party official, a member of the Central Committee, in line for Politburo membership. He's rumored to be out of favor with the Party general secretary, but he's got a large high-level constituency in the Central Committee and throughout the regional Party organizations. He's close to the Soviets and a personal friend of the Soviet ambassador to Tokyo, also a key man in his own top Party structure."

"Yes, I recall that. The take should have been good."

"That's right, sir. Not only for the intelligence we might get, but for the personality info on him, his staff, and his Soviet and other friends. Perhaps he's recruitable. After all, he's been banished to Tokyo."

"Fair enough." The DCI lit his pipe again. Mark wondered if it was a crutch.

"The Rumanians bought this big old house last spring. We got close to the Japanese contractor whose guys were renovating it, early in the game. We got all the plans and specs for the extensive changes—walls knocked down or moved, vaults, strong rooms, the usual. A couple of Rumanian goons watched everything the contractor did, but they went home at night. They hired a Japanese night watchman and installed him in the cottage by the main gate. A German shepherd patrolled the grounds at night. He took the animal into the embassy with him on his rounds.

"I chose the entry time for the operation between the finish of work in the ambassador's study and the Rumanian occupation of the compound. That gave us a window of three weeks, from the ninth to the thirtieth of August. We didn't really need the noise, but we did in fact take advantage of a typhoon that struck on the twentieth, late in the evening. It was the first typhoon of the season, and it was a humdinger. One Japanese TV announcer called it kamikaze—divine wind."

"After the wartime suicide pilots?"

"No, sir. After the great typhoon of the thirteenth century that wrecked the invading Mongol fleet. He was tongue-in-cheek, really, because other than keep people inside, where they watched TV, this one did only harm. It suited us, however. We went in late the night of the twenty-first, with the typhoon still strong enough to keep people off the streets and make a frightful racket inside the building."

Mark stopped. "Most of this has been in the traffic, sir. Shall I spell it all out?"

"Certainly the important parts," said the director. "I want to hear your version, Mark." Mark was warmed by the old man's use of his first name. It made the inquisition less painful, even if the final result would be a personal disaster.

"We knew where all the pipes and wires were, so we could put our audio gear where they would shield it from metal detectors. The dog was a prime obstacle, and the only solution was to put him to sleep for the night. We also had to take out the night watchman in a way that would cause no suspicion. He usually bought a bowl of soba—noodle soup—at a nearby shop late at night. And he often had a Korean girl who stayed overnight. The plan was to dope his soba so he would sleep all night and not do his usual rounds every two hours. One of our best Japanese agents recruited the girl to slip the stuff into his soba and then bed him down securely. She also carried a mini transmitter so we'd know if something went wrong. In addition, the agent rented a room up the street that overlooked the cottage, so we had visual and audio on them.

"In early August, we ran a dress rehearsal. It worked perfectly. The dog took his medicine in fine form. The woman doctored the soba. The watchman drank it. The agent saw and heard it all. The dog and man slept all night. He didn't get suspicious. I decided we should go ahead. Headquarters approved GOLD, including the twenty-first as the entry night. We already had a weather prediction on the typhoon."

"I saw that in the traffic," the DCI said.

"Now, the night of the twenty-first to twenty-second, sir. The typhoon was just right. It pissed rain from the evening of the twentieth on, until at least midday the twenty-second, with a seventy-knot wind. We went over the wall at eleven, after our agent visually checked that the watchman had drunk his doped soup and gone to sleep, woman and all. We'd fed the dog but couldn't see him in that weather. I'd gone over the wall on a solo probe at ten forty-five to make sure, but couldn't find him. I had a can of Mace in case he found me, but he didn't, so I naturally assumed he'd gone off to sleep somewhere, like before. He would had found me if he'd been awake. He could have murdered me in that pitch dark, the wind and rain masking all sound, but I figured we had to know . . . there was no choice."

The old man could visualize it. At least Mark had balls. But was his head still working? Had his assumptions been valid?

"I looked in the window of the cottage. There they were, quite visible in reflected light from the kitchen, asleep in bed. Everything seemed okay, so I decided we'd go ahead. I went back over the wall to get the entry team. They were in the garden of a house that one of our Japanese support agents had rented for the month. Its garden wall was, in effect, the Rumanian compound wall. The guys were wet and cold, more than ready to get on with it. I called the lookouts. We had two of them, plus the Japanese agent watching the street as well as the cottage. They all gave us an okay, so over we went. I went first, then Jim Corbett, my number two. Then a lock-and-key man, and two audio techs. Finally, the Cat."

"Why was he called the Cat?"

"Well, sir, he was amazingly nimble and quick. Thin, wiry, made of rubber. He could get himself through any hole his head would fit through. He had a lot of guts and he seemed to have a charmed life. Once he got stuck between the ceiling of a Soviet's apartment and the floor of the next story up. But he stayed cool, planted his mikes, and eventually got himself out by wriggling out of his jeans, moving very slowly, coming out backwards, his head turned sideways for five hours. There was a very aggressive, fully armed GRU colonel sitting in the room right below him."

"What operation was that, Mark?"

"TELLURIDE, sir. The audio system worked fine for a couple of months, but then the GRU colonel moved out unexpectedly. We hoped another good Soviet target would move in, but they gave up the place. All that work was wasted."

The director looked pensive. "Go on, Mark."

"Another time, the Cat was caught inside a Soviet target. He went out a third-floor window. So help me, he landed on his feet and kept on running. He got clean away. That's what got him the nickname. After that, even his wife called him the Cat. Only she used the Japanese word, *neko*. She called him neko-chan."

"You liked him?" The DCI looked at Mark sharply.

"Very much. One of the best we have. We were good friends. I had nothing but admiration for him."

"Go on."

"In a couple of minutes we were at the front door and the lock-and-key man began his effort to open it. We waited fifteen, twenty minutes and finally Jim and I got sick of it and went around the building, checking. We got a window open and went in. You should have seen the look on that lock-and-key man's face when we opened the front door. He actually fell in, like a scene from a comedy. Total surprise on his face. The others giggled."

The DCI laughed out loud. It was all too rare that he got a glimpse like this of how field operations really work.

"We went straight to the target room. The Cat set up his toys, and his audio boys went to work. A beautiful job. By three fifteen they had the bug installed and the wall closed up again and repainted. There was no trace. We cleaned up, checked and double-checked, and started out, almost an hour ahead of schedule. If we'd been on schedule, the watchman would have caught us right in the middle of it. I've thought about that a lot, sir."

The DCI nodded. He could see where this might lead.

"Our exit began at three forty-five. I left the study last, the others in single file ahead of me, down the main corridor toward the front door. The storm was making a hell of a noise, rain pouring down, winds still howling. We felt our way rather than use flashlights, and the lightning flashes helped. The Cat was leading the parade. We'd agreed on that earlier. Looking back now, I wish I'd gone first."

"Rather you than him, eh? Heroics?"

"No, sir. I have to live with it forever. That may be worse. It seems like it now." The DCI nodded.

"Then, in the main corridor, it happened. I wasn't aware of anything wrong until we were blinded by a very bright light ahead in the corridor. It seemed like the sun because my eyes were used to the dark. Then, over the storm, roaring and yelling. I'd no clue what was going on until I realized part of it was a dog growling, very loud and angry. I thought it must be a Rumanian with another dog. I skated into a side room. We had only socks on . . . our shoes were inside the front door. I ran through three connecting rooms and came out into the main corridor behind the noises. Then I could see it was the watchman and a German shepherd. He had one of those long flashlights full on the Cat's face.

"Just as I came up behind the man, he let go of the dog. I'd heard about this kind of attack, but I'd never seen it. Hope I never do again."

Mark's eyes were glistening, the director realized. For the first time, he caught a look at the man inside.

"The watchman's right hand was free now, but I got him as he was pulling his revolver. I broke his collarbone with a karate chop. He never looked back, never saw what hit him. But that damn dog got the Cat by the throat. So help me God, sir, it was the quickest thing I've ever seen. One second there was the Cat, shouting and trying to reach the light. The next second he was on the ground, on his knees, his whole throat torn out. The dog had it in his mouth, blood and all running out of his muzzle . . ."

Mark stopped. His face was gray and his hands were clamped around his own throat. He stared off at the wall, reliving the dreadful moment. The director, not usually squeamish, felt his stomach rise.

"Oh no . . . what did you do?"

"The dog was going back for another pass. You could tell, he'd tasted blood and he liked it. But he stopped for a moment to wolf down the throat . . . the Cat's throat." Mark looked at his hands in horror. The DCI had his mouth cupped by a hand as he stared at Mark, imagining it.

"I did something I'd not thought possible. I got the dog by its hind legs and beat it like a rug. Up and down on the floor on the stone floor. I beat it to death. On the floor and on the watchman's head!"

Mark sat still, breathing heavily, staring at the director. The DCI stared back. He could think of nothing to say as he listened to Mark's breathing settle down. Of all the fearful stories he'd heard in this room, this was unique.

"We left the watchman and the dog there, sir." Mark's voice was thin now, and flat. "We had to get the Cat to a doctor. Although I thought it unlikely he'd survive. I radioed the lookouts and had the cars meet us at the main gate. I carried the Cat from the corridor. That's when I knew it was hopeless. His blood was all over the floor. All down my front and legs. I looked for a pulse, but there wasn't any . . . or even a windpipe. I've carried dead and wounded in wartime. You know, sir. You can tell when a fellow's gone. He just feels different."

"I know," said the DCI.

"We tried to help, but it . . . the watchman survived?"

"Yes. He did indeed have a broken collarbone, plus some busted ribs, and a concussion. The Tokyo newspapers speculated it was a burglary. They reported someone died, based on the amount of blood. But there were no non-Japanese aspects to the media stories. The Rumanians declined comment. Didn't you know?"

"No, sir. I left Tokyo immediately. The Honolulu press had nothing on it."

"What happened next?"

"We drove him to the station doctor's house in a station wagon. He's the regional medic. His house is on a quiet street, trees all around. You can't see the garage from the street or the house. He was waiting for us in the garage. He checked for signs, but there was nothing he could do. He said even if he'd been with us, he couldn't have helped.

"We left him in the garage with two of the guys. I called his wife, Linda. It was about four fifteen in the morning, but she came over in a few minutes. I sent the rest of the entry team home, and the lookouts. Then I told her. She sat there a very long time, white as a sheet. No movement, not a word. They were very much in love, sir."

"No children, I gather." He'd done his homework.

"No sir. They planned a family in about a year."

"How do you know that?"

"We were close friends, sir. All three of us."

"Linda's Caucasian?"

"Yes. Very blond. French and Norwegian parents. She's twenty-seven, with her whole life ahead. Then she asked to see him. I'd been dreading that, but she insisted. The doctor came with us, in case. But she's a strong girl. She went straight to the Cat and pulled down the blanket. She looked at him for a very long time. Maybe ten minutes. She was oblivious to us. She looked at it all . . . all of it.

"After that, she put her hands on each side of his head. She was crying silently, shaking all over. And she said, very simply: 'Goodbye, Neko-chan. Goodbye. I'll be coming along soon, I promise you.' "

Mark was standing now, at a window. His back to the DCI, to hide his tears. It wasn't possible and the grief in him welled over. He had difficulty speaking the next words.

"Linda was wonderful. She signed the papers to ship the body to Okinawa by military flight. Then she went home and packed, arranged for shipment of their things, and was ready to go by noon. We went to Okinawa that afternoon, then transferred to a civilian flight for Honolulu, with the coffin in the hold. I talked to her on the trip, and a lot in Honolulu. I don't think she'll keep her promise to the Cat. She's too solid to kill herself."

"We buried him in the military cemetery at Punchbowl. His parents were as good as anyone at such a time. They're devastated, of course. But dignified, in control. They treat Linda as their daughter, and asked her to stay—to live with them as their sole surviving child. But she said no very gently."

"Oh? What does she want to do?"

"Stay with us, sir. She worked in Tokyo. She's a very good IA [intelligence assistant] and she wants to work up to field case officer."

"Has she got what it takes?"

"I'm sure of it. All she needs is the chance."

The director nodded. He'd look into her case fully. He charged his pipe. "Well, Mark, what do you think happened?"

Mark tensed. "I really don't know, sir. Perhaps the dog wasn't loose, so he didn't take the hamburger meat. Perhaps they'd just acquired a second dog, unknown to us, and it was locked up somewhere. But then there's the night watchman. Perhaps he slipped the girl his soba and drank hers. If so, he had to know something."

"Something she said, maybe?"

"Not as far as we can tell. We had audio on them, remember. She played her part perfectly. She didn't write him a note either. Our agent had them under his eyes until they were asleep. He must have woken up, turned out the kitchen light, and then started on his rounds. She was still asleep at three forty-five, by the way. Our agent could hear her snore on the audio. He knocked on the window and got her out of there. She was completely confused. I don't see that she would have tipped him off even if she'd found a way. Her reward was going to be too big for that."

Mark paused. "It's almost as if they'd been reading our mail, sir. Expecting us. Aware of the drugs and the woman. As if they knew we'd be in there, and knew how to lull us into going in. They even knew when to catch us hard at it."

"Why not put ten Rumanians on it and really smear you?"

"If they didn't want us to realize they knew about it, they'd make the watchman's arrival look like an accident—like bad luck. Or they'd try to lead us into suspecting our own agents. But they'd keep the Rumanian hand from showing."

"You'd prefer to think someone read our mail rather than

that you made a mistake? Of all the explanations, the least likely one is that the Rumanians knew about the operation."

"I've looked at it from all angles, sir, for three days now. I just have a gut feeling that I was taken. I think the Rumanians knew exactly what we were up to."

He'd gone further than he'd intended, but he had to trust the DCI. He sighed and sat back, waiting for the ax to fall.

"You'll have to prove it." The director leaned forward.

"Give me a chance, sir, and I will. I promise you." Mark's eyes met his.

"You sound convinced."

"There was something different about the dog we met in there, Mr. Director. I know it sounds like wishful thinking, and I can't really put my finger on it. My intuition tells me there were in fact two dogs. I think the second one had a little more tan than black and a slightly longer coat. But I admit I never saw them together. It's a just a hunch, really."

"A good case officer's nose is important, Mark. But you're guessing. You'd have to make the case. I don't see how you can from where I'm sending you."

Mark was now convinced that he'd be reassigned to the archives.

But the DCI had a better idea. He wanted to punish Cameron, not lose him. Mark spoke fluent French, almost like a native. He had guts. And he had no choice. The trick was to make him feel motivated for it.

"I don't know how we find people like you, Mark." The DCI's mood switch startled Mark. "You go into the damnedest places, against cruel risks, on the off chance you might bring in some useful intelligence for us. If you're unlucky you may be jeered by your colleagues, crucified by the press, hounded by Congress. Even fired by me for a mistake you didn't make. If you're lucky, you may get a medal you only see once, can't show anyone or talk about.

"You're a good officer, Mark. Your GOLD was a good operation. Not brilliant, but reasonable. The plan was okay, no obvious flaws. But you lost a life. A very important life, owned by one of my best officers. In any event the risks you took—calculated, I know—were too much. It's so easy, son, to want too much too quickly. You should have made sure the dog actually took the meat. You should have made sure the watchman couldn't surprise you. One extra man watching the front door of the cottage. Then you'd have been sure."

Mark shrugged. He'd thought of all that, but the new lock-and-key man had refused to leave the team, even to stand guard inside the front door. It seemed unlikely now, in a cozy Langley office, but fear made a trained man refuse orders during an operation. Mark wasn't about to tell the DCI that, however. Let the techs take care of their own dirty laundry.

The director already knew about the lock-and-key man. He'd written him off a day ago. He was interested in Mark, a man with real potential. There were so few real leaders, even among the elite of the Company.

"Mark, I've decided to banish you. Put you away for a while—some years. I don't want you around headquarters for a spell."

He changed pipes. Another moment of puffing and sizzling.

"No service is immune to penetration, but you've no evidence. A lot of officers would laugh at you for invoking this specter as a way of defending yourself. I'm not laughing, however. There's a thin chance you may have something. It's up to you to follow it up. If you do get a sniff of something solid, let me know. Nobody else. Just me. Meanwhile, you're going a long way away."

So he wouldn't be doing archives work. It was sounding more and more like Siberia or Tibet.

"While you're in exile, think about this problem. I got a jolt recently. One of our most sensitive agents told us the KGB had prior knowledge of at least two of our more delicate operations. Nothing more than a whiff of the problem. He overheard it in, of all places, a KGB men's room in Moscow. He can't get any more on it without almost certainly getting caught. That's all we know, and it's for your ears only. If you get any sniff of a penetration, let me know by your special channel to me as DCI. Don't forget, contact only me. I'll guide you after that."

"I understand perfectly, sir." A special channel to the DCI meant he'd be on his own somewhere. Good news or bad?

The director grinned and waved his pipe. "I wish I understood it better, but from my chair the world is always ambiguous. There's no such thing as perfect understanding. You'll know what I mean if you sit in this chair one day."

Mark laughed. "Not likely, sir. Maybe you're about to make it even less likely than before."

"No, I'd never do that. My punishment for you can be turned into redemption. Depends on what you do with it and how you look at it. A lot of officers would hate the place. It's primitive, seemingly unimportant. But you may make it a way to restore your career. Let's see what you do with it."

He paused. "I'm sending you to Gitabwanga. It's the capital of Bwagania, in central Africa, where if you pull out the plug, all Africa will run down the drain. You'll open a station there. Just you and an IA. You'll leave as soon as possible, without returning to Tokyo. I want you there by, at the latest, the middle of September. We've never had an officer stationed there, and only a few have visited the place. Go via Paris, where you'll get an orientation. Paris station can arrange for you to get some info from the French, although liaison isn't at its best these days."

"Thank you, sir. I'll do as you say."

"Of course. You won't be considered for promotion for twenty-four months from the date of the Cat's death. But you will officially be the first station chief in Gitabwanga. You'll be a consul in our new consulate general there, then a first secretary when it becomes an embassy on January first. While you're there, reflect on risk assessment. Keep a weather eye out for a mole, although I hope there isn't one. Come back a better field case officer, and we'll wipe the slate clean."

The director stood up. He shook hands with Mark, slapped his shoulder. The DCI had solved two problems.

"Good luck. I mean it."

"Thank you, sir. Thanks for the second chance."

When Mark had gone, the director told his secretary to have the medical staff assess Linda Takahashi's mental state as part of her returning physical exam. Then she was to report to him. The DCI called Frank Wales and told him to process Mark for Gitabwanga. A directed appointment, with a two-year promotion freeze. "No, Frank. I won't consider any other candidates. I'll tell you why one day."

Then he sat quietly for a few moments, looking blankly at the national estimate he'd been reading earlier. Was there a mole somewhere in the building, reading the same top secret document, preparing to send it to Moscow?

Gitabwanga: the royal wall—1930 hours, 26 August

The French call Bwagania the Pyrenees of Africa, a lovely land of mountains and a vast lake and only a few flat places. The country is blessed with perpetual spring; the sun shines throughout the year. At night, cool air drifts down from the hills and mountains to the huts and farms in the countryside and the buildings in the towns. Until the middle of this century, crocodiles occasionally crept into the streets of Gitabwanga from the lake, the herds of elephant were thinned out by the police when they damaged nearby crops, and big game roamed the hills and valleys with little hindrance.

The French took Bwagania from the Germans after World War I and ran the colony with a relatively benign hand. Love was more important than discipline. White and black mixed easily, and the children of wealthy Bwaganians were schooled in France. Troops of the French foreign legion were stationed there: They and the French-supervised police protected the people from each other, made them obey the laws, and kept them safe from invasion.

Behind the royal palace, where the gardens slope abruptly to Lake Tchagamba, there is a low stone wall wide enough to sit on. Below it is a narrow sand beach. Then the great lake stretching beyond sight, to the shores of Chad and Niger. In the rainy season, the storms mutter over the water, with lightning so frequent that you can almost read by it, even if the thunder is inaudible.

By tradition, the king of Bwagania sits on the wall every other night for an hour or so, his back to the lake, soon after dusk. People come along the beach, one after the other, to whisper to their ruler. Some petitioners complain. Some ask for guidance. Some seek the king's help to settle grievances, quarrels, land or water rights, or inheritance claims. Some praise the king or his family. Gossip, a Bwaganian hobby, is often the topic brought to the king for his information and amusement.

The wall was one of Bwaga VI's main sources of intelligence. Anyone under the wall, talking to the king, had to tell the truth or be struck dead on the spot by the Leopard. Everyone knew the deadly power of the ghostly Leopard, the reality of the threat. The king, too, had to tell the truth. Some kings, they claim, had said almost nothing when they were seated on the wall. But Bwaga VI loved the royal wall and used it with an honesty and humor that had become legendary.

King Bwaga VI sat on the royal wall waiting for the next petitioner. Tonight the lake was as still and silent as he had ever known it. This was at least the hundredth time he had sat on the wall this year. He'd enjoyed each petition, and also the periods of vigil between his visitors. His clients, he called them. Bwaga VI was a popular king. He made everyone feel welcome and at ease when they came under the wall to speak with him. They understood that they were his family.

He could hear the old man limping along the sand long before he sat down with his back against the stones. By his voice, he was old enough to command the king's respect no matter what his status in life. They greeted each other with the ritual singsong words and hymnal phrases that tradition had laid down, a routine that took several minutes. Then the old man was quiet for several more minutes. Finally, his whispers were clear, if faint, to Bwaga VI.

"Bwaga VI, I knew your father and your grandfather. I am a devoted member and servant of your family. I bring you dreadful words from darkness, but I must speak. If I hold my tongue, our nation can not survive."

The king heard many dire predictions from atop the wall, most of them much exaggerated. But he kept silent and listened.

"I am in the service of a cabinet minister, Bwaga VI. I am known for my complete discretion, and anyway I am old and harmless. So, much is said in my hearing. The minister is, secretly, an opponent of yours. He wants to force you off the throne. He wants to be the first president of what he calls the Republic of Bwagania. He doesn't want any more kings, Bwaga VI. He has young men, army and government officials, who believe in him and will follow him. They plan to send you away to another country and send away all the French. Then some other white men will come and they will be the 'true friends of the people'. I tell you, I've heard all this with my own ears, many times. They think I'm too old to understand or to care . . . too old and too stupid. But I've listened and they frighten me. They are serious, my king."

Bwaga VI was suddenly wide awake, alert to every sound. He'd heard vague whispers before, but never with any names. He said to the old man:

"You are wise to come to me. I already know about their plan, but of course I always need more information." The king was skating close to the edge of truth, and he paused for a moment to say a brief silent prayer of atonement.

"Who is the minister, and who are his supporters?"

"Yes, sire." But there was a long silence.

"Go on," said the king. "I'm a big king now." They both laughed. It was an old joke in the kingdom, from the days when Bwaga VI had ruled as a child with a regent acting for him.

The old man sucked his breath in and his whisper was almost lost.

"The minister is your oldest son, Prince M'Taga. May the Leopard strike me if I have lied."

For a long time the king said nothing. He sat on the wall and stared out across the palace gardens. The old man gazed at the lake, content to keep quiet. He knew the king believed him, and he knew that he had done the right thing.

The king thought about his son, the inheritor, Prince Simba M'Taga, who was destined by custom and law to be Bwaga VII when his father died. The king was accustomed to intrigue within the royal family, traditionally split into several hostile factions. Royal murder of family members had been routine into the early twentieth century. The royal family of Bwagania was widely known in Africa for its greed, deceit, lusts, excesses, savagery, and vendettas. Educated partially in France, Bwaga VI had risen far above his ancestors, even his father, and had put the family on a road to dignity and grace. In addition, he had started a tradition of care for the Bwaganian people.

Prince M'Taga was tall, over six feet six inches. Good-looking, athletic in his youth, a marvelous public speaker, he could be the perfect inheritor as king of Bwagania if he wanted to be. The population adored him as crown prince. Wherever he set foot in the kingdom, he was joyfully acclaimed. Not because he was prime minister. That was only a modern invention. It was because he would one day be Bwaga VII, and he looked and acted the part.

It was well known that the king dearly loved his twenty-six-year-old son M'Taga. He loved him as much as he despised his only other son, twenty-two-year-old Prince N'Gobi.

The inheritor was only four when the queen died. The king had doted on him, ignoring his younger son. Bwaga VI played mother as well as father to the crown prince. They hunted, swam, rode, and later they flew airplanes and parachuted together. No secrets or discipline divided them. Ten years ago, when M'Taga turned sixteen, the king had procured a mistress for him from Europe. A pretty blonde with superb breasts and buttocks. As though it were natural, Bwaga VI had shared her with his son. Now and then, for a change, they would leave the kingdom, father and son, and together they laughed, drank, and whored their way all over Europe.

The king had been sustained, warmed by the knowledge that one day the kingdom would pass into M'Taga's care.

"Are you certain that these are not stories put about by his brother, Prince N'Gobi?" The king had never hidden his distaste for N'Gobi, whose birth was the direct cause of the queen's death—a three-day agony that still brought sweat to the king's forehead.

"Prince N'Gobi is in no way a part of them, sire. I've seen him at Prince M'Taga's house only once, when a cousin died. Prince M'Taga does not seem to enjoy his brother."

Bwaga VI expected the answer, although he dreaded it. He had heard rumors before of M'Taga's plots, but they were vague and made no sense. Now he felt a metallic chill fill his insides, like a thunderclap. In the rubble of his love and friendship for M'Taga there was the icy thought that one of them would have to die.

"Prince Simba M'Taga, my oldest son, is planning to remove me and abolish the throne? You are sure, old man? Your accusation may cause you dreadful punishment!"

"You may kill me if you wish, Bwaga VI, but I have told you the truth."

The old people of Bwagania, especially, could not lie under the royal wall. The king didn't doubt what the old man said.

"How did the prince come to these ideas? Who's behind this?"

"The prince has been much influenced recently by young Bwaganians schooled in Europe. Also by a man from Europe who is called Pierre. It is a French name but he speaks with many snorts, like a hippo in the lake."

The old man snorted and grunted a few times, and he sounded surprisingly like a hippo. The king laughed despite the pain in his belly.

"This man Pierre often speaks to the prince and the others in the house, when they meet at night, about something very important which he calls socialism." The old man pronounced it badly, but there was no doubt what he meant.

It made sense, and the king hated it. He knew that the communists would be his biggest danger in independent Bwagania. The idea that they had captured the soul of his own son almost choked him.

"When did the prince come to accept their views?" He asked it patiently, but he wanted to scratch all over.

"Perhaps four months ago, sire. Pierre came from Europe, where he had become friends with some of the young Bwaganians. Students in Paris, I think, who are often at M'Taga's house. Pierre promises all kinds of things. Money, arms, training, food, medicine, people to teach us here, gifts so our young people can go to socialist schools for Africans. Some of us in the house don't like the man Pierre. We call him Tofi na n'Zolo, manure of a chicken in Chiluba, because he is cold with the servants."

The king laughed. "Well, we'll call him that too. Tofi for short."

And we'll call my prince traitor, the king said to himself bitterly.

"The prince believes Tofi as if he were God, my king. M'Taga believes that the French will keep Bwagania for their tribe after our independence, whereas the socialists are our real friends. The prince thinks you will help the French and that is why you must go. The socialists do not like kings, Pierre says. That's why M'Taga wants to be president-for-life, he says."

The moon was bright now, and the king could see the old man crouching below, a blanket over one shoulder, a bare arm hanging down with the hand around one ankle. A pipe glowed as the man sucked on it, the scent of tobacco strong. For a moment, the king had a wild urge to throttle the old man, but he shook off the thought.

"Listen carefully, old friend. Go back to my son's house. Do nothing to arouse suspicion. Go about your duties as you always have. Listen to what they say, remember their names, memorize what they wear and what they look like. Pay especial attention to this Tofi man and what he says and whom he contacts.

"Then come to me each time you have something to tell. Make sure you are not followed. Come after the time when I usually leave the wall. Listen for this clicking noise." The king clicked his gold cigar clipper. "You will be rewarded."

The reward would be the traditional gift of cattle and perhaps a young wife. The old man muttered his thanks, and they ended with the customary singsong phrases of Bwaganian parting. The old man left silently, walking slowly along the sandy shore.

Gitabwanga: the royal palace—2030 hours, 26 August

Leaving the wall, the king walked thoughtfully through the gardens to the palace and stopped for a snack in the kitchen, chatting absently with the night cook. Then he mounted the stairs and took his new Swiss mistress to bed.

Bwaga VI was very pleased with this girl, usually quite gentle in bed with her. The chamberlain had found her for him at a

Swiss finishing school. She was a real blonde, a requirement of the king's. Her name was Madeleine, but she liked to be called Muffie. She was very pretty, also a requirement. Slender and athletic. A slight lisp and a sparkle in her bright blue eyes. She was half the king's age. As the chamberlain had reported after her "trial period," which he'd enjoyed greatly, Muffie made extravagant, more than appropriate noises and wild motions when she rose to her frequent and impressive orgasms. Sometimes she trembled all over and cried afterward, which made Bwaga VI feel strong, invincible. He was delighted with her and showed her off as often as he could.

This evening the king made love to Muffie as if it were his last time. He was as erect and hard as stone, and he entered her half a dozen times, trying each time with deep and rhythmic movements to bring himself to a climax. Muffie cried out with pleasure as she did her part to perfection.

But all the king could think of, over and over, was to squeeze a new baby boy out of his penis. After half an hour he rolled away and got up, furiously angry with his son M'Taga and disgusted with himself. Muffie wept and begged his forgiveness, blaming herself for the king's failure. In her youthful way she loved this strange, powerful African. She adored his exotic features, his velvety golden brown skin, and the muscular physique that belonged to a man half his age.

The king thought little of Muffie's anguish and blamed her not at all. Bwaga VI liked her better than any of his previous mistresses, but he had never loved any woman since his queen.

Paris: the Elysée palace—1600 hours, 27 August

The director general of the SSR—the French Service de Sécurité et de Renseignements—was precisely on time for the meeting at the Elysée palace with the president of the French Republic. The president was a tall and formidable figure. French military and civilian officials, like the French population, either respected and liked him, or they feared and loathed him. Few were neutral.

The director general had served as a young tank officer under the president, and then on his staff in World War II. He was one of those who revered the president, who would always think of the president as "mon général," a mark of personal attachment and respect. The president counted on the director general as a loyal friend, which was why he entrusted the SSR to him.

Friends or not, the director general always stood to rigid attention when he stood before the president. The Elysée palace is huge and elegant, and when you are in the presence of the president of France, it is easy to be awed, quite natural to stand to attention. Tonight, however, the president waved the director to a chair.

"Dubois, I want you to make sure things go as they should in Bwagania." The president always began without fanfare or frills. "The government of Bwagania will ask that French troops stay there indefinitely. I want a treaty that binds them politically and militarily to us. It must be publicly announced, as their idea, before independence."

"Oui, mon général." Dubois said it as if it would be done today.

"The treaty is to be long-term, and guarantee us an operational base there that we can use as we wish. In exchange we will guarantee them an export market for their crops and French technical assistance. We must help the king remain on his throne, under our protection. Any disorders must be crushed right away, using all means necessary. The foreign ministry has started to negotiate the treaty in advance with the king, and it is almost ready to be signed. Your role, Dubois, is to see that our influence is discreet and that we know what is going on, where, and why, before it happens.

"Above all, no surprises, you understand? Keep the United Nations, the United States, Moscow, and Peking out of our way."

"Yes, my general. I've already started strengthening the poste there. I have an excellent man in mind for chef de poste. Experienced, loyal, dependable."

"Who's that, Dubois?"

"Colonel François de la Maison, sir. You remember him from World War Two, Dien Bien Phu, and Algeria. He never had anything to do with the OAS or any of the other dissident factions. He is intelligent, perceptive, a ruthless combat leader, and a very good intelligence officer—a rare combination."

The president nodded.

"I'm keeping the officers we have there," Dubois went on, "and sending out six more, plus several warrant officers. They'll handle things properly."

The president smiled, hoping Dubois was right.

"Yes, I remember de la Maison. He'll do. Have him go right away, and be sure he prepares the Bwaganians to take over the Sûreté functions after independence. Perhaps we can make this one African country that isn't taken over by crooks and murderers after independence. I'm not hopeful, but we must try. Don't let the Africans run things until they—and we—are ready. At least this country has a king who's used to governing on the local level, and he's had some exposure to international affairs."

"Many affairs, my general, but few of them were conducted on his feet. A great swordsman, my general." Dubois looked sad.

"I don't care what he does with his pecker as long as he keeps his country in order." The president smiled thinly, went to his desk, and sat down. He ended the interview as if there were a flourish of drums.

"Confirm de la Maison in this appointment, to be effective immediately. Tell him I chose him and am counting on him. Keep the king on the throne. Keep him in our corner. Keep a tight lid on the left. We'll make a model of a former French colony. Once again, Dubois, I rely upon you . . . old friend."

The president knew his man. Dubois left feeling warm all over.

Paris: Au Chat qui Pêche—1300 hours, 29 August

Dubois delayed until Colonel de la Maison's birthday. He telephoned François and asked him for lunch: His appointment would be announced as if it were a gift.

They met at Au Chat qui Pêche, one of the oldest and smallest of Paris' fine restaurants.

The director general had always secretly envied Colonel de

la Maison. He was permanently tanned, tall, slim, his hair dark without a hint of gray, and was always in good humor. He never aged. He wore his uniforms as if they were medieval armor. And he was one of the most fortunate of military men—he had no fear. On top of that, he was intelligent, well read, witty, relaxed, a superb story teller, and in all other ways just the kind of man Dubois had wanted to be.

That was Dubois' vision of François de la Maison. François' vision of himself was quite different. In fact François thought of Dubois as an unqualified success and of himself as a limited man with many faults.

Today was a happy occasion, and Au Chat qui Pêche was at its best. They lunched for two hours with lively conversation about old friends, old campaigns, and the catastrophes of independence in Africa.

It was three o'clock before Dubois got to the point. "François, I have some good news for you. You have been selected by the president to be the chef de poste in Gitabwanga. Your birthday is a fine time to tell you."

There was a long silence. François stirred his coffee as he absorbed the news. He would have preferred command of a line regiment, but he knew this appointment was a compliment. He also knew that Dubois had nominated him. The president would never have thought of him without prompting. He smiled. "Thank you very much, sir. Of course I accept, with pleasure. When do I go?"

"Early September, sooner if you can arrange it. We want to be at full strength before independence on January first. There must be no trouble, no surprises. A treaty we're negotiating must be signed. We must have a permanent military base there. We must give them real independence but keep them in our corner. You must establish excellent relations with our new embassy. There is much to do and, as usual, too little time."

"I can go the day after tomorrow if you wish, then come back later to take care of any personal matters that need my attention."

"That won't be too difficult? What about the château?"

"My wife and my oldest son can take care of everything. Michel's quite capable. He's almost an adult now."

The director general nodded vaguely. "A fine boy, that one. Above all, François, you must keep the king on his throne and become his friend. That should be no problem for you, a count with royal blood. Perhaps you know the king already?"

"I met him when Maman gave a party years ago for him. But I didn't keep contact. He didn't seem to be my type."

"Well, try again. This time it will be more important."

Paris: Orly Airport—1915 hours, 31 August

François took the night flight to Gitabwanga. Michel came to see him off, but it was an awkward parting. He was a lank and gangly reflection of his father, his shyness increased by the presence of François's mistress, Géraldine. The boy wanted to be alone with his father, but Géraldine had to say farewell too.

"Take care of the estate, Michel. You're head of the family while I'm gone. Be kind to your mother and fair to your brothers. Write to me regularly, and work hard in school." François had said all this before when he left his family behind.

Michel responded in the same measured voice, "I'll try to do everything you would do, Papa. You'll be proud of me." He felt stiff and silly and red-faced with this unknown lady beside them. His father's chilly relations with his mother were a huge problem to Michel, who, at seventeen, knew nothing of marriage and its complexities.

But he did understand that his father and the lady wanted time together. Michel shook hands with François, longing to kiss him but too shy to make the move. François wanted to kiss his son too, but was afraid to add to the boy's embarrassment. They parted with words that neither understood, each wanting to express his love but unable to do so.

Michel stopped just inside the terminal doors. He watched as François and Géraldine said goodbye. They were twined together like two vines. She was stunning, Michel thought. He wondered why his father didn't ask for a divorce. Why didn't adults organize their lives better? When Michel was ready he would find the perfect wife, marry her, and be happy with her forever. Voilà! So simple.

Géraldine stroked the colonel's cheek. "Goodbye, my dearest François. I'll count the hours . . . the minutes . . . I adore you."

François felt lost in Géraldine's beauty and gentleness, and cheated that he hadn't found her years ago rather than his wife, who looked and acted like a farm horse.

"Au revoir, ma chère." He kissed her. *"Je t'aime . . . je t'adore . . ."*

Moscow: KGB headquarters—2145 hours, 31 August

KGB Colonel Pyotr Aleksandrovich Petrov had just attended a liquid, noisy reunion of his old 284th Siberian Infantry Division, a pitiful sprinkling of survivors from the siege of Stalingrad, and as a result, he was drunk. So drunk that he stumbled several times and fell on the wet dimly lit sidewalk. Still too drunk to care what he did. Drunk enough to be aggressive. He would show headquarters the true colors of the 284th! In short, Pyotr was dangerous to himself and to others.

Now, as he approached KGB headquarters, there was jubilation in his heart. He would show them!

KGB General Vladimir Ossilenko, cousin of the chairman of the KGB, stalked down the main entry hall of the KGB headquarters on Dzerzhinsky Square, passed through the main door onto the sidewalk, and turned left.

Ossilenko and Petrov reached the corner of the KGB building together. To Petrov, Ossilenko's spotless uniform and medals, the black leather briefcase held like a submachine gun, made him look like a Nazi officer. Petrov, to Ossilenko, looked like a disheveled civilian who had drunk too much vodka. Probably not even a Party member. It was a common sight and he paid no attention until Petrov's lurching, spread-eagled arms stopped him.

"Oh, ho! What have we here? A dandy come slumming at the front? Well, you've come too far, you ugly bit of Nazi shit . . . you're in our lines now . . ."

General Ossilenko backed up, suddenly realizing that he recognized this man with the contorted face.

Petrov jumped on the smaller man, beating him to the sidewalk with hammerlike blows of his clenched fists. The black briefcase lay on the wet pavement as the general collapsed. Petrov was still beating his Nazi prize when KGB guards arrived on the double and clubbed him unconscious.

They manhandled him into the Lubyanka basement, where he was chained in a tiny cell, filthy, puking, and terrified when he came to his senses.

Moscow: Kremlin fifth floor—0930 hrs, 1 September

The secretary-general of the Soviet Communist Party looked out of his window onto a Kremlin courtyard below. Behind him stood the chairman of the KGB, one of the most powerful men in the USSR. Dossiers on the Party's leaders were stacked far above their heads. Even the secretary-general's file was up there, and if the terms were right, the chairman might just release it. So while the secretary-general didn't always agree with the chairman, he never said anything too damaging. Meanwhile, the chairman kept the armistice, because, given the right circumstances, he might follow Beria into a cold grave.

"The geographic position of Bwagania makes it a key to central Africa. It is, therefore, a key to your operations in that strategic area." The secretary-general turned and stared coldly at the chairman.

"With all the time in the world to prepare for the independence of Bwagania, you have done nothing. You have one agent of influence there, you say. I accept that he is a good man. But without the support of a *rezidentura*, he is shackled. His communications are difficult. He can be expelled or even imprisoned, since he has no diplomatic immunity. You know we have put in a consulate general there, and yet you've not sent a *rezident* to Bwagania. Do you know something I don't know, Comrade Chairman?"

The chairman sighed to cover his embarrassment. "I've selected the *rezident*," he lied. "He is still in orientation, but he will be there by the middle of this month. I assure you the situation is well in hand. We'll have a controlling influence within a year."

"What, overthrow the monarchy in twelve months? Can you assure me?"

"If all goes as we have planned it, we will remove the king and replace him with a man we control, in less than one year."

The chairman smiled coolly at the secretary-general, thinking that with such triumphs he could replace him.

The secretary-general understood the smile, but he gave no sign. This was only one of the threats he faced daily from his colleagues in the Politburo.

"I will hold you to it, Comrade Chairman."

Moscow: KGB headquarters—
1300 hours, 1 September

The chairman of the KGB made his selection with skilled cynicism. The choice of Colonel Petrov solved one problem and moved another one overseas. It scratched a back or two in the Politburo, made a point with a member of the Central Committee, and covered up his cousin's peccadillo.

Cousin Ossilenko had been carrying a briefcase of the most sensitive documents to the office of the minister of defense. One of them was a copy of the CIA National Estimate on Soviet oil and gas that the CIA's director had been reading only a few days earlier in Washington. There were other documents, too, copied deep inside the CIA only a week ago.

Ossilenko had disobeyed standing orders that a KGB pouch with documents of this level of sensitivity had to be transmitted by official car, with an armed guard. Instead, the general had decided to walk. Then he could visit his mistress, and be back in his office with no one the wiser.

The chairman could not punish one man without punishing the other. So he decided to punish neither man. Instead, he would send Petrov to Bwagania as *rezident*. That way he could leave Ossilenko as chief of the task force that had planned and undertaken a large number of highly successful intelligence and disinformation operations against the U.S. military services, the CIA, and other Western intelligence and security services. Ossilenko might whore around, but he had an archival memory that was vital to the success of those activities.

As for Petrov, the chairman intended to terrorize him and then induct him into the circle of officers on whom he had a complete stranglehold, could count on absolutely.

Pyotr Aleksandrovich Petrov had always been a problem as well as a talented officer: a maverick with a mind of his own, but a record of successful field operations that more than compensated for his independence. In his late forties, he was one of the ablest, most experienced full colonels in the KGB. He was married to Olga Alekseyevna Lapina, daughter and only child of Aleksey Alekseyevich Lapin, former Soviet ambassador to Peking and now a full member of the Central Committee. Lapin had spent a lot of chips over the years protecting his errant son-in-law from the results of his drunken capers. Lapin had covered for him through successive disasters, to avoid embarrassment to himself and his family. But now with a good chance to move up to the Politburo—which was very much in sight at the next Party congress—he needed Petrov out of the country for a few years.

The appointment of Petrov was, fortunately, logical in personnel terms. He was tough, courageous, would shirk at nothing. His KGB career and his fluent French, English, and Arabic made him more than qualified to be *rezident* in Gitabwanga. If he was named immediately, it would preclude anyone from trying to pressure the chairman to appoint some favorite son, someone he couldn't control tightly. Petrov, with all his faults, was a good selection.

The chairman had to wait a half hour while the jailers in the Lubyanka basement cleaned Petrov up and put him in the only uniform they could find that fit, one of a private in the Border Guards. The pale, shaky officer who stood before the chairman had breath like compost and a nervous sweat that smelled of stale vodka.

The chairman was a professional at terrorizing others. Petrov was also a professional, but the chairman had all the cards. Petrov trembled, visibly exhausted, hung over, contrite, prepared for disaster, but still not an easy mark.

"Petrov," the chairman barked. "You have once again disgraced our beloved committee. You've stood on this rug four times in the recent past. Four times I've had to scold you like a small boy! Four times I've been lenient, mostly because of your family. And this is my reward? I spit in your face!"

Petrov thought, No matter what I say, he'll get even worse.

The chairman found he was trembling, too, but with rage. One hand sought the other, and he wrenched it so hard that his knuckles cracked. Beria probably would have shot Petrov. But the chairman was well aware of the power of the Lapins.

"What would you do with the good Colonel Petrov?" The chairman asked the question with sarcasm. Petrov was silent. "Well," the chairman shouted. "What would you do?"

"Send him to the Border Guards, sir. In Siberia, as a private soldier." He looked at the chairman, hoping to seem cooperative.

"You simpleton," yelled the chairman. "That would be a promotion for someone as dumb as you. I'm going to make you wish you had never been born."

The chairman was warming to the work, and felt mild surprise at how much he was enjoying his righteous indignation. He himself had got drunk the same night as Pyotr, beaten his wife and his eleven-year-old son, and then fallen asleep with a top-secret study on his chest. But then, he was above ordinary rules. He had so much heavy responsibility.

"I'm going to kill you bit by bit, Petrov. I'm going to send you to a place where you will suffer constantly from the heat. Bugs will eat you, poison your system, and ruin your silly mind. You will not drink alcohol. You will work until your body aches for death. You will only get out if I say so, and I may let you rot there forever. If you dare to make one mistake, you will be executed."

Petrov was frightened. He imagined a Gulag camp in one of the sunbelt minority republics, at hard labor, indefinitely. With a prison sentence still to be served after the chairman let him out. His head spun.

Then the chairman pulled his surprise. One that left Petrov gasping with relief.

What the chairman said was: "Petrov, you are exiled to

central Africa. You will go to Gitabwanga, in Bwagania, and open a KGB *rezidentura*. You'll stay there, out of my sight, until I send for you. You will do your best work, and even better. You will not complain or get into any trouble. You will be a strong right hand to the ambassador, but watch him carefully. He will be watching you. I don't trust either of you. You are both shit."

The chairman listened briefly to Petrov's assurances that he would follow the instructions to the letter. No more boozing, no more capers. Just hard work, loyalty, and discipline.

Petrov acted as though he understood and accepted the chairman's harsh words, but he knew one day he'd try to get back at him.

The chairman concluded angrily, "And if you screw up, I will personally see to it that you are successfully prosecuted for treason, and shot. I've given orders that a dossier be started on your treachery. The proof is being manufactured right now, enough to have you executed many times over. Believe me, Petrov, the dossier will be given to the prosecutor general the moment I give the signal. Nobody will question it, as you know!"

Moscow: the Lapins' apartment—
1630 hours, 1 September

After leaving the chairman's office, Pyotr got his ruined suit back and took a taxi to the tiny apartment he lived in with Olga and their ten-year-old daughter, Aleksandra. There was no one there.

He was perspiring when he arrived at the Lapins' apartment on exclusive Kutuzov Prospekt, the opulence of which had always irritated Pyotr, who thought of Lapin as a bureaucrat's bureaucrat. But Lapin always reeked of power, and through his Party connections he could be just as dangerous as the chairman. Pyotr had to keep Lapin's support, even if he had to beg for it. It was a chilling thought, but there was no choice.

He rang the bell and they must have sprung to the door, his slim wife, Olga, and her fat mother. They made a shrewish twosome with teeth and nails flashing. Their screeching voices echoed down the dark hallway before the door slammed and imprisoned him in the huge apartment with them. There was no sign of Aleksey Lapin or Pyotr's daughter, Aleksandra.

Pyotr was suddenly aware of the bizarre scene. Here he was, a KGB colonel dressed as a private soldier, unshaven, stinking, and still hung over. Facing him were two shrieking women, one middle-aged, with frizzy gray hair matching her wild mood. The other was in her mid-thirties, chic, mouth wide open, eyes flashing—his wife, whom he both loved and despised. Instinctively, he did the only thing that could have stopped them cold: He laughed. He simply leaned back against the door and laughed a long, rolling, heaving laugh.

The women stared at him, speechless for the moment.

His mother-in-law asked, "Is it funny?" Olga, his wife, shook her head. Pyotr never failed to surprise her. She had never got control of him. His independent streak exhausted her.

Her mother had admitted once that the only thing she liked about this crazy man was his free spirit. Then too she'd warned Olga that she must discipline him or he'd end up really disgracing the family.

Before they could speak, Pyotr gained the high ground.

"I know you both want to chastise me, but you won't be able to do better than I've already done to myself, and suffered from the chairman."

There was silence while they thought about that. Neither woman knew what had happened, except that he'd been arrested for a drunken brawl and spent the night locked up in Lubyanka. They'd had no idea he'd seen the chairman. Olga stared at him, wondering if his career was ruined and how much it would affect her.

"I've been punished severely for a serious infraction." He looked contrite, but there was no pity in their eyes, only hope that his downfall would be painless for them. Pyotr felt vaguely nauseated, but he went on.

"If I screw up again, I'll be executed for treason."

Olga paled and shook, while her mother sat down, faint and for once at a loss for words. At that moment the front door opened and Aleksey Lapin burst in from the hallway. The ambassador wore a black homburg on his head, a long black raincoat, a navy blue suit and tie. His high collar accentuated his several chins. His dark bulk and his above-average height made him seem larger than he was. His round, jowly face was deep purple with emotion, and he shouted Pyotr's name as he slammed the door shut.

"Pyotr Aleksandrovich!"

Lapin stood dramatically in the hall, legs well apart, looking from one to the other.

"Treason?" Olga's whisper cut in before her father spoke. "Treason? Pyotr, what have you done? How will we survive?"

"Treason?" Lapin yelled. "Treason requires a mind, a thinking brain. There's no question of treason. That's the chairman's way of frightening this madman."

He turned to face his wife. "Our son-in-law has finally gone too far, but we can keep this under control. The chairman called me early this morning. This animal . . ." he gestured at Petrov, ". . . this lush, got drunk and beat up General Ossilenko, the chairman's cousin. Right outside Lubyanka. Ossilenko was carrying very sensitive documents. I concurred that Pyotr should be sent to Africa as *rezident* in a banana kingdom."

"Treason, Aleksey? No treason?" She was shaking.

"Absolutely not. He didn't know what Ossilenko was carrying. He was too drunk to think. But he's a ticking time bomb and we have to keep him from destroying us."

"What about me, Papa?" Olga was, for once, out of her depth.

"You must go also, my pet. Go and tame your maniac." He finally spoke to Petrov: "And what have you to say, Private?"

"I have no excuse," said Pyotr. "I'm ashamed of what I did. I was so drunk that I thought the general was a Nazi wandering behind our lines in the Great Patriotic War. I'm grateful for your intercession, sir, and I'll gladly go to Africa and do my penance."

Pyotr crawled inwardly. He hated humbling himself before this glorified bureaucrat. He changed the subject: "I wonder why the general was walking alone. If he was carrying such sensitive documents, our rules require a car and guards. My offense was to be drunk and disorderly. His could be the real treason."

"Your job is to be grateful and do your duty in Africa without questions. Don't try to bite the hand that saves you." But Lapin saw the point and started wondering, too. He made a note to find out. Perhaps in this there was ammunition he could use to advance his career.

Langley, Virginia: CIA headquarters—1430 hours, 2 September

The director of central intelligence liked what he saw. She was pretty, cool, unruffled. A bright, intelligent look.

"There's no way to tell you how much I regret your husband's death, Mrs. Takahashi. He was a fine man and a first-class officer. We all miss him very much."

She looked into his eyes, willing the tears to stay down. "Thank you, sir. Your personal regrets mean a lot to me. He would have been very pleased."

"I never met him. Wish I had. You called him Neko-chan?"

Mark must have told him her nickname for the Cat.

"He admired you very much, Mr. Director." She wondered where this was leading.

"Thank you, Mrs. Takahashi. About your future. Cameron told me you want to stay with us and work up to case officer?"

"Yes, sir. I do want to be a field case officer. I've been an IA for two years now, and I'd like a shot at outside work. Women are good at recruiting and handling agents."

"They've been doing it as long as men have. What languages do you have?"

"Fluent French and Norwegian, sir. Some Spanish and Italian. Poor Japanese and German. That's all."

"Not bad. Not bad." The DCI knew all that. He was probing for character traits. She was calm, polite, patient, and ambitious. Now, about Cameron. Did she hate him now?

"Tell me about Mark. How's he taking the Cat's death?"

"Very hard, sir. They were good friends. The three of us were good friends, in fact. Mark's very depressed. I think you assigned him to a perfect place. He can stand on his own, recover or crash. It'll be his own doing. I think he'll recover, sir."

"You don't blame him?"

"Not at all. It might have been Mark instead . . . the luck of the game."

"You don't think he took one chance too many?"

"No, sir. I think it was well planned. Nobody could have predicted the watchman would come awake, and the dog, too."

She was discreet, loyal. But deep inside did she blame Mark?

"Why do you think the man and dog were awake?"

"I've no idea, sir. I can only guess the dog was sheltering from the rain somewhere out of sight and earshot of the embassy, until the watchman got him. Maybe all the drugs wore off early, for some reason."

"The Korean woman didn't somehow warn him?"

"Unlikely. She'd too much to lose."

"Someone else warn him?"

"The Japanese agent? No, he's been loyal for years. Besides, there's no incentive . . ."

So Mark hadn't confided his penetration theory to her? Good. The DCI decided to take a chance.

"Linda, how would you like to go out to Bwagania? Follow Cameron out there as soon as you feel rested and ready. Go as his IA. That way you'll get on-the-job training for case officer. Do well, and we'll promote you."

Linda was stunned, but she reacted quickly. It was a great opportunity. She had no fear of hardship posts.

"Case officers go where they're told, sir. I'll go gladly."

"Good. It's settled. By the way, keep an eye on Cameron. Let me know if he gets too depressed about the Cat. If his judgment is affected. He's got really good potential, and I want to be sure he gets all the help you can give him. Also, he's got a theory about this GOLD mess. Tell him he can confide in you. If he's right, we've got a serious problem and he's in the clear. If he's wrong, then there's a problem with his operational judgment. I want to know which it is. Drop me a private line if you come to any conclusions."

It sounded a little like spying on Mark, but Linda wanted to know the answer too.

"All right, Mr. Director. I'll do that."

Langley, Virginia: CIA headquarters—1600 hours, 2 September

Mark and the chief of the special technical division (STD) of the clandestine services were old friends. Mark gave him a complete rundown on the GOLD entry and the Cat's death. Then they discussed the project, looking for clues as to why it had gone wrong. Finally, as the light failed outside, the chief of STD made up his mind.

"I've been wondering whether or not to tell you this, Mark. It's sensitive, very speculative. It'll ring a bell, and perhaps you'll be able to help."

"Go on. I can't wait for the punch line."

"Not only do we have GOLD, but three other cases puzzle me. The common link is that someone's reading our mail. In each case, what looked like sure-fire success became a failure."

"Fascinating. Anything more to go on?"

"Nothing. In each case it could have been bad luck or coincidence. Like your case. But it's just as likely that the opposition knew enough to make the cases fail. We simply have no firm evidence either way. I'll run through them: Rangoon. A bug in the home of a senior KGB officer. He's a known boozer, very talkative, quite open in his taste for reading *samizdat*. The bug should have given us a good look at his recruitability. So, when it's in the wall, we fire it up. Presto! Works beautifully!"

"Then what?"

"Then, Mark, nothing. So help me! He just stops talking. We get the usual background and street noises. Doors slam, traffic roars and horns blow, dogs bark, children shout and laugh, dishes clatter, water runs, the radio plays. He talks, but he says *nothing*! It's totally out of character. No more politics, no more antiregime anecdotes, no clues as to what he really thinks. And that's all we know. Was he warned? Did he know when and where we planted the bug? Or had his boss just disciplined him for talking too much? We don't know."

"If they know the bug is there, why not pull it out and send it to Moscow for analysis? Or play it back to us, feed us disinformation? Why give us a clue that they know?"

"They already have one of this model. And if they don't trust him as much as they'd like to, they'd never play disinformation to us through him. The clues we have aren't clues unless you stack all the cases together. Perhaps the KGB's subtle enough to want to know what we'll do when these operations fail. Perhaps they hope we'll press some buttons in Moscow to try to find out what's going on. They've set more devious traps than that."

"Yes," said Mark. The game of mirrors was a given. "But that would only hold water if they could read *all* our mail."

"Which they could only do if they have a penetration inside headquarters," said the chief of STD. "Someone in Soviet operations."

"That could cripple us."

"Yes. Makes you shudder."

Mark said nothing, only nodding. He had a vivid memory of the DCI's words: *Don't talk to anyone about it . . .*

Then he asked: "The other cases?"

"Rabat, Morocco. We potted a bug into a wall fixture. A beautiful job, almost no way to detect it. Most of it's plastic, and the pinhole for the mike is invisible. The target is a Soviet GRU colonel known to drink heavily and fight with his wife. Doesn't like the regime much, and he needs money. A perfect target.

"This guy goes to the beach every Sunday with his wife and children, so the apartment's empty almost all day. Every Sunday, Mark, except when our technician came to make the entry. They stayed home. We tried again two weeks later, but they stayed home. When our technician wasn't in town, they did the usual Sundays at the beach. It happened four times, so we assumed an agent at the airport was tipping the Soviets off. Next time we brought our guy in by road. He drove down through Spain, across on the Tangier ferry, and on down to Rabat, arriving at seven A.M. Sunday, ready to go to work. He didn't go near the station. They just picked him up in town, in a parking lot. But we aborted. The Soviets were home all day again. Next Sunday they went to the beach, but our man was back at his base by then. That's where that case sits today. No real evidence, but it's pretty obvious to me that they knew what to expect and it didn't come from an airport agent."

"Like Rangoon, we don't know why they didn't let us put it in, and either catch us at it or play it back to us."

"Right. They must have a reason, but we don't know it. The third case is equally ambiguous. The target is a KGB officer under cover of first secretary in their Kinshasa embassy. A juicy target. But he moved to another office as soon as we'd made the installation. The room where we put the bug is now a storeroom, empty almost all day. Nothing of interest goes on in there. It could be bad luck, but we learned later the move was made in a hurry, for 'secret reasons,' whatever that means."

"Have you shared your suspicions with anyone else?"

"Not really. I've discussed each case with the field case officer, but you're the first to hear about all of them. There's a penetration somewhere, but we've nothing more to go on than good operational noses. And I warn you, it's not wise to cry mole unless you've something firm to back it up. The danger's obvious. If we assume a mole at the center of our Soviet operations, then we're paralyzed."

"Is his access mainly in technical operations?"

"Good point. I thought so. But I nosed about a bit and found a dozen officers worried about other non-technical operations that went wrong in the same kind of ambiguous way. They had no evidence."

"A mole, eh? We'd have to suspect every report we acquire, everyone we work with, everything we've done since . . . since when, for God's sake? There's no end to it. I hate to think about it."

"Join the club, Mark." The chief laughed. "I've done nothing else. But if you decide to work on it, let me know."

Langley, Virginia: CIA headquarters—1500 hours, 3 September

Russia division chief Jack Mason watched Mark as he listened to the request, looking carefully for signs of unacceptable stress. For signs of disorientation or of bitterness. He could find none. Mark was holding up well. The DCI's unilateral decision to send him to Gitabwanga looked all right—so far. Jack's nose was out of joint, however. His turf had been violated. By the old man, but, still, violated.

"This defector's just arrived here, Mark. You know how busy we keep them the first few months. There's a line of people like you wanting to question him. They all have good reasons. We try to help, but we've got our own priority questions that come first."

"I know, but I'm leaving in a few days. If I wait to get excerpts from his interrogation, it'll take weeks. All I'll get is a dry paragraph or two, buried among thousands of people he knows or has seen in the KGB corridors."

"What's wrong with that? We'll give you all he has on Petrov. Have you checked the files?"

"Certainly. That's why I made this request."

"They've served together somewhere?"

"Not overseas, but they've overlapped in Moscow, and I strongly suspect it'll be a very useful meeting for me."

Mason sighed. He always had difficulty turning down logical professional requests, even when they were difficult to accommodate. "Okay, Mark. I'll tell them to give you one hour. No more than that. Good luck."

Rosslyn, Virginia: Key Bridge Marriott—1930 hours, 4 September

"He wants me to join you as your IA."

Her words hit Mark like a lash. The director had assigned Linda to Gitabwanga! The implications were myriad.

"Good news," he lied. "How did he put it?" Could a pretty girl like Linda, an old friend, be a fink?

"He said you've got really good potential. He doesn't want you to get depressed. He really wants you to recover and move on with your career."

Mark's dinner was untouched.

"And you, Linda? Your career?"

"I'll be training on the job for eventual case officer status, he said."

"And watching me, eh?" He wondered if she thought he was responsible for the Cat's death, after all.

"Watching in a nice way, Mark. Because the director and I care. And because he wants me to help you pin down your theory about GOLD. Those were his words. He said you could confide in me," she explained, emphatically.

That sounded better to Mark. Maybe the director meant it. He hoped she wouldn't start crying.

"My theory is simple. There's a penetration in headquarters, and that's why GOLD failed. I got a strong hint today that I'm right." He told her about his meeting with the chief of STD.

"Perhaps you're onto something, Mark, but it's dangerous ground. I'll do all I can to help, in every way. Will I be welcome there?"

"More than welcome, Linda. A lovely addition."

But the knot of caution was still there.

Potomac, Maryland: a CIA safehouse— 0930 hours, 5 September

The new defector's cryptonym was ZINC. A week ago he'd been KGB colonel Nikolai Nikolaievich Krasin, assigned to the fifth department of the first chief directorate at KGB headquarters, the department that dealt with Western Europe. On TDY (temporary duty) to Belgium, he'd defected to the CIA station there, established his bona fides beyond any doubt, and been flown covertly to the U.S. He was just beginning interrogation by the agency. It was to be the most arduous year of his life. The memory searches were repetitious, grinding work from morning to night. ZINC was already of enormous value to CIA, and it had been hard for his handlers to fit Mark's hour into the schedule.

Mark expected a carbon copy of the other defectors he'd met: egotistical, arrogant, sensitive, supremely confident outside but very insecure within. Many were childish, angry with the world and with the CIA's refusal to take them into its staff. Most were mavericks—they drank too much and threw tantrums.

ZINC was different. A small man, patient, courteous, undemanding. His handlers had told Mark they'd never known a defector as easy as this one to interrogate, feed, or house. No temper fits, no drunken scenes or throwing things.

Mark was introduced as Mike MacCarran. They spoke in Russian.

"My interest is in two places, Colonel. Japan and Bwagania. And they've given me only one hour."

"Perhaps it will take much less, Mr. MacCarran. I know very little about either." He didn't ask why two such disparate places.

"Have you heard of an operation in Tokyo in which one of our men was killed? Recently?"

"No. Can you tell me against what target it was run? It might jog my memory."

"Against the Rumanians, Colonel."

He thought about that, nodding his head.

"I have never heard anything about the Rumanians in Tokyo. The only thing I've heard about the Rumanian security people recently is far removed from Tokyo. They just bought some guard dogs from East Germany, dogs trained to refuse to eat anything but the food their handlers give them. That was a specific request, I recall."

Mark could feel his skin crawl.

"When was this, and where were the dogs sent?"

"Five, six weeks ago. They were sent to Bucharest. Half a dozen of them. The only reason I know is that we asked for some guard dogs too, for use by our border guards. We had to wait. There aren't that many well-trained dogs being put out by the East German kennels. It's the best training in the world, I'm told."

"No more details? Where were they to be used?"

But ZINC had no more to tell on that score. He did on another subject.

"Paris has just told us that a Colonel Pyotr Aleksandrovich Petrov is going out to Gitabwanga to be the first KGB *rezident* there," said Mark. "According to his visa request, he's taking his wife and daughter. Do you know him?"

"I've only met him a few times, so I don't know him well. We never served in the same overseas posts. We were in Moscow at the same time, but I saw very little of him. He moves in social circles quite outside my own. His father-in-law is Aleksey Alekseyevich Lapin, who was ambassador in China and now is in line for a Politburo candidacy. Lapin has saved Petrov a number of times from severe disciplining. Petrov has talent. He can be charming, and that's the only the side of him I've seen. They say he's a fine case officer, a leader, a linguist. A good observer, reporter, agent recruiter, and handler. I found him bright and likable."

"What did Lapin save him from?"

"Petrov has quite a reputation. He drinks a lot and is always getting into scrapes."

"He's quite senior, according to our files. Is Bwagania a logical assignment for him? It's a tiny country."

"It's hard to say. He looks too senior, yes. But our emphasis is very much on that area right now, so it may be logical. Or he may have had one scrape too many."

"Have you anything to go on either way?"

"Just corridor gossip that one day he'll go too far, use up his credits, even with Lapin."

"Are KGB corridor rumors usually accurate?"

"Nearly always."

"If that's the case, could Petrov recover?"

"Oh, yes," said ZINC bitterly. "The top leaders take care of their own. He'll pull some kind of an intelligence coup in Bwagania. Get promoted and rehabilitated. Go off to the plush Western posts he and his wife like so well."

"She stays with him? What's she like?"

"It's hard to visualize her in central Africa from what I've heard about her. She's spoiled. Very chic. At home in Paris or London. Fluent in English and French. Full of herself. Typical." ZINC waved his hand as if brushing away the Party's darlings. "One of the most difficult things to bear in Moscow is the difference between the treatment of people like me—run-of-the-mill—and those who've gravitated to the top of our 'classless' society."

"That's mainly what brought you here?"

"That, and the cynicism it springs from. The total lack of ethics. I was part of it, and I just got sick of it. You know, Mr. MacCarran, we Russians are still basically a very religious people. The facts we know are offensive to us, even to some of us in the KGB. I speak for the little man, too, from whose bosom I come." ZINC's eyes showed fury.

Mark waited for the man's quiet emotion to pass. "Do the corridor rumors include anything about our operations in Tokyo?"

"Not that I heard," said ZINC. "About our people stationed there, yes. But not about your operations."

"Nothing to indicate that anyone in Moscow Center was reading our mail?"

"Nothing like that. But then if we were, I wouldn't necessarily have heard about it. It would be a very closely held secret. Something only for those with a need to know."

Paris: the CIA station—1030 hours, 8 September

The flight from Dulles had been calm, but he hadn't slept. Now, waiting in the chief of station's (COS) outer office, Mark was fighting a battle against fatigue.

He looked up to see the COS, Daniel Reilly, grinning down at him. Reilly wore thick, soft rubber soles and walked quietly. A large, white-faced man with a vaguely preoccupied air. He was a scholar to look at, but was in fact a hard, practical, professional case officer. He ran the station impeccably, but as if by accident, issuing orders diffidently. But his people obeyed as if they'd been delivered in a parade ground bark. He had excellent rapport with the French, despite the sometimes difficult relationship between France and the United States, as mutually critical allies, with peppery tempers that flared up frequently. The senior officials of SSR admired and liked Reilly no matter what their government's line might be this week. He took them and the alliance seriously, and even when his other station officers were given the cold shoulder, Reilly was personally welcome in the SSR inner sanctum.

"Well, Mark," he taunted. "Getting old? Long trips too much? Where's the coiled spring I used to see?"

They shook hands, laughing. Mark briefed Reilly on GOLD, including what ZINC had said. But he kept silent on his own speculation about a mole. Reilly picked up the thread, however, without any prompting.

"Someone reading your mail? You've thought of that?"

"Certainly, Dan. One of the my first thoughts. But I've nothing to go on except the few clues I've given you. Why? Do you have any ideas?"

"Perhaps, Mark. Before we get to that, I've arranged for you to get a briefing on Bwagania. SSR helped put it together. When do you leave, and how many will be there in your station?"

"I leave for Gitabwanga the eleventh. We'll be just three. A communicator, who's being selected by the director of communications. Linda Takahashi will be the IA. The DCI wanted that. She comes in a week or so."

Reilly whistled silently. "The Cat's widow? Romance?"

"Not at all. We're good friends, but I'm a confirmed bachelor as you know. Anyway the DCI doesn't pimp."

That afternoon Mark was briefed by station officers on Bwagania. History, tribal lore and customs, geography, infrastructure, communications, internal politics, police, French influence now and after independence, and so on. Bwagania went from an imaginary and impenetrable jungle full of wild animals to a living nation of much charm. He could almost smell and touch the people, game, mountains, valleys, deserts, rain forests, savannah, and lakes that the briefers and their photographers described.

Paris: a CIA safehouse—2030 hours, 9 September

Before the French intelligence officer came, Reilly explained to Mark, "He's a senior SSR officer. Very senior. He'll be using an alias. He's goosey—not without reason. He's in charge of SSR operations against the French Communist party, among other things. We're close friends, and I'm sure he tells me more than his bosses would like. He knows the new SSR chief going down to Gitabwanga."

"Jean Dumont" lived up to his advance billing. A roly-poly, round-faced man not five feet six inches tall, he wore a thick Harris tweed suit that added to his bulk.

"A pleasure to meet you, Monsieur Cameron. I hope you will enjoy Bwagania. A little paradise in central Africa. What a change from Washington."

"Actually, almost directly from Tokyo, Monsieur Dumont."

Dumont's eyes widened. "Excellent French, excellent. You didn't tell me that, Daniel. Better than your French."

"He's always been good at primitive languages, Jean." Reilly couldn't resist that one. Dumont laughed, flipping Reilly a crude gesture. Then he was serious.

He spoke for two hours, with occasional comments or questions from the two Americans, filling in the gaps in the station briefing.

Then he described François de la Maison.

"He's my good friend. He left for Bwagania a week ago. A fine officer. He feels the way I do about you Americans . . . our only true allies. You will like him."

"What's he like?" Mark asked.

"A gentleman, a flower of France. Brave, highly intelligent, honest, discreet, and with a good sense of humor. He's a professional soldier, now a colonel."

Then Dumont spoke about Petrov.

"You know from the visa request that he's going to Gitabwanga with his wife and only child. We know a lot about this Soviet, yet we don't really know him. His drunken capers are legendary in the KGB and would have sent most officers to Siberia. Lapin always saves him from all but the most perfunctory retribution. The marriage is turbulent, perhaps cemented by his love for ten-year-old Aleksandra. A talented man, a good intelligence officer and linguist. Perhaps you know all this?"

"Most of it." Mark nodded. He told Dumont what ZINC

had said and what the CIA files had contained on Petrov.

Then Dumont got to the meat.

"Petrov is a revolutionary, kicking against the Soviet system. We know that, but not how deep that spirit goes. Is he liable to defect? To accept being a Western agent-in-place? Or is his smoke without fire . . . would he refuse the concept out of hand? We don't know enough about him, but I believe he's a worthwhile target."

"Have you anything firm to go on, Monsieur Dumont?"

"Only an opinion, but the opinion of one of the leaders of the French Communist party, a man with excellent contacts in the KGB. He said, in confidence, to an agent of ours with a very long record of accurate reporting, that Petrov is a wild card. 'Wild enough,' he told our agent, 'so that I'd not be surprised one day to find him on TV denouncing the Kremlin, after defecting to the West.' I'm satisfied that our agent reported what he heard accurately."

"That is very useful, Monsieur Dumont. You've saved me months of work."

Dumont was silent for a minute. Then he said, "I don't often hear about Tokyo in my work. It's curious, but we did get a report recently that mentioned Tokyo."

Mark sat up straighter. "Unusual?"

"Yes, in fact it was. A German shepherd guard dog in a cage was shipped by air from Bucharest to Paris, then transshipped to Tokyo. The odd thing was that the transaction was heavily camouflaged. The paperwork showed the origin of the animal as Vienna, where in fact the aircraft had stopped. The final destination was shown as Bangkok. The paperwork was changed here by trusted members of the French Communist party, so the link between Bucharest and Tokyo was extinguished. We wondered why it was that important. Just a dog, after all."

Mark tensed. He could see Reilly stiffen, too.

"When did the dog leave for Tokyo, and to whom was it consigned?"

"It left Paris on August fifteenth, consigned to a Rumanian who lives in Tokyo, a certain Ion Pauker. You know him?"

"We do," said Mark. "He's the security officer of the Rumanian embassy in Tokyo. A nasty swine. We owe him one." Mark didn't explain.

Dumont's last topic for this meeting was mainly addressed to Reilly.

"You remember, Daniel, that last time we met I spoke of a hot report we were told we'd get in a few days, one that involves the CIA? We were translating it from Russian."

"I do," said Reilly. "Can't wait."

"My source," said Dumont, "is a leading member of the Fourth International, the organization that is loyal to Trotsky's memory. He has one remaining source in Moscow. They are both old men now. That's all I can tell you about my source and his access, except that the case is so sensitive that I've handled the man at this end, the Trotskyite in France, myself for over thirty years."

He went on. "This is now early September. In May, my source gave me a report that covered certain activities of the Fourth International and their contacts inside the USSR. A rather unique report. I gave you a paraphrased version in French, which you sent to your headquarters."

"Correct, Jean. It's been very tightly held back there, I assure you."

"Perhaps not tightly enough. A summary of it has shown up in Paris, in French CP headquarters. It took months, but it's there. My source's friend in Moscow is furious. It's too close for comfort. Only a very few people in Moscow knew what he'd told my source. He's safe, so far—the man in Moscow. They can't pin it on anyone, because we paraphrased it very carefully. But we're unlikely to get anything from him again."

"Can't pin what on anyone?"

"The fact that it was sourced to us as the origin. The French CP got it from Moscow. My problem is that the summary was in American English."

"My God." Reilly sat staring at Dumont for a few minutes. "Are you certain that it was a summary from the copy you gave us?"

"No question. Here it is. The Brits don't spell *neighbor* without a *u*."

"I'll go back up the line, Jean. We'll find out, I assure you." Reilly's face was whiter than usual.

"Have you other indications of this type?" Dumont asked astutely.

They shook their heads. It was too soon to rock the boat. When Dumont had gone, Reilly said: "I'll get a cable off to headquarters tonight. Ruin their breakfast."

"It'll ruin mine too," said Mark. "Maybe somebody's looking up your tailpipe. But if it's linked with what we discussed earlier, we've got a real problem."

"I won't know if it's linked or not until we get the full story from headquarters as to how they handled it and who they disseminated it to. That may take weeks."

"If it is linked, my advice is that you put the facts into your special channel to the director."

"Sounds wise," said Reilly, smiling, understanding.

Moscow: Sheremetyevo Airport—0830 hours, 10 September

The Lapins' shiny, long, black Chaika limousine slid quietly to a stop and Lapin led the way into the VIP lounge. His wife, Olga, and Aleksandra trotted behind, with Aleksandra in tears, although she secretly couldn't wait to see the most exotic place she'd ever heard of: Bwagania. Pyotr brought up the rear and then stood apart, ignored as Lapin and his wife showered gifts, last-minute advice, and goodbyes on Olga and Aleksandra. Finally, the Lapins graced him with a handshake.

"Be sure to keep your nose clean in Bwagania, Petrov," said Aleksey condescendingly. "You can revive your career if you really try."

"Thank you, sir. I'll do my best."

"It will interest you to know that General Ossilenko, too, has to be careful. His security violations aren't the whole story."

"No, sir?" This was dangerous ground. Why was Lapin telling him this?

"He's a womanizer. No doubt he'll visit you out there. Let

me know what you observe." It was an order, not a request.

"Yes, sir. You can depend on me."

"That'll be new, Pyotr Aleksandrovich. Take care of Olga." He turned his back and strode off.

Paris: a KGB safehouse—2200 hours, 10 September

Pyotr Petrov was beginning to yawn. It had been a very long day, starting before dawn in Moscow at his apartment, then a tedious breakfast at the Lapin apartment, a delayed, noisy Aeroflot flight to Paris, a briefing in the *rezidentura*—where the *rezident*, a major general, had snubbed him by not appearing—an afternoon of collecting their visas and then shopping with Olga to buy—among other things—two years' worth of birthday and New Year presents for Aleksandra. Now this interminable briefing on Bwagania by a KGB agent who was highly placed in the FCP (French Communist party).

His eyes closed as the speaker droned on, his Parisian accent impeccable, his grammar and delivery precious: "One must understand, Colonel, that the masses are anxious for delivery from the colonialist-capitalist oppressors—nothing will stop them now. They ask only your help to rid themselves of their king and become a peoples' republic . . ."

It was the second time he'd made the same statement, and this time Pyotr interrupted him. "Tell me about the police and the armed forces. What equipment do they have? What is the state of their morale? What combat experience do the army's senior officers have? Are they loyal to the king? What is the structure and strength of the Sûreté? How close are the Bwagania leaders to the French administration? Those are the things I need to know."

"Well, Colonel . . . I don't have all the answers to those questions. But if you wish to know about the popular movement . . ."

Pyotr dozed off again, bored by the one-track mind of the armchair intellectual who had been selected to brief him. He would have preferred to hear from a hands-on labor activist, for example, who had lived in Bwagania, knew the people, and understood their problems and the balance between the old and the new Bwagania. Who knew what the key questions were and had their answers.

The next statement, however, opened his eyes. ". . . we in the FCP have never trusted our counterparts in Bwagania. They have no socialist discipline. You schedule a discreet meeting with them, and they are liable to come a day late, with girlfriends, often drunk. They tell their wives or girlfriends everything. Disgusting. That's why I advised Moscow to form a cadre of carefully chosen activists drawn from outside the Bwaganian Communist party. I hope you did that."

"What do you know about the armed forces, the police, and the Sûreté?" insisted Pyotr, ignoring the question, determined to keep his own agenda.

"Frankly, almost nothing, but I can arrange for another person to brief you. He knows the subject better."

"There isn't enough time," said Pyotr. "I've got meetings all day tomorrow in the embassy, then we leave for Gitabwanga at night."

Gitabwanga: Bwaga Airport—
0600 hour, 12 September

Bwaga Airport, named for King Bwaga VI, was quiet when Colonel François de la Maison got there at dawn. Morning doves cooed and scuttled out of his way when he walked from his car, a brand-new Peugeot, toward the terminal. François was happy this morning: alive and well, back in his favorite continent, his own boss. Not nearly as good as commanding a line regiment, but the next best thing.

The terminal was a two-story cinder-block building with a stubby control tower growing out of its corner. A single hangar huddled close by, an overgrown Nissen hut without a front. On the tarmac, a twin-engined private plane warmed up, its noise barely audible in the tower.

François climbed the stairs to the top of the tower, where a tiny room next to the traffic controller was set aside for the Bwaganian Sûreté. One of his warrant officers was already at work.

"Bonjour, Jacques. On se défend?"

"Oui, mon colonel. Je suis prêt." Jacques smiled at this new chef de poste with the bright blue eyes and bronzed face who had so quickly captured the loyalty of the entire SSR contingent in Bwagania.

François inspected the sequence camera mounted on a tripod, its telephoto lens canted downward to where the incoming airliner would park. A venetian blind with one slat gone camouflaged the camera from outside observers.

Satisfied, François nodded approval and walked out onto the deck. Jacques leaned against the wall nearest the camera, bored and yawning as they waited.

Looking out over the flat plain beyond the airport fence, François drank in the sights and sounds. The grass, sandy soil, thorn trees, and scrub were alive with movement. A herd of Thompson's gazelle grazed in full view. A lone Cape buffalo moodily chewed its cud nearby. Weaver birds buzzed around their nests in a eucalyptus. Groups of kudu, giraffe, hartebeest, and zebra were scattered over the plain, and overhead two vultures wheeled in lazy circles as they patrolled for morning prey.

He pulled two visa photos from his pocket, to refresh his memory. Cameron looked the part. Straightforward and a hint of humor. Petrov's visa-application snapshot, on the other hand, had a slightly sinister, chilling look. I wonder if that comes from my instinctive bias? he thought, smiling at his own prejudice, but with no resolve to change it.

Below, on the ground floor, an SSR lieutenant ran through the hidden passport camera routine with a young Bwaganian Sûreté trainee. In just over three months, independence would force France to relinquish all government services to Bwagania. The lieutenant thought the Africans, especially this young man, would have a hard time managing on their own.

"Remember, the passengers can't see the camera. You must be sure each passport is inside the lines or the camera won't get both pages. Don't move the passport when you step on the foot pedal. Take your time, photograph only those pages on which there are visas or entry and exit stamps." Why was this trainee so slow?

The Bwaganian, son of a noble, soon to be a lieutenant in his own right, was deliberately slow. He nodded and smiled at the French lieutenant. He held the practice passport half outside the guide lines, to irritate the Frenchman.

Outside, the Air France flight from Paris rolled to a stop and passengers began climbing down the ramps. François watched carefully from the top deck, aware of the picturesque figure he cast in his uniform, the cloth looking gold in the early sun.

First out of the forward door were two rotund French businessmen. Then an Arab in a Moroccan caftan. Then Mark Cameron, looking around at the plain, the mountains, the airport terminal, and then straight at François. A half smile on his face, he stopped briefly and turned his face left and right, giving the hidden camera a good profile.

Behind the blinds, Jacques exclaimed happily that he got three good shots, one full face and two in profile. François knew Cameron had posed for them.

A few more passengers came out, then the Petrovs. No question as to who they were. Their visa photos were quite good, but today François wanted some really good shots.

"Jacques, those three . . . the man, wife, and little girl. Get all you can of the adults."

"D'accord, mon colonel." Jacques fired a dozen shots, eight of Pyotr, four of Olga.

Pyotr didn't look up at the deck. He was trying to spot the Soviet embassy greeting party. But François hadn't allowed them onto the field.

Inside the terminal, the French lieutenant gave a last warning to the Bwaganian trainee and walked up the stairs to a gallery from which he could observe the scene. François joined him there, and they leaned over the rail.

The Bwaganian trainee had instructions to photograph non-French passports only. But now he was really angry with the French lieutenant. He'd show them when he was airport commander. He'd show them now, too. And he did. He photographed every page of every passport—French, Moroccan, Italian, Greek, American, Soviet. Blank pages and all. The long minutes ticked by, and the line of tired and impatient passengers became noisier.

Mark, then Pyotr and Olga were duly inspected by the trainee and their passports photographed at length. Mark, well aware of the hidden camera delaying the line, smiled at the African and said, *"Fromage."*

The trainee, sweating freely now that he had committed himself, was grateful for the smile. He mumbled a half apology and smiled weakly back. Then Mark was through the line, looking for his luggage.

Pyotr looked on, bored, while the Bwagania trainee turned each page of their passports. He wondered why the French tolerated the photographing of so many blank pages. He decided the French hadn't taught them much during all those colonial years. He doubted they would improve after independence. Pyotr shared the average Russian's contempt for blacks.

François looked down at this Soviet, the first KGB *rezident* in Bwagania. He thought Petrov and his family looked quite civilized. He was glad to see Mark and hoped he and the American could be allies, not antagonists. They would need each other.

As if he could hear François, Pyotr looked up at the tall, slender, tanned Frenchman and noted the colonel's insignia. He etched the face in his memory, aware that this man might be the chief of the security services. Or maybe the SSR chef de poste. But he could detect no sign of any kind on that impassive face. Pyotr looked down at his daughter, then at Olga. He said nothing, having learned long ago not to share his thoughts with Olga unless he had a solid reason to.

It was then that Pyotr and Mark noticed each other for the first time. There was instant mutual recognition. Not because they had ever met, but because each had seen the other's photograph in the files. Neither man showed any sign of having discerned who the other was. A cool stare from each side. There would be time later to meet and joust. Now they merely sized each other up.

Mark thought he caught a whiff of something inside Pyotr that he hadn't expected. Where was the glint in this maverick's eyes that Mark had imagined? How badly had the chairman kicked him?

Behind the two, the French lieutenant watched with delight as the African trainee doggedly photographed every page of all the remaining passports. Fifty furious passengers, many of them his own countrymen, were shouting their anger at the

African. The lieutenant paraded down the line, whispering, "He's training for independence, you know. One must be patient." And to the French passengers, he added: *"Les Africains, vous savez . . . on a fait son possible . . ."*

With a quick word to the lieutenant, François arranged for the opening of another immigration line before the situation got out of hand.

Ivan Ivanovich Raspatov, Soviet consul general and ambassador-designate to Bwagania, had come to the airport to meet his new KGB *rezident* and his VIP wife. He delivered a short, cordial welcome speech in flowery Russian, right at the luggage table. The Bwaganian customs officer trainee waved the Petrov luggage through unopened and listened to the strange language with wide eyes. His father had told him that Russia was made of snow, which the Bwaganian had never seen. He wasn't even sure that the story of water turning white in cold countries was true. Everyone knew that white men told such lies!

From the moment he saw Raspatov, Pyotr could not take his eyes off him. The thin, tall, white-haired diplomat, wearing a baggy pair of trousers and a white shirt with no tie, reminded Pyotr so vividly of his own father that for a few minutes he was back in his family's apartment in Moscow.

His father had been a career warrant officer in the tsar's cavalry. Wounded in 1916, he was recuperating on light duties in a rear-echelon job when the October 1917 revolution took place, followed not long after by the civil war. Petrov senior was a natural for "military specialist" in Trotsky's Red Army and he accepted an immediate commission. He rose quickly to full colonel.

He was still a colonel in 1937 when six burly Chekists came to the tiny apartment to take him away. It was winter and Pyotr could still see them clearly, in their heavy overcoats, filling the dingy living room with the musk of raw power. Every detail was clear in his memory. Pyotr and his two brothers were lined up, their mother beside them, to say farewell. Pyotr, thirteen years old, adored his father. The Chekists waited with growing cynical impatience. They had done this many times before, would do it many times again.

To them, Colonel Petrov was a nuisance keeping them from their after-work drinking.

The old man put on his full dress uniform with his hero's medals. He spoke to each of his family in turn while the six anonymous men scuffed their boots and spat on the floor. He whispered words to each boy, trying to encourage them. Pyotr knew he would never see his father again, and when his turn came to say goodbye, he choked and was unable to speak. He shook all over, his eyes overflowed, and his knees sagged as the seconds ran out and his beloved father was pulled away. Pyotr had wanted to hold him, to put his arms about him and kiss him, to protect him.

But he stood there in utter misery, too young to fight, no weapons to fight with, no guidance from his family. Only a sense of shame and frustration that he would carry with him to the grave.

It is a testament to the cruel Soviet regime that Pyotr eventually became a colonel in the same system, in the KGB, where he too performed similar raids to capture and execute "political unreliables" or "enemies of the people" for a state that had callously extinguished his father for no just reason.

Consul General Raspatov came to the end of his speech and noticed with surprise that Colonel Petrov, KGB, had tears in his eyes. Raspatov was pleased his words had shaken Petrov—or so he thought. He didn't recognize the distance in Petrov's stare.

He had barely heard the words of the welcome speech. Still, he smiled appreciatively at the ambassador, in whom, he decided, he could quite clearly place his trust.

Olga was sickened by the speech and her husband's reaction to it. These men are children, she thought. The men in her family never behaved this emotionally.

Gitabwanga: the royal wall—
1945 hours, 12 September

A breeze stirred the lake and the trees around the royal wall, and it was cool in the evening. This was the season of the "cow rains," the short, sharp rains from towering thunderheads, less brutal than the "buffalo rains" of spring. The evening was full of the scents of tropical plants, charcoal fires, old leather, people and animals, and the fermentation of palm wine.

Gusts of wind blew the smells of Gitabwanga across the royal palace grounds, and the king felt closer to his people the more their scent came to him.

Bwaga VI sat on the wall and waited. His shoulders were cold and his bottom was beginning to suffer from the chilled stones. The cow rains had come quickly and he had forgotten to bring a blanket, but he would stay the allotted hour. He lit his pipe, clicking the trimmer in case the old man was there.

The first he knew of the presence was a quiet cough below him. They began the ritual greeting. One full minute, in sing-song tones, to satisfy their ancestors as well as themselves. Then there was silence for a full minute more.

"Sire?" The soft voice wove wispily through the breeze, but it was audible.

"Yes, old one. I am ready. What news do you have?"

"The European, the one you and I call Tofi, his full name is Pierre Schacht. I saw a note to call him on your son's desk." The old man spelled it for the king, slowly and shakily, for his reading and writing were marginal.

"Have you learned anything else about him?"

"He is said to come from a wealthy, mountainous country named Haut Riche."

The king laughed. "Autriche does happen to be a rich, mountainous country, but the name means eastern kingdom."

"Some of the servants in Prince Simba M'Taga's house have met people from there. They say he is not like them."

"How does he differ?"

"They say he speaks and acts differently from the others, sire. All I know is that this man is cold inside."

"Can you say more about that?"

"A cold spirit in him, my king. Not a warm one."

"And my son, the prince?"

"He is like a chicken facing a green tree snake, sire. Prince Simba believes everything that Tofi says. He is slowly changing, becoming a stranger to us older ones. He uses words that are new, like *enemies of the people*, *people's revolution*, and *socialist brethren*. Words I do not understand, really. Words you would never use, Bwaga VI."

"And the young men who support my son?"

"They were all students in Europe, sire. They come from the best families in Bwagania." He reeled off half a dozen names, all young nobles.

"Finally, Bwaga VI, they often go secretly to a place up in the hills. They take guns and other weapons, to practice shooting."

"Where do they go? How many times a week? When?" The king felt as if cockroaches were crawling over his body, and despite the chill he broke into a sweat.

"They always go on Fridays, in the morning while it is cool, when others are at the mosque. Sometimes they go two or three other days a week. They do this shooting in a ravine behind the village of Bendaga, several kilometers toward the mountains from the village."

Gitabwanga: the royal palace—
2230 hours, 13 September

Sitting in an old leather armchair in his library, King Bwaga VI waited for his hunter. The king was an avid reader, and the walls were lined with novels, history books, travel books and, here and there, leather-bound volumes by the masters of English, French, German, Italian, and Russian literature.

The hunter had had to drive fifty kilometers from the royal hunting lodge, up in the mountains, where he lived in a large cottage next to the king's elegant stone lodge. Bwaga VI drank a scotch and soda slowly as he waited, a copy of *Le Canard Enchainé* open, unread, on his lap. He could think of nothing but his oldest son.

The Sicilian came into the room without a sound, as the king's hunter should. The king felt his usual mild irritation, mixed with amusement, when he finally realized that the Sicilian had been beside his chair for some time.

"Well, hunter, you can still stalk on carpets, I see. How does it go in the bush?"

"Better with age, sire. We Sicilians improve, like good wine, as time opens before us." The Sicilian always spoke as if he were acting in a Shakespearean play. It was his only foible. Otherwise he was a deadly, coldly merciless killer.

The king was tired and he made it short.

"I have a job for you. One that must be kept in your head only. Swear to me you will speak not one word to anyone but me. Not anyone, understand?"

They had been here before. The Sicilian bowed and put his hand over his heart. *"Je le jure*, Bwaga VI."

"Good. There is a ravine behind the village of Bendaga, toward the mountains. Go there this Friday and after that go every day until you succeed. Go at dawn, leaving your horse well away from the ravine. Take a camera with a long lens. Photograph anyone who comes there to practice with weapons. My son M'Taga may come, and you must photograph him also. Do not let them see you. Then photograph their cars, showing the license plates. Bring the film to me, undeveloped."

"It shall be as you say, sire."

"It had better be. Our lives will depend on it."

The Sicilian slipped away without a word. As long as he was alive, he would do exactly as the king had said.

Gitabwanga: Bendaga village—0545 hours, 14 September

It was still dark on Thursday morning, with the first hint of dawn showing in the east, when the Sicilian drove slowly through Bendaga village in his battered Land Rover. Mud obscured the license plates. His two German shepherds lay quietly on the floor behind him, trained to move only when he told them to. His tanned face and wide-brimmed hunting hat made it impossible to see him from outside the vehicle. He had cased the place and was gone before anyone was awake.

Next, the Sicilian drove along the gravel road to a point

one mile from the Bendaga ravine. He pulled off well into the bush and set off on foot, rifle at the ready, dogs obediently behind him, to scout the area. They walked quietly, the dogs sniffing the still morning air, ready to growl softly if there was a reason.

By full light he had cased the entire area and had decided how he would do the job the king wanted, unobserved, with ease. He was back at the royal hunting lodge by noon.

The Sicilian had been in Africa since 1940. As a sergeant in Mussolini's army, he was captured by the British in Abyssinia and taken to Kenya in 1942 to work on the roads. He elected to remain in Kenya when the British released him, and a British coffee planter took him on as assistant farm manager. The Sicilian stayed there for five years, turning out to be a natural shot, an instinctive hunter. He soon set out on his own and became the first and only Sicilian "white hunter" in East Africa.

But one dawn the Sicilian "accidentally" shot and killed an American client. The client's lovely wife stayed on in Kenya after the funeral and lived with the Sicilian—even on safari. There was an investigation, the Sicilian's native trackers and servants told stories of a love affair that predated the American client's death. Nothing could be pinned on the Sicilian, but he was expelled from the colony.

Nor was the Sicilian welcome in any other British colony. The American woman stayed with him, and they wandered together across Uganda, Rwanda-Urundi, the Kivu and Maniema provinces of the Congo, and eventually fetched up in Bwagania. They arrived in Gitabwanga one afternoon, complete with red Rolls-Royce, two Land Rovers, two drivers, a cook, a steward, a Great Dane, tents and guns and a small mountain of baggage. The beautiful American woman was now his wife. They pitched camp and settled into their tents on a vacant piece of city land on the shore of Lake Tchagamba.

Government was primitive then in Bwagania, and the Sicilian got a license to set up in business as a white hunter, a profession still generally unknown in the country. The Bwaganian who issued the license was unaware of what the words *chasseur blanc* intended. Rather than show his ignorance, he approved the application. He thought it might mean that a man had been sent to Bwagania who was approved to execute whites, a rare occasion. He pretended to shoot a rifle and asked: "*C'est à descendre les blancs*?"

The Sicilian's French was rudimentary and he laughed and nodded vigorously, thinking he was being asked if he hunted for a living: "*Oui, Oui,*" he shouted. "*Baff, Baff, beaucoup!*" They clapped each other on the back, and the Sicilian went off with his license.

As it turned out, the license was never used. There was no other Rolls-Royce in the country, and people came from long distances to admire it. Even the king had to be content with a Mercedes for state occasions and a souped-up Bugatti for fun. When the king heard about the strange new license, and the red Rolls-Royce, he drove himself into the Sicilian's camp. Staring at the Rolls-Royce as he drove, the king clipped the pegs for the guy ropes of the cook tent and collapsed it. There was muffled bellowing from inside the stricken tent, where the cook's face was jammed into the salad he was preparing.

The king loved amusing scenes, and this one tickled him. He got out of his car and leaned against it, laughing uncontrollably. The Sicilian, not in the least upset, joined him and he, too, laughed at the scene. The cook crawled out of the fallen tent and, recognizing the king, clapped his hands and bowed in respect. The Sicilian, realizing this must be the king, bowed too. Then Bwaga VI saw the Sicilian's wife, and he kissed her hand with a flourish. A red Rolls-Royce and a beautiful woman. . . . He commanded them to dine with him at the palace that evening.

Within a week, the Sicilian was hired as the royal hunter, a new job that the French paid for with much grumbling. Within two weeks, his wife was hired as the royal social secretary, with the old one sent back to France. The Sicilian ran the royal game collection and put game on the royal table. He was out of town enough to make his wife an easy mark, and she became an enthusiastic visitor to the king's bed.

It didn't take the Sicilian long to find out about the king

and his wife, but it seemed a small enough tribute to pay for his new start in life and the security the king gave them. That, and an occasional loan of the Rolls-Royce for royal occasions.

Gitabwanga: the Bendaga ravine—0900 hours, 15 September

The ravine behind the village of Bendaga is deep and sheer, the floor of the ravine dry and sandy, with some grass and a lot of bushes and trees. Near the mouth of the ravine a shallow draw leaves the main cut and ends in a cliff some fifty feet high. In the morning the eastern sun rises directly behind the draw and against the cliff. Weapons fired at the cliff are inaudible in the village. One lookout on the road outside the ravine can command the approaches from the village. Except for a narrow gully, almost an invisible slit, that cuts into the ravine from the east opposite the draw, the same lookout can also command the mountain approaches.

The Sicilian had found the gully, and its approach from the hills high above the ravine, late on a Wednesday. Now it was Friday. He lay on the sand where the gully joined the ravine, relaxed as a resting cat. He wore a bush hat, camouflage shirt and pants, and safari boots. His brown face and hands added to the effect, and he was invisible from two meters away. When he moved, it was slowly and steadily, and even nearby birds and small animals were not alarmed.

The Sicilian had selected a calm horse. He left it feeding a mile away, reins trailing on the ground. The horse had evaded a dozen attacks by leopards and lions in the past. Bush-wise and silent, it too was a survivor.

He had his favorite .357 magnum rifle leaning against a nearby rock, and he watched the scene in front of him through the 400 mm lens of a Nikon camera. The long lens brought their faces up clearly from 150 feet away.

Prince Simba M'Taga had arrived with the party, and now he coached them on the firing line. There were seven young men, all of good Bwaganian families. In between rounds of firing, they chatted and laughed as if they were on a picnic outing. But when they faced the targets, they were deadly serious.

The Sicilian noticed that all the weapons were British- or American-made. A good selection of small arms: revolvers, rifles, semiautomatic rifles, submachine guns, grenade launchers, bazookas. On a folding table there was a display of plastic explosives complete with fuses and detonators. A flame thrower, which they used only once, taking care not to ignite the grass, completed the arsenal.

When there were questions about the weapons that the prince couldn't answer, a man the Sicilian had not seen before was at his elbow to help, a brown-haired European, maybe fifty-five years old. The European spoke softly, and his voice never carried to the Sicilian. The European handled weapons with easy skill. The young man knew him, and they called him Pierre. Their respect for him was evident.

The Sicilian photographed everything: the prince, Pierre, and the seven young men; the table with its display of explosives; the flame thrower in action. He exposed two rolls of film, and then wriggled back into the gully, returned to his horse to comfort it and excuse himself for another long absence. Then he reloaded the camera, circled to the road, assuming the sentry would be facing west, away from the morning sun, bored, maybe even asleep.

He was right. The sentry was asleep, his face turned west, away from the Sicilian's approach. The hunter came up on him from the east, the sun behind him, the wind in his teeth. He moved slowly, deliberately, with the silence of patience, stopping often to watch. Finally, he was ten meters from the sentry. He photographed the two cars, the van, and the sentry, with details of the license plates, car makes, and colors. The sentry eventually rolled over to face him, and he, too, was photographed face on.

Then the Sicilian put down the camera and took up his loaded rifle. He laid it on the crotch of a bush and sighted the sleeping sentry through the telescope, putting the cross hairs between the young man's eyes.

The Sicilian watched the rise and fall of the breathing, and a fly that walked slowly across the man's forehead. His finger fondled the trigger and in his imagination the blossom of red appeared where the sights were aligned and spread across the forehead in a burst of retribution that left the Sicilian gasping with sexual fulfillment.

New York: Kennedy Airport—2030 hours, 15 September

The week's leave in New Canaan had been a healing time for Linda, seeing old friends, visiting old haunts, talking until late at night with her parents. The week had gone quickly, yet now it was time to go, Linda felt a little guilty that she wanted to get it over with and be on her way.

She stood between her parents, taller than they, a blonde who looked as if she should be going to vacation on a California beach rather than leaving for a CIA post in Africa.

"Linda, do you have to go? I'm so afraid for you. There are cannibals in Africa." Her mother pulled at her sleeve, as if that might stop her. She was smiling at the joke they'd shared, but her eyes were moist.

"They have marine guards at all our consulates and embassies," her father said. "Linda will be in no danger at all." He looked hopefully at her.

Linda put her arms around them both, willing their parting to be casual, not frightening.

"There's nothing to worry about." She didn't mention that Gitabwanga had no marine guards. She hated leaving her parents, yet to stay with them would be to stifle in their web of love. She hugged them both, shifted out of their clutch, and went through the gate for ticket holders only.

The plane arrived in Dakar at dawn, which broke out over the Atlantic in a yellow haze of Saharan sand that filled the sky for a hundred miles over the ocean. The landing at Yof Airport was sharp enough to jog Linda into full awareness that for the first time she was in Africa.

She left the aircraft feeling that she was departing a cocoon of protective American security, to enter an alien world of hostiles. It was a relief to see the smiles of the Senegalese officials who shepherded the passengers into the Yof terminal. She had

had no idea, before, that the Senegalese were so welcoming.

The onward Air Afrique flight to Gitabwanga brought her to a different world. The Sahara gave way to a gently rolling savannah as they flew east into the very center of Africa. She was surprised to see the size and extent of the mountains, as well as the long stretches of forests and plains, dotted now and then with villages. Her girlhood vision of Africa as a jungle from ocean to ocean vanished instantly.

The aircraft made a long descent into a flat valley between two mountain ranges, across a lake she knew would be Lake Tchagamba, and then they were landing at Bwaga Airport.

Mark met her at the baggage-inspection tables. He had an even deeper tan than usual, and looked fit and handsome in a short-sleeved white shirt open at the neck, tan trousers and safari boots.

"Welcome to Gitabwanga, Linda. I hope you'll like it here. It's a charming old colonial town, sort of a mixture of Provençal extended village and Beau Geste desert town." He hugged her gently.

She felt suddenly very much at home, comforted by his warm welcome.

"Do you know, Mark, in this charming village of yours, they photographed my passport? Nekko-chan told me once what to look for, and sure enough the immigration officer did all the telltale things."

"Cheer up, Linda. Perhaps he got it upside down."

She grinned. "Don't tease me, Mark. That wouldn't make any difference."

They walked out to his car, several men giving her admiring stares. "Aren't you supposed to have diplomatic plates, Mark? I was briefed on that."

"I bought a used car, to avoid having dip plates," said Mark as he pulled away from the terminal.

"Can you get away with it?"

"So far they don't mind. We're a consulate general. Maybe after we become an embassy on January first, they'll object, but I doubt it."

Linda was looking into her tiny hand mirror. "Lucky they

don't mind, because they're with us right now. Are they Bwaganian Sûreté or French SSR?"

Mark laughed: "Bwaganian Sûreté. They're practicing surveillance on me. I'm used to it. They're not much good at it. I just ride along, let them be comfortable on my tail. By the way, don't let them see you using the mirror. They don't like dirty tricks, like using a store window to see behind you or looking back when you tie your shoe."

"Then what?"

"Depends on how mad they get, how basically hostile they are. These people would probably just close up on us, try to crowd us, make it uncomfortable to work, and make people uneasy to be seen with us. If we were in Moscow, the KGB would start harassing us. Maybe some pushing and shoving, shouting abuse, even detaining us for a while. But the Bwaganians are friends . . . at least for now."

"And we'll keep it that way." She smiled, snapping the mirror shut. "I'll be good, but why not practice on the Soviets instead of friends?"

"Because they're not yet good enough for sophisticated targets. So while they're being trained by SSR, they practice on birds like me, who won't react. The Soviets would identify them and their cars—they have so few it isn't funny—and run rings around them."

"And you won't? Suppose they lock onto you before an agent meeting?"

"I know most of them and their cars already. When we have agents to run, I'll just drift out of their view. But by then I'll have access to other cars, rentals, cars owned by support agents, and so on."

Linda nodded, thinking that she had a lot to learn. She knew a good deal about technical operations and the theory of agent operations, but she had no practical experience.

"What about Bwagania so far, Mark? Any comments after a few days?"

"It's early to say. The Soviets are here and, as I suspected, they're very accessible. Unlike Paris or London or the other big capitals, where they keep to themselves if they want to, here in this overgrown village there are so few places to go and things to do that we almost fall over each other."

"Have you met Petrov yet?"

"Not yet. But it's only a matter of time. We'll both meet him. And we'll find people with access to him and recruit them so they can help us assess him. If he wants to get out and meet people, to recruit agents for the KGB, he'll inevitably meet the same people we do. Doctors, dentists, government officials, businessmen, teachers . . . they're in short supply and easy to meet."

"For him as well as for us. He has the same cast to work on."

"I know. But while you and I are not wondering whether to flee to Russia or not, Petrov is a misfit, a maverick. He probably spends a lot of time wondering what life is like if you really belong in the West and don't just operate against it." He told her what Dumont had said in Paris.

Gitabwanga: Hôtel du Lac—1900 hours, 16 September

The hotel was a classical French colonial design: two stories, corrugated iron roof painted green, wide verandahs all around. Inside, a wide hall with the reception desk faced the front door. On the left, a formal dining room. On the right, Gitabwanga's longest bar, in a huge barnlike room with booths around the walls and tables in between. Above, twenty rooms with double beds, available by the year, the month, the week, the day, or the hour.

Madame Petarde ran the hotel. She had three pure white German shepherds and four slut daughters, and the eight of them constituted one of Gitabwanga's most venerable institutions. The dogs were the hotel's security. The four daughters, with other girls imported from Europe, ministered to the clients' wishes, and now and then Madame Petarde herself allowed one of the older French colonials to board her, more as a relictuary of the past than a monument to the present, for Madame was pushing sixty years of age and two hundred pounds in weight.

Pierre Schacht had lodged there for a year. He courted anonymity, and the Hôtel du Lac was Gitabwanga's most discreet establishment. At the bar, where colonial governors could pass ostentatiously unnoticed, Pierre Schacht was the supreme mouse. He usually sat on a bar stool, watching, waiting, cautiously polite. He never openly judged, although inside his instinctive distaste for bacchanalia warred constantly with his operational selection of the best bordello in Bwagania as his headquarters. He despised drunkenness and lechery, but he profited much from his seat at the bar, to observe, assess, and meet selected customers.

The clientele included the majority of the shakers and movers of Bwagania, black, brown, and white. Some brought only a thirst, others brought women and rented rooms, while the regulars came to wrestle with the daughters or with the other girls, who came and went in a dreary procession. Most of them signed contracts in France, unaware that their debts would always be higher than their incomes: an arrangement that is the core of the white slave trade.

After a few weeks, almost nobody paid any attention to Pierre Schacht, except now and then to comment on his weird life-style, for he barely drank and never asked for sex. They had tried young girls, mature girls, young boys, men. Madame Petarde had even offered herself. Pierre merely shook his head, mumbled gratefully, "*Non, pas ce soir, merci.*"

Once, a French rancher, in from the bush, had offered to bring him a sheep. Pierre scuttled up to his room, to the amusement of the crowd at the bar and Madame Petarde, who said she wanted no competition from sheep, thank you.

As usual for the hour before the evening meal, the bar was full of men, mostly French. A few Africans. Not so many of them could afford the hotel's prices, although they were reasonable by European standards.

Madame Petarde was circulating among the tables, greeting regulars, welcoming a few newcomers, and telling the girls to get more drinks ordered. Two French bartenders and two Bwaganian waiters handled the orders. The girls sat at the tables and provoked the men to buy drinks. The girls drank fruit juice, by order of Madame Petarde.

Pierre Schacht sat on his usual bar stool, drinking a Coca-Cola. He didn't like Coke all that much, but it could be mistaken for *mazout*—the name the French had given to bourbon with Coca-Cola.

Tonight, so far, no one had paid him any attention. That suited him, because until the coup, he wanted a low profile. After the coup, when the prince would become president-for-life, Pierre would come into his own. Until Moscow Center sent him on another assignment, he would stay in Gitabwanga, slowly shifting the strings of power into the hands of hard-core KGB agents—some already in the prince's entourage. The prince, in his turn, would be eliminated at the end of his usefulness. He was too independent.

Pierre was pondering these thoughts, and running through his coup plans again, when he realized that the man next to him was speaking to him.

"I'm sorry, I was thinking. What did you say?" Pierre smiled ingratiatingly, acting his part perfectly. With his brown hair, middle-aged face, and slightly musty trousers and white shirt, he looked like a seedy businessman.

"You don't look as if thinking is your line." Pierre's antennae went up instantly. The Frenchman, a very tall, beefy planter, was tipsy, eager for a fight. Nearby, a couple of Frenchmen at the bar heard the harsh tone and laughed, hoping for trouble. The drunk planter, encouraged by their laughs, probed deeper.

"What are you doing in Bwagania, anyway? Answer me or I'll knock you off that stool."

A bland response might defuse him, Pierre thought. "I'm a businessman. From Austria."

"What kind of business?" The room was quieting as people realized that the big planter was provoking something.

"I'm still setting it up," Pierre said. "There are so many possibilities . . ." He smiled politely, hoping the reply would stop the man. It didn't. The planter took it as an evasion, the smile as scornful.

He shouted: "Perhaps you're really writing a book about our country. I've watched you sit here, snooping. You're not like us, you little turd. No sex, no booze, just a big pair of ears and eyes. There's no need for you here. Go back to your mother in Vienna."

There was a shout of laughter from around the room. The men loved to see a bully at work on his victim. They loved to see the victim face up to the bully, too. But Pierre wanted only to keep a low profile.

Madame Petarde came to his rescue. She bustled up and said to the planter: "Stop it, or you'll have to go. He did nothing to you." But she joined in the general laughter when Pierre bowed to her, red-faced, and went up to his room. A mild booing followed him from the disappointed crowd. But he was right; they forgot about him next minute.

As he walked up the stairs, Pierre decided he'd hang that French bastard after the coup.

The cost of containing his anger was high. Pierre was shaking with rage when he got to his room. The knowledge that he could have beaten, even killed with his bare hands, anyone in the room below was usually enough comfort—the KGB had trained him well—but tonight the unfair nature of the provocation got to him. He took a drink from the vodka bottle in his suitcase. It helped a little. Then he went into a familiar routine that always settled his nerves. In a locked closet, in a corner of the shabby room, was his battered portable typewriter. It traveled with him everywhere.

He brought the typewriter, locked in its case, from the closet. He placed the machine on the concave double bed and opened it. Using a knife with a special set of watchmaker's tools, he removed the cylinder. It was hollow and at one end the axle unscrewed. The cylinder was an eleven-inch-long, one-inch-diameter concealment device. In it Pierre kept his large bills of cash, his ciphers, and some supplies for writing invisibly between the lines of innocuous letters he sent to various accommodation addresses in Western Europe. From those addresses his reports and recommendations went to Moscow Center, and their coded responses and instructions came back to him by equally devious means.

The cylinder had been machined and put together by the Czech intelligence service, frequent fabricators of miniature or delicate devices for the KGB. Pierre himself had designed the cylinder's hidden access and he was proud of it. You needed a powerful magnifying glass to find the hairline where the cylinder's threaded end unscrewed. Just to open the device made him warm as he compared himself to those crude, unthinking, useless animals in the bar below.

Inside the cylinder, down at the bottom, was a small soft leather pouch with a drawstring. Pierre Schacht held it up reverently for a minute, smiling with pleasure. Now he felt calm and proud. He opened the pouch and drew out a gold medal in the shape of a star. In the center was a ruby-red circle, with a gold hammer and sickle. Around the circle were the words: *Hero of the Soviet Union*, the USSR's highest award for valor.

Pierre Schacht, whose real name was Colonel Oleg Arkadievich Petrosian, KGB, had been awarded the medal for his role in helping Yuri Vladimirovich Andropov, then an ambassador, crush the Hungarian revolt of November 1956. As Johann Bund, a KGB illegal under cover of East German liaison with the Hungarian CP, Colonel Petrosian had performed a miracle of covert action. At a key point of the revolt, his team of paramilitary activists had given quick, deft support to Soviet troops, taking and holding vital river crossings and killing a large number of leading Hungarian patriots. Their role was virtually unknown outside the KGB.

Andropov went on to head the KGB, and eventually the USSR itself. He never forgot that Petrosian had made him look good, and it was Andropov himself who gave the medal to Pierre at a secret ceremony in Moscow a year later. It was Andropov who personally dispatched him as an illegal to Vienna, and then later instructed him to spend six months a year in Bwagania, to bring Bwagania into the Soviet bloc.

The medal was supposed to be in a safe, in Moscow Center, where he could look at it on the rare occasions when he was in Moscow and could talk someone into bringing it to the safehouse. Pierre had snatched it on one of those occasions, replacing it with an imitation he had made himself of gold-plated brass. He still smiled when he thought of how easy the exchange had been as he handed the medal back to its keeper. Pierre could have been a professional conjuror had his life not been dedicated to the KGB.

Pierre mumbled as he fondled the medal. At the award

ceremony, Andropov had made a speech about his devotion, skill, and courage. Pierre was a machine, a Party man to his core. Nothing would ever stop him from doing his assigned duty. A medal every ten years, and he would go until he dropped.

He reassembled the cylinder into the typewriter, and as he got ready for bed, he wondered what the incoming KGB *rezident* would be like. He had never met Colonel Pyotr Aleksandrovich Petrov, but he had heard plenty of rumors about him: a good case officer, married into a powerful family, a hard drinker, a tough-minded maverick. A man who might be easy to work with but who would bear watching carefully. Pierre's world was populated not by friends but by a sea of enemies, ranging from superhostiles down to friendly enemies.

Gitabwanga: Mark's house—
1930 hours, 17 September

After a few days in a hotel, Mark moved into a house rented for him by the consulate general. It was on a steep hillside overlooking the city, an older structure, stucco and wood, with a green tin roof, a large living room, and a wide covered verandah that circled the entire house. The building and its hectare of garden were nestled between a banana grove and a manioc field.

The next day, an old African stood in the doorway of the house and coughed quietly to get Mark's attention. He was relaxed, attentive, respectful. He had gray hair, was probably sixty years old although he looked well over seventy. He was stringy, and his bare feet had deep fissures reaching up the heels from underneath.

"Oui? Qui êtes vous?"

"You will need a cook-houseboy, monsieur. I wish to be that man."

Mark smiled. This main certainly didn't waste time getting to the point.

"How did you hear about my taking this house? It was only yesterday."

The old man shrugged, beaming: *"C'est l'Afrique, patron."* His French was rubbery but understandable.

"Did anyone send you to me?" Mark didn't want to hire a Sûreté agent.

"No, sir. My friend works next door." He waved down the hill, where a red tin roof showed among the trees. Then he volunteered: "I'm Congolese, patron. But I've been here for twenty years. Look, my work permit and some references." He showed Mark some grubby, torn papers.

Mark waved him into the living room, read the papers. They were in order. The latest reference was from a Greek family living in Gitabwanga. It was dated only yesterday.

"Why are you leaving the Greek family?"

"I'm not, sir. They are returning to Greece. They leave tomorrow. That's why I came to you."

Mark nodded. He needed a cook, and a trial seemed in order. Mark had his own way of testing cooks.

"What is your name?" It was on the references and the work permit, but Mark asked to see how the man would respond. He did so without expression.

"My name is Jean Baptiste Banongo, but everyone calls me M'Pishi. It means *cook* in Swahili."

"Let's see if you're aptly named," Mark smiled. "Are you free this evening?"

"Yes, patron."

"Cook a meal for two. Choose something you're proud of. If it's excellent, you're hired. If not, we call it quits and I pay you for the evening. All right?"

M'Pishi threw back his head and laughed. A rolling laugh, full of humor.

"Of course, sir. I'll have it ready in one hour. A drink meanwhile?" M'Pishi's eyes sparkled.

While M'Pishi rattled dishes and spoke to himself in the kitchen, Mark made two phone calls. First to Linda, still in a hotel, to invite her to dinner. She accepted and showed up in half an hour.

The second call was to the Greek family. Yes, they had employed M'Pishi for seven years. He was an outstanding cook and cleaner. He also did laundry, ironed expertly. He was clean, honest, willing, reliable. They had paid him a pittance, housed, fed, and clothed him. They were sorry he wouldn't come back to Greece with them.

The dinner was first-class. M'Pishi served it on the verandah by candlelight, with glowing punk coils to chase off mosquitos. He did it well within the hour. The table was beautifully set with flowers, and his smile was huge when they congratulated him. He cleaned up the kitchen and left at ten, promising to return tomorrow at seven with his suitcase. As he left, he smiled at Linda and nodded to Mark. The meaning was clear. Mark was lucky to have such a charming friend. And such a good cook.

Gitabwanga: the mountain road—2205 hours, 17 September

M'Pishi was bicycling down from Mark's house to town. His light was in order, and his bicycle license was good for another six months. His mood was joyful, and he sang a traditional Congolese song.

Without warning, a long stick was shoved between the spokes of his front wheel, and he pitched over the handlebars. As he lay in the dust, scratched, stunned, bleeding at the palms and knees, he was jumped by two burly Bwaganians. They pummeled him and dragged him into a van, bicycle and all. There was no conversation until they reached the main police station.

The interrogation went on until after midnight. Their purpose was blunt. The two were Bwaganian Sûreté agents, who told M'Pishi that unless he reported to them regularly on the activities and guests of the American consul who had just hired him, he would be deported to the Congo. But first he would be imprisoned for three months. With a jail record, he would never again find work as a cook or houseboy.

M'Pishi refused. They had no legal right to do this. His papers and license were in order. He had broken no laws.

He had resisted arrest, they claimed, and they beat him with a sock filled with sand, so that there could be no proof of their brutality. M'Pishi was violently ill from the pain, but he still refused. They punched his stomach and lungs, until he was sick again. Then they punched his face. But still he refused them. Slowly, they realized that this strange man was praying to God during his ordeal and it sustained him. M'Pishi wasn't going to be a fink for the Sûreté. He had liked Mark and Linda, and M'Pishi gave his devotion quickly and completely.

Finally, they gave up. M'Pishi shuffled his damaged bicycle slowly to his church, where he spent the night under a carport near the pastor's shack. At dawn he awoke in agony. He washed and shaved with great difficulty, then packed his little suitcase.

The African pastor came by and sat beside him. He knew that M'Pishi had been beaten, and he guessed it was by the police. He put his hand on M'Pishi's, looked into his face. "Can I help, Jean Baptiste?"

M'Pishi shook his head to thank him. If he had opened his mouth, he would have wept. He rode off with the suitcase roped to the rear rack of the bicycle.

Gitabwanga: Sûreté headquarters—0945 hours, 18 September

Colonel François de la Maison read the report with dismay. Two of his investigators had tried to coerce a Congolese into reporting on his new employer, the U.S. Consul, who was also CIA station chief, Mark Cameron. It was obvious from the badly written report that they had summarily arrested Banongo, beaten him, tried to intimidate him, and had failed.

François squirmed as he imagined the next step. The U.S. consul general would ask him to explain how such a villainous act could occur in a French colony. An official apology, perhaps restitution to the cook, would be demanded.

The two investigators were standing in front of his desk within five minutes. They were new men and quite junior, but they had political connections and would rise to medium rank right after independence. At the same time François would no longer be their Sûreté boss, but only the senior adviser to the Sûreté, which would be headed by a Bwaganian. It would be wise to teach these two rather than to punish them. The SSR would need their cooperation after independence, not their hostility.

"I've read your report, gentlemen. There is a serious problem."

The two looked defiant.

"The problem is that your target is a diplomat of a country that is friendly to France and Bwagania. Your victim is his employee. You seem to have acted on the spur of the moment. You were watching the American's house?"

"Yes, Colonel. We overheard his employment of the cook. It seemed a good time to recruit the cook. What is the problem?" The older of the two looked genuinely puzzled.

"The problem is not your eagerness to recruit agents. That is admirable." They both looked pleased. "The problem is that there will probably be a complaint from the Americans. It will cite brutal coercion. The French government will have to apologize, and that means we will be asked by Paris how we could have done anything so crude, so childish. Why did you think medieval methods would work in this century, they will ask."

"But they do work, sir. Nine times out of ten they work. We all use force. It's a necessary part of recruitment of Africans." The older man was on the defensive.

"I know. It's understood here. But you must select your targets with greater care now that independence will bring many foreigners with diplomatic immunity. Don't use force on the employees of any foreign installations. It will just lead to trouble, as I explained. Try other means, certainly. But not force. You know that now and then you come across a man who stands up to coercion, although he might well listen to an appeal based on loyalty to Africa." He smiled to soften the words. "From now on, it might be wise to stay away from Mr. Cameron, his cook, and his house."

The younger Bwaganian broke the impasse: "We certainly don't want the world to see us as savages, even if some of us really do belong in the trees." He laughed, digging his partner in the ribs. Africans love laughter, and they left François's office giggling about the event.

Both the incident and its implications stayed with François all day. He believed that violence and cruelty would increase greatly after independence, as Bwagania's leaders strove to harness the masses without the staying hand of France.

Gitabwanga: Mark's house—1100 hours, 19 September

As M'Pishi finished cleaning house and began to prepare lunch for Mark, he broke for a moment to pray for strength. The morning had gone well. Mark had left in a hurry and had only noticed the bruises at the last minute.

"What happened, M'Pishi?"

"Nothing, patron. I fell off my bicycle. It will be all right later today." It was the truth, enough of it to avoid lying, but not the whole truth.

However, the pain and fatigue got worse as the day went on. M'Pishi remembered that Mark had told him to take some aspirin if it was too bad.

M'Pishi had never taken a pill of any kind in all his life. The result was swift and dramatic. At 11:05 he took two pills. At 11:20 the pills took hold, his empty stomach helping. At 11:25 the room began to spin around, and at 11:27 M'Pishi collapsed into a chair. He slept, a serene smile on his battered face.

Gitabwanga: the Petrov apartment—0730 hours, 20 September

Although Olga disagreed, the Petrov apartment was one of the best in the Soviet consulate general compound. On the top floor of the better of the two residential blocks, the apartment had a good view of the city and the steep mountains beyond. There were two bedrooms, a living-dining area, and a small but well-equipped kitchen that was, for Africa, clean.

It was much better than Pyotr had expected. Ten-year-old Aleksandra said they were lucky to have such a roomy, airy place. But Olga complained daily about the "hovel they've lodged us in." Had they been in Raspatov's elegant residence next door, she would have complained.

Pyotr lay in the rumpled double bed for a few minutes, wondering what mood Olga would be in when she woke. He knew he would have to wake her, because she had stayed up, tipsy with Scotch, after he had gone to sleep at midnight.

Aleksandra was already in the kitchen when Pyotr got there, still unshaven and hung over. Her mood was happy, and it helped to lift him up to face the day. And to face Olga.

"Papa, can I make you some manikasha?" Pyotr's face brightened. He loved his little Aleksandra, and although the thought of food was vaguely sickening, he accepted. "Thank you, my little Lapushka. With pleasure!" She had it ready in minutes, a hot cream of wheat that he had trouble swallowing. Aleksandra noticed right away.

"Oh, Papa! You don't like it? I can make a new bowl . . . right away?" She was eager to please him. Pyotr came through like a gentleman.

"No, my sweet. It's just that a hot breakfast seems a little heavy for the tropics. Here, I'll have another spoonful. Must eat something, anyway." He ate half the bowl while she watched, her pretty face alive with good health and love.

"I wondered why you wanted manikasha. It is too hot for this climate. I only had fruit."

They both laughed at the silly scene. Aleksandra liked being alone with her father. She understood the fights between her parents, and she had watched many times as her father drank too much and she sympathized with his reasons. Her mother was always right and almost everyone else was always wrong. Aleksandra saw her father as beleaguered, to be protected, her mother a waspish obstacle to be negotiated. Still, she loved them both.

At eight-fifteen Pyotr woke Olga. The reaction was what he expected.

"Go away, Petrov, it's too early."

"Olga, the office starts work in half an hour. We must be there at least by nine. You have a job."

"Go without me. Nobody will dare to complain about me."

She was right, but Pyotr was determined. "Come anyway, Olga. I'll make you some breakfast. It's not good to use your family's rank to avoid a job you accepted."

"Go away, you peasant." She hid her face in the covers. She looked beautiful in the mornings, even if she'd had too much the night before. He sighed and left her there.

Within ten minutes Olga swept into the kitchen, her hair in a chignon and her bathrobe partially open. She had an attractive body and enjoyed showing it off.

"I'll join you," she muttered. "Just make me some black coffee and skin an orange. I'll be ready in ten minutes."

Pyotr winked at Aleksandra, who tried her best to wink back at him. He burst out laughing at his enchanting child, and blew a kiss to her across the table.

At eight forty-five Pyotr led his little family down the stairs and across the compound to the consulate general offices. They passed the consul general's residence and the other block of apartments, where the lower-ranking staff lived. The compound would become an embassy after December thirty-first, when Bwagania became independent. The *rezidentura* was in the chancery-to-be, on the top floor. Pyotr's cover office as consul, later as first secretary of embassy, was also there, on the second floor near the office of the ambassador-designate, Consul General Raspatov. Olga's desk was on the ground floor, in the Soviet cultural affairs office. She was assistant to the cultural affairs officer.

As he checked his family past the armed guard at the door of the chancery, Pyotr thought that it would take his wife no time to establish her dominance over her boss in cultural affairs. The power of the Lapins was second only to their love of it, and their ability to exploit it.

Gitabwanga: the KGB rezidentura—
0900 hours, 20 September

After dropping Aleksandra off at the Soviet school on the ground floor, Pyotr climbed to the third floor, where the just-established KGB *rezidentura* was essentially a reinforced concrete vault: two small, windowless rooms. The inner room contained safes for classified material: secret reports to and from Moscow Center, and the growing dossiers on persons in Bwagania of interest to the *rezidentura.* There were two warrant officers on duty in addition to Pyotr. They had arrived a week before him. One of them sat in the inner room and guarded the files. He also worked the radio and did the enciphering and deciphering of radio messages. The other warrant officer sat in the outer room, at a small table. He guarded the only door to the *rezidentura* and peered out at would-be entrants through a one-way glass. The other table in the room was reserved for the KGB *rezident.*

Only these three men had automatic access to the two-room *rezidentura.* Pyotr met visitors in his second-floor cover office, where he acted out his cover role, and almost no one wanted to go near the KGB office anyway. Unless you were the chief of mission or the Soviet military attaché, you had no overt business with the KGB. Covert business, yes. Such as reporting on your Soviet colleagues. But that took place outside the KGB *rezidentura*—in locked offices or apartments, late at night, in whispers.

The two depressing *rezidentura* rooms were hot, stark, stuffy. The silence was broken only by soft breathing and the buzz and click of machinery. The floors, ceilings, and walls were painted concrete. There were no books or decorations apart from the usual prints of heroic Soviet workers producing their joyful best for the Party.

Pyotr opened the door to the *rezidentura,* using the cipher lock. He was greeted by the warrant officer in the outer room, and then he knocked on the inner room door. The second warrant officer admitted him. Pyotr asked for the file on Schacht.

He took it back to the outer office and sat at his table to read it. No classified material was allowed outside the *rezidentura.* Only what a man could read in one sitting was allowed outside the inner room. Not even the *rezident* himself could break these standing rules.

This morning, Pyotr had two important meetings to prepare for. One was with ambassador-designate Raspatov at ten-thirty. The other was with the illegal, Pierre Schacht, at eight-fifteen in the evening. The morning meeting with Raspatov was not critical. Nobody's life would be at stake. It was only important because it was the first formal business meeting with Raspatov since Pyotr's arrival. By contrast, the meeting with Schacht was critical. Schacht was a very valuable asset, to be protected at all costs. Moscow Center held Schacht in high regard, and it would be the end of Pyotr's career if he did anything to jeopardize him.

Usually, Moscow Center doesn't allow direct contact between illegals and the local *rezidentura*. But this case was special. Because of the pending coup, close and quick communications between Schacht and the *rezidentura* would be vital. Moscow had allowed direct contact, but on condition that Pyotr use "extreme security caution."

If Pyotr goofed, nasty things could happen. The Bwaganian Sûreté might catch them. Pyotr could be PNG'd, expelled for espionage. Worse, Schacht could be tried, convicted of spying, even executed. On the up side, Schacht could be of great value to Pyotr and his activities in Bwagania. He could help to restore Pyotr's career.

This first meeting with Schacht had been planned by Pyotr before he left Moscow, and the plan sent to Schacht in a microdot, which could only be read with a microscope after it had been lifted off the page of a letter with a solvent and developed. Even then the message was in cipher. It had taken Schacht two hours to lift the dot off a "business" letter from Paris, develop, decipher, and read it.

The plan was a good one. It used information previously supplied by Schacht about meeting sites, times they could safely be used, safety and danger signals en route to the sites, and the best approaches to, and retreats from, them. That Schacht was still alive and serving Moscow Center was a testament to twenty years of excruciating care in his work.

To execute the plan, both men would have to "clean" themselves on the way to the meeting site. Pyotr was to drive about for at least two hours before the meeting, to make sure there was no surveillance on him. During that time, he would change from diplomatic license plates to civilian plates that had been made for the *rezidentura* by technicians in Moscow.

The plate numbers were mythical but in the proper series for Gitabwanga. Registration papers and a driving license were included, in a false Swiss name.

Half an hour prior to the meeting, Pyotr would drive along a predetermined route. His warrant officers would observe his passage and then mark safety signals on lampposts on a different street if there was no surveillance on him. There would be danger if different chalk marks, along yet another street, were not removed from lampposts. Elaborate, but workable.

Now Pyotr prepared for the meeting. There were questions to ask Schacht about local politics, coup preparations, the economy, key personalities, the Western presence in Bwagania, and so on. There were operational questions. How often should they meet? How often pass messages without meeting? When and how to call for emergency meetings?

Finally, there was the unspoken question. Schacht outranked Pyotr, although Pyotr as *rezident* was Moscow Center's chief in Bwagania. Would he accept Pyotr's supervision? Probably with difficulty, so Pyotr would avoid outright instructions. Reaching a modus vivendi was more important than exercising his authority.

Would Schacht report on Pyotr to Moscow Center? Almost certainly. So would Raspatov. So would the Party secretary in the consulate general. It was vital to enlist their friendship.

At ten twenty, Pyotr set off for Raspatov's office. Pyotr had been in Bwagania so little time—he still had no agents, no real information for the consul general. More questions than answers, so far. He looked forward to the meeting, however. He was still intrigued by Raspatov's uncanny resemblance to his father.

Gitabwanga: Raspatov's outer office—
1030 hours, 20 September

Raspatov's waiting room was empty. Pyotr sat on a stiff chair and waited, looking around the room. The usual plush carpet and austere furniture were of no interest. Nor was the unusually tasteful Party poster on one wall, showing the land being tilled by sturdy, happy peasants as the evening sun dropped low in the western sky.

The other walls were bare. On the one desk was an old typewriter, a standard "inside" Soviet compound telephone extension—all calls passed through the main switchboard. There was a photograph of two older Russians, both with pronounced Slavic cheekbones. They were open-looking, simple people. Pyotr had just concluded that they were the parents of the consul general's newly arrived secretary, and that she must be about twenty-two years old, fat, and ugly, when Raspatov's door opened and out she came.

She was a bombshell, a tall, blond girl with a Slavic face. The most lovely peaches-and-cream skin and beautiful eyes that Pyotr had ever seen. Her voluptuous figure was made for love. Her green eyes spoke of cats, fur, smoky fires in log cabins, passion, and devotion.

She smiled at him, and those eyes told him she had noticed his attention. Her voice was as captivating to him as her face and body. "I am Anna Iosevna Karpova, the consul general's secretary. What can we do for you?"

"I am Colonel Pyotr Aleksandrovich Petrov, KGB *rezident* assigned to Gitabwanga, and very pleased to meet you. What a pleasant surprise to find such utter beauty, such perfection, in the center of Africa!"

Anna Iosevna was from the country, the child of peasants, as Pyotr had deduced. The approach—for he had decided to make one—must be firm, forceful, yet not too fast. Pyotr's flattering opening was just right for Anna Iosevna. Just enough of a hint of his power, but not too much metal showed.

Anna asked, "This is your courtesy call, Colonel?" Despite her beauty and her apparent sophistication, she almost curtsied. She was still overwhelmed by rank and position.

"Yes, but there's no hurry. In fact, I would gladly stay here all day admiring you, Anna Iosevna."

Her eyes crinkled, but she gave him a long look to be sure he wasn't mocking.

"Like all girls, I love compliments, Colonel. Especially from men as prominent and handsome as you."

It was his turn to see if she was serious. Full of humor and good will, visibly. But there was no sign of irritation. Pyotr was overcome by her already. He could feel a stirring. He absolutely had to take this lovely girl to bed, both for his own pleasure and because she would be an excellent source of prime, privileged information about Raspatov, his top staff, and their private communications with Moscow and other Soviet diplomatic and consular missions.

"The consul general is on the telephone with Moscow. I expect he'll be a few minutes more. I can't interrupt him."

"No, Anna Iosevna. Not at all. I will wait here and tell you what I see." Anna blushed.

Pyotr made a picture frame with his two hands, squinting at her through it.

"First I see a truly wonderful body, tall and athletic, with excellent muscle tone. You take regular exercise?"

"Yes, sir. I do a lot of aerobics. It's the new American exercise method." She looked at him with wide eyes, realizing what she'd admitted to the KGB *rezident*.

"No sin, Anna." Pyotr liked mavericks. They helped him feel good about his own dislike of authority. "Then I see perfect green eyes, set in a face of perfect beauty. People must have told you this all your short life. Twenty-two years?"

"They've been very kind since I became fourteen, sir. You're right, that's eight years ago."

He went on: "In those green eyes I see profound intelligence, devotion to career, strict attention to Party values." None of the above was accurate. Had he gone too far?

Anna pretended only to average intelligence. She wanted to be a model, but so far no one had come along to help her. She hated Party meetings, which bored her silly. But she loved flattery, and he hadn't gone too far. He could be of great help in her future modeling career. He must know everyone in Moscow. She blushed as she thought, I might even have to submit to him to get what I want. She imagined herself lying back in his arms, her fingers toying with his medals, his erection. . . . Anna Iosevna was an accomplished daydreamer.

Pyotr had hooked a willing victim. It took only a moment

more to get her apartment number and the best hour to find her there.

A buzzer sounded on her desk, and she became businesslike: "The consul general is free now, Colonel. You may go in."

As Pyotr walked past her, she very slightly pursed her lips. The effect on Pyotr was electric.

Gitabwanga: Raspatov's office— 1040 hours, 20 September

Raspatov had been a friend of Lenin's and Stalin's. He was one of the few old Bolsheviks who survived Stalin's purges. He became a major general in the Great Patriotic War. Wounded and decorated several times, he was a survivor, and he deeply understood the long struggle within the Party between the old guard and the new generation, between the conservatives and the reformers. What set Raspatov apart from the other conservatives was his lack of fear of the reformers. He saw the struggle as inevitable, the reformers as beneficial, cleansing. He enjoyed the challenge of the hungry new power seekers. Let them be put to the test, just as he had been.

"Come in, Pyotr Aleksandrovich. Don't be formal with me, even if this is your courtesy call. Are you enjoying Gitabwanga?" Typical of Raspatov to be abrupt, direct.

"Yes, Comrade Consul General. Thank you. We will enjoy it here. My wife is already at work, and our daughter in school." The resemblance to Pyotr's father was amazing.

The consul general and his new KGB *rezident* talked about Bwagania. Raspatov was an encyclopedia on the USSR and the CPSU, but after a month in the country, he still knew almost nothing about Bwagania. He spoke none of the languages used in the area and didn't expect to learn them. He freely admitted that Africa and the Africans were a mystery to him, and would remain so until they were communized and learned to speak fluent Russian.

"Do you think we'll ever see that day, Comrade Consul General?" These two, the renowned old revolutionary and the younger KGB *rezident*, could be honest with each other on political matters. As long as they didn't pronounce heresy.

"Not really, Pyotr Aleksandrovich. I don't think the Bwaganians are capable of being good communists. They lack the essential qualities, the discipline. Nor would they be anything but a burden to our country. But I must play the game. It would never do to tell the Africans the truth. Or Moscow either, for that matter."

He laughed, but his eyes were watching Pyotr. He was testing for reactions, trying to see where Pyotr fit into the younger generation. A stolid Party liner? A rigid technician? A flexible conservative? A reformer? A true maverick, as rumor had it? Who was this KGB *rezident*?

Pyotr was ready for the question. "Sometimes the truth is very hard to face, sir. Even Moscow has that problem. I will try to tell them the truth without being brutal. Then if I'm sent home, at least I will have done my best. First I must find out for myself what the truth is."

"Be sure to tell me, Pyotr Aleksandrovich." Consul General Raspatov smiled, softening his ploy. Pyotr wore well, he thought. Was he really part of the questioning younger cadre he'd feared might never appear in Mother Russia? It seemed possible.

"You can count on it, sir." Pyotr was enjoying the gentle jousting with this paternal man. It was astonishing what could be conveyed in just a few words between men who understood Party jargon and shorthand.

When Pyotr left, neither man had learned anything new about Bwagania. But they had gone a few steps down the road to understanding each other. Pyotr was pleased with the meeting, and he was in a happy mood when he saw Anna Iosevna at her desk on his way out.

The sunlight from outside made her face radiant, and her smile took his breath away. He thought he had never seen such a dazzling, beautiful young woman. He said so:

"Anna Iosevna, your beauty makes this office shine with light."

She was enchanted by this attention from a man so powerful in his own right, married into one of the most powerful families in the USSR. But she tried to look severe, and answered simply: "Thank you, sir."

"Anna Iosevna, if you are going to be so formal in the office, I must talk with you outside this place. I will come to your apartment at ten o'clock tonight. Official business, which I will describe at that time." He said it with a smile, but nevertheless he was the KGB *rezident* and it sounded like an order.

Anna Iosevna wasn't quite sure how to take it, but as she had nothing to hide, she nodded her agreement. Then she blushed as she found herself wondering what he would expect when he came to her room. It was not an inspired place for a tryst. The walls were paper thin and the door locks would not have kept a child out.

Pyotr took the blush for maidenly reticence. "Until tonight, Anna Iosevna." He could barely wait.

Gitabwanga: the Soviet military attaché's apartment—1300 hours, 20 September

Pyotr lunched, by invitation, with the Soviet military attaché, a line infantry officer seconded to the GRU. He was a colorless man who would never deviate from the Party line.

The lunch consisted of chilled vodka and zakuskas, a delicious mixture of various Baltic Sea smoked fish. The vodka was too much for Pyotr's schedule. He nursed one glass throughout the dull hour. A clear head was of paramount importance for his meeting with Schacht.

Pyotr learned nothing new from the military attaché, who had been in Bwagania three weeks. He spoke no French, no African dialects or languages, and didn't propose to learn any. He felt defeated by a culture that was entirely alien and, in his view, subhuman.

During the lunch Pyotr's antennae told him that the military attaché had learned of the drunken caper in Moscow and Pyotr's resultant exile to Bwagania; that much was easy to read in the man's attitude. Being a Party automaton, he would play the game and cooperate with the KGB *rezident*, but would offer neither his friendship nor any special effort.

Fortunately, Pyotr mused as the lunch ended, the military attaché was not likely to be either an effective friend or foe. You would have been a much better Lapin son-in-law than I, Pyotr thought as he shook his host's hand and left.

The military attaché sighed as he put the dishes in the tiny sink. He would survive this tour of duty without tripping over Petrov's dying career. He might even make some points in Moscow by unearthing a juicy scandal that would be the coup de grace for Petrov and a promotion for himself.

Gitabwanga: SSR poste—1705 hours, 20 September

A telephone call from Sûreté headquarters told François that the fixed surveillance on the Soviet compound had spotted Pyotr departing in his car. He turned north toward the center of town. The two KGB warrant officers were passengers in the car.

François sniffed an operational meeting and decided to use both the Sûreté and the SSR surveillance capabilities on this one. François and his senior officers had planned for this ahead of time. None of them had much experience in the surveillance of professional intelligence officers, but they had all worked against a variety of other surveillance targets—criminals, terrorists, drug and white-slave traders, and operatives of Western Communist parties. Only François had a good concept of what Pyotr might do.

He was right. Pyotr drove to several places in downtown Gitabwanga, logical places for a Soviet consular officer to go. Pyotr and his two warrant officers delivered official invitations to innocuous addresses: Air France offices, the U.S. Information Service office, the Spanish consulate and the French Administration, several business houses that supplied the Soviets with goods or services. All overt and all of it to detect surveillance and to stretch the Sûreté and SSR capabilities to the maximum, without seeming to irritate the surveillants deliberately.

At each address, an envelope was taken in by one of the two Soviets. At the fourteenth address, a warrant officer failed to reappear. While Pyotr waited, the other warrant officer got out, poked his head into the building where his colleague had gone, then walked off. At the nearest light he crossed the street and went into the Air Afrique offices, carrying an envelope.

The Bwaganian Sûreté surveillants went wild trying to follow both men and the car, which now drove off, Pyotr alone in it. The Bwaganian Sûreté team lost the car and the two warrant officers. One of the SSR cars, held in reserve until then, kept Pyotr's car in sight for a while. But by six fifteen it was getting dark, and the evening rush hour made it difficult to keep on him without making their surveillance obvious.

At six twenty Pyotr simply drifted out of the SSR car's sight. One moment he was plainly visible a few car lengths ahead. The next he was gone.

François heard it clearly over the radio: *"Merde! Où est il? T'a vu, Auguste?"*

But August, assistant driver of the car, hadn't seen it. They reported "lost bird" and returned to the poste, two embarrassed men.

Gitabwanga: Petrov's car—1820 hours, 20 September

Pyotr was amused by the ease with which he'd slipped away without the surveillance being sure he'd done it deliberately. His technique was the same as Mark's: wear dark glasses so they can't see your eyeballs move. Check your rearview mirror frequently but without moving your head. Don't drive fast or use obvious tricks. Let the surveillants become comfortable with you. Then use the traffic around you to build a shield of cars between you and the surveillants. Before they realize what's happening, turn off on a side street, and make another turn right away. Speed up and go through the "fence" you've preplanned.

Pyotr had found the fence days before. It began with a narrow, winding alley that started twenty yards after he'd turned off the main road. The alley had a prominent SANS ISSUE (dead end) sign. At the end of the alley was a school playground, deserted at dusk. It was closed to vehicles, but there was in fact just room for his little car to squeeze between the steel posts.

He bounced across the deserted, pitch-black playground, bounced over the curb onto a busy street, and was gone before the surveillance car reached the end of the alley and assumed they had taken a wrong turn.

Pyotr drove straight out of town, to avoid being spotted again by surveillance and to find a place where he could change license plates. Soon he was traveling along a dirt road well out in the bush. The moon was so bright that he was able to drive without any lights.

By seven fifteen Pyotr was a good fifteen miles out of Gitabwanga, well beyond even isolated farmhouses. The savannah was liberally dotted with palms, thorn trees, baobabs, and scrub brush. When he had scouted the area two days ago, he had seen no native huts or domestication for miles around. The only risk was from hunting lions.

Pyotr changed the license plates and was back in the car, driving toward town, in two minutes.

Gitabwanga: Hôtel du Lac—1920 hours, 20 September

Colonel Oleg Arkadievich Petrosian, alias Pierre Schacht, slipped out the back door of the Hôtel du Lac. He wore his usual dark blue tennis shoes and dark slacks, and tonight he had on a dark shirt with long sleeves. In his pocket was a thin mesh mask, dyed black, with holes for the eyes and mouth. Schacht could disappear into the night in seconds.

He had no illusions that his departure from Madame Petarde's establishment had gone unseen. Inside, they were all busy with predinner crowd at the bar. But sometimes the garden staff stayed after work and sat under the trees watching the fun inside. In addition, it is a given in central African towns that there is an African under almost every bush, sitting, observing, unseen. The long evenings are more comfortable outside.

What Schacht counted on was that he was doing something routine. He often walked along the lake shore at night and was only casually watched until he was out of sight. This evening the garden staff saw him depart. They joked about the mousy man who didn't screw any of the Petarde girls, the white man who dressed in such dreary clothes. But they paid no further attention to him. Schacht melded into the darkness, walking slowly along the lake shore as if he had nothing on his mind but the cool of this fragrant evening.

Gitabwanga: the St. Louis Bridge—2000 hours, 20 September

At exactly eight P.M. Pierre Schacht was waiting under the St. Louis Bridge, which crossed over a stream leading into the lake. During the two-mile walk from the Hôtel du Lac, he had reversed his course several times, casting back and forth to detect any surveillance. By the time he sat down under the bridge, his back against a buttress, he was sure he was clean.

The road over the bridge led to native farms and was little used at night. Schacht had only a few moments to wait before he heard the distant murmur of a car slowly coming his way. Schacht didn't move until he heard the car slow down. Then he pulled on the mask, edged up the bank, and lay in the bushes. The car stopped and the passenger door opened. Schacht gave a soft whistle, the first six notes of "La Marseillaise." The driver responded with the next four notes, cutting the last one short.

It was the prearranged recognition and safety signal, and Schacht got in the car like a shadow, almost invisible in the shade from overhanging trees. The pickup had taken six seconds. Pyotr headed the car back into the bush, away from town.

Gitabwanga: SSR poste—2010 hours, 20 September

So far, François' trump card had failed to work. It was a limpet with an intermittent radio signal. One of the Bwaganian Sûreté inspectors had attached it to the underside of Pyotr's car while he and one warrant officer had waited in the auto for the other warrant officer to come out of the Air France office. A busy sidewalk, a stumble, and it was in place, a strong magnet assuring it would stay there on the roughest roads.

The limpet had a transmitting range of about eight miles, and would only send out its radio beep when a key was pressed in François' office. François pressed the key at six-thirty, when he learned by radio that the limpet had been attached. But it was some minutes before the radio direction-finding loops began to home in on the signal, and as they did so, it became fainter and disappeared. François cursed the bad luck that had taken Pyotr out of range at the moment they were about to triangulate on him. But he congratulated the men who had seen to the limpet's attachment.

Then he settled down to wait for the beep to reappear. He was sure now that Pyotr was headed for a clandestine meeting. And that he had cleaned himself skillfully.

Gitabwanga: Pyotr's car—2140 hours, 20 September

The meeting had gone well, and Pyotr headed the car back toward Gitabwanga. After they had introduced themselves, he had gone through his whole agenda with Schacht without any problems. Schacht seemed to be accepting Pyotr's role, not interested in his past, only intent on the coming coup d'état.

They had agreed on a timetable for the coup, and on the dates, times, and places of their clandestine meetings from now until the coup was successful. In between meetings, they would communicate through various dead drops that Schacht had spotted and defined to Moscow Center weeks ago. To set up an emergency meeting, either man could chalk a white spot on a roadside garden wall near the Hôtel du Lac. From now on, Schacht's evening walks were to be routine, and Pyotr would drive past the wall every night.

At kilometer six from town, Pyotr dropped Schacht off. It was a mile to the Hôtel du Lac. Schacht began the walk back along the shore to the hotel. Pyotr drove a mile past the hotel, then changed license plates in a lakeside clearing.

Gitabwanga: SSR poste—2145 hours, 20 September

The beep started again at nine forty-five. Now the triangulation was effective and the first report came in. The car was stopped on the lake shore, not far from the Hôtel du Lac.

Within moments it was moving again, stopped briefly a mile past the Hôtel du Lac, then returned to the Soviet embassy. At nine fifty-five François turned off the limpet's transmitter. Silent, it might not be discovered before they had a chance to retrieve it. It was too risky to leave it on the car for any length of time.

Then he radioed for a static surveillance outside the Hôtel du Lac. It was a guess, but he surmised that an agent had been dropped off near the hotel and then license plates had been changed. Now his luck held. The surveillant, a young Bwaganian, had arrived on post just before Schacht got back to the Hôtel du Lac. A question to the garden staff, and now SSR knew that Schacht had left at six twenty and returned at ten fifteen, after Pyotr had got back to the Soviet compound. They guessed that Schacht had been dropped off a kilometer or two away.

It was circumstantial, but on a hunch François ordered a full field investigation of Schacht.

Gitabwanga: Anna's apartment—
2210 hours, 20 September

Pyotr knocked lightly on Anna Iosevna's door. He was still dressed in the dark slacks and sport shirt in which he'd met Schacht. He carried a small briefcase that he'd stashed in the car earlier in the day. It looked official, but inside were a bottle of Stolichnaya, some spicy sausages and black bread, and a wilting blossom.

Anna had been sitting on the bed in her tiny room, reading as she waited for his visit. To impress him, she was reading a French novel but her mind wasn't on it. She felt secure that he had no plan to interrogate her about herself or any of her contacts. She thought he would make love to her. It brought color to her face and speeded her pulse.

Pyotr was disappointed by the noisiness and stale smells of cooking in her corridor, by the thinness of the walls and the fragility of her door. He took it all in with one quick, slanting professional glance as she opened the door to his knock. He offered her the gifts silently, and just as silently she took them, with obvious delight. She bowed him to the only chair. Anna was dressed for the occasion. A thin cotton skirt clung to her hips, and a loose, low-cut peasant blouse showed her ample chest to good advantage. She wore no bra, visibly. Her face was flushed, lovely, with a full smile that melted Pyotr on the spot.

Pyotr moved slowly from the door to the chair, delight and enchantment on his rugged face. He could almost feel this girl clinging to him, her body pressed against his, her face upturned to meet his eyes and mouth. In his imagination they stood there for a full five minutes, gently nuzzling and rubbing against each other. He could feel an urgent erection sliding up in his pants, and her eyes told him that she'd seen it too.

"Don't mind that, Colonel. It is a mark of your appreciation for me and it is normal." She was looking at the bulge in his trousers, gauging its size.

Pyotr almost fell over when she said this. It was so open, so much an ice breaker, that he could barely believe his ears. He sat down, entranced. "Come kiss me, you beautiful flower." Pyotr held out his arms, beckoning her to stand and come over to him. He was seething with physical excitement.

Anna stood up, took two steps to come into his arms. His lips brushed her neck and his hands pressed against the sides of her breasts. She turned in his arms, letting his fingers stroke her nipples briefly, then she stepped back.

"Colonel, I'm afraid," she whispered. "These doors blow open in the wind, even when they're locked. The walls and floor are as thin as paper. We mustn't get too carried away, or we'll have an audience." She giggled as her own words evoked a vision of the four stuffy Soviet families who lived in the little building.

"But, Anna, we could be very quiet."

"Suppose we are reported to the Party or to Comrade Raspatov? Even you have to be careful, don't you, Pyotr Aleksandrovich?" She used his patronymic to soften the remark, and she emphasized *you*, for his ego. Anna Iosevna was a clever girl despite her humble origins.

"You're right. Even I have to be careful. In fact, I must be more careful than others. I must be as white as snow. So we must be as quiet as two little nestlings." He nuzzled her neck, drawing her to him.

As his hands slid over her body, Anna felt her passion rise. It was weeks since she'd had sex, well before she'd left Moscow. Her longing for a man between her legs was almost painful. His rapid breathing and his very obvious erection helped her along, made it almost impossible to resist despite the risks. The knowledge that she could be sent back to the USSR and never again serve overseas eroded as physical desire flowed over her. Slowly, an arm climbed around Pyotr's neck, her mouth came to his, and she pressed full against him.

A door slammed downstairs. A patter of quick footsteps along the lower hall, then up the stairs, sprung them apart. By the time the footsteps stopped outside her door, Anna was seated in the chair and the colonel was standing across the room, pad in his hand, pencil tapping the page.

Anna's visitor pushed open the door. A middle-aged Russian woman, a staff secretary in the economic section who was married to a consular guard, come to beg some tea. The woman was quickly on her way with a few grams of tea in a paper bag, apparently without suspicion. The KGB had a habit of late-night interviews.

But the speed of her arrival and the ease of her entry into the room brought Anna and Pyotr back to reality. They snuggled for a while, but the chill of the visit persisted. Pyotr left soon after, arranging to see Anna in her office the next day when Raspatov was to be out, making an official call.

Gitabwanga: the royal wall—1945 hours, 23 September

The king clicked his cigar trimmer, and immediately the old man coughed gently from below the wall. Even from that cough the king could tell that the old man was excited. But the ritual greeting was unhurried. Neither wanted to hurt the other's feelings by speeding up the traditional phrases.

When it was over, the king asked: "What news?"

"I did what you requested, Bwaga VI. I found out what they intend and when." His voice trembled with pride and with his anguish at what the news conveyed. "They plan to act soon after independence. In late January. The man we call Tofi said he would arrange to have the French army men here called away to Senegal."

"That sounds possible. Go on." The king wondered how Tofi had learned so soon of his secret arrangement with Paris that the foreign legion troops would stay on in independent Bwagania. Probably from a leak in Paris to the French Communist party.

"The plan is to capture the palace, the radio stations, the government buildings, the airfield, and the port. They are sure the Bwaganian army will be on their side. They will send you out of the country in a small airplane, to Algeria. After a time under house arrest there, you will be allowed to go anywhere except back to Bwagania. They will announce your abdication while you're in Algeria, unable to deny it."

It was a long speech for the old man. He said it in uncultured, halting words, but the meaning was quite clear.

"How did you learn all this? Do they suspect that you know it?"

"No, sire. I often listen outside the prince's study now, hidden in the bushes, as if asleep. I can hear everything and they do not know I am there."

"Excellent, my old friend. I will see to it that you are given a good job on the palace staff when this is all over, in addition to the cattle and the young wife you are earning. But meanwhile, I need you in the prince's house. I've brought you something that shows my thanks right now, but will not cause people to wonder. Hide it somewhere until it's safe."

He handed down an envelope, and the old man murmured his gratitude. Not a huge sum, but still more than a month's income.

"I want you to go on with your work, old man. Get me more names, plans, dates, places, even scraps of information that may not seem valuable. But do not take any risks. I want to see you every day when this is over, on my staff."

"One more thing, my king. They call this coup by a strange name: Red Snow. Since a few days, that is the only way they refer to it."

After the old man had gone, the king sat on the wall, thinking about Red Snow. He knew what they were plotting and when it would occur. And they didn't know he knew. The king planned to act forcefully, telling no one just what he intended until he had to. The question was not what to do, but when to do it.

Gitabwanga: Linda's courtyard—1715 hours, 29 September

Shortly after her arrival, Linda moved from her hotel to an apartment the consulate general had rented for her, in an older building with a large inner courtyard. Her two-bedroom apartment was on the third and top floor, with high ceilings, fans, and a wide balcony on the side that faced the mountains. The inner courtyard had tropical trees and plants, mostly in perpetual flower. Birds and geckos kept the courtyard alive with motion and exotic noises.

Linda immediately began helping care for the plants and quickly made friends with the elderly French concierge, Madame Denise, who liked Linda and needed someone to confide in. Linda provided the sounding board.

Within a couple of days there was little Linda didn't know about the building, the other tenants, the schedules of tradesmen and servants, and vacancies.

Early one evening Linda was watering plants when she saw Pyotr Petrov enter the main gate and walk across the courtyard to Madame Denise's ground-floor apartment. He didn't see Linda, tending plants under a bushy tree.

Petrov remained in Madame Denise's apartment for about ten minutes. He came out looking pleased, holding an envelope, which he put in his coat pocket as he left.

Linda did nothing to break her routine. She went on watering and weeding and waited for Madame Denise to come to her. In a few minutes Madame Denise invited Linda in for coffee. They sat in the living room, windows open to the cooling breeze drifting down from the mountains.

"Did you see my visitor, Linda?"

"I saw a man, but paid no attention."

"He wanted to rent a studio," Madame Denise said. "The empty one under yours. It's what he wanted. It's got a combined living and bedroom, with a very small kitchenette. He rented it sight unseen."

"Something is bothering you," said Linda, to hide her own surprise. "I can feel it." She smiled at Madame Denise, inviting comment.

"You're perceptive. The man himself is what bothers me. Pierre Bettrov, a Swiss businessman. He has a heavy accent. Too heavy for a Swiss, even a German Swiss. Perhaps he's not a Swiss, although his passport and other papers are in order."

Linda said nothing, but her eyes showed interest. Outwardly calm, her pulse was racing as Madame Denise went on.

"You know, a concierge is really a security person. We have to train ourselves to be careful of everything and everyone. I've been doing this for over twenty years, since my dear husband died in action in North Africa. My instincts are rarely wrong." Then she brightened. "However, I don't suppose there is any problem. He seems to be a gentleman, and he paid in cash, which is rare these days."

"So you let him have the apartment? For a long time?"

"Six months, with an option to renew for a year. He moves in next week."

Gitabwanga: CIA station—0830 hours, 30 September

"Mark, shouldn't we burn the trash? It's beginning to get in the way."

Two weeks' worth of classified trash—secret and above—was stored in paper bags, stapled shut, in a corner of the communications room. Neither the station nor the consulate general had yet received its own paper shredder or incinerator, and Mark had put off the necessity of burning, waiting for a quiet day with no wind.

He agreed, and they carried the bags out to his car. On the way out of town, they stopped and Mark bought a square yard of chicken wire, a baguette, and some cheese.

They drove along the river that feeds the lake and were

soon out in the bush. Within ten miles there were no longer any people or huts to be seen. Mark stopped the car under a large group of palms, with shade to keep them cool and a sandy clearing with little dry growth to catch fire.

His first move was to take a rifle from the trunk of his car, load it, and stand it against a nearby tree. "We're far enough from the river so we probably won't need it, but the Bwaganian bush is like a zoo without cages. It's wise to play it safe."

Linda grinned her approval. "And nice to be protected."

Mark got an old bucket from the trunk and scooped a shallow depression in the center of the clearing. The first bag of trash went into the hole and Mark put the wire over it, a stone on each corner to keep it down. There was a slight breeze, not enough to worry about.

He smiled at Linda. "Got a match?"

They sat on the sand and watched the fire consume the first bag. The flames danced and little puffs of smoke bounced up as the fire took hold, but there were no sparks.

Linda rested against a tree. "Mark," she said, "I don't suppose there's a KGB bug in the office, but to play it safe, I waited until we were out here to tell you that Petrov came calling on Madame Denise last evening. He posed as Pierre Bettrov, a Swiss businessman. He paid cash up front and rented a small apartment from her. He takes possession next week. What do you think of that?"

"Good work. Definitely Petrov?"

"I've seen his picture in our files, and one day I saw him walking into the Soviet compound. A distinctive walk. He didn't see me. But wait till you hear the bottom line!"

"Come on, Linda. Don't torment me." Mark grinned.

"The apartment he rented is the one right under mine!"

"Jesus!"

"Hold on, Mark. I can't believe I'm a target. I'm not worth their effort and expense. Am I?"

"You are to me, Linda. But it does seem a long reach for the KGB, given their slim assets after so short a time here."

He shut his eyes for a moment, wondering if Petrov already knew who Linda was. It seemed unlikely: too soon after her arrival. While he wondered, she thought about his compliment: You are to me, Linda. It had slipped out so naturally.

"Tell you what, Linda. I'm going to ask for a technical officer to visit for a few days. Tass correspondent Yegorov lives in a building where the TWA manager has an apartment. By luck, they're on the same floor. I've just met the manager, and I'm sure we could use his apartment for an audio job on the Tass man, who as you know is listed in headquarters as probable KGB. We won't tell headquarters about the Petrov apartment yet, but if possible we'll get the tech to do a quickie on it while he's here. Turn the tables on Petrov if he's after you. Better yet if he uses it as a safehouse."

"Okay," said Linda. "Meanwhile I'll try to figure out what he does there."

They turned back to the fire. By now nine bags had been burned without incident, despite the breeze, which was getting stronger. Without warning, the tenth bag began to crackle and spit. Embers were thrown up through the wire and drifted yards away, setting tiny fires in clumps of dry, golden grass beyond the clearing. Mark and Linda stamped out the flames, but two of the fires were persistent. He used their drinking water, but it was quickly gone and the two little fires were still burning.

Mark tried to scoop up sand, but just below the surface the sand was matted with roots, and the rusty bucket fell apart. He was wondering whether to run to the river, at least two hundred yards away, to fill an empty wine bottle with water, when he heard giggling. His pretty, demure IA was squatting, peeing on one of the fires, rear end canted up to avoid being burned.

Laughing, Mark peed on the remaining fire. For a moment they were like two children in their delight.

When it was over, they sat on the sand again, still giggling. Linda smiled. "What a way to burn classified trash."

Mark found himself suddenly acutely aware of her good humor, her original solution to the fire problem, her high spirits. As quickly as it had come, he pushed the thought aside.

Back at the consulate general, Mark drafted his cable to headquarters, sketching out the reason for a tech visit:

. . . TO INSTALL AUDIO DEVICE IN TASS CORRESPONDENT APARTMENT ON ASSUMPTION TARGET WORTH EFFORT AND RISKS MINIMAL. HE GOES WITH FAMILY TO BEACH EVERY SATURDAY AND SUNDAY.

The cable asked for any information headquarters might have on file about the TWA station manager, a U.S. citizen. Mark had some doubts whether they would approve his concept of an audio operation, so soon after his GOLD failure. But it was worth asking.

Langley, Virginia: CIA headquarters—0900 hours, 1 October

The mole read Mark's cable as he took it in to the Russia division chief's office.

"You see this, Jack?"

"I did," said Mason. "I think he's right about it being low risk. The TWA guy checks out okay. The Tass man is indeed probable KGB. The techs can have an audio tech available in a month. It's not as if Cameron is audio happy. He's got some nice contacts, after only two weeks there. Still, right after GOLD . . . I'm a bit leery. What do you think, Sam?"

Sam shrugged as if it weren't really a problem. He wasn't in the command line, but when his old friend Jack Mason asked for advice, he gave it. The KGB would be pleased with this one.

"I'd go along, Jack. Why cripple the guy? He's just had a rotten mess in Tokyo. Let's give him every chance."

"Fine Christian spirit, Sam. Okay, we'll go for the DDO's approval." Sam grinned.

Moscow: KGB headquarters—1630 hours, 6 October

General Vladimir Fedorovich Ossilenko read the mole's latest reports with interest. There was a CIA station now in Bwagania, with a very active station chief. Mark Cameron was known to Ossilenko for his past operations against the KGB and his most recent GOLD failure—one that Ossilenko had orchestrated. The general wondered why they had sent Cameron to Bwagania, as penance or promotion? He would have to ask the mole about that.

It was also interesting that Linda Takahashi had gone to Bwagania. Was it an officially accepted love affair, or was she there to keep an eye on him? And why had the mole sent in all this stuff on Gitabwanga? There was so much hot stuff that he could have sent. Was it possible that the CIA had turned the mole against the KGB? Or that there was some kind of game going on between that Petrov man and the mole?

Ossilenko sighed. One never knew enough. He began to go through the reports. No doubt about it, Cameron was active. Several good contacts already. And now an audio operation targeted against a KGB officer under Tass cover, a man to protect.

When he read that a CIA audio operation was to take place in Gitabwanga—so soon after Cameron had got there—Ossilenko understood why the mole had sent so much about an obscure African post.

It was necessary to warn Petrov, who was so far unaware of the mole's existence. Petrov would have to decide, based on circumstances in Gitabwanga, whether he wanted to let the audio installation go ahead and play it back against CIA or prevent the installation from being made.

Ossilenko drafted a message that put the choice up to Petrov. No mention was made of the mole. Just that a very sensitive source had reported it. Down in the ninth department of the foreign directorate, the message was put into final form. Someone added that Cameron would be worth a close look. He was probably doing penance in Bwagania, hence maybe he was vulnerable. The cable gave a brief summary of the GOLD case.

Gitabwanga: Pyotr's Cover office—1100 hours, 7 October

Tass correspondent Mikhail Ivanovich Yegorov, in reality a KGB major under the supervision of Pyotr, tapped lightly on the door. Pyotr was waiting for him, and waved him to a chair. It was a short interview.

"Mikhail Ivanovich, what I'm going to tell you is very sensitive. You must find some excuse to give your family." Yegorov went pale as he sensed that he was being accused of something and was to be sent home.

"I've done nothing, Colonel. Nothing at all." His voice was hardly audible above the air conditioner. His thin hands clasped his knees and the knuckles showed white.

Pyotr laughed, quickly went on. "No, no. You've done nothing wrong. I was about to add that it has been reported that your apartment is the target for a CIA audio installation. The fact that we know this is very sensitive, as you can understand."

Greatly relieved, Yegorov nodded eagerly.

"We must decide what to do. One option is to let them make the installation and then feed them disinformation. The other options are obvious: To let them install it and then take out the bug and send it back to Moscow; to catch them in the act and get them expelled from Bwagania; to change your weekend pattern so they can't rely on all of you being absent from the apartment."

"We could easily change our beach pattern, Pyotr Aleksandrovich." Yegorov was using the patronymic now that he wasn't on the carpet.

"How would your wife stand it if you were continually being listened to, constantly playing them a line?"

"She's a good sport, sir. But all the time . . . that's a lot, in addition to the children."

"If you're doubtful, Mikhail Ivanovich, she would be even more so. There's no need to put a strain on you so soon after your arrival. Anyway, I prefer not to take on the endless load of playing a bug back to the opposition. Nor do we need the publicity of catching them. We'll tell Moscow Center we prefer to change your pattern. All you need do is not go to the beach when their audio technician comes here. You can go on a weekday instead. Arrange that on your schedule, right?"

Moscow Center approved the plan, warning Pyotr to change things in such a way that there would be no reason for the CIA to suspect that the Soviets had advanced warning.

Pyotr told only two people about the failed operation

GOLD, the Cat's death, Mark and Linda. One was his wife, Olga, while they were both drinking before dinner. The other was Schacht, upon whom he levied a requirement to find out as much as he could about Cameron and Takahashi.

Gitabwanga: M'Taga's house—2030 hours, 9 October

Prince Kalanga, the half-brother of King Bwaga VI, was Prince M'Taga's favorite uncle, and M'Taga was Uncle Kalanga's favorite nephew.

Kalanga was not as bright as M'Taga, or as quick at sports or fighting. But he was very strong and very large, over six feet eight inches and burly. He was also a bully, an idle man who lived on the royal treasury. Prince M'Taga loved this huge, friendly, shuffling, uncomplicated man who never judged him, always spoiled and admired him—and urged him to more innovative pranks.

Since the beginning of M'Taga's drift to the left, Kalanga had ignored the implications. A passing stage, he thought, one that M'Taga had to go through like any other young man. And so Kalanga sat in on many of the discussions and planning sessions of project Red Snow. He dozed, even snored through much of it, and when he heard Schacht incite them to treason, he thought it funny and prankish. He would have clubbed anyone who had suggested that this might eventually lead to the overthrow of the monarchy and the loss of his own revenues and position, perhaps his head.

Kalanga was awake this evening in M'Taga's living room. Pierre Schacht and the group were there. Kalanga disliked Schacht and vaguely feared his cold eyes and level stare. There was a power in the man that seemed to come from a distant, frigid place.

All the discussion about Red Snow was of little interest, and he only half-listened to talk of a post-coup cleansing of the country, of who should get what jobs, and how the peasantry would be reeducated. They were just not educable, Kalanga thought, so why talk about reeducating them?

But he did listen to a briefing on Mark Cameron. It was

part of a discussion of white men in Bwagania, especially those judged to be actual or potential enemies of a coup.

"Mark Cameron is a name you must all remember," Schacht warned. "We must find out all we can about him, for he could be very dangerous to our cause. He is the CIA chief here, working at the American consulate general. He's been here one month and already he is reported to have done a lot of damage. He has been sent here to help enslave all of you."

There were snarls from the young Africans grouped around Schacht and M'Taga. One shouted, "Crotte de singe" (monkey dung), and they all laughed at the crudity.

"Well put," Schacht smilingly agreed. "I can tell you that he is ruthless and has the morals of a pig. He brought with him the widow of a fellow CIA spy who was killed in Asia recently trying to break into the embassy of a friendly socialist country. The thief Cameron was in charge of the break-in, and here he is in Bwagania with the spoils . . . a cute young widow. What a swine! So, let's find out just as much as we can about this man and his spying acts."

Prince Kalanga set his mind to meeting, and undoing, Cameron.

The meeting went on endlessly after that, with frequent murmurs of admiration from the group as Schacht or M'Taga paused between clichés. By ten o'clock Kalanga was snoring loudly, ignored by the group, but the next day he moved fast and brutally. He had cronies everywhere in town and used them to identify M'Pishi and learn his habits. By noon on October 11, he knew that M'Pishi went to the native market on his bicycle almost every late morning.

Gitabwanga: the mountain road— 1215 hours, 12 October

Mark left the consulate general to go home for lunch. Halfway up the long hill toward the house, he saw a small group of police and bystanders. An ancient Mercedes was pulled up just off the road, and a bicycle was lying on the grass. Papaya, mango, avocado, lettuce, and a baguette lay in the dirt.

Mark slowed and would have gone on had he not suddenly

seen his cook lying on the grass. He pulled over and stopped. An enormous Bwaganian was the center of attention. Three policemen and a French uniformed police adviser stood in a ring around him, while the Bwaganian spoke to them in a loud voice. The dozen or so African spectators who had gathered were offering their opinions. No one was paying attention to the agony of M'Pishi, groaning, his face gray with pain.

"What happened, M'Pishi?"

"My back, patron. My back is bad. His car hit me from behind . . . I went into the glass." He had to whisper to avoid more pain. "He is Prince Kalanga . . . bad man . . . please, to the hospital . . ."

"I'll see that you get there as soon as possible." Mark patted M'Pishi's shoulder and went to the French adviser.

"Have you called an ambulance? This man is my cook, and I want to be sure he gets help. His leg looks bad. It may be broken."

"We called an ambulance right away," the Frenchman responded. "But the only one available is out in the bush, on its way back to town."

Mark gestured to the Mercedes, its windshield shattered on the driver's side.

"What happened?"

"That's Prince Kalanga, half brother of the king. He did it, but he will disclaim all responsibility. In fact he will claim to be the victim. We didn't see it, and no one will stand up against him as a witness." He pointed with his chin toward the prince. "Kalanga is a bit drunk, as usual. He's pantomiming his version of the accident. The crowd loves it."

They did indeed love it. One young woman was pretending to be M'Pishi, riding a bicycle backward. She bumped into Prince Kalanga, who staggered back and yelled with fake pain. The crowd of Africans screamed with laughter and approval, and the pantomime was repeated.

"They do it so well . . . pity it's not true." The Frenchman shook his head in frustration. "Kalanga thinks he can get away with anything, and he usually does. Even the police dare not touch him."

Mark, unawed by royalty, walked over to Kalanga. He could smell alcohol on the prince's breath.

"Did you do this?" Mark's anger was clear in his tone. Kalanga sneered down at Mark, irritated by the insolent white man. "No, he did it. He backed downhill into me as I parked there. Too much beer in him, I guess." Kalanga burped in Mark's face, pleased with his response.

The three Bwaganian policemen nodded sagely in agreement. The prince had spoken. There would be no witnesses. The French officer turned away in disgust. He had seen it all so many times before.

Mark was furious. The idea that an old man could ride a bicycle backward downhill was ridiculous. That he could do it fast enough to smash the windshield was patently absurd.

"He's a teetotaler, Kalanga. I know, he's my cook. He never drinks and would never do anything like this. Anyway, it's physically impossible. He cannot have caused this accident, and you know it."

"So," Kalanga shouted. "You must be the American Cameron. You should think twice about defending this lunatic at the expense of my integrity." The crowd muttered their agreement with Kalanga. The three Bawaganian policemen looked coldly at Mark. He had insulted the prince.

The Frenchman, afraid to risk his job by taking Mark's side, advised him to take M'Pishi to the hospital himself. It was a no-win situation. For a moment Mark stood there shaking his head, but Kalanga had begun again to reenact the accident. He steered an imaginary car, parked it, and waited. With great glee, some of the spectators played along with him. With customary African acting skills, some played M'Pishi backing downhill at breakneck speed, looking for the Mercedes to back into. Others played the prince, ducking suddenly as he saw his tormentor bearing down on his windshield. Others wrung their hands in mock pain as they played the stricken Prince.

No one tried to help M'Pishi, or even offer him sympathy. As the old man groaned and sweated, Mark eased him into the car. He made no complaint as Mark drove carefully to the hospital, and later Mark was amazed at the cook's fortitude.

His shoulder and a leg were broken, and he would be immobilized for a while.

Only after leaving the hospital did Mark recall that Kalanga had known his name and position.

Gitabwanga: Lake Tchagamba beach—1200 hours, 14 October

At the eastern end of Lake Tchagamba was a long beach, wide and clean, used by the public. The yacht club was at the southern end of the beach, and the members swam in the lake as well as in the club pool. The northern end of the beach ended in reeds and marshy ponds. People stayed at least twenty yards from the reeds, because they harbored not only the snails that carry schistosomiasis—a disease caused by liver flukes that can be fatal to humans—they also were inhabited by game, including crocodile and hippo. Both animals tended to stay close to the reeds, and keep clear of humans.

Now and then, however, one would stray toward the beach. Most of the swimmers knew about this and stayed on the alert.

Mark and Linda had come to the Lake Tchagamba beach together to have a picnic lunch, swim, sun, and talk about the station's progress. On a weekday the beach was almost deserted: a perfect place to talk. They chose a spot far from anyone, near the reeds. Not too close, but near enough for it to be unlikely that anybody else who came to the beach would pick a spot within hearing distance.

A couple of hundred yards away, a group of French foreign legionnaires were practicing beach landings from two Zodiac speedboats. It was also an opportunity to swim and frolic, and some of the soldiers were playing water polo as they waited for their turn to use the boats. Mark kept a casual eye on them and on the sprinkling of civilians enjoying the beach beyond them.

Linda left Mark for a few minutes to swim. He watched her protectively, having explained that she should keep well away from the reeds.

A white child played along the water's edge beyond the

soldiers, slowly moving in their direction, fascinated by the polo game. Her parents were sunning, not watching.

One of the Zodiacs buzzed a group of hippos out in the lake beyond the reeds, stirring them up. Some of the hippos grunted in rage, opened their jaws showing huge teeth, and made short rushes at the boat. The French soldiers buzzed the hippos again in their boat, their laughter coming through clearly over the engine noise as they selected one hippo for special attention before they circled and came back to the beach.

The hippo, a large one, swam rapidly after the boat, and Mark waved to Linda to come ashore. She came running, splashing him playfully: "What's up?"

"The soldiers have infuriated one of the hippos. It may go after them. Best to be out of the water."

Linda looked over at the soldiers, at the child who was now standing among them, watching the activity, and out at the lake. "I don't see anything."

"Look, there," said Mark. "That line of ripples. He's coming fast." Mark stood up and shouted to the soldiers. But they only looked at him and a few waved, whistling at Linda, not realizing the danger.

Mark started running toward the soldiers. Linda pointed to the line of ripples, now nearing the soldiers rapidly. The group began to scatter, but some of the polo players were too far out and the hippo was almost in among them. The water churned white as the men swam for shore and the animal chased them. The men onshore ran toward their trucks to get weapons. The child, a little girl, was left on the beach, watching, curious, unaware of the threat.

The hippo caught one of the men as he was knee deep, trying to run to shore. There was a scream of agony from the soldier, frantic shouts from his colleagues.

At that moment Mark reached the child, scooped her up in his arms, and continued running until he was well past the danger spot. A man was racing toward them, and Mark handed him the child, panting in French: "Get her out of here, I'm going back."

He went back to the scene of the hippo's attack, but there

was nothing more he could do to help. The hippo had returned to deep water. The soldier was already being carried to the trucks by his colleagues, bloody towels wound around his hips. A sergeant told Mark that the hippo had taken off most of one cheek of his rear end. "He'll survive, but it will be painful and he'll have trouble sitting down all his life. I told them not to tease the hippos . . . this has happened here before . . ."

Mark walked slowly back to Linda, oddly pleased by the look of concern on her face. "At least he's alive. Let's get on with our picnic. I'd like to get back to the office before two o'clock" They knelt down on the sand, spread a large towel, and began to unpack the hamper.

They were interrupted by a polite cough and a man's voice in accented French: "I want to thank you for what you did, monsieur. You probably saved my daughter's life."

Mark stood up, turning, and almost lost his balance with surprise. It was the KGB *rezident*, smiling. They shook hands, silently. Linda watched, sitting on the sand, wondering how Mark would handle this unexpected encounter.

"My name is Mark Cameron. I'm glad I was able to help. You have a pretty daughter, monsieur? . . .

"Pyotr Petrov, consul. Soviet consulate general. Very pleased to know you, and very grateful."

Mark shook the girl's hand. "Your name?"

"Aleksandra, monsieur. *Merci beaucoup*."

"You're ten, I would say," said Mark, knowing it already. "And you speak French?"

"No." Petrov laughed. "She's just beginning. Your French is excellent, Monsieur Cameron. Are you a diplomat?"

Mark grinned at Petrov's open hint that he knew who he was talking to. "This is Mrs. Takahashi. We both work at the U.S. consulate general."

Just then Olga caught up with her husband and Aleksandra. Trembling, she grabbed Aleksandra's hand, intending to upbraid her.

"My wife, Olga." Petrov waved at her, said: "Olga, Mr. Cameron of the U.S. consulate general got Aleksandra out of there."

"I saw it," said Olga coldly, frightened and annoyed that she was expected to be grateful. "There wasn't any real danger to Aleksandra. But we must thank you." She started away with her daughter in tow, wishing she had not been so impolite.

"They can kill," said Linda loudly, irritated. "Mark had just told me so."

Olga stopped and turned, about to say something defensive. Petrov caught her by the elbow: "You must be gracious, Olga. The animal could very well have killed Aleksandra."

Olga smiled reluctantly, nodded her thanks, and turned on her heel. Petrov shrugged at Mark and Linda, smiling, and explained: "Olga was frightened for Aleksandra. Will you be at the king's reception?"

"The twenty-fourth? Yes," said Mark. "And you?"

"I'll look for you there, Mr. Cameron, Mrs. Takahashi. Again, my profound gratitude."

Gitabwanga: the yacht club—1930 hours, 16 October

Without a cook, Mark was eating out most of the time. Linda joined him tonight, and they sat on an open terrace that seemed to float on Lake Tchagamba. Lazy ripples gurgled under their feet, and the mountains showed mistily in the quarter-moon. The candles on their table made the setting romantic, and Mark was pleased to be there with such an attractive girl.

They were talking quietly when there was a discreet cough behind them.

"Good evening, sir . . . Mademoiselle. I must excuse myself, but this is an excellent time and place to say something to you that is important." The European was speaking fluent, barely accented English.

"Please continue, sir," Mark was cordial, but formal.

"I am Doctor De Koening. A Belgian. I am a specialist in tropical medicine. But more to the point, I live next door to Prince Kalanga."

"Please sit down, Dr. De Koening. Will you join us for a drink . . . or dinner?" Now Mark was warmly welcoming.

This was perhaps a break. The doctor sat down, wiped his forehead.

"Excuse me," he said. "I have just had a very humiliating experience. So when I heard you were here, I sought you out. This concerns you, Mr. Cameron."

"Doctor, this is Mrs. Takahashi, who works in our consulate." De Koening bowed to Linda, who charmed him with a sunny smile and a nod of welcome.

"I suspect you were looking for me and asked if I was here, Doctor?" Mark had to know how he had been so easy to find. The answer was simple.

"I have to admit, yes. I have been to nearly every place in town that I thought you might be." The doctor smiled. "You see, Mr. Cameron, we share an enemy."

"A prince, perhaps?"

"Exactly. Now my story. He owns a 1929 Mercedes. The one that struck your cook. I own a 1929 Mercedes. As my neighbor, he admired mine when I bought it a few years ago, so he searched Europe and got a similar car. This morning when I started to go to work, pouf! No windshield in my car. But last night I had seen his car in his garage, with a broken glass. So I suspected him of theft . . . he is a liar, a bully and and thief, you may know. He hides behind the king."

"Admirable character. What does the king think of him?" asked Linda with an innocent air.

"The king is disgusted by him, but Kalanga is older and unable to accept discipline."

"What did you do?"

"I accosted him in his house, Mr. Cameron. I told him that such windshields are not available and have to be flown in from Europe. That takes time, so he must have stolen mine. And then he kicked me from his house. In my behind. I fell in the dirt. It was a scene for animals." He sputtered in his rage.

Mark asked, "Why do you think he ran into my cook?"

The doctor looked at Mark with admiration. "That is precisely why I came to find you. I had heard from my nurses that this accident had happened, and that is how I understood that you were involved, Mr. Cameron. But this evening I was home early, and from my study I heard Kalanga shouting on his telephone. Sometimes he gets so excited I can hear every word—which is usually of no interest. But this evening I was still angry and I made an effort to hear."

Mark and Linda smiled. The doctor had probably gone to the fence to overhear.

"He was talking to his nephew, the king's oldest son, the one who is to be prime minister on January first. They often have long telephone conversations, mostly about women. Sometimes about parties or their childish pranks. This evening Kalanga said something that would normally be quite innocuous. But in view of what has happened, I think it is important for you. He was laughing and he said: 'In twenty-four hours I have arranged for the crotte de singe to be out for every meal, and I have planted my foot where it has been itching to go for a year. A great twenty-four hours.' Double-talk, but if you know the context . . ."

Mark felt a chill. Where did that name come from? Why are they after me? What does it mean? He said: "So it was deliberate, the accident. What do you think it means, Doctor?"

"First, that it was indeed deliberate, and apparently the Prince M'Taga did not know about it but would be pleased by it. Surely, Mr. Cameron, they would only want a newly arrived diplomat out of his house for sinister reasons."

"True, Doctor. But this is my first time in Africa, let alone Bwagania. They know nothing about me."

"But, Mark, others might know a lot about you. Could they have been behind this. And if so, how?" Linda's words hinted of mystery, but the Belgian doctor didn't react.

Mark decided to take a chance. "Doctor, would you help us get back at Kalanga? As a diplomat, I've got far less to fear from him than you have. But I can't do it alone."

"I'd be pleased to help, Mr. Cameron. What can I do?"

Gitabwanga: Hôpital St. Pierre—
1730 hours, 20 October

Mark had visited M'Pishi in the hospital before and had become accustomed to the strange scene. He sat on the edge of the chipped, black metal bed because there was no other place to sit. The bed had no sheet, only two blankets. One to cover the patient, one to cover the lumpy straw mattress. It was warm and humid in the ward, but M'Pishi kept the blanket over him, modesty more important than comfort. He refused to take off his hat, an old trilby a former employer had given him. His surplus French air force overcoat was folded around his trousers and shirt to serve as a pillow.

When Mark arrived, M'Pishi was asleep, lying on his good side. He had a rather benign smile when he slept, which went well with his gray hair and black eyebrows. Mark had brought him a meal cooked by a small restaurant near the hospital. It was M'Pishi's only meal of the day, for the Hôpital St. Pierre didn't feed its African patients. Their families did that.

Mark coughed and M'Pishi woke up. M'Pishi appreciated the devotion Mark gave him. His eyes followed Mark as he moved about the bed, straightening the blankets and helping M'Pishi eat. The eyes of the nineteen other African men in the ward, and the family members who were ministering to them, followed Mark's movements too. The sight of a white man tending to his cook was unusual.

"Are you being well cared for medically, M'Pishi?" Mark asked this question every time he visited M'Pishi.

"N'dio, Bwana. The doctor is a famous Frenchman who serves Africans because we need it. He makes very little money here, but he gets much affection. He's been in Africa over thirty years."

"Yes, I have heard about him. He's something of a saint. And the nurses?"

"All nuns, patron. Some French, some from other European countries. Soon they'll have African nuns here," he said proudly. "In the past, the African women have been cleaners only."

"Any pain?"

M'Pishi grinned: "Only when I laugh, patron."

"Don't laugh, just grin. Looks better on you anyway."

M'Pishi giggled, loving this patter. Then he spoke about Prince Kalanga. M'Pishi had a friend who worked in the prince's household, an old man who was trusted and who heard a lot of talk that the prince and his group assumed went over the heads of the servants.

"My friend came to see me here in the hospital today," said M'Pishi quietly. "He told me that a white man who visits the prince often had told them that you are dangerous and they must find out all about you."

Mark felt his scalp prickle. "Please go on."

"Prince Kalanga was in the room, but he must have heard only part of the talk. He is usually drunk, you know. Kalanga called Prince M'Taga after the accident, to boast about his skill and cunning in putting me in hospital so the group could do something about you."

"Who is the white man, M'Pishi?"

"I don't know, patron. My old friend says they call him Tofi. It means dung in two Congolese languages, Chiluba and Lingala."

Good grief, are we all called dung? Aloud, Mark asked: "Can you find out his European name?"

"I will certainly try, patron."

"What else?"

"They say that Kalanga makes love with the wife of the minister of interior. That is dangerous, even for the bully Kalanga. The interior minister controls the police."

Mark stored that tidbit. Useful. It fitted his plan. "Can you think of anything more that might make some sense out of this, M'Pishi?"

The old man knew nothing more that could help. He could not bring himself to tell Mark what he had heard from his friend about Mark, the Cat, and Linda. M'Pishi didn't want to hurt Mark.

Gitabwanga: the yacht club—2030 hours, 22 October

This time Dr. De Koening was Mark's guest for dinner. De Koening and Linda, working separately, had been busy taking the photographs that Mark had asked for. They handed him the negatives undeveloped, as he had requested. Then De Koening told them what he knew about his neighbor, Prince Kalanga. The doctor was a good student of psychology.

"To sum up," De Koening said at the end of dinner, "he is a bully not so much because of his size and strength, which are beyond doubt unusual. But he is most of all a bully because he is allowed to be. His actions are protected by his royal rank. So he just does what he wants, and because he is still a child at heart, the worst traits of a child come out."

"How does he react when someone faces up to him?"

"He usually crumples, like most bullies. But it rarely happens, because people fear to take him on. Only the king can punish him, and usually, people don't complain about him to the king."

"Would a threat of court action from a diplomat cause him to crumple?"

"In this case, Mr. Cameron, I believe it would. You would have to be very forceful. He doesn't know what diplomats are, really. That will be to your advantage."

Gitabwanga: Kalanga's house—
0600 hours, 24 October

It was still too early for Kalanga to be up or his servants to be in the house. Mark banged on the prince's front door.

There was no answer. Mark banged again on the door, using a stone from the garden. It sounded very important and authoritative. He kept banging until a light came on and the door opened. Prince Kalanga was in the condition Mark had hoped for. His eyes were bloodshot. His breath stank of stale alcohol. He was staggering slightly and had a hangover that was visible at a hundred yards. He also in a foul mood and he barked at Mark: "What in hell do you want?" Then he recognized Mark, and he yelled: "How dare you come to my house? I see no one at this hour, and certainly not you!"

"You had better see me, Prince Kalanga. Or do you wish to be charged with attempted murder and theft?"

Kalanga's jaw dropped, and Mark took the opportunity to walk past him into the house. The surprised prince stepped back, then doubled his fists and came after Mark, who stepped forward until his face was inches from Kalanga's.

"I have something that can cause you a whole lot of trouble," Mark said quietly. "And if you touch me, two things will happen. First, you will go to the hospital yourself. You see, I'm a karate expert."

To emphasize the point, Mark prodded the royal throat with a straight jab of his four fingers, hitting the adam's apple. The jab looked gentle enough, but the prince choked with pain. Mark could see the realization come to him that this smaller man could cripple him. Kalanga had no stomach for an even match, and none at all for a karate chop or two.

"Second," Mark went on, "you will have caused a diplomatic incident, and that will involve the crown in your trial."

For a full minute, the prince stared at Mark. He had never been spoken to with such scorn by anyone outside his immediate family. He measured Mark, every fiber in his body wanting to crush this insolent and frightening white man. But the pain in his throat told him that he could not win a fight. And what was this about a charge of murder and grand theft, and a diplomatic incident?

Mark waited, watching these thoughts race across the prince's forehead, wondering what would happen if Kalanga jumped him. Would his skill dominate this huge man, or would he, too, end up in the hospital? He braced himself just in case, but it wasn't necessary.

The prince smiled with sudden cunning. He would listen, then deal with this bastard later—on his own terms. He waved Mark into a chair, then sat himself in a leather armchair.

Without a word, Mark pulled a small envelope from inside his shirt. He laid out some black-and-white photographs on the coffee table. The envelope went back inside the shirt. The photos were small, somewhat fuzzy, but clear enough. They showed a 1929 Mercedes in various poses. And a man riding a bicycle. Then the car, a crowd, and a man and bike lying in the road. Finally, the prince's house and a fuzzy figure with a windshield scurrying around the corner of the garage.

Based on photos taken for him by Linda and De Koening, Mark had done some photomontage. The results looked authentic, and as he explained them, the prince was completely taken in. He followed Mark's words with childish interest.

"This was taken by a man who happened to be following you up the hill . . . these also. The man came to my office to offer the pictures afterwards. They show your car hitting the bicycle and the cook flying through the air. Notice that your car was doing the same speed as my witness, thirty-five kilometers per hour. And your car did not leave the road. You were not parked. Then here is either you or your servant stealing the windshield."

Mark only allowed the prince to look at them briefly, then returned them to the envelope, which he patted meaningfully.

"I also have a photograph of you and the wife of the minister of interior misbehaving. It was taken some time ago by a man who has since left the country. I understand that if the minister saw this, he would let his police go after you."

Mark was prepared to take out the photo and show it. It too was a montage, using two dummies and the De Koening car. It was very grainy, but it would pass quick inspection by a hungover prince. But as it turned out, Kalanga was thoroughly convinced. He waved it off, accepting Mark's word.

"What do you want?" Kalanga was resigned to what was coming. He thought it would be a request for money.

"This is what you must do," Mark said. "You must pay for my cook's hospitalization. You must buy him a new bicycle. You must pay him damages of one million francs. And you must buy a new windshield for Dr. De Koening."

The prince was aghast. He didn't have that kind of money. He whispered, "And for you? You'll want something too?" There was scorn in his voice. "I'd rather go to prison than pay anything to a man like you."

"Nothing for me. You must have a wrong impression of me, Kalanga. I am not blackmailing you, only asking for justice for M'Pishi and De Koening." Mark was trying to tease out some clue as to why Kalanga had gone after him in the first place.

"I thought you were a crook as well as ruthless. But anyway, I don't have the money."

"What made you think I'm a crook and ruthless? We'd never met until the accident."

"I was told you were, that's all."

It was enough for Mark to hang his hat on. He said: "Kalanga, I'll strike a bargain with you. I'll pay your costs for M'Pishi and De Koening, pay them directly to you. And we'll destroy the photographs together, right here. All you have to do is tell me in detail how you came to have this impression of me. From whom, when, and where?"

Kalanga could see nothing wrong with that. He had no inkling of the sensitivity of the information. So he related in detail what had happened in the M'Taga living room. Mark listened with increasing excitement until Kalanga stopped.

"What is the name of this Austrian?"

"Pierre. Pierre Schacht. The servants there call him Tofi na n'Zolo. It means manure of a chicken in a Congo language, I'm told. One of the servants came from Zaire. They don't like him."

"Why not?"

"They think he's leading M'Taga into a trap. Toward a coup against the king. But I think it's all just children's talk. Just young men playing at grown-up games." He laughed.

It was getting more interesting, and it turned out to be Mark's easiest recruitment ever. Kalanga wanted money. The idea of a regular payment in exchange for gossip was a lark. All he had to do was tell Mark about Pierre Schacht. No secrets of the kingdom of Bwagania. Just the group that had formed around Schacht. He didn't perceive any disloyalty to M'Taga. In fact it might be fun and profitable to ask Schacht for money in exchange for information about Mark. It never occurred to him that Mark accepted this risk, in fact assumed that Kalanga would work both sides of the street.

Mark was happy when he left Kalanga's. He had solved the mystery of why Kalanga had run down M'Pishi. He had a new, albeit substandard, asset. He had wind of a coup against the king. He had—he was certain—identified a KGB agent: Schacht. And above all he had another clue to the mole. How else could Schacht have learned about the death of the Cat, and Linda's situation?

He would, however, have to tread with care.

Gitabwanga: the royal palace—
1930 hours, 24 October

The king's official birthday reception was unlike any other Mark had attended. The palace was full of people of all descriptions: the diplomatic corps, business people, farmers, military, the clergy, academia, the medical profession, French and Bwaganian administration officials.

Out in the garden, the royal drums played softly.

Eight Soviet guests came from their consulate general: Raspatov and his senior officers, with their wives. They arrived together and stayed together, silently watching the crowd, as if they felt isolated in the swirling, noisy mass. Only Petrov smiled and nodded to passersby.

Mark caught his eye and grinned. Pyotr returned the greeting, and he and Olga drew away from the rest of the Soviets. Mark and Linda strolled over to join them. Linda edged Olga aside, to talk with her separately. Olga went along, trying, in her own way, to make amends.

"I meant to call you before this evening, Mr. Cameron, but it got away from me. Anyway, I knew we'd meet here. I want to thank you again for risking yourself to save Aleksandra. She talks about it a lot and wants to see you again."

"I'd be delighted, anytime, although I feel thanked enough." Mark smiled. "I'm pleased you're here tonight, Colonel. Linda and I don't know many of the guests."

"Nor do we, Mr. Cameron. By the way, I'm a consul, like you. But if you want to call me colonel, I accept the honorary title." He grinned. They both knew the truth.

"Sorry. Consul from now on. Colonel is often used as a mark of esteem in the south of the U.S., whether you have the rank or not. It must have been a Freudian slip."

"Thank you, Sigmund." Pyotr laughed. "As to our work, I'll be first secretary and political officer when our consulate general becomes an embassy, Mr. Cameron. What about you?"

"The same. We'll see each other on the diplomatic circuit. Perhaps we can exchange notes?"

Petrov's eyes widened with surprise, but he smiled and rose

to the occasion: "With pleasure. But it would be one-sided—you must know a lot more than I do."

"What makes you think so?"

"American friendship with France. Your support for this kingdom. We've only had a presence here since August this year."

"Perhaps," replied Mark, grinning to take the sting out of his expression of doubt. "But you'll make up for that quickly. I bet you're an excellent political observer as well as a fine linguist."

Pyotr, pleased by the flattery, wondered how much more Mark knew about him. Undoubtedly, a lot. "Are you a linguist also? Do you speak Russian, for example?"

They were talking in French, a language Mark handled almost as well as English. "Yes," he said, switching to Russian. "I enjoy it."

Pyotr's face brightened and his body relaxed. "You have an interest in Russian culture?"

"Not only, but in your country as a whole—the economy, the political system, everything."

Mark was stating a fact. Pyotr knew it and grinned. He liked this kind of frankness. "The Arab world is my specialty," he volunteered, finding himself increasingly comfortable talking to Mark. "But of course the U.S. is of great interest. I have a lot to learn about it."

"You haven't been stationed there?"

"Not yet. We look forward to it one day."

"Meanwhile, Mr. Petrov, I hope you enjoy Bwagania. Do you hunt?"

The ladies reappeared, Linda looking unusually pale, but before Mark could query her, Pyotr—eager to go on uninterrupted—led him out onto a verandah.

"Yes, I hunt. Bwagania's a good place for hobbies, Mr. Cameron. What do you enjoy?"

"I like to hunt, sail, swim, keep my karate up to snuff, and I play chess. And you?"

Pyotr was smiling warmly now. "I like the same things, except sailing. I've never done it. Is your chess good?"

"Not particularly, but I'd be happy to play with you."

"I play very unconventionally, and I enjoy blitz."

"Great," said Mark. "So do I. We'd better nail the board down."

"Two mavericks, eh?" remarked the Soviet. "That should make for some interesting games. When shall we start?"

Mark was pleasantly surprised by his invitation. He responded casually and without hesitation. "I'll call you during the week and we'll set a time. I know some good places to hunt, too. Want to go with me?"

"Absolutely. But I've only shot birds. I know nothing about African game."

"We'll manage all right." Mark grinned. "Mind you don't shoot me. After all, I am the principal enemy."

Pyotr stared for a moment, surprised that Mark had used the KGB's label for U.S. intelligence. Then he laughed. "First, mavericks are an endangered species. Second, you're a valuable protector against hippos. Third, I like your style and I like you."

Mark laughed, clapped him on the shoulder. "It's mutual." They talked on for an hour more, each man probing for a solid picture of what made the other tick. Pyotr came away pleased by Mark's friendliness, an attitude he was certain was honest, surprising as that was. We got along well, he would tell Moscow, and I learned a lot about him. I'll pursue the contact, see where it leads.

It was late before Mark and Linda got a chance to walk out onto the palace lawn, far enough away from everyone to whisper unheard.

"Get much out of him, Mark?"

"We're going to exchange notes. Play chess. Go hunting. He said he likes me. Most defections are based on friendship, you know, so this may be a start. I know a good bit more about him, despite what the old guard in the Russia division will say: 'You know very well, Cameron, that eyeball-to-eyeball confrontation with KGB officers is at best a waste of time. At worst it plays into their hands.' I don't agree with them. I'll do it slowly and carefully, but it'll be my way. But what about you, Linda? You came back from your chat with Olga looking unhappy. What's up?"

"Mark, she knows about the Cat and me. She knows his nickname, for God's sake." Linda looked shaken.

"What did she say? Did she come right out and tell you?"

"No. She asked me about my husband, since I was introduced as Mrs. Takahashi. I told her he'd died quite recently. She just murmured, 'Some cats don't have nine lives,' with quite a triumphant little smile, I thought."

"Holy mackerel," Mark said. "Unless it's just a very unusual coincidence, which seems doubtful. I wonder why she'd know something like that, let alone give it away. I wonder if she did it for him. What did you do?"

"I changed the subject without making anything of it. But she had to be referring to Neko-chan. My woman's intuition tells me Olga can't resist putting people down. She has to parade her power and her knowledge. She might be very hard to take. His life could be hell!"

"No wonder you were rattled. Okay now?"

"Of course. I'm pretty solid, Mark."

"Both, Linda. Pretty and solid." He meant it.

Gitabwanga: Mark's office—1430 hours, 30 October

The voice on the telephone spoke French; the words were classic. All case officers have received, suspected, and often rejected unsolicited approaches. Too many of them are provocations.

"Monsieur Cameron?"

"Oui. Ici Cameron."

"I have an important message for you. I must see you at once."

Uh-oh! A pusher, thought Mark. Who does he work for . . . Kalanga? Petrov? "Who are you?"

"Paul. You don't know me, but it's vital that I see you."

He'd given no last name. Mark played him along, to tease something out. "What's the nature of your message, monsieur . . ."

"Not on the phone, Monsieur Cameron. I'll be at the Café Tchagamba in five minutes. Look for a leopard hatband." The phone clicked, hummed, and the man was gone.

Instinct, the brother of a good case officer, told Mark to go along. The café, two minutes' walk away, was an unlikely spot for an ambush. Perhaps Paul was legitimate. If not, perhaps the truth might show through.

"Linda, I just got a must-see-you-ASAP call. Paul God-knows-who, a Frenchman. Café Tchagamba in five minutes—four now. I'm going. Wish me luck."

"Be careful. Could be a trap."

"I know."

Gitabwanga: Café Tchagamba—1438 hours, 30 October

Under a wide bush hat with a leopard-skin band, the Frenchman was short, muscular, tanned dark brown. Black hair, brown eyes, heavy beardline, hairy arms a shade too long. He radiated a strong sense of purpose, and there was a vague smell of burning grass around him. His handshake was firm, dry.

"Afternoon, Monsieur Cameron. My full name is Paul Passatu. I came to Bwagania twenty years ago and have built up a ranch about twenty kilometers from here. I love this country, and will die here. I also happen to be a friend of King Bwaga VI." He stopped, waiting for Mark to react.

At least he was direct, up front. Mark liked that.

"Delighted to meet you, Monsieur Passatu. How did you hear of me? I'm new here."

"Monsieur Cameron, I have a long story to tell you. It involves the welfare of this kingdom, which is certainly of interest to your country. It also involves an incident of last week with Prince Kalanga. I have been instructed by the king to contact you and expose to you certain facts. But it must not occur here. I invite you to come alone to an apartment I have here in town, this evening. From there we will go to meet a very important personage."

That was something Mark couldn't refuse. "I will be there. Please tell me the time and the place and what to wear."

Passatu smiled. Mark's tan trousers, safari boots, and

short-sleeved white shirt didn't look very diplomatic. A good sign.

"Come as you are, say at six-thirty. Be prepared to go on until midnight. The address is rue Gambetta, number eleven. Go through the tunnel, to the back. Cross the courtyard and take the stairs to the second floor. Just open the door. I'll leave it unlocked." He got up and left.

Back in his office after meeting Passatu, Mark thought it unlikely that this was a bushwhack engineered by Kalanga. But he would take along a weapon just in case.

"Linda, I'm going to meet Passatu this evening. If I don't call you by two in the morning, take over and call headquarters." He described Passatu carefully to Linda, so that she could almost see the swarthy, tough-looking man.

"Mark, I'm afraid for you." It was in fact a stronger fear for him than she had expected. The idea of losing Mark was suddenly terrifying.

"Linda, I smell a good contact here, one that could lead me right into the center of local politics. There are always risks. They're part of our profession. I know how to take care of myself."

"It didn't work for the Cat, Mark."

He listened for a hint of bitterness, but there was none. Just concern.

"Bad luck can come at any time, just like a traffic accident. Careful tradecraft lessens the risks. That's all."

"Let me come too, Mark. It'll be safer with two."

"Sorry. It just might put the man off. I don't know enough about him to take a chance like that. But thanks. A great offer." He wished she could come.

"Mark, you know nothing about him. Why not at least get a trace on him from headquarters? The regulations require it."

"Linda, a trace would almost certainly result in nothing known. We're only just beginning out here, and so far they've come up with a blank on all our traces on Europeans and Africans. Anyway, I have the discretion to do this if I feel it's useful. And last but not least, I trust my instincts. I bet you twenty dollars everything will be okay."

Linda knew she was beaten. "All right, Mark Cameron." She touched his cheek.

"I'll be back. You can count on it." Mark suddenly wanted to kiss her, then thought better of it.

Gitabwanga: Passatu's apartment—1830 hours, 30 October

It was dark when Mark parked his car four blocks from 11 rue Gambetta. First he walked in the opposite direction. Then he stopped to listen for footsteps. There were none. Then down an alley to a parallel street, and eventually to 11 rue Gambetta—certain that he wasn't being followed. Prior to parking, he had driven around town and out of town for forty-five minutes to be sure he was clean.

The tunnel was a narrow passage between buildings, with an arched brick roof. Its mouth, set in a white wall, made the tunnel entrance as black as if it had been painted there.

Before he entered this forbidding hole, Mark shifted his weapon to his left hand, where it disappeared in his closed fist. It was a plastic bottle of DO powder, a strong form of Mace. A squeeze of the bottle and a thin stream of the powder shot out ten feet, surprisingly accurately. A silent, nonlethal defense better than a firearm. You just had to be sure you didn't squirt it upwind. He'd done that once, and been on his knees retching for twenty minutes.

There was no sound in the tunnel, almost no light. Mark edged along the right-hand wall, ready for action. Keep to the right, Passatu had warned. Sometimes people sleep on the floor of the tunnel. Mark felt very visible against the lights in the street behind him, and vulnerable.

He stopped a couple of times, but there were no sounds that he could identify. He had brought no flashlight, not realizing it would be so dark. Finally, he could discern a vague lighted area ahead, and he was in the courtyard. Just the reflected lights from the city, but no light in any window. At least it was fresher in the courtyard and he could see the sky.

Mark walked very slowly across the court and into the entry to Passatu's apartment. He crept up the stairs, not using the timed stairway light. It would have gone on and off (too soon) with a loud clank and left him in total blackness.

At the head of the narrow stairway he felt only one door. It had to be Passatu's, but there was no light showing under it. Mark pushed it open anyway, and there was a thin, nerve-twanging squeal for oil from the hinges. A light came on, almost blinding him, and there across the room was Paul Passatu in a large armchair. He was staring right at Mark, unblinking.

A cocked and loaded crossbow was pointing at Mark's chest. The bluish steel quarrel looked hungry.

So it was a trap. Mark's body stiffened.

As he tensed for a desperate leap at Passatu, the crossbow was slowly lowered and a big smile rode across Passatu's face.

"I just wanted to see what a professional would do in a tight spot. Hope I didn't alarm you."

"You bastard, you owe me a big one." Mark sat down slowly, deliberately, in the nearest chair. He could feel the tension leave and the trembling begin, and knew it would last a few minutes. With luck, it wouldn't show.

"Alarm me? Of course not. It happens several times a day." Mark was angry and sarcastic. "You are a lucky man, Passatu. Another second and I'd have killed you. I don't recommend that game unless you're prepared for nasty results." He wondered if Passatu would accept the ploy. He did. He was an amateur playing a game.

Passatu put the crossbow in a rack with two others, slipping the quarrel into a quiver. Then he poured Mark a tumbler of Scotch and water.

"Sorry, no ice. I ran out today."

Mark smiled. "Your Scotch is more important than your lack of ice just now."

"I'm forgiven? To business," said Passatu. "I speak all the local dialects and I have close friends among Africans at all levels. They know I keep my mouth shut and can be trusted. Including the king, they value my advice. You see, I'm partly African too. My mother was Algerian."

Mark nodded. Passatu's credentials sounded okay. "How do the French administration and you get along?"

"A good question. Without stress, but there's a certain distance because of my Algerian background. I don't have contact with the Sûreté or SSR."

He was making it easy by volunteering necessary information. Hopefully, it was accurate.

Passatu went on. "Recently I began to hear stories of a new movement among certain younger Bwaganian men, all from good families. I was in the French army in Indochina, and the words I hear are the same dogma that the Viet Minh taught. A professionally led young communist cadre has been secretly formed. We're seeing the tip of an iceberg that has never existed here before, largely because of strong traditional values."

"Are those values eroding?"

"All human values erode if they aren't protected."

"Doesn't the king want them to remain intact?"

"Oh, yes. But the younger men are divided. Many think the monarchy obsolete."

"Won't the crown prince defend his future role as king?"

"That's part of the problem, Mr. Cameron. Our sources claim that the prince wants to force the king to abdicate soon after independence, and make himself president-for-life." Passatu shook his head. "M'Taga might very well fall for this kind of thing if it is put to him with skill."

"By a man like Pierre Schacht, for example?" Mark was taking a calculated risk. It worked. Passatu sat up in surprise. "You've heard of that man?"

"I am a professional, Mr. Passatu."

"Call me Paul, please. I'll call you Mark. Yes, you are indeed a professional. What do you know about him?"

"Not yet, Paul. First, your story."

"My information is that M'Taga is already convinced that a coup is needed. His cadre group is coached by this mysterious Pierre Schacht, a hard-core Marxist. Prince Kalanga is on the edges of the group because he's M'Taga's favorite uncle. Kalanga went after your cook, trying to please M'Taga. He jumped the gun and made a mess of things. They're angry with him, but they won't harm him. They just think he's irritating and got what he deserved. But you aren't out of danger. I imagine they're wondering what to do about you right now."

"Why me especially?"

"Because Pierre Schacht told them that you're the prime enemy here, the CIA representative."

The initials CIA hung in the air. Mark rarely used them. It was a shock to hear them pinned on him by a French farmer in Gitabwanga. He wondered whether to deny the label or let it ride. Maybe more would be gained by letting it ride.

"Paul, what do you know about Schacht?"

"Almost nothing. He discloses very little about himself. He's said to be Austrian, age about fifty-five. He lives at Madame Petarde's Hôtel du Lac, a bordello. But he never plays around with the girls. He frequents M'Taga's house and has great influence there. He is definitely a communist—although that's not against the law here."

"How long has he been here?"

"He started coming a couple of years ago and spent about half of each year here. Since a year ago, he's spent most of his time here. The rest of the year in Vienna, they say."

"What do you think will happen? Will the king move against the plotters, and if so, when? Can he beat them if he wants to? What would he do to his son?"

"So many questions, Mark." Paul laughed. "The king is tough, cunning, well-informed, and very determined. I think he will move when he can catch all the leaders. We're identifying them now. If he keeps the army in hand, he wins . . . especially if the French troops are still here. As to his son, I simply don't know. They have been very close all of M'Taga's life. But you never know in Africa . . ."

Then he looked at Mark and waved his finger. "This brings me to this evening. The king needs as much information as he can get. He is also willing to provide information in return. He trusts the CIA more than he does the SSR. So he wants to meet you, to arrange to have liaison with your service. He wants to start it tonight."

Mark did some quick thinking in a hurry. The king undoubtedly had a channel to the SSR but also wanted one to the CIA. There would be substantial advantages to having a discreet liaison with the king—formal, informal, whatever. On the minus side, it might draw Mark into a tight liaison that could diminish his other options. On balance, however, the opportunity to hear what the king wanted was too good to miss.

"Fine, when do we meet him?"

Paul looked at his watch. "At eight o'clock tonight. In fifteen minutes. We must start now."

Mark stared at him with mock irritation. "You knew I would go along. How?"

"Intuition!" Paul laughed and his joy was infectious.

As Paul led the way out of his apartment, Mark was thinking that if Bwaga VI knew that Mark was trying to find evidence of a mole in CIA, he wouldn't be so quick to put his faith in the Company.

Gitabwanga: the royal palace—
2000 hours, 30 October

The drive to the palace in Paul's car took only a few minutes. The sentries at the main gate knew the car and waved it in. Paul drove around the palace to a small, single-story brick building with a green tin roof.

Jean Prosper M'Bouyé was a tall, gaunt, ascetic man. He was chamberlain to the king and principal confidant. He was also Bwaga VI's first cousin and lifelong friend. Among his many duties was management of an informal network of sources, Europeans as well as Africans, of great value to the monarch.

Paul introduced Mark as "my CIA friend."

Mark said, for the record: "I've been presented as a CIA officer. That is not necessarily the case, but I do have contacts of that sort."

"I'm sure we can avoid too many initials, Mr. Cameron." The chamberlain smiled.

"*Chapeau,* Monsieur M'Bouyé! A good choice of words. Now, how can I help you?"

"His Majesty learned of your adept handling of Prince Kalanga, and wants to meet you. He was considering contact with the United States on a discreet, very discreet, level and so he wants to combine the two. I believe that such a meeting is acceptable to you, Mr. Cameron?"

"It will be an honor, Monsieur M'Bouyé. As it has been to meet you." Mark bowed slightly and in return received a broad grin. It wasn't often that M'Bouyé was told that meeting him was an honor.

"The ground rules, before I take you to him: The king is friendly and informal. He loves to talk and to listen. To save him time, we try to handle all details and leave only the policy to him. So I will make some remarks first."

Mark nodded, and the chamberlain went on. "It is critical that your country understand what is happening here and that you give us your advice and possibly your help. The great majority of our people love the king. They want him to be succeeded by Prince M'Taga. But we are not being left alone by the communists. They're training a cadre to conduct a coup against our king and our most sacred institutions. Until recently, we thought this was a long-term activity, but now we know the cadre is almost ready to move and an armed coup may be only weeks away. We know this from many reports." He waved to include Paul Passatu as one of the sources. "One of our principal, and reliable, sources is right inside the cadre. From him it's clear we need all the help we can get."

M'Bouyé looked sad as he continued: "Prince M'Taga is the principal plotter. There is no doubt of the prince's treason. He was recruited by an Austrian, one Pierre Schacht."

"Mr. Cameron already knew about Schacht," said Paul. "He's well informed on all this."

M'Bouyé smiled. "I had hoped so. Here's a copy of Schacht's passport, Mr. Cameron. Also copies of his various requests for visas, and his business affiliations. He is a remarkably well traveled man. Do you know much about him?"

Mark shook his head. "Almost nothing, but I expect information on him from Washington at any time. I presume that any information I give to you will go no further than His Majesty?" He didn't explain that he had buried the trace request on Schacht in with a dozen others, hoping a mole would overlook it.

"No further." M'Bouyé nodded. Then came a bombshell.

"We have an urgent request, Mr. Cameron. We need enough strong poison to eliminate forty men. It must be a painless death, and quick, and leave no traces of poison. Our native poisons do not have these qualities. We hope yours do."

"Monsieur M'Bouyé," he answered quietly. "Despite the impression left by our media, the U.S. doesn't conduct or support assassinations." Then he softened the blow. "But I sympathize with your position, and there's a lot we can do to help. I can exchange information with you. I can advise on matters in which we have more experience than you. I can ask Washington for specialized training and equipment for your Sûreté. In exchange, we would want information on the coup leaders, their plans, their support from outside Bwagania as well as inside the country. I'll give you every scrap of information I learn about this potential coup and what we know about other communist-backed coups."

"Then we agree. Mr. Cameron, it is impossible to overstate the urgency of our situation. I hope you can meet Paul or me regularly, starting at once."

Mark smiled. "I will do my best, Monsieur M'Bouyé."

The chamberlain led the way across a lawn and into the palace by a side door. He said, over his shoulder: "The king seems relaxed and unworried. But he is very concerned."

On a broad terrace at the rear of the palace, King Bwaga VI was seated motionless in a lounge chair. In light slacks, white shirt with short sleeves, no tie, he was clearly visible in the moonglow.

"Sire, this is the young American who got the better of Kalanga." There was laughter in M'Bouyé's voice.

Mark bowed, murmured: "*Bon soir, majesté.*"

The king got up and shook hands. With a bubble of glee, he said: "I learned with pleasure of your . . . approach to Kalanga. Compliments, Mr. Cameron. My half-brother takes advantage of his position and I have no real leverage. I do not control his purse. He needed a reminder that he is human, and you gave it to him. I would decorate you with the Order of the Elephant, but we'd best keep all this in a cocoon of discretion."

The chamberlain appeared with drinks, and they sat in a tight circle, their voices quiet in the still night.

"Thank you, Your Majesty. I am delighted to meet you. I've heard wonderful things about you."

The king's eyes glistened. He loved compliments. "Tell me what they said, so long as it's kind." All four laughed.

"I know the mounting danger your kingdom faces from the communists. I know their methods and how to counter them. I'll do all I can, working with Monsieur M'Bouyé, to help, within the limits of action and ethics of my own country."

The king thought, his head bent over sideways in characteristic gesture. Then he spoke slowly.

"This monarchy is devoted to the welfare and safety of its people. I will keep it that way. If someday the people want a republic, they will have the chance to vote for it and I'll abide by it. But I will not step down in favor of a self-serving group of communists whose only goal is to enslave the country for their own benefit. I will step down only if the country makes its own choice, after we are independent for a few years. You are said to be a man of honor, integrity, and great skills. Those are vital ingredients for success. We are glad that you will help us."

He motioned toward M'Bouyé and Passatu. "They will be your daily contacts. You can see me when you need to, but it's better for me to be able to deny it if I have to."

Mark laughed. "I'm used to that, Your Majesty. We call it plausible denial. My government will treat this with complete discretion." Mark wondered if he sounded as pompous as he felt when he said this. But the others nodded gravely.

The king stood to dismiss them. As they left, he said: "Next time, Mark, tell me the nice things you heard about me."

Gitabwanga: Passatu's tunnel—2200 hours, 30 October

On the way back to his apartment, Paul drove Mark past a number of places with good potential for being meeting sites, dead drops, and signals for them. In half an hour they had planned their next six meetings and run through gaps in information that Mark needed to have filled at once. Paul took to it as if he'd been trained at the farm.

It wasn't often Mark found such good contacts. He was both delighted and suspicious. Was Passatu too good to be true?

It was just ten-thirty when they started into the tunnel. They had stopped outside it to accustom their eyes to the dark, but the moon was up now, its light making the tunnel seem totally black.

"Why doesn't the owner put lights in there?"

"Too cheap, Mark. I have unusually good night vision, so I don't find it a problem."

Halfway down the tunnel, Paul stopped. Mark stopped too, holding his breath, listening to the blackness. A distant dog barked, the sound flat and distorted. Then there was just the sound of breathing. Paul resumed his slow movement, but immediately there was a gasp of surprise, a series of grunts, sounds of fists hitting flesh, then a long groan and a body hit the stone floor. Mark crouched, waiting, his DO dispenser in his fist.

Silence for a few moments more, then Paul whispered: "I need help." Mark felt his way forward, seeing movement and vague outlines only. Paul caught his hands and guided them to a pair of ankles on the floor. "Back to the street, please."

They carried the body to the sidewalk, dragged it into the gutter between two parked cars. The man's neck was broken.

In Paul's apartment, glass in hand, Mark said: "You must have really good night vision. I could see almost nothing."

Paul was busy with the wallet: "He's African. John Wilson M'Bili. Tanzanian passport issued in August this year. Visas and frontier stamps for Kenya, Burundi, Zaire, Cameroon, Ivory Coast, Chad, and guess what?"

"Hong Kong?" Mark grinned.

"An entry stamp for Bwagania, yesterday. Then look at this, Mark." He put a long, stilettolike dagger on the table. The grip had heavy brass rings for the four fingers.

"How did you get him?"

"He struck at me, upwards, from the side of the tunnel. A polished strike. But I could see his hand, and I was able to block him, like this . . . and break his neck like this . . ." He refought the brief encounter, then looked at Mark for approval.

"Where did you learn that?"

"I took a karate course here in Gitabwanga. This is the first time I've had to use it."

"I'm glad you said that. I was beginning to wonder if you were a professional killer."

Paul laughed. "No, just a farmer. But I'm very serious about protecting my farm and myself. Bwagania is my only home. I've nowhere else."

He was gutsy. Tough, competent, with a reason to stay in the country forever. Just what the station needed.

Paul went back to the papers on the table. "M'Bili was thirty-two. Born in Ujiji."

"What else?"

"A couple of other men's wallets, money still in them. Looks as if he was a professional robber, doing the rounds where he isn't known."

Mark went to the phone and dialed Linda. It was a brief, discreet call. "Linda, just to let you know that I'll be in on time tomorrow."

He could hear the relief in her voice. "Oh, great, I'm so pleased you called. Thank God." He felt a warm glow. It was suddenly important that she cared.

"Paul, will my contacts with the king and M'Bouyé remain discreet? I've heard that in Africa you can't expect much in the way of secrecy."

"In Africa we say *Tout fini par se savoir*. Everything ends up becoming known. There are very few lasting secrets. I'm sure the palace is a sieve. Not that the king or his tight circle are loose talkers. But you can expect things like that to leak out eventually."

Mark drove home thinking that Paul Passatu had the makings of a first-class agent. Bwagania was full of surprises.

Gitabwanga: Restaurant Victor Hugo—1400 hours, 1 November

Mark arrived a few minutes early for lunch. Colonel François de la Maison had reserved a table tucked away in a corner, almost a separate alcove, and the colonel swung into the restaurant at precisely two o'clock, looking cool and distinguished. His invitation had stipulated casual clothes, but his open-necked shirt was so impeccable that he might as well have been wearing his uniform.

"I am sorry to be late, Monsieur Cameron. I should have been here before you, as your host."

"Please, Colonel. I came early to avoid keeping you waiting." He'd seen de la Maison before but he couldn't remember when or where. He sat back to get a better view of him and asked the waiter for a Campari with soda, guessing that the colonel would order the same as his guest. He was right. A gentleman, just as Dumont had said.

"Is Bwagania old territory for you, Colonel? Or is this your first posting here?"

"My first time posted here, although I visited here several times in the past. I arrived the first of September this year," he volunteered. "Have I seen you before, Mr. Cameron? Something tells me we met a long time ago. It has been in my mind since I saw you at Bwaga Airport."

Mark hunched over the table, elbows apart, face in his hands, looking intently at the colonel.

"Yes," he said, "I've got the same feeling. You weren't by chance in Korea?"

François suddenly grinned, slapping his forehead. "Of course. We met in Korea. I was with the French army there, in the infantry. That was it. I remember seeing you, but not where or when. Can you fill in the gaps?"

"I'm trying. I was a very new infantry second lieutenant. Were you in the hospital?"

"Ah, I recall your face now. It was a traumatic time for me. My first wound." The Frenchman rapped his left hand on the table. Both were made of wood. "I was a company commander, a captain. A couple of months after we got there, there was a nasty firefight and suddenly I had no left hand."

He looked at his wooden hand and went on. "I recall we were in the same hospital tent together, for a week, I think. I was very impressed by your French."

"And I was very impressed by your good humor, in spite of your wound. You had us all laughing . . . great stories."

"You were very quick to learn some of our bawdy songs, Mr. Cameron. You entertained us all."

"Now that I look at you, I can see the French officer in his bed, laughing a lot. You were a frightful mess when they first brought you in. You're a lot more presentable now."

De la Maison laughed. "My mother always said I looked well in uniform. I'm glad she didn't see me then."

They dawdled over their drinks, enjoying the unexpected basis for companionship. To Mark's pleasure, it was François who suggested that they use first names. "After all, we are both *anciens combattants* from Korea!"

The waiter, a pompous Corsican, served their lunch with a flourish reserved only for Colonel François de la Maison. The colonel took the trouble, Mark noted, to nod his appreciation.

When the waiter had gone and they had begun to eat their tournedos Rossini—exquisitely cooked—Mark asked François: "With your greater knowledge of Africa and especially of Bwagania, what do you think will happen after independence?" It was an obvious question, and François nodded as Mark posed it.

"I'm sure Bwagania will remain in the French family of nations, allied to us, and will be a member of the pro-Western countries of the third world, like Senegal or the Ivory Coast. But only if the king remains in power."

"Is there some doubt of that, François?"

"Yes, there is doubt. We have information from several sources that indicates a strong effort by the Soviets to put Prince M'Taga into a presidency of the republic of Bwagania and force the king out. Some of that information comes from local sources, some from the French Communist party. Taken together, it is a very real threat."

"I agree, from what I've heard in the short time I've been here, that the KGB is behind M'Taga's coup plot," said Mark. "How do the plotters get away with it?"

"Partly by using clandestine techniques. We know little about them to date. We began hearing about them just before I got here. And, too, the laws here are similar to those of France. It is not a crime to be a communist, to meet with other communists, or to meet with KGB agents—unless you give them classified information or otherwise help them damage the country. So far we have no firm evidence of that."

"How much real power has the king?"

"Theoretically, very little. He's a constitutional monarch. In reality, he is a true African traditional king. He usually gets what he wants. But even he must move with care, particularly when the chief plotter is his own son, who is well liked by the people.

"Until recently, this was the most untouched, most primitive of all our African colonies, Mark. Our troops never really pacified the mountainous areas—and that means most of the country—until after World War Two. Like the Upper Voltans, the Bwaganians are formidable soldiers. They were staunch allies when they weren't fighting us. Many of them fought in both world wars plus Vietnam until the nineteen fifties and Algeria until the late sixties. They are amazing trackers, and their bravery matches that of the Gurkhas."

"So I've heard, François. I understand the king has the same streak of bravery." Mark wanted to get de la Maison back on the subject of the king, the key to stability of the realm.

François laughed. "Yes, he's brave. Quite possibly, he has no fear of anything. But you won't get a clear picture of him. The king is as changeable as Paris weather in April. You can count on only one thing from him. There are many anecdotes about it. It's a fickleness. He's never the same two days in a row. He'll approve something today and reverse himself tomorrow. He'll joke about it, blame himself, and you may laugh with him. But it can be very frustrating."

"Is this fickleness less pronounced in any field?"

"No. Not in politics, administration, public relations, internal security, or family relations. Not even in his field of specialization."

"What's that?" asked Mark. "I didn't know he had a special field. Is he like Japan's emperor?"

François laughed. "Our king a marine biologist? No. A biologist yes, but not marine. His specialty is women. He adores them, mostly white women, as you must have heard.

He changes them regularly, but to give him credit, he's had this one—the Swiss girl called Muffie—more than a year. Maybe he's getting less fickle."

"Do you see other signs of a more solid approach?"

"Not really, but I'm hoping they'll start appearing. After all, Bwaga VI is over sixty now."

"What's the biggest danger?"

François thought for a moment. "It's not that the king would lose in an open confrontation with his son. I think then the army, the police, and the masses would gather behind the king. The son must know that, too. He's no fool. No, the biggest danger is that the king takes it into his head to abdicate. That he gets fed up with the problems of staying on top and says to his son: 'You take it, M'Taga. It's yours.' He might do that, and maybe regret it later. But it would of course be irrevocable. Once in charge, the prince would stay there. Even if he were to die soon after, the leftists would retain power."

"Schacht would see to it?" Mark was gambling on this revelation of his knowledge.

"You have been busy, Mark. Very busy. Yes, I mean that Pierre Schacht would see to it that power is consolidated for Moscow."

"I've only just learned of Schacht's existence,"said Mark. "It came about through an incident in which my cook was the victim of a traffic accident." Not the whole truth, but enough for the time being.

"I know," said François. "When I heard about your defeat of Prince Kalanga, I sent you the invitation for lunch."

Mark looked disappointed. "I had hoped that you were going to propose field collaboration between us, François."

"For obvious reasons, I want such liaison. It makes good sense for us to pool our resources and information when we can. I suggested it to Paris after you arrived. I had heard nice things about you from mutual friends."

"What did Paris reply?"

"They approved, but with a caveat. Our relations must be ostensibly social and limited to unclassified information. I'm infuriated by their reaction."

"Disappointing," Mark agreed. "We would both profit from local liaison. That door is closed?"

"Yes. It is ridiculous, and I shall ignore it." François rapped the table with his wooden hand.

Mark was astounded. "You will?"

"I'm going to bend my orders and give you a piece of highly classified information. It illustrates my point."

"I'll respect your classification, François, and keep the information here in my station. You're sure you want to go around your orders from Paris?"

"Without a doubt, Mark. My SSR poste here has a penetration of Prince M'Taga's inner circle. A brand new source, untested, and there's no way to check out his reports because he is the only source that we have in that circle. A young Bwaganian intellectual, a convinced Marxist, but he distrusts the Soviets. So far, he's given us what looks like excellent, authentic reporting on the inner circle of the coup plotters and on the advice that Schacht gives them. Perhaps you can help us confirm what he's telling us."

"Right inside the cadre of plotters? Sounds like an excellent source."

"Yes," said François. "He has first-class potential for the long haul. But it's a tightrope we're walking, in view of his political convictions."

"Why does he report to SSR? He's a convinced Marxist, even if he dislikes Schacht's influence or his motives."

"We're using a false flag, Mark. He thinks he's in contact with a secret wing of the French Communist party. That's an approach that we use with great success."

Mark grinned. "It gives you a great advantage. I've used that method, too. It can get tricky."

"It gets complicated. Sometimes the agent handler has trouble remembering he's supposed to be a communist. He's a conservative businessman, doing this as a patriot. In his most recent report, he said that Schacht has been warning M'Taga and his group about you, Mark Cameron. By name and title: 'CIA station chief here, masquerading as an American consul.' That's why that idiot Kalanga went after your cook. He thought it would help his nephew."

"I can confirm that in this case your source is accurate. I got the same story from a different source."

François was impressed and pleased. "Thank you. I wish Paris would understand that this kind of field collaboration is useful to us both."

"Maybe you can get him to change their policy. Have you traced Schacht with Paris?"

"They list him as a possible KGB illegal. I think they're right, and I've started full surveillance on him day and night."

"I'll let you know what I hear about him from my headquarters," said Mark. "Any details of what Schacht said about me?"

"One thing sticks out. He told the coup cadre that his information about you comes from Moscow, where 'everything the CIA plans or does against the socialists is known within days; the CIA is an open book to the Kremlin.' Puffery, I'd say." He laughed. "What do you make of it, Mark?"

"Sounds like it. Why crow about a good operation if they have one?" This new clue to a mole was curious. Why indeed, Mark wondered, would Moscow Center tell Schacht and Schacht tell the cadre? To increase their respect and allegiance? Or was it disinformation?

By the end of lunch François had committed himself to meeting regularly with Mark. But discreetly: "If Paris learns I'm bending their orders, they'll be very angry."

"Then why take this risk?" François' motives must be spelled out, his commitment certain.

"Because I believe in what I'm doing. If we in the West don't stick together as closely as we can, the Soviets will separate us and eat us one by one. It's as simple as that."

"Thank you, François, for your candid answer. I'll do my very best to keep our cooperation low-key. Let's meet at your house or mine from now on. Except for a purely social lunch now and then—for appearance' sake—next week, maybe. My treat."

François smiled. "To show Paris we're doing what they ordered?"

"And anyone else who's interested."

Moscow: KGB headquarters—0900 hours, 5 November

General Ossilenko looked at the incoming message from the KGB *rezidentura* in Washington with satisfaction. The mole had come through with a copy of an outgoing CIA message to Gitabwanga:

AUDIO TECH JOSEPH PALMYRA ETA GITABWANGA 0700 7 NOV. PLS MEET AND HOUSE ONE WEEK.

Ossilenko sent a cable to Gitabwanga:

CIA AUDIO TECH PALMYRA JOSEPH ETA GITABWANGA 0700 7 NOV. EXECUTE PATTERN CHANGE.

The reply came back from Gitabwanga in hours:

APPRECIATE YOUR ADVICE RE CIA AUDIO OP. WILL INSTITUTE AGREED-UPON PATTERN CHANGE WITH DUE REGARD TO AVOIDING OBVIOUS

Ossilenko nodded approvingly. At least that drunken ass Petrov was doing his job.

Next was a cable from Bonn:

CIA AUDIO TECHNICIAN PALMYRA JOSEPH BOOKED TO DEPART FRANKFURT 6 NOV ETA GITABWANGA 0700 7 NOV AIR FRANCE.

The airport watch at Frankfurt was working effectively, at minimal cost, thanks to the Badwasser gang.

Gitabwanga: Bwaga Airport—0700 hours, 7 November

The audio technician selected for the Tass job in Gitabwanga was, to Linda's delight, an old friend of hers. Uncle Joe, as he was known, was one of the best in the business. A gangling

Southerner, he had a laid-back approach to his exacting trade, a well-developed sense of the ridiculous, and was said to be immune to fear. That was, of course, not really true. He did, however, operate on the Shakespearean thesis that a coward dies a thousand times, a brave man only once.

Linda met him at Bwaga Airport as he was picking up his suitcases from the luggage area.

"What a pleasure they sent you, Uncle Joe. I haven't seen you for two years."

"You're a sight for sore eyes, Linda. Just as pretty as ever." Then his smile disappeared. "Can't tell you how sorry I am about the Cat. We all miss him."

"It's not been easy. But thankfully, I love it here. It helped to plunge into a new life."

"I've only met Cameron a few times, but he has a good reputation. You enjoy working for him?"

"Yes, very much. Perhaps too much." That slipped out, but Uncle Joe caught it.

"Too much? Linda, are you in love?"

"I don't know. We were all three great friends. I've known Mark for years. It's just that I feel so wonderful when he's around. Do you think I'm dreadful?"

"Negative, Linda. You mustn't blame yourself for what's natural. Do you want to mourn forever?"

"No. I did that for a month, and it turned into self-pity. The Cat's gone . . . nothing will bring him back. I survived: I have to live normally. Thanks for understanding." She clutched his hand tightly.

Gitabwanga: TWA manager's apartment—0830 hours, 8 November

The TWA manager had an apartment on the same floor as Yegorov's. A bend in the corridor hid one front door from the other, making the manager's apartment a good jumping-off place to enter the Tass reporter's apartment.

Mark and Uncle Joe were in the TWA manager's apartment by eight-thirty A.M., with two suitcases of audio-related gear and tools shipped from Washington a week earlier. The TWA manager had gone to Paris for the weekend at CIA expense, to distance himself from the operation. In fact, the TWA man had no idea what his apartment was to be used for.

The plan was to make the installation and activate the bug while Uncle Joe was still in Gitabwanga. The LP (listening post) was to be in the station itself, and the signal from Yegorov's apartment would be scrambled, making no sense to anyone without the equipment to unscramble it. The bug could be switched on and off from the station by remote control. A simple, routine audio operation involving minimal risks.

By eight forty-five Linda was in a restaurant across the street, dawdling over breakfast. She could see the front entrance of the apartment building and the driveway leading to the parking lot behind the building. Her job was to watch and report when the Yegorovs left.

A ten, Linda began to think she had missed the Yegorovs when they left for the beach, which they usually did between nine and nine-thirty. She dialed their number, using a public phone in the restaurant.

"Da?" A man's voice. They were still there!

"Bonjour . . . Pharmacie de la Liberté?" Linda's accent was not too bad; Yegorov's French was marginal. The pharmacy number was one digit off Yegorov's.

"Allô, Allô. Vous demandez la pharmacie? Allô. C'est pas le Docteur Poitiers? Allô, allô."

Thinking quickly, Linda said: *"Allô, allô, Docteur Poitiers? C'est la pharmacie ici . . ."*

Yegorov was taping and logging all his calls today, but this one confused him: *"Vous êtes le bureau du Docteur Poitiers? Venez . . . ma fille est malade."*

"Oui, monsieur. Attendez . . ." Linda hung up, satisfied she'd not made an obvious call to see if the Yegorovs were home. She called Mark at the TWA manager's apartment.

"Sorry, the newspaper didn't come today."

"Okay, thanks a lot. Perhaps later." He understood, and would wait for her second call, an hour later. If the Yegorovs were still home at twelve-thirty they would abort the installation. At eleven ten, Linda called Yegorovs' number again. This time from a boutique next to the restaurant.

"*Da*?" The same voice.

Linda hung up the instant he said it, even before he had finished the word. That way it could seem like an accident. But to Yegorov this was almost certainly a call—perhaps the second—to see if he had gone to the beach. Now he was certain that the information Petrov had given him was accurate. CIA was trying to bug his place. He perspired, wondering how the KGB had obtained this forewarning. His pride in his KGB, and his dread of ever tangling with it, soared.

Linda got into her car and drove to the street behind the apartment building, then up an alley to the parking lot. Yegorov's car was still there. It was better to drive in and check every half-hour than to keep making phone calls.

At twelve-thirty Mark called the operation off for the day.

Gitabwanga: François' house—1500 hours, 8 November

Mark met briefly with François de la Maison: "I have a lead. A Dr. Poitiers may be treating some of the Soviets here. I imagine Poitiers is French."

"I know him," said François. "He is very French. I suggest you let me handle this." A gentle way of saying, hands off this one.

"Can you find out who he treated today and for what? I need it soonest, if possible. Details can come later."

François smiled. In return for not touching the Frenchman, Mark was asking immediate action. "I'll call you at home, by five."

It was just before five o'clock when François called: "He's seeing three of them. One was today, but the malaise seems to have disappeared mysteriously. Thanks for the tip."

"And many thanks to you, my friend. Just what I suspected. I'll fill you in later." No names had been used in the short conversation.

Gitabwanga: Mark's house—1900 hours, 8 November

Linda made a cold dinner of meat, salad, and a French baguette. It was cool on the verandah.

"Dr. Poitiers' report makes me think Yegorov knows we want to bug his apartment, used the kid's mythical ailment as an excuse, and spent the day at home. Until now they've gone to the beach every weekend." Linda shook her head, looked at Uncle Joe.

"This has happened twice to me recently, at two other stations," said Uncle Joe. "I went back to the stations several times, and each time the target stayed at home. It's a pattern, and patterns usually mean something."

"Want to speculate?" Mark asked it casually, but inside he was churning. There had to be a mole—no other explanation made sense. If the KGB could read all CIA cable traffic, then all audio operations could be compromised. But if a mole was feeding the KGB, only a portion of the operational traffic would be affected. Maybe only a part of one area division's traffic. That could explain why some operations were successful, others not.

"I think we're seeing either the results of our traffic being read by the KGB, or they've got a penetration at headquarters. That's what I think, Mark." Uncle Joe was emphatic. "Admittedly, we always get some excuse for the changes in their patterns. The excuses are usually reasonable, so you can't prove anything. But in my experience, we've never had a failure rate like this. It's more than just bad luck. Look at what happened to you two in Tokyo."

"Have you discussed this with your division chief, Uncle Joe?" Linda wouldn't take his suspicions lying down.

"Yes, I saw him about it. He just listened and thanked me. No reaction."

"It's a rough one. What do we do? Stop all operations until we find a mole?" Remembering his own discussion with the chief of the technical division, Mark went on: "Unless we can give the DDO or the director firm evidence, we'd best keep quiet, I'm afraid. All we'd do is cause a riot without offering a solution." As he said this, Mark decided to make more of his own tests to find such evidence and then ask permission to search for the mole himself on a leave of absence from Gitabwanga. Until then, he would share his own suspicions only with Linda.

"You're right, Mark. But it's frustrating." Uncle Joe scratched his chin.

"Let's agree on two things, just to be positive," said Mark. The other two nodded. "Let's keep track of your suspicions, Uncle Joe. Let us know what else you run across, and meanwhile, leave us a note of details of those other aborts. And let's do a quickie while you're still here, one that headquarters knows nothing about. I suspect this one will work."

"Petrov?" Linda asked Mark.

"Yes, I think he'll use it regularly." And to Uncle Joe: "Would you install a sequence camera, a simple mike, and a viewing screen in the overhead of the local KGB *rezident*'s safe apartment? It's right under Linda's pad, so we don't even have to make an entry. It can all be done from her place."

Sure," said Uncle Joe. "Happy to. But how do I get another medal if there's no danger?"

"We'll strike one for you here," Mark laughed. "The Order of the Banana Snake."

"Done," said Uncle Joe. He made the installation the next day.

Gitabwanga: Linda's apartment—0900 hours, 9 November

It took him hours to prepare a cradle for the camera, the bug, and the screen. He pried up a board and made it into a hinged trapdoor in Linda's floor. It was next to impossible to see. It opened only if a magnet was placed on the wood and rotated counterclockwise, to pull back a steel locking pin he had installed inside the wood. Then he carefully pierced the ceiling below, with a trio of pinholes, sucking plaster dust up through the center of his special drill. When he was through, the camera and bug assembly were hidden between the floor of Linda's apartment and the ceiling of Petrov's safe apartment.

Linda watched, ready to turn back Madame Denise should she knock at the door. Linda had told her that Joe was an uncle, visiting for a few days. Madame Denise guessed he might be a lover. A man, she thought, would do Linda a world of good. Madame Denise left them alone.

Finally, Uncle Joe was through. The camera worked perfectly. In a display of improvisation Linda had never suspected, Uncle Joe shot half a roll of film at various speeds and exposures, then developed the film in a coffee cup. He mixed a unibath developer with black coffee to keep out the light. It worked, and the negatives showed a couch, a bed, and a coffee table with two side chairs. He showed Linda how to use the viewing screen, through which almost the entire room below her was visible. He drilled her on the camera and the audio bug, and by the end of the day they were ready for Petrov and whoever he would meet there.

Gitabwanga: the Soviet compound—1900 hours, 9 November

They met in the dark, beside his car. Pyotr had told Olga that he had an agent meeting and would be late. Suspicious, but with no evidence, she just grumped: "Go!" They had finished their dinner in silence. The wives of all case officers hear their husbands claim late agent meetings, true or not.

Tonight Anna Iosevna was in a clinging black dress with no shoulders. Pyotr held her hard against him and she could feel his swelling. He turned around and slipped the top of her dress down. Her nipples hardened in his fingers, and he caught his breath as she turned her head to kiss him. They were lost in the urgency of their feelings, their breathing loud under the low carport roof.

Pyotr had often cursed his little car . . . too small and uncomfortable to make love in. But now he loved it. It was their magic carpet to the apartment. He helped her into the backseat, where she crouched down out of sight when he drove through the compound gate. The gatekeeper saluted the *rezident*'s car. She stayed hidden until the car turned the first corner and Pyotr said: "All clear, Anna."

Then she climbed into the front seat and unzipped his trousers. "Oh Pyotr. It's lovely. . . ."

Gitabwanga: Linda's apartment—
1930 hours, 9 November

Uncle Joe had thought of everything. When the KGB safe-apartment door opened, a red light came on in Linda's hi-fi. She telephoned Mark's house. "Don't forget, you're going to Djimana early tomorrow."

"Thanks, Linda. See you in the afternoon." It was a simple code. Mark was there in five minutes. Madame Denise watched from her seat in the courtyard, invisible behind the plants. A busy night, she thought. She sipped her beer, the ache for a man as strong as it had been when she was sixteen. She smiled when Mark used the service stairs. Her Linda was in for a good evening.

"He's there, all right, Mark. With a girl. They're sitting on the couch." Linda had already opened the trapdoor in the floor. The ground-glass screen glowed eerily when she flicked off the only lamp in the room. They lay on some pillows she had spread on the floor, watching the Soviets below.

Pyotr had spread some bread, sausages, and cheese on the table, but they were ignoring it. There were full glasses, too, but after the first sips they had set them aside. Pyotr and Anna were kissing furiously, hands all over each other.

As Linda watched, she felt guilty of peeping tommery, but was fascinated. "How strange to be paid to watch people make love," she whispered to Mark.

"We'll learn who she is and how he plans to use her. And a lot about him."

Down below, clothes were coming off. Then Pyotr had Anna pinned to the bed and they watched as his bottom rose and fell, faster and faster, and Anna began to scratch Pyotr's back and moan with joy.

Suddenly, Linda realized that her own hips were rising and falling in time with Petrov's. She looked at Mark, hoping he hadn't seen. But he was looking at her in the green glow, not at the Soviets. No longer listening to the sounds from below.

Without thinking, he took Linda's hand and moved closer,

their bodies touching. "I'm sorry," he said. "I have to be with you, it's important."

"Mark don't worry, it's important to me too. You've become such a part of me."

The words came more easily than he'd expected. "Oh, Linda, I'm so in love with you. I need you all the time."

"Let's start now," she whispered, kissing him.

She gently touched him through the thin trousers, and then they were racing to undress. For the time being the camera, tape recorder, and ground-glass screen were forgotten.

Much later, as he and Linda lay on her bed gazing fondly at each other, Mark's thoughts turned to the Soviets below. This was an operation he hadn't reported to headquarters. Uncle Joe had installed the equipment without prior approval from Washington. Unlike the Tass operation, this one had worked.

In the days that followed, after Pyotr and Anna made love, they talked of their lives, their affection for each other, and the embassy and its personnel.

Not even the KGB *rezident* could be sure that Ambassador Raspatov's secretary wasn't secretly reporting to someone else, but despite that, he slowly opened up. With amazing speed the Soviet community, its players, and Pyotr's personality unfolded before Mark. The closed Soviet compound came alive. Its individuals, their likes and dislikes, their daily activities were revealed with humor or anger as Pyotr and Anna gossiped.

Pyotr never spoke directly of his KGB work. Nor did he criticize Soviet policies. But as their lovemaking sessions went on, a clear picture of the KGB *rezident* took shape. The words, the facial expressions, the tone, the body language enabled Mark to fill in many of the voids caused by Pyotr's training and instinctive caution.

Over the days, Pyotr came through as a bitter, passionate, sensitive, cynical maverick. His distaste for the arrogance and the selfishness of the top-level Soviet "Vlasti" was very clear. Most interesting of all was Pyotr's suppressed fury at what had been done to his father. He confided this to Anna, without directly showing his anger. He told her that Raspatov reminded him strongly of his father, and that he had begun to look upon him as a sort of father figure . . . one of the rare Vlasti he could admire for his honest patriotism. He told Anna: "At least Raspatov doesn't believe that the Russian people exist only to be exploited by the Vlasti. He may be an old mastodon, but he's a breath of fresh air."

Down below, Anna nodded agreement as she lay on her back, a satisfied smile on her face. Above them, Mark was amazed at Petrov's criticism of the Soviet Union's top leaders. Amazed and pleased. Even if Petrov's in-laws guaranteed him immunity from charges of heresy, Pyotr had given Mark a reason for optimism. A Soviet with such views was a prime target for recruitment.

Gitabwanga: Mark's office—1100 hours, 10 November

Concentrating on the draft cable he was writing for the director wasn't easy. Mark found himself thinking about Linda all the time, now and then jumping up and going to her desk to look at her, touch her cheek. Then back to his desk, where the tape recorder told him what he'd missed of the conversation last night between Pyotr and Anna.

Finally, after two hours, the cable was ready, its privacy indicators ensuring that only the DCI would receive it. He could then make his own distribution as he saw fit:

> HAVE WHAT APPEARS TO BE MOUNTING EVIDENCE OF MOLE, BASED ON CONVERSATIONS IN HQS, PARIS AND GITABWANGA SINCE WE TALKED. SUMMARY BELOW, DETAILS FOLLOW BY DISPATCH YOUR EYES ONLY. WILL TRY SMOKE MORE OUT AND ADVISE ASAP.

The cable gave the DCI a brief description of the new evidence. The longer dispatch took Mark until later afternoon to prepare and write.

At the end of the day the DCI's rely came in:

> GOOD WORK. ADVISE ONLY ME REPEAT ONLY ME IF YOU NEED HELP.

Frustratingly, the director had not indicated if he'd learned anything new about a mole from other sources.

Gitabwanga: Radio Nationale Gita—0830 hours, 10 November

Charles Djoulaba was known by almost everyone as Petit Charles. The senior announcer of the principal radio station, he was a tiny, skinny, ebony Bwaganian of almost forty years. He spoke fluent English, German, Italian, and Spanish, as well as French and a dozen African languages.

Petit Charles was one of Bwagania's true intellectuals, as well read as any man. He made a fetish of knowing what was going on in the world, of the issues as seen from all sides. He had attended the University of Paris, then Cambridge.

Petit Charles was better informed on the events and the actors in Bwagania than 99 percent of the elite of the country. He knew everyone who would or could make policy. People loved this diminutive man who was uncompromisingly on the side of the little Bwaganian. For twenty years, he had struggled and fought for justice and fairness for the masses. He had trod on a hundred toes, had been ridiculed, even beaten, but never ignored.

When independence approached and Prince M'Taga began to gather young intellectuals to his salon, Petit Charles became a useful catch. The prince's entourage wooed him, and for a while they won. He was an early member of the cadre and attended a lot of soirées at the prince's house.

But after Pierre Schacht arrived on the scene, the talk became less obtuse, more focused on breaking down old disciplines, on "socialist reality," and class hatred. A smaller, inner group formed, meeting more often in planning sessions with M'Taga and Schacht—a tight little communist cadre, all with jobs to come in the postindependence "peoples" government.

As he saw clearly where Schacht was leading them, Petit Charles grew painfully uneasy. He listened and watched, curled in his chair like a cat. Now and then he offered an idea—always a good one, always in favor of the masses.

Mostly he listened, somberly noting the drift away from his objectives toward the goal of total, permanent power for the inner group.

It was impossible to divine his thoughts. Petit Charles's glasses were dark and the left lens was cracked clear across. He wore a tiny pointed beard, like Leon Trotsky, and a black beret, like Che Guevara. A deep scar on his right cheek gave him an exotic, conspiratorial look. To most of the young men on the cadre he was a mysterious, distant riddle. To M'Taga he was a steady, quiet associate. To Schacht he was baffling but not an apparent danger. None of them knew that inside, Petit Charles was twisting in pain, his distress growing as time slipped away and the masses were just as much, or more, at risk than ever. He saw himself as increasingly isolated, drawing antagonism as a web draws flies: There was no one in Bwagania he could talk to safely about M'Taga's chilling plans.

Tonight, his first newscast of the evening finished, Petit Charles headed for a reception at the U.S. consulate general. He accepted invitations to receptions because it was his business to do so. Most of them bored him, however, and he expected this one to be the usual tedious hour of pompously delivered gossip that overfed, ill-informed officials traded back and forth.

For the first fifteen minutes it was precisely that. But then he was introduced to Mark by a French journalist.

"*Monsieur Cameron, je vous présente Monsieur Djoulaba.* Petit Charles, as we call him, is an encyclopedia on Bwagania."

"A pleasure, Monsieur Djoulaba. I hope you will share some of your knowledge with me. I know very little about your country or about African affairs in general."

Petit Charles was pleased by Mark's warm, dry handshake, his admission that he had much to learn, and his fluent French. It was quickly apparent that Mark knew a great deal about Bwagania, far more than the usual diplomat. There was immediate affinity, and they talked for an hour. Then they went to Petit Charles's favorite restaurant, to drink coffee and talk some more. They were there until Petit Charles had to go back to the radio station to prepare for the late newscast.

They agreed to meet again the evening of the twelfth, "a private seminar to discuss the realities of Bwaganian politics," as Petit Charles put it.

Here was a man who really understood liberalism, socialism, communism, and the Soviet empire, who ardently believed in democracy. And who, he suspected, had the capability of helping find some way to stop M'Taga and Schacht before it was too late.

Mark's cabled request for traces on Petit Charles Djoulaba came back from headquarters negative, early on the twelfth.

Gitabwanga: Restaurant Baobab—
1900 hours, 12 November

Petit Charles made up his mind soon after they sat down to eat his favorite fish, Nile perch. He told Mark about Red Snow, about M'Taga and Schacht and their plans, and about the cadre meetings. He explained his dismay and suggested that Mark might be able to help.

"How can I do that, Monsieur Djoulaba?"

"Call me Petit Charles, Mark, everyone does. Anyway, we're friends already. First, I need someone I can trust to talk to. I trust you instinctively. Second, if your government knows what's going on, maybe you can convince the king to take notice and act against them. I can't. He won't talk to me."

"You've tried?"

"Dozens of times. He thinks I'm crazy, just peddling rumors. If I'd told him his youngest son, Prince N'Gobi, was plotting, he might have listened. But N'Gobi isn't involved."

"When did you last try?"

"Months ago. There's no use."

If you tried now, Mark thought, I'll bet he'd listen. But I want you for myself. I'm going to let you recruit yourself. Aloud, he said: "I know what you've told me about Red Snow is accurate. Other people have mentioned it, discreetly. I can get information to the king, through a secure channel."

"Good. Here's what you should tell him . . ." Petit Charles talked nonstop for an hour, giving Mark details on the plotters, their strengths and weaknesses, their precise coup plans, and their intentions for the country after the coup.

When he stopped, Mark asked: "What else can I do to help?"

"Bluntly," answered Petit Charles, "money. I have several sources who depend on me for their expenses. My salary is not so big, and it's a strain. Can you help there?"

Keep coming, Petit Charles. "Yes, I can help there. Provided you tell absolutely nobody about it."

"Absolutely not. The money is a necessary evil. I'm not proud of having to ask. Are there any formalities?"

"Delicately put. Yes, I must know who your sources are. And you must sign receipts. It's routine. They can be in an alias we choose right now."

Petit Charles smiled, thought for a moment. "How about Parsifal?"

"Good choice. And welcome to a rather exclusive club."

Gitabwanga: Restaurant Agadez—1400 hours, 13 November

Mark grinned across the lunch table at Petrov, feeling both pleased and curious—pleased by the chemistry that was bringing them together in friendship—a Western friend was a key to most Soviet defections—and curious as to how the Soviet would react. Mark knew what to probe for, now. He had set himself a short-term goal for the lunch: to get Pyotr to open up about the similarity between his father and Raspatov. To talk, if he would, about his father's death and his feelings about it.

Their lunch finished, they were starting a chess game, the set provided by the Bwaganian owner of the Restaurant Agadez, a chess buff. They agreed on thirty seconds to a move. Long for blitz, but they didn't know each other's game.

Mark moved a pawn: "What's your favorite lunch when you're at home?"

"Dark bread, butter, smoked fish, and onions," said Pyotr without hesitation, responding with a pawn. "And you?"

"French bread, onions, Swiss cheese, rough mustard." Another pawn went out. "Just like my father."

"My father liked borscht and sausages. Heavy stuff."

"You liked him?"

"Very much. I admired him."

"What did he do?" Mark backed up his first pawn with a second.

"He was an army officer, a colonel. He taught me chess when I was still little. We did all kinds of things together, my brothers and my father and I—swimming, camping, hiking . . ." He brought up a knight, testing Mark.

"Wonderful memories, Pyotr." Mark brought up a third pawn, limiting the knight's field. "I hope he survived the war."

"Yes, wonderful memories. No, he died before the war." Pyotr moved up a second pawn.

Mark moved a third pawn. "I'm sorry. You must miss him." He thought: That's far enough, now let him open himself up, if he will.

Pyotr wanted to tell Mark: Stalin's men killed him. He brought out a bishop and said: "Your father is still alive?"

"No." Mark blocked the bishop with a pawn. "He was killed in 1941. His destroyer was torpedoed at Pearl Harbor. I was seven then."

"I'm sorry," said Pyotr, sad for them both. "You were so young. But at least he died with honor. Mine was killed too . . ." He couldn't stop himself. "By Stalin . . ."

"Political murder?" The game was forgotten as they looked at each other.

"The favorite sport then. I can't tell you what it was like."

"Worse that the Western media portrayed it?"

"The Western press was being fed a line, and mostly gobbled it up in their eagerness to look at the silver lining."

"Knowing what I do about the media, I believe it. Was there any silver, Pyotr?"

The Soviet shook his head. "Not for my family, not after that. We just existed until the Great Patriotic War. Then I joined the army and sometimes we had enough to eat."

"After the war? . . ."

"I was the only one. Mama starved to death. My brothers were killed, one by one: 1941, 1942, and 1944 . . ." His eyes clouded. He could almost touch them.

"You were bitter? . . ."

"Oh, yes. I hated what had happened. It seemed so unfair."

"Your move," said Mark.

Pyotr glanced at the board but made no move. "I spoke some German by then. I was able to stay in the army. I had no home, you see. Nobody. Then I was lucky . . . college." He didn't mention that the GRU had recruited him at the end of the war, that he'd eventually been selected by the KGB, and that they had sent him through their academies.

"Then foreign service . . . would your father have been pleased by that?"

"He was the most generous soul I've ever known. He would be proud that I'm here, that I've survived so far."

"And the government that killed your father? . . ."

Pyotr understood, and he answered—in a whisper: "He hated it . . . so did I, but in the end it saved me."

"Older people like your consul general, how do they feel?"

"Raspatov? A wonderful man . . . reminds me of my father . . ." He shook his head, bringing himself back to the reality that he was talking openly to a CIA officer, a man he'd only known for a few weeks, yet a man he already felt close to. He looked at the chess board, laid down his king: "I delayed the game. I lose."

"We both did," said Mark. "It's a draw. No winner, no loser."

Pyotr smiled at Mark. "You have all the right reactions."

Instinct told Mark to leave it right there. He'd achieved enough for today.

Moscow: KGB headquarters—
0945 hours, 19 November

The latest batch of mole reports included a copy of an information report cabled to headquarters by Mark after his second meeting with Petit Charles. The source was identified only by cryptonym and a vague description, but the mole remembered the trace request. He put two and two together, then took the trouble to find out who Mark's source was. A note added to the report told General Vladimir Ossilenko that the source was a well-known Bwaganian radio announcer, Charles Djoulaba.

Ossilenko cursed: Charles Djoulaba, of all people, going over to the other side. Ossilenko drafted a cable to Schacht and sent it to Vienna, where the KGB *rezident* himself, specially cleared to support the Red Snow operation, converted it into a cipher and sent it by commercial telegram to Schacht.

The telegram took over twenty-four hours to reach Gitabwanga.

Gitabwanga: Hôtel du Lac—0930 hours, 21 November

Pierre Schacht locked his door and opened the cylinder of his typewriter. He deciphered the telegram in fifteen minutes:

> CADRE MEMBER CHARLES DJOULABA AKA PETIT CHARLES RELIABLY IDENTIFIED AS CIA SOURCE, POSSIBLE RECRUIT. YOU MAY TERMINATE RPT TERMINATE. YOU MUST ARRANGE "LOCAL DISCOVERY" OF CHARLES'S TREACHERY. REZIDENTURA NOT TO BE INVOLVED.

Schacht calculated the options: play Petit Charles back against the CIA, or simply get rid of the traitor. He chose Moscow's preference, termination. The vehicle: M'Taga.

Gitabwanga: Prince M'Taga's house—1900 hours, 21 November

M'Taga listened to Schacht with disbelief. "Petit Charles! A firm socialist, if not a Marxist! There must be some mistake . . . known him for years, he'd never do this."

Then M'Taga got furious. He believed Schacht. He listened to Schacht's scenario and politely agreed with the plan. A simple drowning in the lake, then pass the word that Petit

Charles had betrayed the cadre. It was cold, clinical, but not at all Bwaganian style.

M'Taga did it his own way.

Gitabwanga: Radio Nationale Gita—
2100 hours, 22 November

Petit Charles left the studio for a coffee break. He sat alone outside the building, under a huge baobab tree. In fifteen minutes he would go in and start preparing his last news broadcast of the day, due to begin at ten P.M.

Three heavyset men with thin sandbags, came at him silently from different sides. They were on him before he noticed them. They gagged him and taped his mouth. His hands were tied behind his back, the thin wire cutting to the bone. A cord was slipped over his head and drawn tight around his neck—tight enough to hurt and frighten him, but not enough to choke him.

Petit Charles struggled weakly, but he was too little and too frail. They had him in a car within seconds, a burlap sack over his head. They stopped half an hour later on a narrow bush road that was deserted at night. The gag came out, and there was a quick interrogation. Why was he an American spy? Who was his American contact, Cameron? What had he told the American? Petit Charles made no outcry. He sat motionless between them on the sandy ground and told them that brawn was no match for brains. He had nothing to say to them.

They beat him with the thin sandbags and with their fists, shouting at him to talk. He was sick on his own knees, and he wet himself, but he didn't talk. Petit Charles was sustained by his own acceptance that this had always been destined to happen. Even the pain that made him vomit was in a sense a welcome distraction; a reminder that his crusade for the little man was like that of his Savior.

Irritated by his silence, they beat his eyeglasses into his eyes, grinding the broken glass into the sockets. Petit Charles whined in agony until they tightened the noose and he died slowly, flopping on the ground like a chicken.

They sewed the body into a large American flag, much as a dead sailor is prepared for burial at sea.

Gitabwanga: Mark's house—2315 hours, 22 November

The car came silently, lights out. It was windy, and Mark only heard it when the engine roared as it bounced away down his driveway. There was no light on the rear license plate.

A body, in a makeshift American flag, was in the middle of Mark's lawn. A placard stuck into it said, "Ton mouchard" (your stoolie).

Before he called the police, Mark burned the flag and the placard. In a pocket he found a crumpled, handwritten letter. It was addressed to Prince M'Taga and begged forgiveness for his humble servant's treachery.

Mark had a sample of the real handwriting of Petit Charles. It didn't match.

Gitabwanga: Prince M'Taga's House—2030 hours, 23 November

Pierre Schacht had to be careful with the prince, show no anger, just gently chide him for doing it his own way: "I thought we'd agreed on what to do with Djoulaba."

"That drowning scenario? That's un-Bwaganian. My guys wanted some fun, that's all."

Schacht sighed. There was no point in pursuing it. There was a more important point to get across.

"There will be an investigation. It may stir things up. I'm not sure they won't eventually find out who did it and why. We'd better set the date for Red Snow earlier rather than later."

"What do you have in mind?"

"We have to wait until Bwagania is independent and the French troops are temporarily out of the country. A month of total quiet after independence, then a diversion that draws the troops over to west Africa. I can arrange that. Perhaps the very end of January?

M'Taga mulled it over. He loved his unpredictable father, but to wait until Bwaga VI—so healthy—died, would waste half his life. It wasn't easy to press the button. But Schacht had a good point.

"All right," he said reluctantly. "We'll do it on January thirtieth."

"A special day?"

"My birthday. We always have a great big party at the palace on my anniversary. Papa will have had too much to drink when the fireworks start."

Gitabwanga: the royal wall—1940 hours, 24 November

The old man's reports to Bwaga VI had, for several weeks, been more of the same information: Red Snow was still being discussed, the firing practices at the Bendaga Ravine still took place, a few more names were added to the king's list of conspirators. But Red Snow still seemed remote, a threat that just might go away. Tonight, however, the king's clicks brought a different story:

"My Lord, they have set a new date. Red Snow will be on January thirtieth. By then, they say, calm will have existed since independence and they can achieve surprise. Especially as it's your son's birthday."

"Good work, old man. Keep on top of this. Any change of date must be reported to me at once. Also the details of their plans to take over."

The old man was gone within a minute.

**Gitabwanga: Paul Passatu's car—
2030 hours, 25 November**

There were no streetlights behind the cathedral. Mark waited for only ten seconds after he got there. Paul Passatu was finally using an accurate watch.

Once inside the rickety car, they drove out of town without a word. Paul parked well off the road, out of sight. They could see each other easily by moonlight. The bush around them was still.

"The coup, Red Snow, is set for January thirtieth, Mark. I just got this from M'Bouyé. It's reliable."

"What will the king do now?"

"I don't know. They may change the date again. I suspect he'll wait until after the independence ceremonies, but not much longer. It would be wise for us to get together and work up a counterplan as soon as possible: You, the king, M'Bouyé, me. I'll set it up?"

"Yes, please. Meanwhile, I'll try to get confirmation through my own sources."

"We have the names of most of the cadre." He handed Mark a paper. "And here's a list of the buildings and key points they will capture or destroy. They plan to use flame throwers to demoralize army units that oppose them."

"They won't leave the king unmolested?"

"Oh, no. They plan to seal him up in the palace with a heavy guard. Then they'll fly him out to Algiers and refuse him reentry."

Mark thought: If they run true to form—if Schacht really runs this his way—they'll kill him. He asked: "Will the king exile his son when he puts the coup down?"

"More likely than a trial and imprisonment. The king would see M'Taga in jail here in Bwagania as a continuing threat. In Europe, a threat but not so immediate."

"What does the king need that I can provide?"

"Information about the coup, about similar coups. All the information we can get. Also a lot of claymore mines for defensive purposes. We have none in the kingdom."

"I'll do what I can. Let me know when we meet again." Paul let Mark off in an alley four blocks from the cathedral.

Gitabwanga: Mark's house—2130 hours, 25 November

Mark's phone was ringing when he got home.

"Mark? Leclerc here."

"Yes. Point A?" François wanted to see him right away. Leclerc was the code name they had agreed on for an emergency meeting, Point A was Mark's house.

François got there in ten minutes: "Are you alone?" "Yes.

M'Pishi doesn't come back until tomorrow." No need to tell him that Linda was coming over later.

François got right to the point. "We have a date now, for this wretched coup. It's to be January thirtieth."

Mark nodded. "I heard the same thing. Apparently they only just decided on it."

"Our agent handler just gave us the report. They've increased their weapons training. The cadre is bigger but more disciplined. They killed a radio announcer who they believe was spying on them for the CIA." François smiled at Mark when they said this, but his eyes were questioning.

"I wonder why they thought that?" An ambiguous reply.

"Schacht told M'Taga, according to my source."

Schacht again! That SOB. But Mark gave nothing away to François. Even dead, good agents deserve protection. "I suspect that Schacht is an expert disinformation peddlar."

The Frenchman nodded. Mark's failure to admit anything was understandable.

"François, it's critical that we exchange notes on this as often as we've got something new. I was about to call you when you called me. My confirmation of your coup date is from a different original source, I'm sure. And the intermediary is reliable as far as I can tell. By the way, do you know anything about their weapons?"

"British or American. No East Bloc arms, obviously."

"Right," said Mark. "They'll try to pin the worst of it on us or the Brits."

Gitabwanga: Tchagamba plain—
0700 hours, 30 November

"There's a small group. Four adults, three calves," said Mark, standing on the driver's seat, his upper body through his Peugeot's sliding sun roof. He pointed, handed the binoculars to Pyotr, who was standing next to him, on the passenger seat. Behind them, in the backseat, a Bwaganian tracker sat patiently, watching the two foreigners.

"I see them. They look small." Pyotr had never seen Cape buffalo before, outside a zoo.

Mark laughed. "They're a mile away. In fact, they're very big. Quick on their feet, and mean when they're threatened. They've killed a lot of hunters."

"Where do I place my shot?"

"The shoulder or the upper chest. Try to break a major bone, or get the lungs and heart. Never aim for the head."

"Why not?"

"There's a very thick bone protecting the brain."

Mark spoke quietly to the Bwaganian. Then, to Pyotr: "We'll walk from here, downwind, keeping above them. Along the reverse side of that ridge." He pointed, and the Soviet nodded.

They started off in single file. The Bwaganian tracker first, carrying a spear and a large machete, hoping the two white men knew how to use their heavy rifles. Mark followed the guide, then Pyotr. They walked in silence, the hunters in safari boots, the Bwaganian in bare feet. He stopped now and then, motioning them to crouch and be quiet while he surveyed the landscape.

The small herd of buffalo moved as it grazed, keeping a tantalizing mile ahead of them. The sun rose and the heat set in. The buffalo were often invisible in the shimmering mirages of grass, thorn trees, and brush. The tracker occasionally used his toes to turn over a dung heap to see how fresh it was.

At ten they stopped to drink and eat a snack, tired, hot, but still eager to catch up with their prey. They sat on a flat rock, the tracker a few yards off to one side, watching them silently, discreet and patient.

Pyotr was fascinated by a big black beetle rolling a manure ball larger than itself along the ground. "What is it, Mark?"

"A dung beetle. They get inside fresh manure and literally have a ball. They take it off to their nests."

Pyotr laughed: "*Chacun à son goût.* I hope he likes it."

"He does it to amuse us," joshed Mark. "A comedian." He looked at Pyotr. The Russian was relaxed and enjoying himself. Mark had a goal for the morning: to get Pyotr to talk about the Soviet regime . . . even a few words will give a clue as to whether he's sick of it. He likes frankness, but go at it carefully.

"Pyotr, I've thought a lot about what you told me. About the way your father was taken off and killed. Wasn't it difficult to go to work for the same regime?"

Pyotr smiled. He'd expected this, although he hadn't thought he'd find himself wanting to tell Mark what it had been like. Perhaps it was the African bush, the hunt, his growing fondness for this straightforward American . . . whatever it was, he saw no harm in telling Mark about a long-ago problem.

"I went to work for the regime, in a way, when I joined the army. The Nazis were trying to colonize Russia, so everyone went up against them: loyal Party men, the few surviving dissidents, farmers, workers, intellectuals. Many of them would have welcomed the Germans if they'd been trying to free Mother Russia from the Soviets. I would have welcomed that, then."

"You would have?"

"Yes, I was still bitter about my father."

"Then?

"Then, after the war, the only thing I could think of doing was to stay in. I had no other way to go."

"The bitterness was . . . ?"

"Less so. Time had built up some scar tissue. But I hated Stalin, and when he died, I was very happy. I waited for things to improve."

"They did . . . enough for you?"

A long silence, then no came out as "Yes." Another long silence, then Pyotr slipped away with an ambiguous remark: "We each love our country."

Mark tried again, standing up and speaking as casually as he could: "I'm not sure I could have reconciled myself."

Pyotr stood, too, looking Mark in the eye: "We go on?"

"For as long as it takes," Mark replied, grinning.

Pyotr laughed and patted Mark on the shoulder.

The tracker stood up and they filed down the hill, the little herd now out of sight.

In midafternoon they halted again, and Mark said: "I don't think we'll catch them today. They know we're here, and they'll just keep ahead of us. This isn't like a game park. The big animals here are widely scattered. Let's bag a couple of dik-dik and call it a day."

"Dik-dik?"

"A tiny antelope, but its meat, especially the filet, is delicious. Olga and Aleksandra will love you for it."

The next evening Pyotr called Mark at home. He sounded delighted: "You were quite right, my friend. The dik-dik was superb, and the girls think I'm a professional hunter. They ordered me to go out again. You want to?"

"Of course. I'll call you."

Petrov had once again surprised Mark. He told Linda, "Pyotr frustrates me. He knows who I am and he should just fence with me, yet he's gone further than I expected this early."

"Schacht is the point man for Red Snow, but Pyotr's basically in charge of it, isn't he? You don't expect him to let slip any clues about that."

"No, obviously. It's his attitude toward the regime I'm after. He's fed up and wants to reason about it with someone who understands, I'm sure. He's got nobody to talk to over there—Anna Iosevna can't react at the level he wants, and anyway, he can't trust her very far. I'm his only friend outside the system, but I'm also the enemy. We get to a certain point and he can't go on."

"Be patient. Eventually he'll open up. You've played chess, you've been white hunters. Now take him sailing. Maybe the water will help."

"You're serious?"

"Yes. Maybe you're his Waterloo . . ."

PART II
December 1972–January 1973
The Chase

Gitabwanga: Mark's office—0830 hours, 4 December

Mark sat at his desk, thinking. Using a mole to prove there is a mole requires both ingenuity and luck. The bait has to be strong enough to provoke him to action yet not so blatant as to arouse his or her suspicions.

Luck is needed, because a mole cannot possibly see every cable and dispatch between headquarters and the field worldwide. He can only screen and select the cream out of the daily flood of paper to and from the field. The bait has to be the kind of item a mole looks for—valuable intelligence or operational information that indicates a danger to the KGB.

Mark had no truly valuable intelligence to offer, but he did have operational information, and he could try to slip it to a mole without approval of headquarters. It took him another twenty-four hours to work out the details.

The bait consisted of two quite separate items, and Linda composed and typed the dispatch while Mark made up the attachments. Twelve carefully selected photographs, blown up to eight by ten inches, with negatives. Seven selected tape segments. The dispatch itself provided an incomplete account of the activity from its inception. The dispatch carried special sensitivity indicators that should catch a mole's eye.

Mark was willing to sacrifice the operation. The meetings between Pyotr and Anna had become less productive for the station as the two lovers concentrated more and more on each other and less on the outside world. For the time being, the place seemed unlikely to be used by Petrov to meet his operational contacts or agents.

"I hope it works, Mark, you fiend." But Linda was laughing at him. She kissed him as he left for a quick clandestine meeting with Paul Passatu.

Gitabwanga: kilometer 26—0930 hours, 5 December

Mark and Paul met thirty minutes out of town, off the road, a mile from the nearest dirt track. Mark enjoyed bouncing around in Paul's car, zigging between trees, flushing game from the grass and bushes.

"Do you know the Hôtel du Lac?"

Passatu looked curiously at Mark: "Yes, why?"

"You know Madame Petarde?"

Paul was visibly uncomfortable: "Yes. Where's this leading, Mark?"

Mark laughed. "I've got no interest in why you know them or how well. This is business. I just want to know if you can get her to do something for you."

"Oh, it's business. Monkey business?" Paul grinned.

"In a way. Here's what I have in mind . . ."

It was enough for Paul Passatu to know that he was doing something against Schacht. He didn't ask for details about Mark's plan, sensing that it was part of something very complex.

Gitabwanga: François' house—1230 hours, 5 December

Mark had told François nothing over the phone, only that he would much appreciate half an hour together.

François sent his servant out shopping, and Mark explained the ploy, telling him only that headquarters would arrange for the story to get into KGB hands. No mention of a possible mole. François liked the concept and told Mark so.

"You certainly have an active mind, Mark. If it works, you'll qualify as genius, my friend." François laughed at the thought of what might happen as a result.

"Do you think you can do it?"

"Oh yes. With no doubt. I know the bank manager well, and he's sure to cooperate. You can count on it."

Together they went through the envelope that Mark had brought. The contents were simple but unambiguous. Two thousand Swiss francs. Ten thousand French francs. One thousand U.S. dollars. No counterfeit; the real thing. There was a "carbon," a sheet of chemically impregnated paper used to produce secret writing. This carbon, however, was a throwaway—its chemical formula was already known to the KGB. Finally, there was a list of requirements, including a request for information about M'Taga's cadre.

"Eventually, he'll be able to convince them it was planted purposely, to shaft him," François said.

"I know," said Mark. "But think of the hoops they'll jump through before then. They might just postpone the coup."

François smiled. "That would help."

"Then they'll make a real effort to find out what's going on. Either Petrov will investigate or, more likely, they'll send someone out from Moscow Center."

Gitabwanga: Banque d'Afrique— 1730 hours, 7 December

The Banque d'Afrique branch that Mark chose was across the street from the U.S. consular compound. It was a busy branch, but the toilets were too small. That was what had given Mark the idea.

By five-thirty there were no more employees in the bank. The manager and François had finished their talk, and now the manager watched while François taped the envelope behind the tank of the men's toilet. There was only the one throne in the minuscule men's room. You couldn't see the envelope once it was taped there, because there was so little space between the tank and the wall.

A tiny thread, fine enough to break under any real strain, was caught under the tape. It connected to a microswitch, and when the envelope was removed, the switch would activate a light and a buzzer on the manager's desk. The bank's surveillance cameras would do the rest.

The manager grinned. "I hope you identify the bastard, Colonel. I can't stand communists."

François smiled. "If you're at your desk, we'll catch him. I'll call you when they leave their building."

They shook hands. François was satisfied that the manager was discreet and would tell no one. Not even his wife.

Gitabwanga: Hôtel du Lac—1945 hours, 7 December

Madame Petarde introduced Paul Passatu to the French planter, the man who had picked a fight with Schacht on September sixteenth.

They instantly recognized each other, and the planter was happy to help Paul, a fellow farmer. Madame Petarde left them, not interested in what Paul had in mind. Paul only told the planter what was necessary in order to make it work.

That was at seven forty-five P.M. By nine o'clock, the planter, who was tipsy, had apologized to Schacht as they sat at the bar. The planter was tipsy. He detested Schacht; the apology and the subsequent conversation would have been impossible had he been sober.

"Personally, I hate communists," said the planter. They'd been talking politics for an hour, ever since Schacht had been grabbed by the planter as he crossed the hall and pulled into the bar. "And the worst of them are the Soviets. They're a bunch of cannibals, right?"

Schacht knew what would happen if he disagreed. He would be the center of a shouting session again. He had to live his cover: an apolitical Austrian businessman, no threat to the French in Bwagania.

"I agree," he said, clapping his new friend on the shoulder. "They're man eaters, all right." He thought: We'll eat you when we take over, you shit.

Schacht and the French planter suffered each other for another hour, during which Schacht made some very anti-Soviet remarks. He even agreed he wanted to live in the U.S. one day.

Gitabwanga: Mark's office—1100 hours, 8 December

The cable was not very long, but should catch the mole's attention. A French planter, the cable said, had reported that

> PIERRE SCHACHT, KGB ILLEGAL, IS DISENCHANTED WITH SOVIET REGIME AND TALKING ABOUT DEFECTING. WANTS RESETTLEMENT IN U.S. STATION PASSING HIM FUNDS, CARBON AND REQUIREMENTS TO HELP DETERMINE HIS BONA FIDES AND WILLINGNESS STAY IN PLACE AS LONG AS POSSIBLE BEFORE DEFECTION . . .

The cable went on to describe the dead drop in the Banque d'Afrique

> . . . WHICH SUBJECT WILL SERVICE AFTERNOON 18 DECEMBER.

"What will actually happen, Mark? Will the KGB let Schacht service the drop?"

"I think they'll send someone to pick it up late in the morning, on the assumption that it might be ready then. And because that's safer for whoever services it. Then they'll watch the bank to see if Schacht goes there."

"Will he?" Linda was laughing.

"I think he will," said Mark. "François is asking the manager to invite Schacht to a lunch at the bank that day. Schacht will probably respond, because he'll sniff a good contact. Bankers are very useful to the KGB."

"Who do you think will service the drop?"

"A man, obviously." He dodged her slap, blew her a kiss. "I'm hoping we'll smoke out another KGB asset. But if not, Petrov will do just fine. It'll give me what I need." Mark shared all his thoughts about a mole with Linda. It was Linda who thought up the final touch. Mark agreed, and she added a line to the cable: "BELIEVE TARGET WORTH RISKING Z-212 CARBON." It was, in fact, a nonexistent carbon, the code number of which had just been invented by Linda. But the KGB would want that Z-212 badly. It was a juicy addition to the bait.

Langley, Virginia: CIA headquarters—1700 hours, 8 December

The Bwaganian desk officer frowned at the cable. It wasn't like Mark to cut them in on an operation halfway through. Who was this French planter? Why hadn't Mark asked for traces on him? And what was Z-212? He called the special technical division—STD.

"Hello? May I speak to a carbon expert? Anyone will do." He was just back from the field and didn't know any of the technical people now at headquarters.

"This is a carbon guy. What can I do for you?"

"What's your series Z-212? Is it hot stuff?"

"Z-212? Never heard of it. Must be a garble. A cable, you say? Probably it got screwed up in transmission. Ask for a correction and call me again."

The desk officer hung up. The puzzle was getting thicker. It was quitting time for mattress mice, so he followed their example, locked up, and went home.

A floor below, the mole read the cable with great interest. But he had no reason to wonder about Z-212 or about the fact that the cable wasn't the successor to others on the same subject. So he put it in the stack of cables, dispatches, and other documents that he was going to take home and copy.

Langley, Virginia: CIA headquarters—1400 hours, 13 December

Gitabwanga station's dispatch on the Petrov safe apartment, with the photographs, got a mixed reception in headquarters. Some Russia division officers considered Mark's audio operation against Petrov a brilliant coup: Without headquarters' permission, Cameron had given the division a welcome early Christmas present. Others, who hadn't served overseas in the so-called "armpit" posts, thought he should be disciplined. Luckily, the two interested division chiefs—Russia and the special technical division—agreed Mark had scored a coup. No cost, no risk, no paperwork, and high return potential!

Mark had flagged the dispatch as sensitive and priority,

and so it caught the mole's attention. He added it to the growing pile for Moscow Center. There was no difficulty getting extra copies of the overhead shots of Pyotr and Anna making love, because the pouch room had made dozens of them. Copies quickly became collectors' items.

Arlington, Virginia: the mole's house—1800 hours, 13 December

The mole used a standard camera and standard film, which he bought at a neighborhood camera shop. The mole coated the film in his darkroom before using it, with a special chemical supplied by the KGB. He stored the chemical in the basement, in an old wine bottle marked ANT POISON. The formula of the coating was known only to the KGB laboratory in Moscow. Only after the coating was dissolved away could the film be developed. The KGB had urged him to use a variety of sophisticated espionage equipment: rollover cameras hidden in cigarette cases, or microdot equipment neatly concealed, or even their newest copying device. But he had refused. He didn't want any compromising stuff around the house. The mole knew his agency well and was—he felt—safest telling any guard who looked in his briefcase that he was taking work home. Many officers did it, especially senior ones. The guards knew many of them by name, all of them by sight, and never searched them.

Once home, the mole turned on the hi-fi, drew the curtains, and went to work to the accompaniment of medieval music. He made notes on many of the documents he'd collected during the day; some in the margins, some on separate pieces of paper. Often, he wrote reports covering information he'd learned from colleagues, friends, briefings, lectures, or summarizing documents too long to be copied. He printed so as to shield his handwriting from easy identification.

The mole had a job that gave him access to all of the Russia Division's communications, as well as those of other divisions in the clandestine services. In addition, he knew where to go for "extra" copes of sensitive cables, dispatches, reports, and intelligence studies.

His wife, one of his subagents, helped him. She contributed

documents and other information available to her in her own job in the clandestine services, and she made sure the neighbors neither saw nor heard anything to make them suspicious. She ran the house and tended their little garden and told the neighbors that her husband was writing a book. "Long hours, you know. Such a tedious subject, the history of medieval musical instruments, but he's fascinated by it." The mole, who prided himself on his attention to detail, had taken the trouble early in his career as a KGB agent to become a recognized expert on the history of medieval musical instruments, and had learned to play the sackbut quite respectably.

It sometimes took him until after midnight to photograph his daily take, and often he produced over a thousand frames of unprocessed film for the KGB in a single week. Two thousand pages of highly sensitive strategic, tactical, and operational intelligence weekly, from deep inside the CIA.

Tonight the mole raced through his loot, in a rush to get the take ready for a nine-thirty meeting with his KGB case officer. He ate a sandwich as he worked, and by eight o'clock he had prepared the entire package. There were six rolls of film; thirty-six frames each, two pages to a frame. The 432 pages he had photographed included nine pages of his written notes. Usually, his packages included only tightly rolled film in a special container. Tonight, however, there also were a tape cassette and the eight-by-ten photographs carefully rolled in a tube. The package was bulkier than usual, but it fitted into a folded newspaper. He taped the newspaper around it, to be sure.

At eight forty-five he left his house and drove by a circuitous route to the meeting site. It was to be a brush meeting lasting only a split second.

Washington, D.C.: the Dogwood Hotel—2127 hours, 13 December

Both the mole and his KGB case officer had set their watches to radio time before the meeting. A brush contact, more even than a regular agent meeting, must occur at a precise, present time. The danger mounts for each second of delay.

The mole entered the Dogwood Hotel garage three minutes

before the meeting. He was positive that there was no surveillance on him before he turned into the hotel driveway. At 9:28, he parked his car and locked it, the package inside a newspaper. There was nobody in the garage, and the KGB officer was due at the stairwell at 9:30 exactly. At 9:30 less ten seconds, the mole opened the door of the stairway. He stepped inside and started up the narrow stairs. On the first landing he met his case officer, right on the dot of 9:30. The Soviet was coming down the stairs. Without breaking pace, the Soviet gave the mole a newspaper—that morning's edition of the *Washington Post.* The mole exchanged his paper for the other, smiled bleakly, and continued upward.

By 9:32, the KGB officer had walked out of the garage and down into Rock Creek Park, unseen by anyone. The mole went into the lobby, jettisoned his newspaper in the first trash can he found, and went into a phone booth. The envelope he'd found in the newspaper was inside his shirt. He would open it at home and fondle the five thousand dollars happily. Right now he telephoned his home, spoke a few words to his wife. He would be home in twenty minutes.

Washington, D.C.: KGB *rezidentura*—
2200 hours, 13 December

The mole was prolific and his reports were of great value. Their secure, immediate handling was required by General Ossilenko.

The *rezident* himself, in Washington, a KGB major general, had to wait as much as a week to see what the mole produced—after Moscow Center had processed the film and decided what he needed to see. He didn't see most of the hottest material: It was reserved for the customers in Moscow to whom the precious take went routinely. A small amount of the take never left Moscow Center, where it stayed in General Ossilenko's vault. That was, generally, the portions of the take that didn't fit the official Party line—that, for example, demonstrated conclusively that the United States was not bent upon world domination or was not being thrust toward war by a small clique of greedy capitalists.

Tonight, the film was repackaged, as usual, into a secure, booby-trapped canister for the courier—a KGB officer under diplomatic cover—to take to Moscow Center. The audio tape cassette and the eight-by-ten photos, however, required special handling. They were encased in thick plastic, sealed, and closed into a locked steel box. But the KGB warrant officer who packed them saw the shots of Pyotr and Anna Iosevna making love. He called over his best friend, who eyed the photos with appropriate comments. Soon a half dozen men were passing them around, wondering who they were and what nifty piece of blackmail Moscow Center was cranking up. The late-watch supervisor had to get them back to their tasks by threatening to report them to the *rezident*.

Moscow: Ossilenko's office—1730 hours, 15 December

General Ossilenko had a love-hate relationship with the mole. The mole's take was so enormous and so valuable that a special office had been set up to handle "this gold mine to be protected with all the resources of the KGB." Ossilenko had a half dozen officers assigned, under his personal direction, to plan and execute support for the mole. They were supported by three secretaries and two couriers. There were follow-up questions to be asked of the agent, requirements to be levied on him, the mole operational and support budget to handle, his meetings to be planned, his Swiss bank account to be serviced.

All this took place in a heavily reinforced and guarded vault area consisting of four offices. General Ossilenko's office was the largest one, with a barred one-way mirror in the wall that gave him a view of the vault door. He had a conference table, and a private WC. It took Vladimir Ossilenko almost full time to read, absorb, analyze, comment upon, and personally distribute the mole's take to those customers who had the need to see it: the chairman of the KGB and his deputy; the chiefs of the various Soviet armed services; the Party general secretary and two other Politburo members; and a few ministers with portfolios that required them to have some of the information. Only a senior KGB officer could handle the job. It had to be done by someone who knew everything going on in the KGB, GRU, foreign ministry, and the armed forces—at least roughly, if not in detail.

It was a demanding job and Ossilenko's sharp eye and fast, accurate work habits made him uniquely qualified for the work. No other senior KGB officer had quite his grasp of the mole's product, its history, its enormous value to the USSR, and the pitfalls of not reading between the lines.

The mole was a constant complainer. He whined about his pay being too low, how his case officer was incompetent, that his work was too demanding and dangerous, and—always—that Moscow Center was not sufficiently grateful.

Ossilenko, a man of considerable courage as well as sound operational experience, occasionally lost patience with his hysterical, whining mole. But the product was worth every moment of agony and more, and the general would bite his knuckles and writhe in anguish as he suffered the insults and mentally consigned the mole to Siberia for life or a firing squad or, better yet, a slow death by torture in the basement.

He'd even gone down once to the basement of Lubyanka to watch an enemy of the people being prepared for interrogation, and he had greatly enjoyed mentally putting the mole on the stainless steel table.

He sighed and turned to the newly arrived pouch. This pouch was different. There was the usual canister containing rolls of coated 35mm film, undeveloped. Ossilenko sent the can to the lab immediately, unopened.

It was the plastic enclosure in the steel box that was different. He cut the seal and examined the contents: a large manila envelope and a small rectangular carton. Ossilenko set the envelope aside while he opened the carton. He pulled out the tape cassette, put it into the cassette player on his desk, and switched it on.

General Ossilenko sat there with his mouth hanging open. "Someone in Washington has gone mad," he said aloud. He listened some more, hoping the tape would eventually make sense to him. But it didn't. Why would the mole have sent in a tape of a man and woman speaking native Russian, talking nonsense, talking sex, and then quite obviously making love? Over and over again. With no apparent rest in between. One full hour of it, and no clue as to why.

Then he opened the envelope, hoping for something to clarify this idiocy. On top was a sealed envelope addressed to the chairman, EYES ONLY. Ossilenko opened it carefully. It contained an unusually vitriolic note from the mole: "Am risking my life daily for the Great Cause of Democratic World Revolution," the mole had written, "yet my case officer is a crude message carrier, nothing more . . . not fit to be associated with the great SVYET operation. The peasant has been late twice for meetings—once as much as twenty seconds late. Why doesn't he know how to set an accurate watch? Only the chairman of the KGB really understands and appreciates me . . . the others are lax, stupid, lazy, disinterested. A recent defector to the CIA has hinted about a mole in Washington! Can't Moscow Center keep a secret? Are they trying to get me killed?"

Ossilenko leaned back, eyes shut, wondering which of the recent defectors might have known something about SVYET. Or was the mole making this up to provoke a further tightening of security? It could be either, and would have to be researched. Only after Ossilenko was ready would the chairman get a look at his EYES ONLY note.

At that moment an armed guard brought the film back from the lab, the prints already dry. Ossilenko shut his door and locked it, and riffled through the prints until he found the one that referred to the tape and the envelope.

"Received 13 December," said a brief covering note from the mole. "From Gitabwanga. One of our people! Have you people gone crazy?" The next few prints showed a copy of Mark's dispatch about Petrov and Anna. Ossilenko scanned it, horrified. He opened the envelope and there they were, naked as jaybirds. Ossilenko almost jumped out of his chair. That monumental idiot Petrov! Was this what he had wanted the safe apartment for?

With shaking hands, Ossilenko put it all together. He laid out the photos on his table, noting as he did the exquisite beauty of Anna and her obvious enjoyment of Petrov. Then he read the dispatch again and found it hysterically funny, incredibly sexy, and infuriating. That man Cameron had pulled a real coup, had reported on Petrov in enormous detail and with great humor.

Ossilenko ground his teeth and laughed at the same time. Cameron was superb at his job. But as he studied the pictures and listened again to the tape, Ossilenko became even more enraged as he felt his own passions rising in response to the sounds and pictures of this beautiful young woman who enjoyed Petrov so much. Ossilenko was envious, and the more he studied Anna's lovely body, with its voluptuous curves, the harder his penis became.

Finally, it was too much. He snatched up the best shots of Anna writhing in ecstasy and went into the tiny toilet and brought himself to a fiery, if lonely, climax.

Later, while Ossilenko was going through the rest of the mole's pouch and, at odd moments thinking about how to handle Petrov's stupidity, he came across Mark's cable about Schacht. The general felt slightly nauseated as he read the cable. The CIA had identified Schacht as an illegal. Worse yet, the trusted illegal was talking defection. Schacht had been reliable for twenty years or more, or was thought to be. Had he been a double for all that time? Of which service? It was hard to tell from the cable just how Cameron had made this discovery. Perhaps SSR told him? Most likely, although it might have been some other source.

Ossilenko had no reason to speculate that this cable wasn't one of a series on the matter. The mole could only catch a certain percentage of the CIA's Niagara of paper.

But the general did want a look at that Z-212 carbon. So he sent a cable directing Petrov personally to unload the drop in the Banque d'Afrique, late the morning of 18 December.

> . . . CUT A THIN SLICE OFF ANY BLANK PAPER IN IT BUT LEAVE EVERYTHING ELSE UNDISTURBED AFTER YOU PHOTOGRAPH THE CONTENTS. RETURN THE DROP TO ORIGINAL CONDITION.

Ossilenko's cable said nothing about Schacht. That would have to wait for a full investigation, as soon as possible, but it couldn't begin to happen by the eighteenth.

The cable also instructed Petrov personally to stake out the bank the afternoon of December 18, from some discreet observation point outside the building, ". . . AND ADVISE IF ANYONE YOU RECOGNIZE ENTERS THE BUILDING." It was an unusual message that would raise a lot of questions in Petrov's mind. Unless he saw Schacht enter the bank. Then Pyotr would understand.

Ossilenko telephoned Schacht's case officer and asked for copies of all Schacht's reports for the past five years. It would be heavy reading, but the general read fast and he had to find out what the trends had been: how Schacht's reports might have changed, even in the slightest manner. He would have to stay up all night, but there was not an hour to be lost in determining if Schacht's exposure and reported defection were fact, and if so, what damage was done.

Cameron's guarded reports about his relationship with the SSR chef de poste in Gitabwanga were of little interest to the general until the idea came to him. He could get rid of Colonel de la Maison and in so doing close one of Cameron's eyes! The idea took shape quickly, and the last thing Ossilenko did before lunch was to write another cable to Gitabwanga. This one instructed Petrov to have a member of the *rezidentura* photograph a lunch on December 21 that—the mole had penned in a casual addition to his reports—Cameron had scheduled with François de la Maison, "as a sort of Christmas celebration."

Then Ossilenko went to see the KGB chairman.

"Look at these, Comrade Chairman! That asshole Petrov has done it again." He shoved the photos under his cousin's nose, forgetting to tell him about Mark's report and the tape.

"Pretty girl," the chairman said, licking his lips. "I'll bet she's a fabulous lay. Much prettier than most Russian girls. What are you doing, cousin, using her to keep Petrov off the vodka?"

"Sir, these pictures came from SVYET, with a tape of the proceedings and a full report by their station. The CIA took these shots."

The color drained from the chairman's face. He hammered his desk with a balled fist: "That's it! Pull him out and bring him back for trial! That stupid man has no sense whatsoever!"

But the general wanted a piece of Anna. "Let me go there immediately, Comrade Chairman. The mole also gave us this." It was a copy of the Schacht cable. "I must go there and see if we've got to lose our two key men just before the coup. Any change now could upset things irrevocably. We need to know much more, and right away."

It took some time, but finally the chairman agreed to let Ossilenko do it his way. Had Cameron reported how Pyotr had criticized the regime, the chairman would never have agreed. But Mark had only reported the love affair. He wanted his recruitment attempt on Petrov to be successful, not to become known to the mole and so be lost.

Gitabwanga: Lake Tchagamba—
1000 hours, 16 December

For the first hour, Pyotr sat in the stern of the boat and watched Mark prepare the twenty-two-foot craft, hoist the sails, cast off, and set out across the lake in a stiff breeze. He was fascinated by the process and by Mark's ability to do it alone.

"You borrowed this boat?"

"Yes, from a French friend," responded Mark. "I wish I owned it."

"Have you sailed it before?"

"Never, but they're all somewhat alike. You just have to study the rigging first, before you do anything."

"Will you teach me? I'd like to help, to be able to sail."

"Of course. There's not much to sailing on a lake like this. You just have to know the basics: how the equipment works, how to set the sails so they bisect the wind directions, and the direction you want to go in, that sort of thing. The problems come in storms, sudden violent winds, if you're becalmed, or if you get out of sight of land and have no compass . . ." Mark gave him a fifteen-minute beginners' course, including how to jibe and how to come about, then handed him the tiller.

They were silent for a while as Pyotr concentrated on handling the boat. He turned out to be a fair sailor, quickly at ease with the basic principles and with the boat. He relaxed, enjoying himself thoroughly.

This was a good moment for another probe. Mark's goal today was to try to get him to open up about his marriage—not necessarily to explore ways out of his marriage, but at least to reveal the problem. Just as Mark's knowledge that Pyotr was uncomfortable with the Soviet regime was exploitable only if he would talk about it, so the fact that Mark knew Pyotr was having an affair—was unhappy with Olga—was only valuable if the Soviet could be brought to discuss it. If Pyotr would talk about one problem, perhaps he'd talk about the other.

"It's a great sport, Mark. I should have done this years ago."

"Would Olga and Aleksandra enjoy it?"

"Aleksandra would. I think Olga would be concerned about her skin being damaged by the sun and the wind."

"She takes care of her appearance." Mark avoided taking a position. "That's probably a good reason to be cautious."

"She's not the cautious type, Mark. She's impetuous, even aggressive, in most things."

Interesting. He wanted to talk. Mark repeated the word: "Aggressive?"

"Sure of herself, sure of her position. You've noticed that?" His cheek muscles were working, his knuckles white on the tiller.

"Yes. Unusually so?"

"It can be infuriating." Pyotr stopped, realizing once more that he wanted to talk, this time to tell Mark about his growing unhappiness with Olga's constant, harping tirades against their posting to Bwagania—against Pyotr for having caused it. He couldn't contain the urge. "She hates it here."

"That must be very difficult."

"You're a lucky man, Mark. Linda's not only pretty, she's nice about everything."

"That's perceptive. She's wonderful about everything."

"What about Mr. Takahashi?"

"He's dead." Mark knew that Pyotr knew it, so rather than hide it, he used the fact to advance the conversation: "He died last August, in an accident. We were friends, the three of us. I started out trying to take care of her. Now I'm in love."

"I can see that. And she?"

"She too. It's a great feeling."

"I know," said Pyotr. "I've been there twice."

"Olga, and . . ."

"And someone else." He stopped short of telling Mark about Anna Iosevna, but Olga was another matter. "Olga much prefers it if we're stationed in the great capitals—Paris, Rome, London. She's not the outdoors type, and she's uncomfortable in an unsophisticated society."

"That doesn't bother you?"

"Living in a relatively primitive society? Not at all. I like the sense of being unstructured."

"France, Italy, and the UK are very free societies. One's personal life can be unstructured there."

"For most people, yes. Not for diplomats."

"You mean, not for Soviet diplomats?"

Pyotr stared at Mark for a moment, then realized there was no point in denying it: "Yes. My life there would not be the same as here."

"You're pretty much on your own here."

"Exactly. A lot more than there."

"Not much fun for a maverick," Mark grinned. "The places she'd like to be."

Pyotr shrugged. "There's nothing I can do about it."

"That depends on you, surely?"

Pyotr nodded, but he said nothing.

Gitabwanga: the king's vault—
2100 hours, 17 December

From a secret basement room in the royal palace, a passage led under the gardens to a hidden exit deep in a dense grove of trees. Bwaga VI had had this built "just in case" and had never had to use the passage. But he did use the secret room for sensitive discussions. It had a stainless-steel vault door with a combination lock that only the king and the chamberlain knew. The walls were six-foot-thick reinforced concrete.

The first line of the king's defense was his rudimentary but effective network of informants. The second line was the French military presence, which he was negotiating to extend after independence. The third line was a palace guard. It consisted almost entirely of men who, although they were in the regular Bwaganian army, were personally loyal to the king. The vault in the basement was the final line.

They asked Mark to speak first, about coups d'état in general and this one in particular. Mark was intrigued to be in this eerie setting with the king, his chamberlain, and Paul.

First Mark gave them a thirty-minute sketch of the KGB and its role in recent coups and other forms of political covert action. He bore down hard on the KGB's disinformation program, the skill and ruthlessness with which it was run. He ran over the history of overthrow of monarchs, the tactics used, and then a sanitized version of the CIA's role in countering the Soviets. Finally, he told them what he knew of the Soviet mission in Gitabwanga, what it might be expected to do, how the *rezidentura* might support and then control the coup and its successor government. It was succinct, clear, and compelling. As he finished, Mark asked them to consider several simultaneous actions.

"You could stock this room with army rations, ammunition, and weapons. Put in telephones and a radio transceiver. Get a wall map of the country and a large map of the city. Give the palace guard a special training session on how to handle attack from inside as well as from outside the palace. Make them take a special oath of loyalty. Use upcoming independence as the excuse, but require them to say nothing to anyone. I'll try to get you the claymore mines in time."

The king and his chamberlain nodded agreement.

"Then I would select an elite group of snipers from among your best hunters, people whom you trust, and train them so they know each other and can work as a team. Have four of them sleep in the palace each night from now on. They would be sent out from here, if they aren't needed for defense, to harass any groups trying to capture key points or buildings.

You'll need quick, accurate tactical intelligence, so arrange for good observers who live overlooking key points, to get their information to you by phone, radio, or runner."

"All that in such a short time!" The chamberlain looked unhappy, but the king shot him a glance and said, "Sshh."

"Those are just some of the defensive things that would help if you plan to let the coup attempt occur and arrest or kill the plotters then. But if you intend to preempt the coup by striking first, you might want to pick a date. Maybe January tenth, three weeks before Red Snow. Take command of the army and the police that day, without warning, and arrest all the plotters. And I'd rake in Pierre Schacht and try him for attempted murder, sedition, provoking revolution, whatever. He's got no diplomatic immunity. This way you wipe out the coup completely before they have a chance to act."

"I like the idea of the snipers," said the king. "They will be useful no matter what. My Sicilian hunter can form them up and lead them. Want to volunteer, M'Bouyé?"

M'Bouyé smiled. His total incompetence with firearms was a palace dining table joke.

"I also like the idea of making this room my command center." He nodded to M'Bouyé. "Keep all this in your head." To Passatu, the king said: "Can you arrange for the observers? I think they should mostly be Frenchwomen who don't work. They have the time, and they are not likely to support my overthrow." Paul grinned and bobbed his head.

And to Mark: "Can you help by bringing in the radio, rations, weapons, and ammunition? I don't want to raise suspicions by asking our military for them."

"I'm sure I can, sir. And an emergency generator. You'll want power for light and communications."

"Have you done this sort of thing before, Mark?"

"Yes, Your Majesty. Once. But we lost."

"Why?" asked M'Bouyé.

"Because the president—it was a republic, not a monarchy—lost his nerve at the end. That's not likely here, I know."

The king grinned at Mark. "You can count on that, young man. But let's keep moving, or we'll be all night."

The session went on until two in the morning of December 18. Mark leaned back and listened as the king discussed the problem. Bwaga VI looked like a shiny brown athlete despite his balding head and the slight paunch that showed as he strode around the table, arms waving, loose shirt and baggy pants adding to the picture of informal strength.

"Gentlemen, be in no doubt that we face a skilled and determined enemy, the KGB and its assets. They've turned my own son and his cadre of young men against me. As you know, I do not plan to let the coup occur and then defeat it. We will preempt it, but not before I know who all the leaders are and exactly what they intend. You now know my plan for preemption, and your roles in it. I'm deeply grateful for your cooperation in this."

He bowed to Paul and Mark, who bowed in return. "I will keep my decision as to when we move against Red Snow to myself until the last minute. That way, word of our plan can't get out. I trust you all, but there's no reason to take even the slightest risk. So, gather more intelligence and when I give the word, we'll crush every last one of these traitors."

The king spoke through clenched teeth, one of the few overt signs of his rage. Then he finished his thought, his neck veins bulging: "No matter who they are. M'Taga too will have to pay."

Gitabwanga: Banque d'Afrique—
1030 hours, 18 December

The Bank of Africa—La Banque d'Afrique—dating from the very first years of the French occupation of Bwagania, was a solid, comfortable two-story building: large stone blocks and a red tile roof. A prime symbol of European colonialism, it was not the kind of place Pyotr would have chosen for a dead-drop site.

When he saw the men's toilet, however, Pyotr understood the practicality of this drop. The back of the tank was so close to the wall that it was impossible to see the envelope without using a mirror. It was, in fact, so tight a fit that he had to slide a knife in to unstick the tape from the porcelain tank. The thread tripped the alarm in the manager's office without Pyotr's noticing the booby trap.

The manager could see the men's room door from his desk in a corner office, his door open on purpose. The security cameras took several excellent shots of Petrov as he walked across the main floor. Then he obligingly changed some notes into smaller denominations, to account for his presence in the bank. It gave the manager enough time to phone François, and François to phone Mark, who took a photo of Pyotr leaving the building. Even from across the street, from his cover office on the U.S. consulate general's second floor, through the glass window, the telephoto lens gave Mark a good close-up of Pyotr.

François called again a few minutes later, to announce that Petrov had removed the envelope from the men's room.

"There's no doubt now, Mark," said Linda. "The KGB knew the contents of our cable. There is a mole."

Mark was sure, too, but more conservative. "They know what was in that cable, Linda. That isn't proof positive of a mole. If the dispatch on the Petrov bug-and-camera thing brings a reaction, then I'll be certain there's a mole. A machine can read our cable traffic, theoretically, but only a human can intercept our nonelectronic communications."

"What kind of a reaction would you expect, Mark? Would they bomb my apartment?"

"Very doubtful, Linda. They're more likely just to stop using it. However, just in case, you'd better vacate the place for a while. Come on over to my place, my love. Tell Madame Denise you're getting strange phone calls and you're going to bunk with a friend for a while. Ask her to take your name off the hallway register."

Linda nodded. "That'll make it harder for them."

"Meanwhile, I'll set the camera and tape recorder to shoot when the door of his place opens. Maybe we'll catch him saying goodbye to his nest."

Using the rear entrance, Mark went to Linda's apartment, reset and reloaded the system. Madame Denise was snoozing in an armchair in the courtyard and didn't see him. He was back in the office in twenty minutes.

Gitabwanga: Banque d'Afrique— 1145 hours, 18 December

Pyotr went back to the bank at eleven forty-five to return the envelope to the drop site in the men's room. Bwaganian Sûreté reported Pyotr's passage from the bank to the Soviet compound, his forty-minute disappearance into the compound, and then his appearance again in his car.

François de la Maison received the radio reports and alerted both the bank manager and Mark. The bank cameras again photographed Pyotr entering and leaving the bank.

This time, Pyotr made it easy for everyone. After visiting the toilet, he changed a Swiss banknote at a teller's cage, remarking casually that he'd forgotten to do this earlier. The teller made out a money-change form and asked to see Pyotr's passport—a routine requirement, but one that quite clearly identified him as an officer of the Soviet consulate general.

Later that afternoon, François and Mark met briefly. François laughed as he returned the envelope to Mark. "Schacht won't need this. He doesn't know it exists. I just love your trap, Mark. How did you arrange it?"

"I don't know. Headquarters has some way of inserting it into KGB channels, but they aren't telling me how."

"Anyway," said François, "I left an empty envelope in its place, just in case Petrov checks again to see if it's there. But I would love to see Petrov's face when Schacht goes to the bank."

Mark smiled: "Things do seem to be falling into place."

Gitabwanga: Banque d'Afrique— 1250 hours, 18 December

Pierre Schacht was early for the lunch. He paced up and down the sidewalk for a few minutes, perspiring in his suit and tie. His Panama hat made it duck soup to recognize him.

Mark watched from the second floor, unseen behind the venetian blinds, and took several telephoto shots of the KGB illegal. He also spotted Pyotr watching from a café window. He, too, had a small camera and took some shots of Schacht. Pyotr's face was flushed: the almost irreversible process of distrust had taken root in his mind.

At five minutes before the hour, Schacht went through the bank doors. Pyotr crossed the street, passed the bank's front doors, and tried to see inside, but he clearly didn't want to risk being seen by Schacht. So he kept on walking and, as Mark's vision was about to be obscured by an adjoining building, ducked into a Soviet mission car and was driven away.

Gitabwanga: the KGB *rezidentura*—1730 hours, 18 December

Still shaken by the sight of Schacht entering the bank, Pyotr had taken longer than usual to write his short cable. "Ten minutes per word," he said to himself. "It's too long. But it's so delicate. Perhaps there's a good explanation."

The problem was that Pyotr didn't know enough. He was certain that there was a connection between the dead drop and Schacht. Logically, it meant that Schacht was a CIA agent. But suppose Moscow Center knew that all along? Maybe they'd instructed him to let himself be "recruited" by the CIA. Perhaps even years ago. But then again, perhaps this cable was to be very unwelcome news to Moscow. He looked at it again. It had to be completely neutral. Finally, it seemed safe:

> RE YOUR MSG 9-12 DROP CONTAINED ONE SHEET BLANK PAPER, OF WHICH THIN SLICE POUCHED TO YOU. ASSUME IT IS CARBON SHEET. ALSO IN DROP U.S. DOLLARS ONE THOUSAND, SWISS FRANCS TEN THOUSAND, FRENCH FRANCS TWO THOUSAND. RED SNOW 001 OBSERVED ENTERING BANK 1250 HOURS 18 DECEMBER.

Red Snow 001 was, of course, KGB Colonel Oleg Petrosian alias Pierre Schacht. Pyotr suspected that the effect of his cable would be electric in Moscow Center.

He was right. General Ossilenko was stunned when he read it. It took the general a full day to compose himself and three more to decide what to do.

Gitabwanga: Restaurant Victor Hugo—1315 hours, 21 December

Pyotr had briefed the Tass correspondent, KGB major Mikhail Ivanovich Yegorov. There, in an alcove, were the two men—Colonel François de la Maison lunching with CIA station chief Mark Cameron. The assignment was simple: Photograph the two together. If possible, get a shot of them passing documents to each other. Conceal the camera.

For once, Pyotr had given Yegorov the reason for the exercise. Moscow Center said that de la Maison was passing classified information to Cameron against SSR orders. The pictures would be used to "get rid of de la Maison." So, Pyotr had told Yegorov, "use your excellent photographic skills to the best advantage. . . . we must remove de la Maison from the scene, he is a real threat to Red Snow."

Yegorov used an old and simple technique. He got to the Victor Hugo, with his wife, fifteen minutes ahead of de la Maison and Cameron. The camera was a tiny Minox concealed in a package of Gauloise cigarettes. Yegorov could take passable photos without using the Minox's viewfinder. Just lift the package, take a cigarette or offer one to your wife, and at the same time press the switch several times. The camera lens could view the target through a small hole in the package. Among two or three dozen shots there would be one or two good ones. Ones in which, for example, a gesture of an empty hand by one of the diners could be changed to show an envelope being passed.

François recognized Yegorov, even nodded to him, but thought nothing of it. The Soviets had been there when he and Cameron arrived, and left long before they did. He said nothing to Mark about seeing the Tass correspondent. They concentrated on their plans to counter Red Snow.

Pyotr sent Yegorov's photos by special diplomatic courier to Moscow.

Moscow Center: Ossilenko's office—1830 hours, 23 December

KGB General Vladimir Fedorovich Ossilenko enjoyed lecturing at KGB training schools and seminars, and he did it often. His favorite subject was disinformation—planting deceptive information designed to make the opposition believe something or do something that the KGB wants.

"Make it simple," he would say. "Simplicity is the key to good disinformation. It must be plausible, seem to be accurate and true, including the apparent source. Only the ultimate source, the KGB, must be hidden. Make it short, so that even dull minds such as yours can grasp it."

The students always laughed at that, which amused him because he knew they didn't like to be called stupid. They weren't, in fact. They had some of the Party's best minds.

Whether you liked Ossilenko or not, he was recognized throughout the KGB as a master of disinformation. Now he checked the photographs Tass correspondent Yegorov had taken of Mark and François in the restaurant Victor Hugo. They were perfect for the job. He checked his buzz lines again, on a notepad. They were spare and to the point:

1. Doctored photos, copies of SSR reports initialed by de la Maison, must *prove* de la M is Cameron's agent, verifiable at least for short term
2. Cite trusted source . . . disgruntled SSR man?
3. Cause immediate recall of de la M, before Red Snow
4. Severely damage SSR-CIA relations

The package he had been working on for hours was finally ready. It included two SSR documents that had been passed to the CIA station chief—Daniel Reilly—in Paris and copied by the mole in Washington. Ossilenko perceived no danger to the mole, because the apparent source of the documents would be an unidentified SSR employee in Gitabwanga. The KGB lab added a set of François' initials to the upper right corner of the documents.

One expertly doctored photo showed François handing an envelope to Cameron over the luncheon table in the restaurant Victor Hugo. Another showed Mark handing some Swiss money to François. All Ossilenko had done was to spell out a distorted version of the lunch meeting, add documents that the nonexistent envelope supposedly contained, and now he would feed it to the SSR. Simple, neat, with the ultimate source—the KGB—nowhere visible.

He sent off the package to Brussels with detailed instructions.

Ossilenko changed gears and turned his thinking back to Gitabwanga and the problems of Petrov and Schacht. He would have to take care of the Schacht inquiry himself, in Gitabwanga. There was the whole Schacht file to go through first, all twenty years of it, not just the last five years of his reports, but every single document in it: a huge undertaking. In addition, Bwagania was no place to do business in a ten-day span that included Christmas and the Bwagania independence ceremonies. He decided to go after the first of the year. His brief cable to Petrov was unambiguous in its wording, but it would leave Petrov wondering about what was going to happen.

> ARRIVING GITABWANGA 1400 HOURS 3 JANUARY VIA UTA 7765 FROM PARIS. MEET AND ARRANGE HOTEL REPEAT HOTEL FOR MIMINUM ONE WEEK.

Before he left that evening to visit his mistress on his way home to his wife and children, Ossilenko opened a wall safe in his office and took out two items to take with him to Bwagania, "in case of need." They had been made especially for him by the secret KGB laboratory that created devices to kill "enemies of the state." Only members of some of the more esoteric departments of the KGB could order items from the lab, such as officers in the "wet affairs" (mokrie dela) from department v of the first chief directorate. Ossilenko was among a few senior officers not in department v who could have special "tools" made. His were a hypodermic needle neatly disguised as a fountain pen, and a thin steel wire coiled and hidden inside the base of a pillbox. One end of the wire was welded to the pillbox lid, the other to the box itself: The result was a lethal wire loop that could be dropped over a victim's head and tightened to choke him, then locked tight by rotating the ends of the wire several times, like the tie of a trash bag.

Gitabwanga: the KGB *rezidentura*— 0930 hours, 24 December

Pyotr read Ossilenko's cable with dismay. No mention of the reason for this visit could only mean trouble. An official visit in six months would be routine. But for a man of Ossilenko's rank to come to Bwagania so soon into Petrov's tour was chilling. And why hadn't the cable said something about Schacht?

Pyotr could think of nothing he'd done that would make Moscow Center suspicious of him or mad at him. He spent a lot of time worrying during the next ten days.

Brussels: Restaurant La Ferme— 1300 hours, 24 December

Colonel Paul Edouard Vilmaire, the SSR chef de poste in Brussels, watched his lunch companion with mixed emotions. Vilmaire didn't like Dr. Victor Martini. But the good doctor was one of SSR's most trusted HC's, a volunteer "honorable correspondent," who sometimes performed better than any fully paid and controlled agent Vilmaire had known.

There was a creepiness about Martini that got to Vilmaire every time he looked at the tiny physician. It wasn't so much that a Frenchman should choose to spend his life in Belgium. That wasn't so bad, really, although to Vilmaire it was a dumb thing to do. It wasn't even the small stature, potbelly, wet handshake, and smell of sweat, although they too added to the colonel's unhappiness. It was just that his antennae told him that deep down inside there was something rotten about Martini. Paris had scolded him for even suggesting an update on Martini's security clearance and a field investigation to go with it. This little shit, said Paris: ". . . is too valuable to risk by insulting him, and that's it."

Martini had just given Vilmaire a useless account of NATO medical facilities and some of the new tropical medicines being developed by the Université Libre de Bruxelles. (SSR had all this information already through its contacts in the NATO medical office and its liaison with the Belgian services.) But Martini's next subject gave Vilmaire a nasty shock.

"I have an acquaintance who is close to your poste in Gitabwanga, Colonel. Not all the employees and agents there are fond of the chef de poste, a Colonel de la Maison. One of these unhappy employees gave a package to my acquaintance, who just brought it back with him from Bwagania. I took the liberty of opening the package, and I believe it's dynamite." He smiled at Vilmaire and said softly, "Dynamite."

Vilmaire and de la Maison had been close friends for over twenty years, and Vilmaire had a good idea of what the package must contain. By opening it, Martini had made sure that Vilmaire would have to send it on to Paris.

They were at a corner table, and only two other tables in the large room were occupied. Vilmaire opened the package slowly, making sure no one could see it in his lap. A quick glance and his fears were confirmed. De la Maison had gone too far; he would be ruined by this. Ironically, Vilmaire would probably have done the same as de la Maison, in a small post where one needs all the help one can get. He struggled to keep his food down as the meal meandered on for another hour.

Martini, reading him like a book, thought that Vilmaire might make the next target for Ossilenko: just slip word to Vilmaire that the CIA chief in Brussels would like discreet contact with him. Slip similar word to the CIA chief, and presto! Sit back and watch another SSR chef de poste go down the drain.

Gitabwanga: Mark's house—1900 hours, 24 December

"Christmas Eve in Gitabwanga, Mark. We've only been to the office once today. Let's celebrate."

"Good. I'll pour the drinks. Eggnog?"

"We have it?"

He laughed. "No. A glass of wine?"

"Please. What do you suppose people are doing in town tonight?"

"François told me. The French have a round of parties, sing their carols, trade bûches de Noël, some attend church, just like in France at Christmastime. The few Bwaganians who are Christians observe the usual customs with a few local additions. The Christ child and his family are black, their clothes African. The crèche animals are distinctly Bwaganian—goats instead of sheep, donkeys instead of horses. Most Bwaganians, being Moslem, officially ignore Christmas, but in fact they join in because it's a holiday. Whether or not they can afford to celebrate or believe in Christ, almost everyone believes in the Christmas spirit."

"No snow or ice, people in light clothes . . . it seems unreal for Christmas. Anyway, I love you and I've got a special present for you. Ready for it?"

"Of course."

"They'll be here at exactly seven," said Linda, looking at her watch. "Right now."

"They?"

"The Petrovs. I couldn't think of anything you'd like better than a quiet evening with him. I asked her last night. She was surprised, but she seemed pleased. She checked with him, and said they could come. M'Pishi cooked a goose for them—that's Russian tradition."

"You amaze me, my love. The Soviets don't celebrate Christmas—they've moved their traditional Father Frost to New Year."

"I know, but they want to see how we do it. You're pleased?"

"I'm delighted. Did you invite his girlfriend, too?"

"Oh, Mark, that's silly. Well, come to think of it, I did."

"Good grief . . . Anna Iosevna? You couldn't."

"Gotcha, for once. No, they're bringing Aleksandra."

The Petrovs arrived with a chilled bottle of Stolichnaya and a can of beluga caviar. They were touched by the goose and its ring of traditional baked apples, and pleased to dine outside the Soviet compound. Aleksandra thanked Mark formally for saving her life, and gave him a box of Russian chocolates. Then she sat in front of the tree, enchanted by the lights, decorations, and the presents scattered under it.

Before they sat down to dinner, Mark set the ground rules: "No serious talk tonight. Just friendship, Christmas spirit, and a game of chess if you ladies don't mind." The ladies didn't mind; Olga was surprisingly friendly and lighthearted: "It's good to have a night off . . . so many diplomatic parties. I'm so pleased you invited us."

The men played until midnight, barely speaking a word, but Mark learned more about Pyotr from his chess. He was a tough, calculating opponent, thinking far ahead, moving fast, and above all making unexpected plays that sometimes worked. There was tension in him, like a coiled spring, but he seemed to have it under tight control. He drank a few Scotches with soda, but there was no sign of excessive drinking.

Pyotr won six games of blitz out of eight, but lost a one-hour-long standard game to Mark. "I know nobody I'd prefer losing to," he remarked graciously.

After dinner, Aleksandra was absorbed by a photographic essay on life in the U.S. while Olga and Linda gossiped about the diplomatic corps in Bwagania. "Most of them are cretins," Olga said at one point. "It's nice to know you two." Then she spent some time lauding her family and its prestige, without identifying them. Finally, as the time to leave came near, she described their apartment: "We'll have you over, but you must excuse it . . . so small and primitive, not at all like we're used to."

As they left, Pyotr gave Mark and Linda a bear hug and said: "We may be on opposite sides, but I genuinely like you two." Aleksandra curtseyed, thanking them in a serious voice but with a big grin and a twinkle in her eyes. Olga smiled at Mark as she led Pyotr and Aleksandra through the front door: "We will meet again soon. Linda will arrange it."

"I'm sorry for him," said Linda after they'd gone. "She's all wrapped up in herself, his career's unimportant."

"No doubt of that. No wonder he went after Anna Iosevna."

"What's next?"

"The hardest part of all. We know how he feels about the regime, but we've still got to tease it out of him. He's got to tell us frankly, so we can make him face the next step . . . doing something about it. The French have a disgusting expression for teasing information out of someone: '*Tirer les vers de son nez.*' "

"Is that what I think it is?"

"Yes—pull the worms out of his nose."

"Yuk. Can I help?"

"A woman's touch? It might work. Unless we push it—and that's not wise—we meet next at the palace on independence day. Give it a try then."

Gitabwanga: Mark's house—0800 hours, 1 January

Independence day came quietly to Gitabwanga. The Bwaganians took to the streets later than usual, in their most colorful clothes. The women wore their brightest, most flowing gowns and long cloth headdresses. The men wore large turbans, or fezzes, and loose desert robes over their trousers. Children were dressed in their best clothes and were treated with more than the customary tender care on this very special day. People strolled along the main streets in family or clan groups, talking noisily and hailing other groups until the town buzzed with their happy chatter.

French troops from the foreign-legion camp patrolled the town in company with Bwaganian gendarmes. Beggars and robbers had been rounded up before dawn, driven in trucks many miles into the bush, and released on foot.

Mark and Linda could easily hear the growing clamor from the breakfast table on the veranda as she read the celebration schedule to Mark. "We're to be in our seats at the stadium at ten. From then until noon, there'll be various sports: racing, spear throwing, boxing, wrestling, jumping, and so on. At noon, the French hand over the kingdom to the king, as a sovereign nation. Then there are parades and speeches through the afternoon. At five, the king gives a public reception, then at dusk there'll be the royal drums and fireworks. Finally, the palace VIP reception at seven. A long day, but it'll be interesting."

Gitabwanga: the stadium—1100 hours, 1 January

In typical African style, the VIP stands were still almost empty at eleven o'clock; so were the public bleachers. Thousands of laughing, shouting Bwaganians were walking around on the playing field, and it took the gendarmes another half hour to clear the field—good-naturedly, using persuasion, gently pushing.

When the games finally began at eleven-thirty, the master of ceremonies, a jovial man with a deep belly laugh, announced that all the games would be run at the same time so that the noon independence ceremony could be on schedule. He was an optimist: in fact, it slowed everything down.

Runners, racing bicyclists, spear and javelin throwers, wrestlers, boxers, and jumpers raced and flashed in among each other, and the floor of the stadium was a mass of movement, color, shouts, and laughter. Although no events were properly conducted or timed, everyone had a good time, which was what counted most in Bwagania. The officials, assisted by grinning police, worked patiently to clear the field for the second time, urging the competitors and their friends and relatives back to their seats in the bleachers.

Finally, the VIP stands were full of people, half white and half black. The king arrived in the Sicilian's Rolls-Royce, followed by the government leaders in open cars. They circled the floor of the stadium at walking speed, avoiding the remaining competitors, cheered by the thousands in the bleachers and the VIP stands.

The king's car did three turns around the stadium and then stopped. Bwaga VI got out and stood there, unprotected, waiting for his son. Prince M'Taga's car did another circle, and the inheritor joined his father on the floor of the stadium. They stood there for a minute, the beloved king and his popular son—soon to be prime minister—while the crowd roared. Then they climbed together up the carpeted stairs to their seats in the center of the VIP stands. The VIPs, including the diplomatic corps, stood and applauded them until they sat in their gilded chairs.

The official independence-day ceremonies started an hour late. Nobody minded, for in Bwagania time wasn't taken too seriously. The crowd passed the time talking to each other and singing. The master of ceremonies got tipsy and had trouble getting to the microphone.

First, he introduced the French governor-general, who would hereafter be the French ambassador. Then he introduced the French deputy foreign minister, here from Paris for the turnover of sovereignty. The deputy foreign minister made a brief speech, pledging eternal friendship between France and her erstwhile colony and ending with a solemn declaration of Bwagania's independence: "France hereby solemnly declares that Bwagania is henceforth a sovereign, independent state within the family of nations, no longer subject to the benign stewardship of the Republic of France."

The band played "La Marseillaise," and then the Bwaganian national anthem—written for the occasion by Bwagania's premier composer. The new Bwaganian flag was unfurled on a pole higher than that holding the French tricolor. The crowd didn't recognize the national anthem, but the brilliant green, gold, and crimson flag was greeted with a huge roar of pride and joy. The warrior's shield in the center of it was striking.

A unit of the French foreign legion paraded, led by a major with glinting medals. They met a unit of the army of Bwagania in mid-stadium, led by a Bwaganian major with a long record of courageous service in the French army. The two officers shook hands, symbolizing Bwaganian acceptance of its own defense responsibilities.

Then it was time for Bwaga VI. The master of ceremonies, a cousin of the king's, made it simple: "People of Bwagania," he bellowed, "I give you our much loved Bwaga VI, the spirit of our lovely land!" He hiccupped and, missing his chair, sat heavily on the steps of the podium. The crowd roared its laughter and its greeting to Bwaga VI.

The king stepped up onto the podium from the other side

and waved, turning in a circle. He was magnificent in a white uniform as commander-in-chief of the Bwaganian armed forces, with a wide red sash and a chestful of glinting medals that gave the uniform colorful splendor. His father's white sun helmet with cockade and ostrich plumes, and large fly whisk of rhinoceros hide and a horse's tail, had been taken out of the royal collection for this day's celebrations, and now he took off the helmet and placed it over his heart, waving the fly whisk in a slow half circle to include all the crowd. Bwaga VI had thought about this day for a long time.

He began to speak, using the fly whisk to emphasize his words. Bwaga VI was at his best. The sun shone on his people, and this was the first day in his lifetime that his country was free to do what he and it wanted—in that order. He felt wonderful, and it showed in his face and the way he used his hands and moved his body. The uniform, sun helmet, and fly whisk helped give a dramatic impression of strength and tribal autocracy tempered by humor and tolerance: the new and the old Africa. Bwaga VI was a highly amusing and effective public speaker at any time. Today, he was outstanding. He spoke in French, for all the crowd understood it. But he larded his sentences with liberal use of the Bwaganian language, in the words that were reserved for royalty speaking to the people. He did it so skillfully that the non-Bwaganians in the stadium could understand everything. It was masterful bilingual eloquence.

First he thanked the French deputy foreign minister for ". . . the priceless gift of independence, for which we fought so hard against such odds." The minister, unsure how to take that, bowed courteously in response.

"My people and my guests," Bwaga VI continued, in a deep paternal voice that blasted the stadium with loudspeakers at full volume. "We are here today for one purpose: to celebrate our independence. We will do it in peace and dignity. It is my royal decree that there will be no fighting today." The crowd roared its approval.

"There will be no drunkenness." The crowd booed and jeered, laughing uncontrollably.

"It is forbidden to eat anyone." The crowd screamed in

mock horror at this reference to what had happened after independence in other central African countries. Mark and Linda laughed until their eyes teared. They had spotted a nearby Bwaganian army colonel pretending to eat the hand of his neighbor, a French foreign legion major. The Frenchman replied with a simulated bite at the African's sholder, both laughing, obviously close friends.

"No pocket will be picked here today." As the king said this, his son M'Taga ostentatiously reached up behind Bwaga VI and pantomimed stealing his wallet from his pants pocket. The crowd went wild with laughter and whistles. The king caught on, looked around, and with a big grin clapped his son on the head with the fly whisk. The crowd stamped, bellowed, whistled, and shrieked its amusement and love for the royal pair.

Jean Prosper M'Bouyé watched impassively, pleased that Bwaga VI gave no hint of his fury at his son's treachery.

The French ambassador watched with a sardonic smile. He had gone from being governor-general this morning to being ambassador this afternoon. The abrupt change of role would, he thought, be difficult to handle. Especially the transfer from power to persuasion. He liked the king and wished him well, but he thought it entirely possible that M'Taga would win. France would have to appear uninvolved while covertly acting to support the king.

The South African trade commissioner watched the royal pair caper and the crowd loving it, with cynicism. This morning the new Bwaganian minister of trade had given him an order for a year's supply of South Africa's famous Outspan oranges. In exchange for the order and a healthy kickback, the minister had committed himself to a similar order next year if the price and terms were right.

The Spanish ambassador watched the various pantomimes in the VIP stands and in the general crowd with tolerant good humor. He saw them as remarkably good actors, cheerful and friendly. He wondered idly why there were no Bwaganian bullfighters.

The Soviet ambassador sat stolidly, baffled by what he saw. He judged the scene as proof that Africa was an undisciplined zoo whose inhabitants would never make good communists.

Pyotr, sitting next to the ambassador, spent most of the afternoon with an equally blank expression, trying to fathom the dynamics of the Bwaganians and their French colonists. The pieces didn't fit: Despite the Party line about French masters and African slaves, they didn't seem to hate each other. For the most part, the crowd, white and black, Christians, animists, and Moslems, sat together and chatted as if they were friends. He wondered if the man who wrote the Party line had ever been to Africa. Probably not.

Having put the crowd in a good mood, the king moved on to more serious things. He told them what to expect for the rest of the ceremonies. He explained the various parades and speeches that were to occur, and then invited the entire crowd to a buffet under the giant baobab trees outside the stadium. The crowd yelled its approval.

Then the king told them that he was going to make a long and boring speech. The crowd hollered its disbelief. They knew he might be serious, but he would never be boring or go on too long.

"My people, my guests, my friends, my children!" He included them all with the sweep of his fly whisk. There was a huge smile on his face, but his words were serious. "I want you to listen with great care. We are a small but important nation, at the crossroads of Africa. The eyes of the world are on us. People say that we Africans are not competent to receive independence, that we are children who cannot play adult games. The riots, mutinies, civil wars, and general disorders among our neighbors are cited as proof that Bwagania will go to pieces as soon as it is independent, that a small clique of elite will rule, with only its own selfish goals in mind.

"Well, people of Bwagania, that's not going to happen," he went on. "We're simply not going to go to pieces. If any of you want to do that, do it now. Here in front of me. Then you will see what your king is really like." There was a roar of laughter and applause. The crowd accepted the challenge. They loved the king's directness as much as they appreciated his sense of fun. At that moment there was no one who would have gone against the king. Bwaga VI turned and grinned blandly at his son M'Taga, who looked back coolly at his father, a smile on his lips.

"My fellow citizens, let us act like true sons and daughters of ancient Bwagania. Let us be a model for Africa." The king's noble words rolled into the stadium with Shakespearean pomp, achieving the effect he wanted. There was dead silence.

"Let us live as free people, in complete peace and harmony. Let our government work for all the people, not for a favored few. Let us respect the foreigners in our midst as we wish them to respect us. We admit we need their help for years to come—not because we are uninstructed or incompetent, but because we have much work to do and too few trained people to do it. Our French friends did not go far enough with the training programs in foreign technology . . . and that's the only area where we are lacking."

He closed this sentence with a shout, and the crowd yelled its agreement that Bwaganians were capable of any heights. "Work as hard as you can, my children," said the king. "Learn as much as you can. Those who can, teach others. Each one who reads must teach others to do so. Those who can see must lead the blind, and those who can hear must be the ears for those who cannot. The strong must support the weak. Those who see a crime must report it. The brave will stand in front of the fearful. In this way we will go forward together and the unknown will no longer cause us to shiver."

Then the king laid a curse on those who might break his commands. In a loud, deep singsong voice that rolled up and down the scale in traditional tones, using traditional words, he repeated a complete litany of don'ts.

No Bwaganian could cheat, lie, steal, maim, murder, or eat another person. The king called down the Leopard to strike infractors with its dreadful claws, and a chill went through the crowd. The Leopard was a symbol of vengeance and discipline throughout central Africa. Its claws, simulated by sharp steel grips used by witch doctors, have deeply scarred numberless dead victims, but the people believed in the legend and its curse. It was tradition that the monarch could invoke the Leopard, a terrifying threat to the believers.

Even M'Taga felt a cold shiver at the ancient invocation, and a dozen young Bwaganian men—nobles, officers, intellectuals—turned to watch the prince. They, too, wondered how their secret leader would react to his father's words. They studied him for telltale signs. A change of expression, a facial color or body language. They depended on him for their lives from now on.

But the prince was an apt pupil of his father. He hid his reactions and sat as immobile and placid as a Buddha.

The king, who rarely missed anything, spotted eight of the young men scattered in the VIP stands. Meanwhile, he had a job to do. The people wanted a perfect day; he would ensure they got it. There was no room for concern about tomorrow. Bwaga VI closed his speech with a string of hilarious stories about the confusion and disorder in other African countries as they were given independence. Guinea, Senegal, Upper Volta, Nigeria, Cameroon, the Central African Republic, and the Congo all came in for anecdotes. The king left out the pain and bloodshed and concentrated on the amusing. His gift for telling tales was inspired, and by the end of his speech the Bwaganian crowd was roaring with laughter, even though with each story there was a lesson to be learned, a parable to be understood, taken home, repeated.

The king turned the ceremonies back to the tipsy MC, who passed a troop of Bwaganian hunters in review, a colorful lot in monkey, lion, or leopard fur headbands and wristbands, spears, cowrie-shell necklaces, and long bows. Then Prince M'Taga spoke. He gave a brief, witty, and well-delivered speech wishing the nation and the people well for the future. He avoided political subjects, which was not his usual style. The king noted this, for he had expected M'Taga to give the crowd some idea of how he would conduct himself as prime minister. The omission was sinister, indicating M'Taga was under pressure, perhaps expected by his coconspirators to show a distance between himself and the king. Perhaps M'Taga was a reluctant leader, the king thought, clutching at straws. Oh, if only that were true! Just as quickly, he jerked himself back to the reality of RED SNOW.

It was time to swear in the new cabinet members, including the prince. The justices of the supreme court lined up facing the king. The royal ceremonial ax was placed on a folded Bwaganian flag, in front of the king. The crowd was silent, and the chief justice swore in each cabinet member in turn, ten of them. The king took a salute from each in turn.

The last was M'Taga, prime minister. In a sudden move that stunned the onlookers, the king took the microphone from the chief justice after the legal phrases had been read that bound the prince to his office. His son's hand held in his own, high for all the crowd to see, the king chanted:

"May the Leopard of our ancestors hear you swear most solemnly that you will perform this office with utter devotion to your king and your country."

The king shouted the oath with such force and apparent goodwill that the prince automatically shouted, "I do," and the crowd roared and stamped its joy.

The same dozen young men who had checked for M'Taga's reactions when the king first invoked the Leopard checked him again. The king spotted two more, for a total of ten. He waited for a few minutes, then signaled to the chamberlain to come over. He whispered the ten names into M'Bouyé's ear. The chamberlain knew them all.

He nodded when the king said: "I want a one-page summary on each man, including as many of his friends as can be identified. At the bottom of each page tell me who would avenge him if he were murdered." The chamberlain was a pro. He smiled as if the king had just shared a joke with him.

Gitabwanga: the baobabs—
1700 hours,1 January

The king's buffet was a huge success. There was food and drink enough for all who came. It was cool under the giant trees, and a breeze stirred the paper tablecloths. There were large bowls of all kinds of native foods, endless plates of dried sandwiches, edges curled and butter melted. Hundreds of gallons of warm juices and beer, including the famous Bwaganian sorghum beer in paper cups, each with its busy little tiara of flies. Monkeys jumped and ran between the baobabs and the tables, excited by the crowd, snitching food from the tables and from children's hands. The crowd was festive and tolerant, and the monkeys weren't chased away.

The king, Prince M'Taga, and dozens of officials wandered through the crowd, talking and laughing with them. The diplomatic corps followed, some amused by the scene, some aghast.

Later, in the gathering dusk, the king's three great bands of royal drummers met in a field between the stadium and the palace, the rattle of their sticks on the edges of the drums setting off the thunder of the skins. Chanters from various parts of the kingdom sprang into the circles of drummers and chanted folk stories describing events of ancient Bwagania. The smoke, the torchlight, the dark, the sweat, the flagrant and generous smells of the crowd combined in a fantastic and eerie image of old Bwagania.

"Linda, look." Mark pointed with his chin to Pyotr and Olga, standing a short distance away. Pyotr was watching the scene with a smile, but Olga had her nose wrinkled and a scowl on her face.

"That's the essence of those two," Mark commented. "He likes it because it's different and everyone's happy. She thinks it's noisy, smelly, undisciplined."

"She'll always be unhappy," commented Linda.

Gitabwanga: the royal palace—1900 hours, 1 January

It was the kind of party the king loved to host. His Royal Highness King Bwaga VI's Independence-Day Reception, as it was billed on the invitation cards, was to bring together everyone who mattered in Bwagania: senior government officials, French and Bwaganian army officers, the diplomatic corps, United Nations officials, businessmen, clergy, academics, airline representatives, and leading ranchers. It would include the first official gathering of the diplomatic corps and the United Nations emissaries. Bwaga VI planned to introduce them to each other formally, "to open the season," he told Muffie with a laugh.

The king's plan to have Muffie, who had not been deemed appropriate to sit beside him in the stadium, act as his hostess at the reception had been opposed by Chamberlain M'Bouyé. But Bwaga VI was firm on this one. The palace was, after all, his dung hill, he told M'Bouyé, and grinned when the chamberlain winced at the crude term.

All the palace windows and french doors were open. Smoke from the torches in the grounds drifted in and with it the smell of the hundreds of cook fires lit by Bwaganians camped around the city. The lake seemed especially still and haunting for the occasion, a full moon reflected on its surface.

The first guests were prompt, the receiving line ready on time, Chamberlain M'Bouyé first in the line, to announce the guests. Next to him was the French ambassador, invited to receive as a courtesy because he was former governor-general. After him, stiff in a cutaway and ascot, Prince M'Taga in the dual roles of crown prince and prime minister. Finally, the king in a fresh white uniform that gleamed with brass buttons, medals, and sashes. A little apart, a step behind the king, not in the receiving line, was Muffie—at her charming best tonight, her lively face and slender figure perfectly shown by a form-fitting white evening dress.

At seven-thirty Chamberlain M'Bouyé clapped his hands and announced in a booming voice: "His Majesty invites the diplomatic corps to join him for a few minutes in the state dining room. Other guests will please just enjoy the party until we return."

The diplomatic corps trooped into the state dining room, members asking each other what this was all about. Nobody knew. When the doors closed and silence fell in the large room, the king welcomed them, asked a special guest to step forward, and told the group:

"This is the Indian ambassador from Kenya. There is no Indian embassy here yet, so he drove more than two thousand kilometers just to attend our reception. I invited him because of my respect for the memory of Dr. Mahatma Gandhi, who, like me, opposed colonialism without using violence."

The French ambassador rolled his eyes up and asked God to forgive the king, who had profited far more from the French mastery of Bwagania than he had suffered from it.

"Ladies and gentlemen," the king went on, ignoring the Frenchman's act. "I present his excellency Jawaharlal Kumar."

The Indian was a tiny, impish man with a twinkle. He thought of himself as a gentle man of great wisdom, inheritor of the quill of Gandhi. He beamed at the circle of diplomats and inclined his head benignly. When the nodding and bowing had ceased, the Indian cleared his throat importantly.

"His Majesty has very kindly given us this moment together before the festivities continue so that I can tell you a truly wonderful story." He spoke in English, knowing no French.

The king understood English and looked surprised. He had intended only to introduce the Indian. But the assembled diplomats seemed interested. Anyway, there was no stopping the Indian.

"As you know, Bwagania is throbbing with the thrill of its independence," the Indian said. "I drove here through hundreds of miles of Bwaganian countryside. To my amazement and great pleasure, the name of our prime minister was on every tongue. As soon as the people saw the Indian flag on my car, they shouted our beloved prime minister's name . . . Gandhi, Gandhi."

The king thought: Gandhi? My peasants don't know about Gandhi, neither Mahatma nor Indira. I'd better listen to this.

The Indian had stopped, giving them a solemn stare. "I was so moved that I sent a telegram to Prime Minister Gandhi telling how much she is loved in Africa. She will be thrilled."

Everyone in the room who understood English—most of them—understood at once what had happened. The people were using the Bwaganian word for independence: *n'gaanti*. The Indian had mistaken it for Gandhi. There was consternation.

Mark stole a quick look at Pyotr and silently congratulated

the Soviet: He had understood and was shaking with muffled laughter, like many of those in the group.

The Spanish ambassador was laughing openly. The French envoy's eyes were streaming with the effort of not laughing. The American and British ambassadors were grinning broadly. Soviet ambassador Raspatov, his DCM, and the military attaché, smiled politely, but clearly it had gone past them.

The king had caught on and was doubled over, a diplomatic coughing fit covering his wild laughter. Finally, His Majesty stood erect, grinning broadly, his tummy heaving with smothered gasps.

Jawaharlal Kumar surveyed the group with intense pleasure. His story had been a great hit. He perceived the red faces as showing honest emotion, the streaming eyes as shared happiness, the grins and honking laughter as open enjoyment of how Gandhi was so widely loved in Africa.

No one told the Indian what the natives had been shouting, or that—far from identifying the car as Indian—they probably were wondering if it was the vehicle bringing them their independence. Independence, many believed, would come as a basket of valuable goods, in an airplane or a car from Europe.

The king had a statement to make. As the diplomats quieted and watched him, he said:

"I will be brief. We are a small country, perhaps amusing to the larger countries. Most of my people can neither read nor write. They do not worship a god known to you, and many are animist. They are noisy, poor in material things, ignorant, often dirty in appearance, and vengeful."

He looked at the ring of surprised faces. It was his second serious statement today, blunt and out of character.

"We may never be historically important, but we are people, just like you. Our ambitions are the same, and when our freedom was taken from us, we suffered just as you would. We want to be taken seriously, just as you do. When you laugh at us, we are as dismayed as you would be if people laughed at you. But we will not have developed bombs to kill a million people in a millisecond."

The Indian ambassador applauded briefly, thinking that he

could not have said it better himself. The Spanish ambassador, a royal count and a compulsive big game hunter, was daydreaming as he stood there. He had asked for, and got, Bwagania rather than a plush Western capital, which his rank could have secured, because he loved to hunt. He had spent his life at the top and had no fear of being thought of as a second-class diplomat.

Right now the Spaniard was staring at the king with a fixed, piercing gaze. He saw the king as a leopard crouched in a thorn tree. The leopard was in profile, his chest fully visible in the open sights of the Spaniard's rifle. Wind, ten kilometers per hour from the left. Distance, 175 meters. He sighted carefully, a shoulder shot. The spot he meant to strike was, in his actual stare, the center of the king's forehead, just above the eyes. Slowly, he squeezed the trigger, not breathing now that he was making the kill.

King Bwaga VI noted the concentration on the Spaniard's face. He was sure that he'd found an ally in him. They were both of royal blood.

At that moment Muffie burst in through the closed doors, alive with excitement, doing her best to be a perfect hostess, and her bright and tinkly voice broke across the group like a wave on a beach.

"Come, Your Majesty, ladies and gentlemen, you've denied us your presence long enough. We can not do without our king and his diplomatic corps."

There was a moment of silence as the corps wondered if she had overstepped, but the king smiled and said to them: "Tell your governments what I said," and led the way into the great salon. They danced and drank and ate his superb food for the rest of the night.

They had no choice. The king had ordered the palace gates locked. No guest could leave until dawn. Long before then, the less intrepid spirits faltered and could be seen lying on couches in the hallways and on the lanais of the palace. The Indian ambassador slept like a little mouse, curled in a huge armchair in the main hall. The Spanish ambassador was an early dropout and found an upstairs bedroom, where he locked himself in and slept until noon the next day.

Olga and Linda lay in deck chairs on a palace verandah, Mark and Pyotr close by, sitting side by side with their backs against a pillar. At times all four dozed as the long night stretched out and the drinks took effect. At times they chatted about life in Bwagania, in the USSR and in the U.S., the rift between the two Soviets temporarily closed by the subject matter.

Olga, fascinated by the king's two speeches, had suddenly become aware that Bwagania contained real people. She wanted to know more about them and their king. She ignored Pyotr's efforts to answer her questions and concentrated on Mark and Linda.

"This Leopard, does it really kill people? What is it? Can the king use it?"

"I don't think it's more than a myth," answered Mark. "But here in Bwagania, if you believe you'll be killed by it, it seems that you are liable to be. Many Africans have died from the fear of it. All the king has to do is make the threat."

"The king's strange. Does he really love his people?"

"He seems to, and they believe it."

"He can't last. Monarchies have to go."

"What would you do here?" asked Linda.

"Socialism, of course."

"It can't work, Olga. Neither can capitalism."

"Why not?" asked Pyotr.

"The extended family," said Mark. "Its mechanics won't allow any real accumulation of capital. Those who earn have to cough up whatever's needed for their relatives—no matter how many they are or how much they need. They literally camp in the compound, and the earner has to support them."

"That's true," said Pyotr. "One of the ministers told me that the more he earns, the less he has. The family takes it all. He's got over fifty of them in his compound now."

"Which minister, Pyotr?" Mark was laughing. Pyotr gave him a finger.

Olga went on: "How can anyone love a king? He didn't work for his job, he was born into it."

"Born into it," said Mark, "then trained for it. He's better than a lot of European leaders. If Bwaga VI wanted to, he could screw this country. But he doesn't want to, so his people are lucky."

"Why doesn't he want to?" asked Olga.

"Maybe he thinks things are okay as they are," replied Linda, grinning. "I think they already have socialism, Olga: From each according to his ability . . ."

"But there's no discipline; they never do what they're supposed to."

"Not in your terms," said Mark. "But from their viewpoint, there are plenty of rules. Anyway, I don't see any reason anyone'd try to change the system here."

Olga snorted: "They'd be much better under communism."

"Why peddle something that doesn't work?" asked Linda bluntly, looking at Olga, but hoping to elicit a reaction from the man running Red Snow.

Olga shook her head in disbelief but said nothing.

Mark watched Pyotr out of the corner of his eye. The Soviet was grinning, nodding his head slowly, obviously enjoying Olga's discomfiture but, after a while, frowning. He seemed to be pondering the question, perhaps feeling obligated to respond.

But in fact there was turmoil in Pyotr's head: He could find no safe way to say that he thought Linda had a point. He was silent.

Gitabwanga: the king's bedroom—1330 hours, 2 January

King Bwaga VI had a deep-toned, powerful snore that was famous in the palace. At their peak, his snores sounded like a tuba and there was no doubt anywhere in the palace that the king was asleep.

Usually, he slept in his own bedroom, the largest of the ten bedrooms in the palace. Muffie joined him there most nights, and sometimes for an after-lunch nap. Sometimes, not very often, the king slept in another bedroom to avoid waking Muffie. Sometimes they slept in her room, at the other end of the bedroom wing. No matter where the couple slept, the palace servants and guards knew just where the king was.

The king and Muffie had lunched early and had drunk a bottle of wine between them. When they got to his bedroom, Muffie went to sleep right away. The king was a fastidious man who always brushed his teeth and showered before he made love. Then he walked around the bed and kissed Muffie.

She stirred slightly in her sleep, and her scent came to him. Bwaga VI leaned over again, gently nibbled her ear and stroked her cheek. He slipped in beside her, firmly erect, and slowly Muffie came awake. His hand between her legs stirred her and she opened for him like a flower.

The king slept afterward, his snores reverberating off the walls and ceiling. Muffie was wide awake now and wanted more of her beloved Bwaga VI. She whispered her love in his ear, but he was too deeply asleep. She lay beside him, her head on his shoulder, wide awake and imagining him on top of her again. The curtains in the open french doorway shifted gently in the breeze.

It was then that Muffie saw the spear, a cruel barbed point on a dark wooden shaft. At first she thought nothing of it, since there was a crossed set of them on the wall near the door. But when it moved she sat up, wondering why, still unaware of danger.

Her movement provoked the attacker, and he leaped out from behind the curtain, silently aiming the spear at Bwaga VI. Muffie rolled on top of him, protecting him, shrieking his name: "Bwaga, Bwaga, look out . . ."

The spear struck her in the back, and the barbed tip bit deeply into her lungs. Even as the pain caught her, she heard the assilant grunt with the effort.

The king woke instantly and reached for the revolver under his pillow. The assailant broke the shaft of the spear trying to jerk it out of Muffie. She writhed with the pain, her arms reaching uselessly behind her to take out the spear, pink froth bubbling from her mouth. It gave the king time to fire twice into the man's chest.

The room was full of palace guards and servants within seconds. A guardsman, trying to help, grabbed the broken shaft and pulled the spear out of Muffie. He was a large, strong man, but even so it came out with difficulty.

The barbs tore open her lung and heart, and what had been a serious wound she could have survived with careful treatment became a mortal one. Muffie gave a long scream, her grip on the king's hands like a clamp, blood pouring from her mouth, and then she died, shuddering with agony, her eyes staring into those of Bwaga VI.

After the two bodies had been taken from his room, the king allowed himself a few minutes of private grief. Sorrow and pity for Muffie, who had laid down her life for him, and grief for himself. He had neither Muffie nor his son; the future looked bleak, lonely, without reward. He wept for Muffie and for himself, and then quickly his mind turned to the imperatives of self-protection.

He quickly met with Chamberlain M'Bouyé and the Sicilian. The assassin was a palace guardsman, they reported, a twenty-year-old, newly hired, and a distant cousin of the king's. It was routine to employ poor relatives of the royal family in the palace.

The young man's body, naked, muscular, was laid out on the main kitchen table. Bwaga VI stared at the dark face with a hint of beard, the clenched teeth with the pink tongue caught between them, and the yellow, staring eyes. It was infuriating that he'd died with no chance for questioning. Why had a young relative been willing to die to kill his king? Why had Muffie been willing to give her life to save his? Two young lives gone for opposite reasons, and an old man survived. He shook his head, again close to tears.

"We'll find out what this was about, sire." M'Bouyé rubbed the king's shoulder. "His family will know something. They'll talk." His voice was deep, hard, and he looked meaningfully at the Sicilian.

"He was not only my cousin. He was M'Taga's."

M'Bouyé caught the implication. "I hope there's no connection. In any event, don't let the heat of this moment cause you to act too fast, something you may later regret."

The king forced an unhappy smile. "All right, Jean Prosper. I'll wait until we know."

Then the king turned to the Sicilian: "Do an 'African interrogation,' hunter. Find the right hut. Go in at midnight, when everyone is asleep. Wake them with bright lights, in the king's name. Have your dogs snarling at their bedside. Don't touch them, but give them no time to think, no room to move. Come back as soon as you've finished, and come back with the name of the instigator of this." He gestured at the young man's body.

The Sicilian nodded. The king's name was usually all it took. They would talk. Their village was only two hours away from Gitabwanga.

"It shall be, Your Majesty. Tonight." He wanted to put his arm around the king's shoulders and comfort him, but protocol forbade it. The Sicilian was a friend, confidant, bodyguard at times, an honorary officer of the palace guard, and the royal hunter, but he was still an employee, not a relative. He was sorry that Muffie had died. He'd had her twice, in silent (and it turned out very pleasant) protest against the fact that the king had slept numberless times with the Sicilian's own wife. His conquest of Muffie had wiped the books clean so far as the Sicilian was concerned, and his loyalty to the king was intact. He would avenge Muffie: once for the king and once for himself.

Before the Sicilian drove away, he whispered to M'Bouyé: "It might be useful to let no word of this get out. Swear all the palace servants, gardeners, and guards to silence. Then see who tries to find out what happened."

M'Bouyé nodded, a hungry grin on his face. He remembered his trial period with Muffie and the happiness she had brought Bwaga VI. "We'll find out."

N'Sabaré: Robinet 5—0020 hours, 3 January

It took the Sicilian much of the afternoon to locate the assassin's family huts. They were in a small compound, walled by wooden fencing to keep out predators, near the tiny village of N'Sabaré. The village had a crude but serviceable water system, and the compound was near tap No. 5: that was its address.

From dusk on, the Sicilian waited in a rocky gulch a mile from the village. He could see the lights in the compound from a ledge on the rock face, and he saw the last one go out at about ten. He waited another hour for them to fall asleep. Then he roused his two German shepherds and began the descent toward the compound. He could see clearly in the bright moonlight, and he skirted the village until he could approach against the breeze. His footsteps were soft, and the dogs were trained for silent hunting. He carried a .38 revolver in his belt, and a sjambok—a short, thick whip made of cured rhinoceros hide.

At twenty minutes after midnight, he opened the compound gate and left one dog there on guard. No one would pass that gateway in either direction while the dog lived. A few strides and the Sicilian was in the main hut, his flashlight sweeping around the single large room. There was the usual tidy array of food-storage baskets on shelves against the walls, neat piles of clothing on a wooden chest, and half a dozen well-used sandals on the floor; in the center, a wide bed holding an older man with a young wife beside him, both fast asleep. There were no guards, no other people in the hut. He listened briefly to the rustling of insects, sniffed the pungent smell of wood smoke mixed with old leather and sweat, and decided to find the senior wife and bring her in. He left the second dog on guard in the main hut, picked up the old man's spear and his banana knife, and headed for the next biggest hut. There he found the oldest wife, asleep.

Quickly, he had the senior wife awake and stumbling into the main hut. He stuck the spear into the ceiling of reeds, threw the banana knife into a corner away from the door, and gave a sharp command.

The second dog began to bark. The noise in the little hut was like gunshots. Then the Sicilian stopped the dog, and cracking the sjambok repeatedly on the wooden chest, he began to shout at the older man until he awoke, looking blearily into a powerful flashlight. The younger wife stared into the light, fear in her eyes. The senior wife, her arm gripped by the Sicilian, trembled and screamed, a high, thin scream that went on and on like a steam whistle.

"In the king's name," the Sicilian roared in Bwaganian. "Up, on your feet, quickly. I am the king's hunter, here on the king's business. Up, get up!" He quickly had the older couple standing in front of him, shaking with fear, completely rattled by this noisy, official invasion.

"Your young son, Daoud, made an attempt to murder the king. Why? Who was behind it? Hurry, the dog is hungry." The dog growled.

The younger wife had run out of the hut, and all around he could hear the compound coming alive. Some younger men and boys came into the main hut, carrying lighted lanterns. But the Sicilian paid no attention to them. He had no fear, and they could sense that. They stood in the doorway, paralyzed, eyes wide, bodies swaying, watching the dog and the Sicilian. Now and then they whispered to each other, like the wind in high grass, but no one threatened him.

As the drumbeat of the Sicilian's shouts ground them down, the older couple pled for a moment to talk. He gave it.

"What has happened? Where is Daoud?"

"First tell me why he tried to kill Bwaga VI. Was it his idea, or did you put him up to it?"

"No, no! We would never do such a thing, the king is our cousin. Daoud would never do it. Never!"

"But he did. And you will have to answer for it. Now, tell me the truth. Who was behind it?"

"We know nothing . . . nothing. Truly, nothing . . ."

"Was it a European? Answer quickly, I don't have all night. Quickly. Was it a European?"

A voice from the doorway: "He much admired a European, he said that to us. A white man."

The Sicilian spun, caught a young man full in the face with a beam of light. "Who? His name? Quickly."

He kept up the insistent pressure, but it was hopeless. No one knew his name. No one had seen this European. The Sicilian tried one last time:

"Was he French? Do you know that?"

"I remember that Daoud said he was an older man, and his French is not the same as other French people."

"What else can you remember?" The flashlight swept across them all, but it was clear that he could learn no more from the family. Daoud hadn't been home for almost a year.

To the Sicilian the case was solved, his mission accomplished. The unknown European had to be Pierre Schacht. Schacht, an enemy of the king, had somehow convinced Daoud to attempt an assassination.

The Sicilian told them: "I will explain to the king that this family tried to help." He whistled up his dogs and left.

Gitabwanga: the royal palace—0615 hours, 3 January

The Sicilian spent the rest of the night in the quarters of the palace guard. Shortly after six A.M. the king stopped snoring. He was awake, the Sicilian was told. He went to the king's second-floor bedroom, knocked, and went in.

Bwaga VI was at a small desk in the room, wearing trousers and a dressing gown, his feet bare. He greeted the hunter with raised eyebrows.

"It was Pierre Schacht, sire. A European, they said, an older man whose French is not the way French people speak. They didn't know his name, but that's clear enough to me."

The king nodded. "Yes, it's clear. What about M'Taga? Did they know anything about him? Was he involved?"

"They didn't know, sire. Daoud hadn't been home for close to a year. Why would Schacht try that without M'Taga's knowledge? Has M'Taga tried to find out anything?"

The king's face was as unhappy as the Sicilian had ever seen it: "I'm certain he did, hunter. He telephoned yesterday, in midafternoon. I answered the phone myself, because I wanted to hear what anyone who called would say. M'Taga seemed surprised: 'Oh, Papa, it's you! How are you?' Nothing you can really put your finger on. But like the Schacht thing, too much is at stake for us to make a mistake. Intuition must guide us."

"Then shall we go ahead, sire? If so, it had better be right away. This evening."

"One more day, hunter. Tomorrow evening. Our own private plan. Let no one know about it. I'll appoint a witness."

"A witness, Your Majesty?"

"Of course. A witness to testify it was Schacht."

Gitabwanga: Mark's office—1900 hours, 3 January

Mark looked at the two reports again, pleased that Paul Passatu had managed to get them to him so quickly. He had found them in a dead drop that he and Paul had arranged in the cathedral grounds: a hollow tile high up in a wall, hidden by a bush, in an unused corner of the gardens.

The main report was dated 3 January and it spelled out the attempt to assassinate the king. It was printed in Paul's casual lettering in secret writing between the lines of a love letter from "Paula" to "Jean."

The second report was also dated January 3. It was brief, quickly scribbled on a small piece of paper. Paul had done it quite well with his version of French double-talk:

> Mon amour,
>
> According to boss, it was caused by Tofi, almost certainly with her son's accord. Rather than take any risks, the timetable will be moved up. See you tonight.
>
> Your darling Paula

The missing element was a logical reason for Schacht to incite a cousin of the king's to jump the gun on Red Snow. It didn't fit the pattern. It put Red Snow in jeopardy.

Gitabwanga: Bwaga Airport—1420 hours, 3 January

When he reached Paris, General Vladimir Fedorovich Ossilenko was already papered—in alias documentation—as Gleb Uspensky, Soviet foreign ministry analyst of African affairs. With tongue in cheek, he had chosen the name Gleb Uspensky, after a leftist acquaintance of Anton Chekhov's. The general had a sense of humor, and he liked to test the cultural level of others. He was fair, and enjoyed being tested himself.

When SSR headquarters cabled details of the only Soviet

visa issued for Bwagania for the week and the arrival data, François decided to be at the airport. Since independence, he was no longer chief of the Bwaganian Sûreté. Instead, he had new dual roles: principal adviser to the Bwaganian Sûreté, and SSR chef de poste under cover of the French embassy.

He explained to the Bwaganian Surêté inspector on duty who Gleb Uspensky was. Luckily, the inspector had read Chekhov in French. "I have no idea who this man may be," said François, "but he's probably not using his true name." The inspector nodded, enjoying the moment. It was much better being advised by the French than being employed by them. They seemed more human after independence.

François went up to the balcony to watch. After a few minutes, he saw Pyotr walk into the large main hall of the terminal. Petrov was alone and frequently looked at his watch. The flight was half an hour late.

François went into an empty office and called Mark: "We've a Soviet visitor, Mark. One Gleb Uspensky. Just arriving now. When could you look at his photo?"

Mark laughed. "Gleb Uspensky, eh? Born in Moscow?"

"Aren't they all. Yes. Title: African analyst, ministry of foreign affairs. Petrov's meeting him."

A thoughtful pause, then Mark's voice again. "How about my place at four? I'll have my Chekhov primer ready for our meeting." François grinned as he turned back to the scene below. It was good to work with an educated man.

When Gleb Uspensky got to the immigration booth, the Bwaganian inspector was there.

"Passport, please."

"Certainly." Ossilenko spoke fairly good French, with a strong Russian accent.

"Gleb Uspensky, eh? Who's your conservative friend, Mr. Uspensky?"

It was so unexpected that Ossilenko burst out laughing. An African who'd read Chekhov? Not possible. The man was coal black and looked as if he couldn't read or write. But he could: He could also understand and feel human vibrations, and he was not amused.

"All right, Gleb Uspensky, what is your real name?" The general came down to earth quickly. He had no diplomatic immunity. He was on an official passport, not a diplomatic one. He looked at the African and realized that the man was busily photographing all the pages of his passport.

"Well, Uspensky, I'm waiting for your reply. Have you forgotten?" This was quickly getting out of hand. What had started as a lark was backfiring.

"That is my name. My parents named me that in honor of Anton Chekhov." It was a prepared reply, but the Bwaganian was irritated by this Russian who'd laughed at him.

"I don't believe you. It sounds unlikely. Come with me." He motioned brusquely with his head toward a door marked OFFICIALS ONLY.

Ossilenko had no choice. He was in a foreign country, without immunity. Pyotr stepped up to intervene, saying:

"I'm from the Soviet embassy. This man is an official visitor from our foreign ministry. Our ambassador is waiting for him." Pyotr sounded serious, but the inspector was not swayed.

"We have the right to question visitors, except those with diplomatic status. So please stand aside and wait until we have finished." He brushed Pyotr aside and requested the general to identify his luggage. Then general, inspector, and luggage disappeared behind the OFFICIALS ONLY door.

François de la Maison appeared at Pyotr's elbow.

"Anything I can do, Colonel Petrov?"

Pyotr was rattled by the use of his KGB title. A blunt reminder that he was being watched in Bwagania.

"No thank you," he said. "A protest would do no good."

François shrugged and went back to the balcony. He stood there for thirty minutes, watching. Petrov got more and more anxious. He could think of nothing to do but pace up and down. He couldn't leave or go through that door. A phone call to the embassy would do no good and would make him look ineffective. He could only wait, his belly hurting with tension. Ossilenko would blame him, undoubtedly.

An hour later Ossilenko came out of the door, his face bright red with anger. He ignored Pyotr's hand, said not one word in reply to his greeting, and simply motioned to Pyotr to pick up his heaviest suitcase. In the car, he burst out:

"I suppose you arranged that little farce, Petrov?"

It was so unfair as to be alarming. Pyotr wondered if Ossilenko was losing his marbles. If the general wanted to play games with a phony name, he had to be ready for things like this to happen.

Aloud, he said: "Of course I didn't arrange it, general. That's an outrageous idea. What happened in there?"

"Well, he did pay some attention to my name," Ossilenko conceded gruffly. "He looked carefully at everything I had, my notes, money, papers, clothes. Looking for initials other than G.U., I suppose. All the while he asked me my real name. Naturally, I stuck to Uspensky. None of his business what my real name is. What impertinence. I never suspected Bwagania had people who've read the Russian classics."

Ossilenko didn't tell Pyotr that the African had looked with obvious scorn at the general's pornographic books and magazines, bought in Paris. And his corsets, made in London. But he'd missed the killing devices.

"What news from Moscow, Comrade General?"

"Time for that when we get to your office," Ossilenko growled. "After I've seen Ambassador Raspatov."

The rest of the drive to the Soviet compound passed in uneasy silence as the general took in the sights, and Pyotr drove as carefully as he could.

Gitabwanga: Mark's house— 1615 hours, 3 January

Mark looked at the prints of Gleb Uspensky's passport and the new airport shots. There was no mistaking that face.

"That's KGB General Vladimir Fedorovich Ossilenko! A big fish, François. He's the fourth- or fifth-ranking officer in the KGB. He's also a cousin of the chairman's, so he's got close ties all the way up. He's here to investigate Schacht's CIA links, I'll bet, and see what's up with Red Snow."

François whistled. "A KGB general! What an honor for my poste. Paris will be impressed, unless they know already."

"I'm sure they know by now. They've had time to look at his passport photo. Of course, if you cable them first you'll look very alert." They grinned at each other.

"He listed the hotel Las Palomas as where he'll stay. That's unusual. Normally they stay inside the compound. I wonder if he's got some plan to go around Petrov."

Mark nodded: "Probably. He'll be ready for surveillance by white men, but hasn't much experience with Africans. Is your Sûreté group ready for something like this?"

"I think so, Mark. Some of them have several years of practice. They're good at melting into the background and changing clothes as they move around. They're okay."

"We'll also need a close watch on Schacht and on Petrov. Do you need any help there?"

"Not with Petrov. But Schacht is a different story. I can handle him around Madame Petarde's, but maybe if you have a really good man, he could lock onto him if he strays too far from the Hôtel du Lac. Our people have lost him too many times. He's very good. You never know if he's slipped away from you on purpose or by accident." François looked a bit unhappy that he had to admit this.

"You know about the attempt on the king?"

"I just heard it. I've no details yet."

"Any idea who was behind it?" asked Mark.

"Not yet, but it'll come out soon enough."

"I'll try to take care of Schacht, then," said Mark. They shook hands and François left, wondering if in fact the Bwaganian teams would be able to stay locked onto Ossilenko and Petrov.

Gitabwanga: the KGB *rezidentura*—
1630 hours, 3 January

Immediately on his arrival at the Soviet compound, Ossilenko paid a courtesy call on the ambassador. Anna Iosevna was sitting at her desk, looking as radiant and full of youth as she'd ever looked and Ossilenko was captivated by her at once. She was prettier, with a finer figure, than he had believed possible. The photos hadn't done her justice.

The general was too experienced a campaigner to display any emotion, however, and went on into the ambassador's office, where he greeted Raspatov with the routine high-level Kremlin statements. Before they settled down to talk, he did a brutal thing: He dismissed Pyotr as if he were a flunky. "I'll catch up with you in the office later on, Petrov." Pyotr left, his ears burning red.

Ossilenko gave the ambassador news of mutual friends, added some recent insider Kremlin anecdotes, and lastly gave him some words on recent foreign ministry policy changes. Then the general set about his main purpose. He wanted some sort of complaint about Petrov from Raspatov.

When the conversation was over, Raspatov had no idea that he'd lodged an official complaint against Petrov. He might, if pushed, recall a mild objection to Petrov's frequent hangovers, but it was very mild, really only to humor Ossilenko. Yes, it was true, Petrov sometimes smelled like a brewery, but it didn't interfere with his work.

Now, sitting in Petrov's chair in the *rezidentura,* it was time for Ossilenko to unload. Pyotr had hoped for messages of greetings from friends in Moscow Center, some kind words of encouragement from senior KGB officers, insights into the latest successes of the KGB in other areas, and maybe even a pat on the shoulder from Ossilenko. When that was over, they would sit back and go over this strange Pierre Schacht incident . . . as two senior officers discussing a problem. What actually happened was a shock to Pyotr, as brutal a blow as a slap in the face.

A diplomatic pouch had arrived marked for Ossilenko's eyes only and been held in the embassy mail room until Ossilenko retrieved it on his way from Raspatov's office. He opened it without speaking, one eye on Pyotr, who began to feel uneasy.

"Petrov, I thought you were a bright maverick. Now I find that you're a stupid fool. You have no idea of personal security, of ethics or morality, and no common sense. You violate every instruction given to you, and even Ambassador Raspatov is sick of your hangovers and your idleness. He just told me so himself." Ossilenko had no idea that

Pyotr had begun to think of the ambassador as a father figure.

Pyotr was horrified. He had been betrayed. He sat mutely, looking at his knees. He shook his head.

"Smelling like a brewery, and an idle attitude. What a performance! And to think, the chairman trusted you to perform above average."

"Only once or twice, General. I think that's all. The ambassador surely didn't make an official complaint."

"He did. But that's not the worst of it."

Pyotr looked blank.

"Here's the worst of it, Petrov." Ossilenko pulled out the large color prints and a transcript of conversations between Pyotr and Anna Iosevna.

It took a moment for the truth to sink in, and then the shock was total and deafening. Pyotr just sat there, sick with horror. So the chairman had unleashed his dogs, and the charge was to be treason. No doubt, as the transcript was in English. All Pyotr could think of was that the KGB had pulled this stunt in order to put him away. At first he only half understood when Ossilenko explained: "Whatever went on in that room, Petrov, was photographed and taped. It went to the CIA by the most rapid means. Our operational apartment, which you use for your own sexual escapades, is totally unsafe. Every time your silly mouth opens, to talk or to make love, it becomes part of the CIA files. How näive can a senior officer be?"

Now Pyotr understood. "The CIA did this, not KGB?"

"Exactly, Petrov. Your opposite number, Mark Cameron, did this to you. He must be laughing his head off. You make me ill!"

"Then we have an excellent penetration of CIA?"

"Right again, Petrov. Slow, but right. Perhaps you will recall mistaking me for a Nazi officer?" He said it with heavy sarcasm.

"Of course, General. To my everlasting shame." Pyotr was truly contrite.

"You didn't know it, but I was carrying a briefcase full of that man's take. Our agent's reports. We very nearly put you away on suspicion, I can tell you. Now you have to know about that agent, because we're going to use this for our own purposes. We're going to feed disinformation to the CIA through that apartment. We're going to keep you here to do that, although the chairman wanted to bring you back in disgrace. He's furious at you, with your picture in the nude pasted on every wall in the CIA, each wart on your arse plain to see."

Petrov sighed, trembling all over. So he was going to stay in Gitabwanga! That was by now a relief, compared to the threat of a treason charge.

"Another reason you must know about our agent in the CIA, Petrov, is because of Pierre Schacht. I don't know what he's up to, but it looks very bad." Ossilenko described Mark's bait in detail, and Schacht's defection was suddenly clear to Pyotr.

"I don't see how we can come to any other conclusion, General. They've turned him against us. I thought perhaps he was doing it for Moscow Center and I had no need to know. Why not just bite the bullet, General, and write him off?"

"He's the key to Red Snow, as you know, Petrov. He's been an excellent illegal for over twenty years, with a spotless record. It makes no sense that he'd turn now. I want to be quite sure if they've turned him. If it was a provocation designed to make us suspect Schacht, I'll find out. If it was, then Cameron may be suspicious that we've penetrated CIA. Otherwise why do this? So we'll meet Schacht. Both of us. We'll give him an injection, which I've brought with me. He'll tell us the truth. If he has been turned, we'll eliminate him. Don't ever think of just writing off a turncoat, Petrov. That only encourages others."

Pyotr nodded, glad the general had tired of bullying him. Anything, even planning Pierre Schacht's death, was better than Ossilenko's vicious snarls.

They spent the rest of the day talking about Red Snow. What questions to put to Schacht; how to word them. How to dispose of the body if he'd been turned. How to proceed without Schacht if they must.

**Gitabwanga: Hôtel Las Palomas—
1900 hours, 3 January**

Pyotr drove the general to the hotel at seven and stayed while he checked in. Then he was dismissed until eight fifteen.

"Come back fifteen minutes before the ambassador's dinner, Petrov. I need to wash up and change before then. After the dinner I'll need your car, so don't bother to bring me back. In fact, I'll need your car while I'm here. You will remain in the compound while I'm here, except for duties that I approve."

The general turned back into the hotel. Pyotr left feeling ashamed and angry.

Ossilenko shaved, showered, and changed. He liked his room, on the floor above the street. The large french windows opened onto a balcony with lacy cast-iron railings. A municipal park was across the street, the trees and bushes black in the soft night. Traffic on the street was light, the noise level not too high. The room had a large double bed, he noted approvingly. The room's own bathroom reminded him how rare such amenities were in the USSR.

Ossilenko enjoyed walking in strange cities. He spent almost an hour strolling the streets, in the area near the hotel. He looked at shop windows, at the movie-house posters, at the parks and buildings, the people and cars. He had a couple of drinks in a bar, then went back to the Las Palomas and sat on the wide verandah that ran along the street side of the building. He waited for Pyotr, sipping a Scotch and soda, content with the world.

At precisely eight fifteen, Pyotr parked and found the general on the verandah. There was no offer of a drink. They just left for the Soviet compound. Without a word, Pyotr handed the car keys to Ossilenko as they walked from his carport to the Petrov apartment. Olga was waiting for them, very chic in her best silk dress. Aleksandra watched with solemn eyes as her mother received a kiss on both cheeks. The general was a friend of Olga's parents' and had known her since childhood.

Then a hug and kiss for Aleksandra, and a book of beautifully illustrated Russian fairy tales.

They walked to the ambassador's residence, fifty yards across the compound, chatting about family and friends. Pyotr followed a few paces behind, listening to the clatter of their voices and wondering why he didn't join in. It was as if a noose was tied around his neck, pulling him away from them, away from the world he lived in.

Gitabwanga: Raspatov's residence—2030 hours, 3 January

The ambassador's dinner was lively, noisy, festive and, for General Ossilenko, a dream come true. The ambassador had requested Anna Iosevna to be his hostess, as if the old man had read Ossilenko's mind.

Only Pyotr was relatively quiet. He did his best to stay inside the circle, join in the banter and the anecdotes. But his mind was elsewhere, and at first he didn't notice Anna Iosevna's growing fascination with Ossilenko. The general told stories about Kremlin life, the KGB top level, and the Vlasti in general, demonstrating to Anna Iosevna that his friends were Politburo members and senior government officials.

Anna Iosevna was swept into Ossilenko's sphere of influence, her green eyes following each move he made, her expressive face alight with admiration and awe. It was instant conquest, just as the general had intended.

When he finally noticed her attraction, Pyotr's atennae snapped up in a split second. He surveyed the scene, grinding his teeth. His wife, the ambassador, and the general, all showing off for Anna Iosevna, his love. Their cackling voices shredded his nerves. Anna's wide, innocent eyes fixed on Ossilenko made him tremble all over as he counted his losses, fury and frustration mounting. Ossilenko would make sure that Moscow Center kept Pyotr in Bwagania as long as it suited him. Then they would find a way to ruin his career once and for all. Maybe a treason charge would be applied after all. Meanwhile, the general was going to screw his love—using his car and confining him to quarters or the office. Probably, he would recruit her to spy on him. Using his famous disinformation skills, Ossilenko had destroyed the ambassador's affection for Pyotr. And Pyotr would have to use the safe apartment to play Moscow Center's lies to the Americans.

It was loathsome, unfair, and there was nothing he could do about it. He was washed up . . . finished . . . the deck stacked against him. He would have to do something truly spectacular to make a comeback. Something as unexpected as recruiting Mark Cameron. Was there any chance? He could start now claiming there was, and drag it out for months, even years. Perhaps he might be able to get the family to Washington, or so he hoped.

That he'd no real reason to suppose Mark was recruitable was lost in the compulsion to save his career, the imperative of self-preservation. The case officer's nightmare—an inability to distinguish dream from hard fact—was set into motion.

After what seemed to Pyotr like an interminable dinner, everyone said good night. In the courtyard, out of earshot of anyone, Pyotr put his dream in motion. He said softly to Ossilenko, so that Olga couldn't hear: "You should know, Comrade General, that I've reason to think I can recruit Mark Cameron. It will take time, but I'm confident it can be done."

Ossilenko was a subtle, sensitive man under his callous veneer. He did not really want to destroy Petrov, or even be mean to him. He merely wanted to jerk him back onto the right track. He had no idea of the turmoil he had caused in Pyotr's mind. A strong man himself, with an indestructible ego, he assumed that Pyotr could withstand a hard shaking up and would rebound like a rubber ball. It never occurred to the general that Petrov might be deluding himself.

"Great news," he whispered. "We'll get into that one tomorrow. Meanwhile get a good night's sleep." He pushed Pyotr toward Olga and watched while they entered the doorway of their apartment block. Then he went back into the residence. Anna Iosevna was in the hall, wishing Raspatov a good night.

"Perhaps I can escort you to your door, Anna Iosevna? It's dangerous here in central Africa."

Raspatov and Anna Iosevna laughed, but she was willing.

The ambassador turned, smiling tolerantly, and went upstairs to bed. The young woman needed male attention, he thought wistfully, wishing he were younger.

Gitabwanga: Petrov's apartment— 2300 hours, 3 January

At home, Pyotr poured himself a strong Scotch and soda—like many KGB case officers, he preferred it to vodka—and sat down to think. Olga was tired and went to bed without bidding him good night.

After she'd gone, Pyotr walked over to Anna Iosevna's apartment and knocked on the door. There was no reply, just as he'd dreaded. Back in his own apartment, Pyotr drained the bottle, then remembered there was one in the safe apartment. Drunk enough to lose his customary caution, he left the compound on foot, telling the gatekeeper that he was going out for a walk. A mile later, he unlocked the safe-apartment door and poured himself a neat Scotch. He was drenched with perspiration, tie down, collar open, no coat. He looked and felt a mess, and he was profoundly sorry for himself. Sobs of rage and frustration broke out now and then, until in a fit of fury he hurled his glass at the ceiling and stuck out his middle finger at the light fixture, blind to the consequences.

"Fuck you, Cameron," he yelled. "Fuck you too!"

Upstairs, the opening of the apartment door below had triggered the camera and the tape recorder. They whirred quietly, mechanically exact and aloof.

Gitabwanga: Hôtel Las Palomas— 0630 hours, 4 January

Anna Iosevna awoke first, and wrinkled her nose at the smell of stale whisky. Slowly, she realized that she wasn't in her apartment in the Soviet compound and that she'd better get there before it was time to go to work. But first she wanted the general again. He had been a truly excellent partner, slower, more careful, more aware of her requirements, than Pyotr. Older, yes, but much better. And he was a general . . .

She stroked Vladimir Fedorovich. His cheek, neck, chest, paunch, and then . . . the general lived up to her hopes. By the time they finally dressed and left the hotel, Anna Iosevna was in a rosy, relaxed glow, breathing endearments into the general's ear, touching him whenever she could. Vladimir Fedorovich was hooked; pleased with his stunning conquest, and determined somehow to keep her as his new mistress.

Anna Iosevna stayed on the floor behind the front seats of the car until they were in the carport. The Sûreté team on surveillance duty saw her get into the car and hunker down. The Soviet gatekeeper saw only the general. But Pyotr was watching from his apartment. He saw the car drive into the carport, and after a long wait, Anna Iosevna rushed into her apartment block and the car left the compound again.

Pyotr trembled with rage and humiliation.

Gitabwanga: François' office—
0900 hours, 4 January

Almost all people have an innate sense of how to observe others without being seen. The art of observing a moving target while in view of that target, however, can be developed into a skill approaching magic.

Most Bwaganians are natural actors, playing parts easily and with joyful grace. The Bwaganian Sûreté surveillance teams are at their best in the streets of the capital, working on moving targets, using a combination of foot surveillants, men and women on bicycles, and people in an assortment of cars and small vans. The teams skillfully bring together French professional techniques and the Bwaganian hunting skills of being seen but unnoticed.

The first batch of surveillance reports began drifting in around nine o'clock in the morning. They were unanimous on what had happened yesterday afternoon and evening. At three-thirty, Petrov and the visitor had gone to the Soviet compound in Petrov's car. At seven, Petrov drove the visitor (known as Target in the reports) to the hotel Las Palomas. At seven ten, Target had gone out for an hour, wandering the streets near the hotel. He had a couple of drinks in a bar, then was picked up at the hotel by Petrov at eight fifteen. They went to the Soviet compound and stayed there until ten fifty-five, when the visitor was observed driving Petrov's car to the hotel. He entered the hotel with a passenger, a young blond female from the Soviet embassy. They spent the night in the hotel.

To François such reports were old hat, and they made generally boring reading. But one of these was a classic. The surveillant was a resourceful, determined young Bwaganian policeman on loan to the Sûreté. As he read, François couldn't stop laughing:

Report in 2 Parts

Part 1: From 1910 to 2010 hours, 3 January: Target left Hôtel Las Palomas at 1910 hours on foot, dressed in white shirt, dark blue trousers, shiny black shoes, no hat or coat or tie. He proceeded up avenue de la Paix and I followed on Colette (my bicycle). Colette squeaks most loudly when she is ridden most slowly, which is why I named her for a certain lady. At the corner of Paix and Gambetta, Target stood on the sidewalk for 6 minutes. He used glass shop windows as mirrors to try to observe surveillance, an annoyance which I countered by melting into an alley with Colette.

At 1921 hours Target walked down rue Gambetta at a slow pace. I rode Colette past him several times. Once with a coat on and my red fez. Next, trousers rolled up, sunglasses, no coat or hat. Then with a bandanna on my head and coat on, but trousers rolled down, and so on. Colette was in a good mood since I rode quite fast at times. She squeaked a little, but in a low frequency as if purring.

Target stopped at many places. Three times he stopped in front of movie theaters, looking at the posters of pretty girls. One of them so caught him that he played with himself surreptitiously, but without result. At the corner of Gambetta and Joffre he stopped again, for a long time, just looking around at everything. I parked in a large archway and sat on a box. He paid no attention to me, for I am a black man. I looked picturesque with a straw hat I borrowed from a salesboy sitting there.

At 1938 hours he entered the bar Krokodil and ordered a Scotch whisky. I observed him from close outside the bar, behind a truck parked there. He spoke to no one except to order his drink, and made no sign to anyone. At 2005 hours he moved on, thanks be to God, because the driver of the truck was becoming uneasy. He told me to get away from his truck several times. I believe he thought I am *pédale* [gay]. Colette and I rode past Target a few times more, changing our clothes as much as possible, and once again he paid no attention. He returned to the hotel at 2010 hours and five minutes later P. Petrov of the Soviet embassy picked him up."

Part 2: From 2255 hours to 0015 hours 4 January: Target returned to the hotel at 2255 hours, driving the Petrov car. At first I thought he was alone, but after parking his car Target opened the rear door. Out came a very pretty blond woman, age about 20, dressed in a tight sheath that showed off a fine figure. The car was parked in a dark spot by the park across from the hotel, where Colette and I were in a bush. They kissed for a few moments, his hands all over her.

It was obvious that they were going to his room, so I went across to the hotel garden, put on my dark pullover and climbed a tree until I could jump onto the first balcony. From there I jumped across the gaps in the balconies until I was hidden behind the flower boxes on Target's balcony.

At 2301 hours they came into his room. He switched on a dim lamp beside the double bed. I could now see the woman and she is very beautiful. We joke in Bwagania about all whites looking alike, but this one doesn't look alike. She is perfection!

At 2302 he poured them both a drink from a Scotch bottle, mixing in a little water. They toasted each other. Then he opened the balcony doors and I could hear every word.

Unhappily I speak no Russian, but what they did is universal. Target caressed her all over, talking the entire time, and removing her garments one by one. She is a real blond, that one. She was quickly on the bed, legs wide open, moaning and waiting for him. But Target had his own clothes to take off. To my surprise he wears a corset because he has a big tummy. The woman was surprised, too. She sat up and watched, her eyes wide, as he tried to pull the corset down past his erection. He has a very long, thick member and it was a real struggle. Finally, as he pulled and cursed, it came off with a jerk and before I could take a breath he was on the bed with her.

At 0015 rain began. I had to leave because the balconies were slippery and dangerous. In any event I do not believe there was any more to be learned about Russian ways to make love. It had been enjoyable to be paid for watching this little breeding theater, but all good things have to end.

Boniface Djiallo, Gendarme.

François made a note to watch Djiallo's performance for possible early promotion. He was irrepressible, as well as courageous. Those balconies were dangerous when dry, let alone when wet.

Gitabwanga: Mark's office—1100 hours, 4 January

"I'm going over to your apartment," Mark told Linda. "I've got a hunch we might find something interesting."

He was back in fifteen minutes, and Linda developed the film. Half an hour later, it was dry and they could see the negatives on the reader-printer. The tape confirmed it. There was Pyotr, drunk, making a finger at Mark, cursing him, and throwing his glass at the spot where the camera had to be.

"There it is, Linda. Ossilenko must have told Petrov about our dispatch. There is a mole. Now to identify him."

Mark's cable to the director of central intelligence (for his eyes only) was long. Point by point, he laid out the evidence that there was a mole in the agency, certainly in the clandestine services, possibly in the Russia division.

The last point was the most telling: Pyotr's knowledge of the exact location of the bug in the center of the ceiling. The message ended:

BELIEVE EVIDENCE CONCLUSIVE. HAVE NO REPEAT NO PERSONAL DOUBT THAT MY VISUAL BAIT WAS SENT TO MOSCOW CENTER BY A PENETRATION OF HEADQUARTERS, THEN BROUGHT HERE BY OSSILENKO TO CONFRONT PETROV. HAVE THOUGHT OUT TRAP TO SMOKE OUT MOLE. REQUEST TDY TO HQS FOR TIME NECESSARY TO REFINE PLAN, PRESENT IT FOR YOUR APPROVAL, SET UP OPERATION AND CATCH TARGET. ESTIMATE THREE WEEKS. REC-

OMMEND LEAVING LINDA TAKAHASHI IN CHARGE. FYI SHE PERFORMING MOST EFFECTIVELY, WELL QUALIFIED AS ACTING COS. END.

Linda was pleased with the way Mark had worded it: "Thanks, Mark, for the vote of confidence. Flattery will get you everywhere."

"It's far from flattery. It's a fact. Just see to it that you recruit Petrov while I'm gone."

"What about Ossilenko, too? Make it a fleet act."

"Very funny, Linda. He's not just a part of the Soviet system—he is the system. But you're welcome to try. It'll make an interesting three weeks, if he stays that long."

The telephone rang, and Mark picked it up. "Mark?" It was François' familiar voice: "Can you come over to my house at seven this evening? It's something rather amusing."

Gitabwanga: François' house— 1900 hours, 4 January

François showed Mark the Djiallo surveillance report and watched in glee as Mark roared with laughter. Then he said: "Mark, Djiallo wasn't the only surveillant we had out there last night. We also had an SSR officer watching from a building that looks out on the hotel. This man, bless his heart, phoned me to say that Petrov's car would probably be out there on the street most of the night. To cut a long story short, my men got into the car and planted a bug, which we can switch on and off from my office. It sends a garbled signal that we will decode. I'll switch on at five-minute intervals, for a few seconds only, starting when it gets dark. I think it best not to put a watch on Schacht, for fear of scaring him away. This will be a critical meeting for Red Snow."

"What a coup! A bug in the only car likely to be used for the meeting! Congratulations!" Mark was so excited that he walked up and down the verandah, pounding a fist into his other palm. "Great, just great! Of course I'll leave Schacht unwatched tonight. And you'll have your men lose the car quite early, I would guess?"

"Yes, Mark. They have instructions to lose it after a discreet and rather unprofessional try. We want to avoid any chance that they'll abort the meeting."

Gitabwanga: the KGB *rezidentura*—
1800 hours, 4 January

Pyotr had had to pay court to General Ossilenko all day, knowing that his visitor had slept with Anna Iosevna the previous night and would do so again every night as long as he was here. Then if he could, he would get her reassigned to Moscow, where they could go on screwing. All day—as the two men discussed Red Snow, what the *rezidentura* would do after the coup, how to feed Mark Cameron disinformation over the apartment bug, how to maneuver him toward recruitment, and the myriad other things for which Pyotr would be responsible—his hatred grew and his mind was consumed with one theme: how to pay the general back. How to discredit him. But Pyotr acted his part well and Ossilenko perceived no change. Although Pyotr brooded, he still functioned effectively. In fact, Ossilenko was pleased with him and didn't hesitate to tell him so.

"You really have a good grasp of things out here, Pyotr Aleksandrovich. Keep your nose clean from now on and we'll overlook your mistakes. I think you'll handle things well after I've gone back." But it wasn't going to work. Pyotr knew Moscow Center needed him in place or they would have ordered him home, and he knew an enemy when he saw one. Ossilenko had stolen his girl and his manhood, and would ruin his career despite his plaudits.

They discussed yet again the meeting with Schacht for the evening. Both men knew that if Schacht was now working for the CIA, it might be a trap. Pyotr and Ossilenko could be arrested, expelled. It was more likely, however, that the CIA would let the meeting go ahead and rely on Schacht to tell them about it afterward. In other words, that Cameron was taking Schacht at face value.

Ossilenko's plan was to give Schacht the injection as he sat down in the car, to get on with the questioning as soon as possible, and then to strangle him if he turned out to be working for the CIA: simple, quick, brutal. The lake's crocodiles would finish the job.

The discussion about Mark Cameron went well, as Pyotr had hoped. He described their conversations, exaggerating the things Mark had said, embellishing his own role to make himself look like a mongoose with a snake in view, and it was done.

Ossilenko was pleased: "I will make sure that you stay on this case. Well done, Pyotr Aleksandrovich!"

Gitabwanga: Hôtel du Lac—
1820 hours, 4 January

Pierre Schacht left the bordello for his usual evening stroll. Wearing his usual somber clothes, he melted into the night within yards and moved slowly and silently along the shore of Lake Tchagamba, toward the bridge. The watchers in the garden saw him go but thought nothing of it. It was cool, a good hour to go for a stroll.

Schacht's antennae were tuned for surveillants who might follow him, for this was to be an important meeting. He knew that Ossilenko was in Gitabwanga, and he looked forward to meeting his old friend. At last Moscow Center had sent in their first team to support him.

A kilometer away from the Hôtel du Lac, there was still no sign of surveillance. Schacht was going to enjoy the evening.

Gitabwanga: François' office—
1825 hours, 4 January

The radio receiver in François' office picked up voices. The SSR direction finders located the car leaving the outskirts of town, headed for the bush. The voices were faint but quite clear.

". . . give him the injection through his trousers as he sits down. Understand? Tell him sorry, must have been your fountain pen. After we've questioned him, if he can't explain it, I slip the wire over his head from the backseat. Then into the lake, at the bridge. The stream will carry it out."

François' Russian wasn't good enough, so he played the tape to Mark over the telephone. The voices of Ossilenko and Pyotr were clear and chilling. "They're serious, François, they may knock off Schacht. Does your official position require you to intervene?"

"If I can legally do so. But they may not kill him. Petrov has diplomatic immunity. He'd deny it anyway, before the fact. To have the Sûreté make an arrest would blow our surveillance capabilities. Sorry, Mark, but we'll have to let things take their course."

"Too bad," said Mark sarcastically. "That gentle, harmless SOB of a KGB illegal will just have to be executed by his own ungrateful service. Unless he can convince them he's been unfairly framed."

François went back to the radio. The car had turned toward the lake, toward a spot north of the Hôtel du Lac.

Gitabwanga: the lake shore—1845 hours, 4 January

After he left the Hôtel du Lac and made sure he wasn't being followed, Schacht took his usual route on the sandy beach along the lake shore, the placid moonlit waters close by on his left, the dark trees and bushes off to his right.

He was pleased with the report he was bringing to Ossilenko. He had typed it earlier this evening on his battered machine. It was a full account of the preparedness of the coup plotters for Red Snow. It recounted his arrangement with the Senegalese communists to stage an "invasion" of Senegal from neighboring Mali, to draw away French forces from Bwagania. It assessed his ability to take over the new government—by using stooges more malleable than M'Taga, who was to be assassinated some weeks after the coup, by rifle shot while he dined at his habitual Restaurant Lac Tchagamba, at his usual time: between seven-thirty and nine P.M.

Schacht knew it was risky to carry an uncoded report to the meeting, but at least it was in German, without naming any addresses or giving any hint of the Soviet hand. He wanted to read it to Ossilenko himself. Then no one could overlook his role. There would be another hero's medal. It was heresy, but worth the risk.

The first arrow caught Schacht in the stomach. It went in from the right front, and the barbs lodged near the spine, just as the Sicilian had intended. When he saw Schacht go down on his knees, half in the water and half on the sand, the Sicilian broke cover behind Schacht, watching while the stricken man groaned and clawed at the shaft.

"That's for Muffie, you bastard. This one's for me."

He fitted another arrow, and took Schacht in the back. The arrow passed through a lung into the liver. It would only be minutes now before he drowned in his own blood. The Sicilian walked around to face Schacht.

"His Majesty Bwaga VI sends you these greetings."

The Sicilian watched with pleasure as fear and agony continued to sweep across Schacht's face. Satisfied, he fired the third arrow into the man's heart. He left the arrows in the body. They were from a tribe in Nigeria, to confuse the investigation.

Then he searched the body and pocketed Schacht's report for Ossilenko. He left the dead man's wallet untouched, but he added an expended .357 magnum rifle cartridge to Schacht's breast pocket. Then he dragged the body a few meters up the sand, above the lake's edge. He wanted it to be found more or less intact.

Gitabwanga: François' office—1942 hours, 4 January

"Where is that wretched man?" It was Ossilenko's voice, and Pyotr responded:

"He's two minutes overdue. That's not like him."

Ossilenko said, "Drive on a kilometer and come back."

There was no voice for three minutes. Then Pyotr: "He must have decided to abort. He's now six minutes overdue. I suggest we leave and try the alternate tomorrow night."

The car headed back to the Soviet compound. François

played the tape to Mark over the phone. They were both mystified. The stakeout in the bordello had reported Schacht leaving the Hôtel du Lac for his usual evening stroll.

Gitabwanga: Restaurant Lac Tchagamba—1950 hours, 4 January

Just as the king had instructed him at the royal wall an hour ago, the old Bwaganian hid himself in a bush, lying prone. The lake was on his left, glistening as ripples rolled under the moonlight. There was almost no breeze, so it was warm and cozy in the bush. The ants were persistent, but not too much for an old hand.

The old man had watched Prince M'Taga parade into the restaurant like a medieval baron, his huge figure dominating the place. He led his group of six young acolytes and his pretty blond mistress to their usual table on the covered terrace, facing along the lake. The diners, mostly Europeans, had watched when the prince came in, hushed their voices until he was seated, tried to catch his eye for a nod of recognition if they could extract one. He was the prime minister now, the inheritor, the second most powerful man in the kingdom.

It was a round table, and the prince sat facing out toward the old man. The blond mistress, who looked surprisingly like Muffie, sat next to the prince, but she was looking out over the garden, not paying much attention to the conversation, now and then giggling and gently pushing away his idly straying hand. The prince was in an expansive mood. His big secret, Red Snow, was now only days away. It would be a relief to get it over, to be president-for-life and be able to assert his own wishes over the nation. He would have to trim Schacht's ambitions quite a lot, he thought, but that was a few months off. Tonight, he wanted to take some time off, and tell tales.

M'Taga had a huge stock of Bwaganian stories, and larded them with anecdotes designed to make himself look even more important than he was. Tonight, as he waved his knife and fork about and told tales of his hunting skills, his voice boomed as his companions laughed. M'Taga's bulging red eyes were underscored by dark bags of fatigue and drink, a soiled white napkin was tucked into his collar, and in between anecdotes he lectured in short, staccato bursts of clichés, sermonlike statements of philosophy, and allusions to his future activities that wrung adulation from the table. The group was noisy, irritating, untouchable.

Outside, in his bush, the old man was hardly aware of the movement—just a trace of a change in the light, of something dark creeping along the ground. He watched it, wondering if this was the something he was to witness for the king. Bwaga VI hadn't told the old man what to observe, just to hide and watch everything.

The shape became a man with a rifle. He was dressed in dark clothes, wore dark gloves, and his face was black. But he was a white man. The old man could tell by the way he moved, by his body shape. But the man was well disguised, and he couldn't identify him.

The Sicilian, unaware of the motionless old man prone in a nearby bush, found a suitable site to lie in, his rifle resting on a log. He watched the prince, the boy whom he had taught to shoot, to use bow and arrow, to hunt. He had watched the prince grow from a slim youth into a man who had thrown away his ability in sports and become grossly overweight.

The Sicilian watched with approval as the prince drank a whole carafe of red wine with his huge *biftek au poivre,* ate bananas and mangoes for dessert, and finished with a double cognac and coffee. When the inheritor's last meal was ending, the Sicilian made his final preparations. He quietly chambered a round, then he wriggled into position and sighted at the prince. A hunter's shot, right at the breastbone.

Before squeezing the trigger, he swung the rifle slightly to the right and sighted at the young man seated next to M'Taga. An easy second shot, if needed. Then to the left, past the prince, he sighted on the blonde. To his surprise, she was looking right at him. He blinked. She seemed to be staring right into his eyes. The Sicilian raised the rifle and put the sights on her left eye, then down to her breasts. He sighted each one in turn, thinking that they were as big and luscious as the best he'd ever seen. Her eyes were following the barrel, perhaps seeing the reflected light. She made no sound or sign. In a moment she might react, however.

He said a mental Hail Mary, asked forgiveness from God for the execution of his friend and prince, aimed at his breastbone with exquisite care, and fired. The 300-grain bullet crossed the space in less than a twentieth of a second. The deafening bang of the rifle, the flash that seemed as bright as lightning, and the smack of the heavy slug as it hit bone were simultaneous to the diners. And horrifying.

A slug that will stop a charging rhino does great damage to the human body. The prince's upper body was torn almost in two, his flesh and blood spattered all over the terrace.

There was silence for a moment, except for the prince's knife, which spun on the wooden floor with a burring sound. The Sicilian heard it as his orgasm shook him.

Suddenly, the prince's followers reacted, diving for cover and screaming their panic and dismay. Other diners shouted, threw themselves to the floor, or ran into the main room. The Portuguese ambassador sat quite still at his table, a large piece of the prince's flesh splattered on his forehead. Blood dripped from the ambassador's forehead, down his nose and into his plate. Then he was sick.

The prince's mistress was the only person who didn't move. She sat upright, rigid, as if nothing had occurred. Only later was it apparent that she had wet herself.

The hunter left no brass, no useful footprints, no clue as to his identity. But he did leave Schacht's report, neatly typed in German, for the investigators to find. In minutes he was a hundred yards from the scene, gliding away without headlights in the red Rolls-Royce.

The old man followed the king's instructions exactly. He had seen his employer murdered by a white man, and that was what he would tell the police. As he sat in his bush, waiting for the investigators, he perspired and wept quietly. He had never witnessed a deliberate murder, and the shock was total.

The police came just after eight-thirty and found the old man still sitting in his bush, unable to move. When they got him to his feet and into the restaurant, he was able to tell them what he had seen; slowly, stumblingly, but nevertheless accurately. A white man, not a young man, but nimble enough. A trained shot. No, he'd never noticed if the man had dropped the folded notes, but it was quite possible that he had. No, he couldn't identify the man. It was night and he wore dark clothes . . .

Gitabwanga: Mark's house—2130 hours, 4 January

Mark and Linda waited after dinner, willing the phone to ring with news of the meeting between Pyotr, Ossilenko, and Schacht. Finally, François called with unexpected news.

The police had put it all together. It would probably be on the ten o'clock news broadcast. Pierre Schacht had murdered the prince and had then been murdered himself by some unknown African, perhaps a witness who had stalked him along the lake shore. An expended .357 round had been found in Schacht's pockets, but no rifle. Supposedly, he'd thrown it in the lake or buried it. The identity of the murderer was in no doubt. A note in German had been found in the bush from which Schacht had shot M'Taga, apparently a report intended for Ossilenko and Petrov, although there was no proof of that. It was neatly typed, on a typewriter they found in Schacht's room in the Hôtel du Lac. A servant in the hotel had heard him typing in the evening. It was clear he'd planned to assassinate the prince . . . as well as the king.

In his rudimentary German, François read parts of the note to Mark. Then he said: "The king has given the Sicilian orders to take care of the plotters. He knows the names of the cadre."

"What does 'take care of them' mean?" Mark asked.

"I wouldn't like to be one of them."

"No trial?"

"This is central Africa. He'll move fast, leave no trace, but eventually everybody in Bwagania will know what happened and it will have an impact."

"Does it make sense to you that Schacht didn't level with the KGB? Or that he'd jump the gun this way?"

"Mark, Mark, my very American friend," François was laughing. "Remember *'c'est l'Afrique'*? Don't look a gift horse in the mouth, to coin a phrase. It is enough that Schacht, a murdering bastard, was himself executed in mid-act. Think how many people Red Snow would have blown away."

"Of course I'm delighted, François. I'm certainly not about to question this stroke of luck. It's just that there are some loose ends. I'd like to know the truth. It's always so elusive."

"We'll know one day, Mark. Meanwhile have a good night."

"Hold on. Are the Soviets in the clear?"

"I'm not telling the Sûreté or the police that Petrov and Ossilenko planned to meet Schacht. They'd be kicked out, just when we want to know what they'll do next."

When Mark hung up, Linda asked: "Now what?"

"Up to the king, I suspect. I'm going to see Passatu. I think we'll see the king's hand in these two deaths. Despite what he says, he plays his own game, and it's for keeps. Remember M'Bouyé's request for poison? Thank God those two are on our side."

Gitabwanga: Passatu's apartment—
2200 hours, 4 January

They listened to the ten o'clock news broadcast, which carried only a brief account of the two murders, not yet linking them. Then Mark listened carefully as Paul briefed him on recent events.

Afterward he said: "I'd appreciate it if you'd level with me. It doesn't add up either that Schacht made the attempt on Bwaga VI or that he shot M'Taga. Does it?"

"No, it doesn't." Passatu grinned. "It might be wise not to try to find out the truth."

"It may be wise for most people, Paul, but not for me. It's my job to know what happens and why, even if I never use the knowledge. I trust you'll help."

"Of course," said Paul. "The fact is that the king accepted

the Sicilian's assumption that Schacht was behind the attempt on him. It was circumstantial, but logical enough if you're Bwaga VI and trying to be sure they don't knock you off your perch. So he took things into his own hands, without consulting his advisers. He's tough as nails where his kingdom is concerned."

"I'm sure it wasn't Schacht, but I'll keep trying to find out. I suppose we may never know the truth."

"Does that bother you?"

"Not much. Ninety percent of what we attempt to do never succeeds. That's part of this game. What's worse, there's more."

"Like what?"

"Like ninety percent of the time we never know why."

Gitabwanga: Hôtel Las Palomas—
2245 hours, 4 January

General Ossilenko took his time coming down to the lobby. He suspected that Petrov was bringing him news of Schacht, but even so it was embarrassing to be hauled out of Anna Iosevna's arms. He met Pyotr on the verandah, well away from the almost deserted lobby.

"Well, Petrov? What is it?" Ossilenko was gruff.

"It's very important, Comrade General. Yegorov came in late tonight with a report that Prince M'Taga was shot dead at a restaurant, by Schacht. Then after that, Schacht was shot dead by an African with arrows. It's incredible, but true. The radio had it on the ten o'clock news. All they know is that 'the Austrian, Pierre Schacht, lived at the Hôtel du Lac.' That's the news so far."

Ossilenko was stunned. His mouth fell open, and for once the general was without words. After a considerable time, he pulled himself upright.

"Petrov, find out all the details. Arrange it so that Cameron is blamed. After all, he recruited Schacht, so the bastard must have been acting under his orders. Cameron, acting with the king's approval. Then they had an African kill Schacht, to ensure no leakage. That's what must have happened . . . unless of course Schacht simply went crazy."

"Which do you prefer, Comrade General?"

"Get Cameron, Petrov. But I prefer Schacht to have gone mad. That explains to Moscow how Cameron was able to recruit him so quickly. Perhaps we can tie both things together. Work on that, Petrov. Meanwhile, I'm tired. Good night!"

He went back to Anna Iosevna.

Bwagania: the Bendaga ravine—0700 hours, 5 January

As he waited in the bushes, the Sicilian marveled again at the king's cunning. "I had the word passed by whisper, on the phone," the King had said. "They'll come. It's a habit now, so they'll do it despite the confusion over what happened to their two leaders."

The king was right. They did come. There they were, twelve of them, like disciples, gathered in a tight group, discussing what to do.

One of the young men took command. The others listened, accepting him, as he began to sketch out a plan.

It was time to move. The Sicilian pulled up his scarf to cover his face up to the eyes. A single shot from his submachine gun killed the leader. A couple of bursts mowed down the rest. Two grenades stilled all movement. Then he waited for the sentry. The king's orders had been precise: "Roast them, but leave one alive to scare any remnants of the group. I don't care which one."

The sentry came at a run from his post on the road, rifle ready, looking around to see what had happened. An amateur against a professional. The Sicilian stepped out of the bushes behind him.

"Drop the rifle. Don't look around. Put your hands in your trouser pockets, right foot on top of the left foot." When the man was ready, the hunter shouldered his weapon, opened his arms wide, cupped his hands, and slammed them simultaneously against the man's ears. The impact of his two cupped palms coming together burst both eardrums, and the Bwaganian dropped to the ground, screaming.

The Sicilian whipped out a length of cloth-covered nylon cord with a loop at one end, a wooden toggle at the other. He looped it over the man's head, drew it tight, and fastened it at the neck. Enough to half throttle, not to kill. The man writhed on the ground desperately fighting to survive the cord's grip. He half saw what followed, as in a nightmare.

The hunter put on a pair of gloves, picked up a flame thrower, and incinerated the corpses. He laid the flame thrower beside the sentry, knocked him unconscious, and took off the noose. There was no rope mark on the man's neck.

He quickly left a scene that would result in the sentry's trial and eventual execution for mass murder. No one ever believed the deaf survivor's mixed up version of the events.

Gitabwanga: KGB *rezidentura*— 1000 hours, 5 January

Ossilenko drove slowly to the Soviet compound, thinking through what he must do in the coming weeks. To Moscow Center, the ruin of Red Snow would be a serious but temporary setback. The KGB was unremitting in its worldwide efforts to colonize new countries, to dominate them politically, to capture people and land and institutions. Red Snow One would be quickly succeeded by Red Snow Two.

But for General Ossilenko, the ruin of Red Snow One was a double calamity. All the efforts to convert Bwagania into a vassal of the USSR would have to be undertaken again, with new assets, against far greater odds. And all the work done by KGB Colonel Oleg A. Petrosian, aka Pierre Schacht, would have to be reviewed again and painfully analyzed, right back to his first assignment as an "illegal" outside the USSR twenty years ago. Had he gone nuts? If not, how deeply had the CIA bitten into him? For how long, if at all, had the CIA been feeding Oleg information for the KGB? How valid had Oleg's disinformation and political action activities been? Had SVYET known about him and withheld his knowledge?

The mountain of work to be done was depressing, the general was the only one who could effectively do it, and he would now have to watch his back because of the damage Schacht had done to Ossilenko's professional image. The shortcut to redemption would be to recruit Mark Cameron and find out from the horse's mouth what had happened. Then they could use Cameron to ensure the success of Red Snow Two. Petrov must now concentrate all his efforts on the Cameron assignment. The plan was by now lodged in Ossilenko's mind as his own invention: aggressive and brilliant.

Meanwhile, how to dump his old mistress? How to get Anna Iosevna into a good job in Lubyanka and a nice apartment alone in central Moscow? It could only be done from Moscow. There was no official reason for him to stay in Bwagania, anyway. A month without Anna Iosevna would be rewarded by years with her.

He arrived in the KGB *rezidentura* late, tired from an active night with Anna Iosevna. His mood, based on a combination of satisfied fatigue and professional dismay, included a need to torment Pyotr.

"Good morning, Petrov. I trust you spent a pleasant night?"

"Good morning, Comrade General." Pyotr jumped to his feet. "I did, thank you," he lied.

"Nothing like good exercise in the morning, eh?" Ossilenko was rubbing it in. "Well, Petrov, I've got news for you. I'll be going back to Moscow on the seventh, on the afternoon flight. I want to do some shopping today, so I'll go on using your car. Meanwhile, I want you to start on a new plan to replace Red Snow with a program that works. Start on the plan now. We can discuss it this evening. Also, write up the plan to recruit Cameron. Make it in two stages: First, he gets the blame for these murders; then, when he's down, we offer him an inducement he can't resist. I'll see you about six o'clock."

He stopped by the ambassador's office on his way out, to beg the use of Anna Iosevna for the day: ". . . she's promised to help me with my shopping. A woman's touch, you know . . ."

Raspatov agreed. It was a small price to pay for a future favor he might ask the general.

Anna Iosevna was delighted to return to the hotel. Already she could see what life might be like when the general had her transferred to Moscow. It made her insatiable.

Gitabwanga: Mark's office—1130 hours, 5 January

The DCI's reply was just what Mark wanted:

> COME EARLIEST OPERATIONAL CONVENIENCE. REPORT FIRST TO ME ONLY. WAITING WITH GREAT INTEREST YOUR PLAN. APPROVE LINDA TAKAHASHI ACOS. GOOD WORK. END.

"Nice to know we're both wanted," said Linda. "I'll keep the lid on while you're gone, but I'll miss you. What next, Mark?"

"The next move's up to the king. He plays things his way, obviously, and he's tough. Remember M'Bouyé's request for poison?"

Mark phoned François: "I have to leave Gitabwanga for a while. Can I bring someone over to see you this evening?"

Gitabwanga: François' house—1900 hours, 5 January

François had guessed it would be Linda. There was a red rose beside her plate, and he toasted her with a little speech of congratulations: "It'll be a pleasure to work with you, Linda. But I've news for you. Paris has asked me to go back there for a few days. I've no idea why, but I hope they're pleased with our upset of Red Snow."

"Perhaps a promotion, or a medal?" Linda smiled. He grinned optimistically.

"When are you leaving, François?" Mark asked.

"The seventh, on the afternoon flight. I should be back in two or three days. Will you be back by then, Mark?"

"Probably not. I expect to be gone almost a month."

Before they left, François gave them a photocopy of the

report that Schacht had intended for Ossilenko. Mark read it quickly, eyebrows showing his surprise.

"Good grief, it's in more detail than I expected. I wonder why he took this risk. Just to have written it without S/W was a big risk. To have it on him so that it fell out when he shot M'Taga is incredible." He grinned. "Let's not question it!"

"I know." François smiled. "Not at all like a KGB illegal. One wonders what got into his head. Was he getting senile?" He gave a Gallic shrug, tongue well in cheek.

"When can we get a look at Schacht's belongings?" asked Mark.

"They are being held by the police for the time being. I'll get a look after I return from Paris. I'll show them to Linda."

"What will Moscow Center do to Ossilenko?" Linda asked.

"Maybe they'll order him home to stand trial for the failure of his coup," François suggested hopefully.

Mark shook his head. "I think he'll blame Schacht and get away with it."

Gitabwanga: KGB *rezidentura*— 2000 hours, 5 January

Ossilenko and Pyotr had spent almost two hours going over the plan to replace Red Snow with a successful coup, and Pyotr's proposal for the recruitment of Mark. The new overthrow concept was a copy of the standard KGB blueprint: Pick and groom a new leader, preferably a military officer with overtly moderate views, big ambitions. Help him spot, assess, develop and recruit new cadre members. Conduct a campaign to discredit the present regime and the king, and so on. Ossilenko approved it on the spot, subject to later changes, of course.

The proposal to recruit Mark was also routine: Gather as much more information on him as possible . . . "I'll get to know his weaknesses," Pyotr's operational plan read, "better than I do now" (the implication being that he was far down the road already). "Tempt him with double agents that turn sour. Test him with provocative remarks about Marx, Lenin,

Stalin, Malenkov, Khrushchev, and so on. Commiserate with him over the trouble he's in because of the murders of the prince and Schacht, and his rotten agents; trouble that's ruining his already tattered career. Above all, maneuver him into compromising situations that can be used to blackmail him. Then offer him our silence about his misdeeds, a KGB commission as a colonel with full pay in Swiss francs at our most favorable exchange rate, plus a dacha after he defects."

It was a tall order, but Ossilenko wanted to be convinced that the effort had a good chance to succeed. He granted the detailed plan his official approval.

Gitabwanga: Kalanga's hunting lodge—2100 hours, 5 January

It was Pyotr's suggestion that they use Kalanga to sniff around Madame Petarde's. The two Soviets met Kalanga at his ramshackle hunting lodge, miles out of town.

Kalanga listened to Ossilenko's request. It sounded reasonable, and he needed money. For a stiff price, he agreed, and then he described how he would handle the assignment.

"It's a fancy whorehouse, run by a Frenchwoman. That's where I first met Schacht. Sometime later I introduced him to my nephew M'Taga. I go there quite often. Madame Petarde's daughters and some other girls are available, but of course I just eat, drink, and talk with them. I don't have to pay for my sex, you understand."

They nodded, amused.

"They will expect me to come, now that Schacht is dead, to see if they have any clue as to why he killed my nephew. They may even tell me what the police have found out so far."

"It's important to get some idea as to what he did yesterday before leaving the hotel," said Ossilenko. "And above all, find out his state of mind recently—whether he was nuts or not."

"I'll go there right away," said Kalanga. "Tonight. They're open until the early hours."

"Is that all right, with everyone in mourning?" asked Pyotr.

"Nobody questions what I do," answered Kalanga pompously. "I make my own rules, and they'll never suspect I'm there on your account. Besides, I'm angry enough at Schacht that my being there will appear quite normal."

A risk, Ossilenko thought, using this jerk. But worth it.

Gitabwanga: Hôtel du Lac—
2230 hours, 5 January

Kalanga talked his nephew Prince N'Gobi—King Bwaga VI's youngest son—into going with him. "We'll go together," he said to N'Gobi. "It'll double the chances of our finding out why Schacht killed M'Taga."

"What about the cops," asked N'Gobi. "Won't they still be there?"

"So what?" said Kalanga. "They're too dumb to find out what really went on. It takes our kind of brains. You drive, N'Gobi. You're a much better driver than I am." N'Gobi was won over by the crude flattery.

The hotel was quiet, almost deserted, as a result of the two murders. Madame Petarde thought it was tasteless of them to come so soon after M'Taga's death, but she was pleased to have their business, and made a fuss over them. She called to her two youngest girls, both recently arrived from Europe:

"Girls, come over here and meet two of Bwagania's royal princes. We must give them a warm welcome on such a sad night." She left when the girls were seated at the table and drinks had been ordered.

"Why is it so quiet tonight?" Kalanga asked, knowing the answer.

"Most people have stayed home, in mourning for the prince. Your nephew, wasn't he?"

Kalanga nodded. "And N'Gobi's brother."

"I'm so sorry for you both. For all of us. Here at the hotel it's a double requiem. We lost a man who lived here for a long time. Pierre was his name, Pierre Schacht . . . a fixture in the hotel."

"The bastard who shot my brother," said N'Gobi. He

looked sad, but he was thinking, Schacht did the family a big favor. I wonder why?

The girl laid a hand on his arm, trying to console him. "He was such an inoffensive little man. No one ever thought of him as a killer. He just wasn't the kind of person who'd do a thing like that."

"What was he like?" asked N'Gobi.

"We didn't really know him, sir. He kept to himself, was quiet, didn't drink much, never had any of the girls. A really strange man. But he was always polite, paid his bills on time, and never caused a disturbance. But now I guess he'll go to hell forever." She shook her body like a wet puppy. Then she reached over, grabbed N'Gobi's neck, and stuck her tongue in his ear. Nothing like that had ever happened to him before, and he almost fell off his chair. Kalanga burst out laughing, then quieted as he saw the embarrassment in N'Gobi's eyes.

The girl said, "Don't be so serious, let's have some fun." She nuzzled his ear again and stroked his thigh.

"He's never had a white girl," said Kalanga. "He doesn't know how to react." To N'Gobi, he said, "I'll pay for it."

"He's almost a virgin, then," the girl said. "They make me horny as hell." She worked on N'Gobi a while longer, until he went upstairs with her.

Just as N'Gobi and the girl left, Madame Petarde came back to see how things were going. She waved them on and turned to Kalanga: "How about you, Prince? Do you want to take a girl upstairs too? How about this one?" She motioned to the remaining girl at the table. "Or one of my daughters? You know them well."

"Thank you, Madame Petarde. In a minute. I'll sit here with you first."

She laughed and dismissed the girl with a wave of her fan. "What shall we discuss, monsieur? Or would you prefer to play cards?"

"No cards this evening, if you don't mind. Tell me, madame, what was this man Schacht like?"

She knew this questioning would come—de la Maison had briefed her. She'd even prepared her answers. "Quiet, alone, almost scared, I thought. Mousy, but in my opinion there was a man under the mousy veneer, a man who for some reason didn't want to show himself. Something about him didn't hang together—there was a missing facet to him that I never understood."

"Perhaps he had a screw loose?" Kalanga said hopefully

"He seemed quite sane, but there was an aura of mystery about him. As if he were hiding something. He lived within himself, very privately."

"You're sure he wasn't going crazy?"

"I don't think so, although God knows why he killed poor Prince M'Taga and threw the kingdom into an uproar. He didn't seem nuts, however. Not at all."

"Did the cops find out anything useful?"

"They took all his stuff from his room," she replied. "They questioned all of us about him. I've no idea what they concluded, except that his murder was linked to your nephew's. Just what the radio has been saying. I must leave you now, Prince Kalanga. The cook needs my help. It'll be business as usual tomorrow," she said happily.

Kalanga took one of the girls upstairs and was gone for an hour. Then he and N'Gobi left together, paying for the girls and drinks with the money Pyotr had given him.

Gitabwanga: KGB *rezidentura*—0900 hours, 6 January

"Did Kalanga find out anything more?"

"Only a little, Comrade General. According to Madame Petarde, who knew him best of all in the hotel, he seemed sane, but she can't understand why he killed M'Taga: 'He didn't seem nuts,' Kalanga quoted her. 'But there was something missing about him that I didn't understand.' The girls thought he was very strange, but not the type to kill. Not much use, I'm afraid."

What wasn't lost in the translation from Bwaganian French to Russian was lost because Ossilenko ignored what he didn't want to hear. "Exactly! Obviously, Schacht had a screw loose. Well done, Pyotr Aleksandrovich. Your idea of using Kalanga worked. He's confirmed my theory. Without question, the man was crazy. I expect the pressure of his work drove Schacht over the edge—that and his life-style here in Africa. Normally, he would never have considered the idea of defection. I'll explain that to the chairman."

Pyotr was silent. He doubted Ossilenko's facile theory, felt certain there was a more logical answer, but he simply nodded. Ossilenko interpreted his silence as assent.

"He must have flipped completely just about the time I arrived," Ossilenko commented.

Paris: SSR headquarters—0930 hours, 6 January

The single most important quality any intelligence service seeks in its personnel is loyalty. It is more critical than initiative, imagination, common sense, hard work, courage, and perseverance—although they too have primordial values. But they can be in fairly short supply and the service can still function. Given a shortage of loyalty, however, the service might as well be working for another country.

Any disloyalty, even in favor of an allied service, is unacceptable. Even if the person committing the act has the best motives, it can only be regarded as hostile, for a service must be able to trust its own people. And disloyalty in favor of the Soviet Union is, to a Western intelligence service, an act of the highest treason.

When SSR Director General Dubois read the dispatch from Colonel Vilmaire in Brussels, his insides churned. He sat on the offensive message for a day and a half before cabling Gitabwanga to order François home.

Then François' reply came in from Gitabwanga:

> ARRIVING PARIS LATE 07 JANUARY. WILL REPORT TO YOUR OFFICE 1000 08 JANUARY. END.

The cable was terse and gave no offense. But Dubois felt bile rise in his throat, and he perspired all over as if his malaria were acting up. Vilmaire's reluctant message had convinced him that François was guilty of disloyalty, turning Dubois' respect and friendship for de la Maison into anger and suspicion. He had little hope that François would be able to explain his actions satisfactorily, but at least he had to go through the motions of confirming his guilt.

Dubois didn't trust the telephone. He sent a handwritten message to Gitabwanga that night on the last aircraft. It was carried by an SSR courier, who arrived at Bwaga Airport without notifying the SSR poste.

Gitabwanga: SSR poste—0800 hours, 7 January

The courier found François' deputy alone in his office and saluted. The message was in a sealed envelope, and the deputy signed for it. The courier saluted, and the receipt was back in Dubois' office by midafternoon.

". . . you will tell no one of this, except the surveillants whom you select for this job. Move quickly, because he will leave Gitabwanga this afternoon. I want a precise account of all his movements in Gitabwanga today . . ."

The deputy, who admired de la Maison and liked him, was given no reason for this unusual request. A professional army officer, he accepted the instruction without question and set the team in motion. It was not hard to keep it from François' knowledge, because the chef de poste was home packing.

Gitabwanga: Mark's house—1200 hours, 7 January

It was a short but festive lunch. A cold buffet on the lanai. François gave Mark a copy of the police report on the deaths of M'Taga and Schacht and a report on the calm with which the nation had taken M'Taga's assassination. The king, he said, had made sure of that by issuing the news bulletin himself, asking the public to join his mourning.

"I learned a few minutes ago that Madame Petarde had a visit from Kalanga and N'Gobi last evening. Kalanga was there to find out what he could about Schacht. He was told Schacht must have gone nuts to kill M'Taga, but nothing much more."

"I wonder how she came to that conclusion, François. Did she have any help from you?" Mark was laughing.

"The possibility was mentioned to her, I believe."

"Nice work, François. Kalanga was sent by Ossilenko and Petrov, I'm sure. They'll blame everything on Schacht. And then they'll have to reassess Schacht's take for years back, trying to figure out when he was sane and when he was crazy. It'll cost them man years of work. I love it."

As the meal drew to an end, Mark asked François if he wouldn't mind delivering a gift to the U.S. Embassy in Paris.

"The package is in two parts. One is for you, and one for our COS Paris. It's perishable, so I've put it into dry ice. But even so, it should be delivered tomorrow morning if you don't mind. You should use yours the same evening, too."

"What is this mysterious package, Mark?"

"It's two filets. One is impala, the other Thompson's gazelle. Take the one you want and give the other to Daniel Reilly. Do you know him?"

"No, but I know of Reilly. He's a very effective man. We have excellent liaison with him, I believe."

In the bushes facing Mark's lanai, the SSR team's photographer got a telephoto shot of the police report being passed to Mark and Linda and then the package being handed to François. Shots were taken of François' car parked outside Mark's house. Finally, several shots of the three walking down the steps, saying goodbye.

Gitabwanga: Bwaga Airport—
1630 hours, 7 January

François' deputy saw him off. It was a strange scene, the deputy thought. De la Maison was, unwittingly, carrying with him to Paris a report for Director General Dubois on his meeting with Cameron and Takahashi. The report was in a routine SSR sealed pouch, to be collected from François by an SSR courier at the airport in Paris—so that François could go directly to Géraldine's apartment. The deputy knew that François was carrying his own time bomb. He crossed himself inconspicuously and breathed a prayer as his chief passed through the gate.

Petrov, there to see Ossilenko off on the same aircraft, saw François and smiled grimly to himself. He shook hands with Ossilenko, who marched through the gate after François. As he watched that straight back ahead of him, Ossilenko reveled in the knowledge that de la Maison was being recalled for punishment, just as Ossilenko had planned: I hope they cut off your balls, de la Maison, he said to himself.

Paris: Géraldine's apartment—2100 hours, 7 January

Inside the warm apartment, Géraldine had a candlelight dinner waiting for François. She scented the air with pine needles, and played his favorite Mozart piano concerto softly on the hi-fi. Her favorite dress glowed in the dim light, and she was beautiful. They kissed passionately to salve the long abstention, and she danced in and out of his arms as she brought drinks and food, froze the impala filet, and listened to his stories about Africa while they ate.

After dinner, François told her about the defeat of Red Snow and what it might mean: "I don't know, but I believe there may be a commendation or a medal for me tomorrow."

"Wonderful," she said, eyes damp. "I'll pray for you." It was the perfect welcome-home night that François had dreamed about in his lonely house in Gitabwanga.

Outside, an SSR staff surveillance team watched from their car as the lights went out. It was bitterly cold, but the team had strict instructions to remain on watch throughout the night. And to be extra careful: this bird was a professional—an SSR colleague. They weren't able to run the motor to keep warm. The exhaust might be noticed by the target.

"What's he done?" asked the driver, an SSR warrant officer.

"The rumor is he's in bed with either the KGB or the CIA," a lieutenant in the backseat said. "Probably for the money."

"I saw her this afternoon when we first got here," said the

driver. "She came in from shopping. I wish I were in bed with her, she's good-looking."

The lieutenant laughed. "Not that one up there. She's only his mistress. The rumor is about his relations with the KGB or the CIA people in Bwagania."

"Everyone goes bad in Africa." The driver shrugged.

Paris: the U.S. Embassy —0915 hours, 8 January

Daniel Reilly met Colonel de la Maison in his "overt" office. They had heard about each other for years but had never met.

"You have a very good man in Gitabwanga, Mr. Reilly. Mark Cameron and I have become friends. He asked me to deliver this package to you this morning."

"Well, thank you, Colonel. Do you know what's in it?"

"A filet of Thompson's gazelle. A true gourmet's delight, as you must know. Please freeze it as soon as you can, or eat it tonight. The dry ice is about finished."

"Thank you, I will. What news of Bwagania?"

François explained the Red Snow affair, ending with the deaths of M'Taga and Schacht, and departed fifteen minutes later, having agreed to dine with Reilly if time permitted.

After François had left the U.S. embassy, a member of the surveillance team telephoned to SSR: "Target just spent fifteen minutes in the U.S. Embassy, where he had left a package that he'd carried from the apartment this morning."

Paris: SSR headquarters— 1000 hours, 8 January

François was not expecting surveillance on him in the capital of his own country, by any service, and he arrived at SSR headquarters unaware that he was leading a tail two hundred meters long, consisting of seven well-trained men and women. They bunched up when he reached the door, welling in just behind him as if they were coming to work. Their orders were to see him into the office of the director general. They did it simply. One man and one woman rode up with him in the elevator, talking to each other about "les archives," a most boring conversation, and he paid no attention. They broke off and went to the team postmortem after he had closed the director general's door behind him.

There was no delay. François was pleased when the door to the inner office was opened for him immediately. He didn't notice the security man behind the outer door, ready to stop him if he broke for the corridor.

He strode across the carpet, smiling broadly at his friend, and reaching out his hand:

"Good morning, General. So good to see you." That ended François's illusion. The director general stood up, but he didn't offer his hand. He said in a harsh voice:

"Have you any idea why I ordered you back to Paris?"

"No, sir." François was astounded by this greeting. His stretched right hand slowly drooped. "I had hoped you would be pleased with the decapitation of Red Snow."

"Normally I would have been delighted, de la Maison. But not in the light of your other actions in Bwagania."

"What other actions? I do not understand, General." Still François had no idea of what the director general meant.

"Can you think of nothing you've been doing that constituted disloyalty? Nothing that grossly violates your standing orders? Nothing that might cause me to abandon my friendship for you, to distrust you forever?"

François could think of only one thing, but it was not possible that the director general knew of it. He shook his head. But the general did know.

"Then I will remind you, Colonel. You have been engaged in liaison with your CIA counterpart, one Mark Cameron. You have been giving him copies of our classified material. You gave him one as late as yesterday at noon, while your deputy was supposed to think you were at home packing. Then, to thumb your rotten nose at me, you even took a package to the CIA station chief here in Paris, this morning, while I waited for you to show up. Classified documents, no doubt. De la Maison, you and your actions are a stain on the honor of France, and you will be dealt with accordingly."

The director general was trembling from head to toe with rage, his hands clasping and unclasping.

The effect on François was calamitous. No matter what he said, it could be misinterpreted. He had to try, but with little hope of a fair hearing. His mind was in shock as he contemplated the shame that his family might have to bear.

"There is no need for an investigation, de la Maison. We have absolute proof, with photographs and eyewitness accounts. A confession has been drawn up and is being put into final form right now. You are under arrest, and your rank of colonel is suspended. You will sign the confession this afternoon, and then I will pronounce the punishment. Have you anything to say?"

François nodded. "Yes, sir. I do."

"Then we will bring in a witness. I have chosen a man who is of your former rank and is impartial. He will be allowed to plead on your behalf if he feels so inclined."

He pressed a button and said to his secretary: "Please admit Colonel Peletier. And come in yourself, to take notes.

"Whatever you say, de la Maison, will be recorded by tape as well as by my secretary, and will be appended to your confession and become part of the record."

As the secretary and Colonel Peletier came in, François nodded to them and said to the director general: "I understand." For both François and Peletier, it would always be a mystery why the director general had chosen a firm friend and believer in de la Maison. For Peletier was the real name of the man Mark had met as Jean Dumont when he transited Paris en route to Bwagania. Was it because the director general wanted to warn Peletier also, in a friendly way? Or did he want to be excessively fair?

He could have merely fired François, but instead he was giving him a staunch defender.

"Begin," said the director general.

"What is the charge, sir?" Peletier asked.

"He is charged with providing classified information, both orally and in writing, against explicit orders, to the CIA on a regular basis from September last year until now. It is an act of disloyalty punishable by a maximum of imprisonment and/

or dismissal." The director general looked François straight in the eyes as he stated the charge. The secretary took it down verbatim, as a backup to the hidden tape recorder.

"Your statement, de la Maison?" said the director general.

"Sir, I admit the fact of passing classified information to Mr. Cameron. But it was information that was developed in Bwagania, by the Sûreté or by my poste. It was local information, of value to an ally in the common cause against communism. In exchange, I received equally valuable information that Cameron obtained locally. I did this in order to make our defeat of Red Snow more likely, General, not because I had no respect for your orders. It was a field expedient, done in the spirit of the Atlantic alliance, in order to counter the KGB. I believe that most of my colleagues in the SSR would have done the same thing in my place, in that very unstable situation."

Peletier raised his hand, received a nod. "Sir, from my knowledge of what's going on in Africa, it's very useful to exchange information of purely local value with our allies, and indeed many officers would have done the same. It's not as if he gave away any classified information from Paris, sir."

The director general slapped his forehead. "But you both seem to have overlooked that it was done against my strict instructions. We shall have discipline in the SSR."

"Like the army, General?" said Peletier. "But in an intelligence organization we want intelligent handling of local situations, not just blind obedience."

"Beware, Peletier," retorted Dubois. "I don't like insubordination. Nor do I like being told what SSR needs."

"Quite, sir. But can we afford to lose a good man just on the basis of a technical violation?"

François intervened. Peletier was on a collision course, trying to save him, and it wouldn't work.

"My General," François said. "I have no defense. I did it for what I consider to be our cause—yours and mine. The cause of France. No doubt Cameron did the same thing, perhaps against the CIA's orders, for similar reasons. Technically I knew it was wrong when I did it, and I know it was wrong now. The only question is how you will dispose of me, because I would do the same thing again, given the same circumstances."

Peletier flung up his arms, a Gallic gesture of total despair. "Oh, mon cher, you have cut your throat!"

Despite himself, the director general laughed. It was a bitter laugh, and it had despair in it. He would have to decide what to do with a very good officer whose motives were completely understandable. Perhaps, in Gitabwanga, even the director general would have done the same thing. He knew it, but it was his job to impose discipline, demand loyalty, and to see things in black or white. These two men could indulge in such luxuries as ideals, but he had to run a tight ship, produce a trustworthy product, and be the ultimate judge of what was the best for the SSR. Not for any one officer, but for the organization.

"De la Maison, you will remain in Colonel Peletier's company and in this building, until fifteen hundred hours this afternoon. At that time you will both return here to receive the sentence." General Dubois' tone was uncompromising.

Gitabwanga: Mark's office—1100 hours, 8 January

It was Pyotr on the line. Mark listened carefully, his antennae up.

"Mark, may I ask you to lunch with me tomorrow? If not tomorrow, then the next day?" To Mark, Pyotr sounded unusually persistent. Did Moscow already know Mark was leaving TDY? Had Pyotr somehow convinced Ossilenko—based on nothing—that he could set up Mark for a recruitment pitch? Or was Pyotr beginning to depend on Mark? The latter, he hoped.

"I can't, Pyotr. I would have loved to, but I'm off to Washington this afternoon. I was just going to phone you to tell you. Perhaps when I come back?"

"Oh, I'm really very sorry. But pleased for you, Mark. Washington is such a beautiful city. When will you return?"

"I'm not sure. Perhaps in a month, perhaps two. They didn't say." Mark wasn't giving anything away. Let the KGB wonder how long I'll be gone. If I return sooner, it may catch Pyotr off balance.

"Well, Mark, I'll miss our talks." He sounded as if he really meant it. "I wish you a successful trip and a speedy return. Will you be in Washington the whole time?"

Mark smiled to himself. Pyotr was doing what professionals do, trying to smoke out what the trip meant. "I suppose so. They didn't say."

Pyotr's optimism read the reply as yes, not perhaps.

"Good. Very good. Then I'll wait for your return, my friend. You will call me?"

"Yes, Pyotr. You'll be the first to hear about it."

Gitabwanga: Pyotr's office—
1120 hours, 8 January

Right after talking to Mark, Pyotr drafted a cable to Moscow Center:

> CAMERON ADVISED TODAY HE WILL SPEND SEVERAL WEEKS IN WASHINGTON COMMENCING NOW. ETD GITABWANGA 1630 HOURS 8 JAN.
>
> FYI CAMERON, ALTHOUGH PLEASED WITH HIS TDY TO WASHINGTON (WHICH MAY RESULT IN CAREER IMPROVEMENT), MADE IT CLEAR HE WILL MISS OUR CONVERSATIONS.
>
> VIEW RAPID PROGRESS THIS OPERATION AND OUR PRIORITIES URGENTLY RECOMMEND I TDY WASHINGTON TO CONTINUE DEVELOPMENT OF CAMERON WHO COULD BE KEY TO SECURITY AND SUCCESS OF RED SNOW TWO. SUGGEST YOU CONSIDER SENDING SENIOR REPLACEMENT FOR ME WHO COULD STAY GITABWANGA UP TO TWO MONTHS.

That last paragraph, although ambiguous, was the clincher. Ossilenko would have a fit if he knew that the long discussion was a two-minute phone call.

Moscow: KGB headquarters—
1500 hours, 8 January

General Ossilenko read Pyotr's cable with mounting interest. He was particularly interested in the fact that a senior replacement for Petrov was suggested. His face darkened with excitement as he thought of more nights alone with Anna Iosevna. Sixty nights!

The chairman agreed reluctantly, based on Ossilenko's able detailing of how he alone could step in at this critical moment in Gitabwanga, to structure Red Snow Two as an unbeatable military coup.

Ossilenko's cable to Pyotr was brief:

> AGREE YOU TDY WASHINGTON ATTEMPT RECRUIT CAMERON. I WILL REPLACE YOU IN GITABWANGA BUT NOT MORE THAN FORTY-FIVE DAYS. YOU WILL RETURN GITABWANGA AS REZIDENT WHEN CAMERON RETURNS. WILL ARRIVE GITABWANGA 10 JANUARY.

Paris: SSR headquarters—
1515 hours, 8 January

Peletier broke the silence as they sat in the outer office of the director general: "What was it, François, that you gave to Cameron? I have a feeling we should talk about those classified documents. And the package for Reilly that you just told me about—what was in it?"

"I gave Cameron only my own locally generated materials," François said. "Nothing that was really sensitive or that I thought would cause a problem. And the package for Reilly was simply a filet of a very unclassified Thompson's gazelle. I don't suppose Dubois would believe that, however."

"Don't be too sure, old friend. I've got a hunch we should ask to see those documents he spoke of. Perhaps they will speak for themselves. Do you agree?"

"Well, yes, of course I do. I was shocked into silence when I first met the general, but you've got me wondering now."

"My nose," grinned Peletier, "is usually right."

The director general kept them waiting until three-thirty, the added half hour to help them stew. Then he told his secretary to admit Colonel Peletier and Monsieur de la Maison.

Before the director general could say a word, Colonel Peletier asked for leave to speak: "I have a question, sir, that seems reasonable since punishment is being considered for de la Maison."

"Your question, Peletier?"

"May we inspect the documents that he is reported to have given to Monsieur Cameron?"

"You realize that these are only samples? Most of what he passed is not available . . . we don't have copies. But he has confessed, so it is an academic question."

"Even so, General, we would like to see what you have. It is only fair to let us examine them."

"Very well." Dubois handed them the package. Peletier quickly found two documents that Ossilenko had selected: "These two documents, François—did you receive them?"

"Yes, I did." François studied the documents for several moments. "But not these copies. Look here, we have a stamp that's always used by our mail room in Gitabwanga, and it's not there in the corner where it should be." He pointed to the upper right corner. "Anyway, I didn't give these to Cameron." He pointed to the upper left corner, where there was a stamped block of printed initials and lines where readers were to sign. "The printed initials on the distribution ladder are correct, including mine, but here, where I supposedly wrote my initials in my box to indicate I'd seen the documents, the handwriting isn't mine."

Peletier also studied the papers. Suddenly, he jumped up and brought the documents around to the general's chair. "Look, sir, these coded marks show that these papers are copies of documents circulated in Paris. Look here. We can see that they went to four French government offices and to three foreign intelligence services."

The director general stared, reddening as he realized he hadn't known about the new coding system or taken the time to check François' handwriting against the initials on the distribution ladder. While he was making a mental note to get briefed on the Paris coding system, François let out a shout of surprise.

"Look, General! These photographs in the restaurant. They had to be taken by Yegorov, a KGB officer in Gitabwanga! I remember well, he and his wife sat at that very table near us. These photos must have been doctored in Moscow. How did you get them?"

"From a very good source of ours, a man who's info has been reliable for years. Martini, in Brussels."

Peletier wrinkled his nose: "That little worm. Vilmaire has always said that Martini's playing games with us. This proves it."

"Where did Martini get it, sir?" François wondered how the director general would handle the question.

"From one of your own men in Gitabwanga," he said. "But now I suspect it was planted on Martini."

"Perhaps Martini has links to the KGB." Peletier nodded toward François. "In any event, we owe this man an apology."

Dubois was receptive. De la Maison had been indiscreet, even disobedient, but at least it wasn't a question of loyalty. He was the victim of KGB disinformation.

"François, I can honestly say thank God you're clear. I regret the incident. You're reinstated in your rank and position." He shook François' hand. "Go back to your poste, but in the future, be more careful how you deal with Cameron."

To Peletier, he said: "Jean-Luc, you must ascertain to which of the seven organizations these documents went. That'll tell us where the KGB has a penetration."

Peletier pointed out: "The coded marks are distorted by the copying, but I'll get the lab to work on them."

"See that you brief me on those marks each time they're changed," said Dubois defensively. He turned to François: "The sight of your initials at the head of the Gitabwanga distribution ladder made me lose my temper. I regret I didn't check it."

"Yes, sir," replied François coolly.

They left the director general staring out the window, still pink with embarrassment. The incident was closed, but it had blighted the director's friendship with de la Maison.

Gitabwanga: KGB *rezidentura*—1730 hours, 8 January

Pyotr looked at General Ossilenko's cable with disgust, as if he'd got hold of a snake that was going to twist out of his hand and bite him. Ossilenko himself was coming back to Gitabwanga to steal Anna Iosevna away from him for good. How he hated the bastard! His TDY request should never have suggested a senior officer as acting *rezident*. Ossilenko must have grabbed at it. Pyotr wondered how on earth the general had managed to convince the chairman to let him go for as much as forty-five days. Moscow was putting a great deal more importance on Red Snow Two than he'd thought.

On top of Ossilenko's maneuver, Pyotr would now have to face Olga's fury. She would see his TDY in Washington as something he had contrived to leave her alone with Aleksandra in primitive Gitabwanga. She would rail at him for hours, while Aleksandra would weep quietly at the prospect of her father's long absence. The best thing to do was to leave as soon as possible, giving Olga only tonight to work on him.

Pyotr left on the first flight on January 9, a man full of hidden anger and bitter frustration.

PART III
January–February 1973
The Trap

Langley, Virginia: the DCI's office—
1700 hours, 9 January

"Sir, I believe I've devised a scheme that has a good chance of smoking out the mole, plus any subagents he or she may have."

The DCI smiled at Mark's implication that it might be a woman. A man seemed more appropriate. "What do you have in mind?"

"To start some corridor rumors that, added up, indicate two facts. First, that a KGB officer in Washington is negotiating to defect. Second, that I'm running the case and that the Soviet is about to identify a mole to me."

The director nodded.

"It's going to require good timing and a lot of luck, but I think it's worth the effort. I've assumed that the mole is now working in headquarters, in fact he's usually stationed here, perhaps permanently. He has routine access to most of our Soviet operational traffic. I've also assumed that the mole has one or more subagents, and they're included."

"Reasonable assumptions."

"If the rumor campaign doesn't bring results, then we distribute a document to the prime suspects that should prompt a mole to act—a report of my supposed latest contact with the defector."

"If the recipients aren't in the need-to-know category, they'll smell a trap, surely."

"Some of them would in fact receive copies, even of a case

with this sensitivity. That's one of the reasons they're suspect. The others will get copies by mistake . . . the kind of distribution mistake that is rare but credible."

The director nodded. Everyone knew such mistakes were impossible to avoid, no matter how careful people were.

"The rumors and the contact report will be worded so that even though it makes a mole and his subagents panic, we become aware of their panic and can use it against them before they can bolt and escape. The mole mustn't sense the acuteness of the danger early enough to escape it."

The DCI grinned. "I see where you'll need some luck."

"The core of the idea is to use bait that both scares and entices him. The mole must feel that he has to take the bait, has to move to see what's behind it, or risk his head by sitting on his hands. The case will apparently be very closely held, and the indication is that the Soviet hasn't given me any details yet. He's feeling the ground, making himself attractive to us so he can get the best terms. He's promised details about the mole, but he's not giving away the store now. He will soon, however. He's pretty much committed."

The DCI smiled. "Sounds good, Mark. It should scare him into action. Go on."

"He'll have to act, sir. He may warn any subagents that danger exists, but he'll want them to sniff about for him so he'll avoid frightening them into inactivity. They'll cast about, trying to find out more about my 'case'—hopefully, from me directly, or from my assistant. If so, our antennae should pick up signs of unusual tension, questions, persistence, and so on. I'll have other trip wires around too, the widest net possible without alerting the mole."

"It won't be easy. He's a pro."

"There are only a few candidates, sir. We'll look at them all. Somewhere we'll catch the telltale signs of fear, of efforts to find out what's up. Hopefully, we'll find traces of emergency contact with the KGB *rezidentura* here, direct or indirect."

"Won't he avoid his usual case officer, a prime suspect?"

"I think he'd like to meet him at least once, sir, to see if his instincts will tell him if that's the defector. Then, if he wants to go around his case officer, he'll probably have to take a chance, use a signal that we too can spot."

"Like sending some kind of signal to the *rezident*'s house?" The director looked dubious.

"Anger and fear will drive him to make a mistake, I believe. It's done it to KGB agents before. With luck, it'll be an error we can detect."

"Who are your suspects?"

Mark gave him a handwritten list. There were seven names on it. "I don't like to point the finger, sir . . . but there's no other way. They're only on there because they fit my criteria."

The DCI nodded: "I know of nothing against them, either. How big a team do you want, and who will be in it?"

"I brought a list, sir."

The DCI laughed. "Good for you." He looked at the list. "You've got it. I'll tell them to help you. You've proved there is a mole, so you can have first crack at him . . . or her. Good luck!"

Langley, Virginia: Mark's office—1400 hours, 10 January

By early afternoon Mark had his bait in final shape, on paper. The principal element of the bait, the corridor rumor campaign about Mark's hot case, called BRASS, was carefully constructed so as to be believable and not arouse suspicion. Rumors abound in all intelligence services, and people listen to them with great interest. Mark needed the right person to start the rumor, someone he could trust completely.

The fake contact report of a mythical meeting between himself and the potential Soviet defector (cryptonym BRASS), looked real and would, Mark thought, pass muster. The report indicated he had known the Soviet overseas, but the overseas location wasn't cited. The Soviet promised details on a hot case, a mole in the CIA, to prove his bona fides. The information would be given to Mark in a week or so.

Mark had never knowingly written fiction before as part of his job, and the process was more laborious than he'd expected. Finally, he typed the documents himself, and carried them to the office of the deputy director for operations (DDO).

Langley, Virginia: DDO's office—
1600 hours, 10 January

"The DCI moved quickly," said Frank Wales. "The director of security just called me. It may stretch his people a bit, but the surveillance teams you wanted are ready. They're standing by to put in the phone taps and bug the houses, cars, and offices of whoever reacts to your bait."

Mark nodded. "Thanks, Frank. Here is the bait, in final form. Would you approve it?"

Mason looked over the two documents carefully. "They'll do fine. Hope they work. Anything else you need?"

"Only one thing. Clara."

"Clara Brunswick? A great gal. She's yours. I'll have her report to you right away. Why did you choose her?"

"I know her. She can do it, and she wasn't in headquarters when I was shafted in Tokyo."

"I was, Mark. What about me?"

"You were still COS Rome when two of the other incidents took place."

"The other members of the team the DCI approved?"

"Same thing. Either they weren't in headquarters each time we know the mole struck or they had no access to what he stole."

"That let's you out, too," said the DDO with a grin. "I couldn't resist that."

Langley, Virginia: Mark's office—
1615 hours, 10 January

Mark greeted her with a hug: "Hi, Clara, wonderful to have you aboard." He offered her the chair next to his desk.

"Mark Cameron, young man, is that gray hair I see peeking through the brown?" She kissed him as she sat down. "You haven't been working for a change, have you?"

"I'm so glad I asked for you." Mark laughed. "You always put things in context."

"Well, I'm here to work. What's up?"

Clara Brunswick, senior secretary, had served for over twenty years in the Russia division. She was neither young nor decorative, but she was solid and bright and by now she knew more about the division's personnel than did its senior officers. Two of her overseas tours had been in Berlin, as secretary—in fact, she was special assistant to the chief of base. Her boss's explosive temperament, crude but colorful language, and iron discipline—which earned him the nickname Beast of Berlin—had brought out in Clara a protective, motherly attitude toward the base's case officers, especially the juniors, most of whom were twenty years younger than she. They loved the warm brown eyes in her rather forbidding brown, craggy face. Her toothy grin and no-nonsense, friendly scolding of the chief of base when he went too far helped them when they faced the Beast for one of his famous chewings out. There would be an ally to complain to, afterward, in the Beast's outer office. Mark had been one of those young case officers.

"This doesn't get outside this room, Clara," said Mark quietly. "The KGB has a source here in headquarters, probably in our division—a mole, a staffer. You're part of a trap for this mole."

Clara nodded, without changing her expression. She was shocked, but contained it and listened silently while Mark ran through the evidence, the mole's apparent level of access, his assumptions, and the nature of the trap.

"When does the action start?"

"Tomorrow morning, first thing. Please lock these envelopes in your safe overnight. They're stage two of our bait. We'll distribute them only if stage one doesn't work fairly soon. Tomorrow you start a rumor campaign, then come back here and watch who makes a move. This is what's in each envelope." He let her read the contact report.

"Is this a fake, Mark?" she asked astutely.

"Yes. It's the basis of the rumor you'll spread. Do it as believably as you can, to people you know won't be able to shut up about it."

"There are some of those around," she said grimly. "And for once, we may be grateful for their loose talk."

"Exactly. Now, read this. It's what the rumor has to say, word by word. We'll get the bastard."

She read the wording of the rumors she was to start. "Your optimism's infectious. I think it may work. Are we alone in this?"

"Good question. Here's a list of the team the director has approved. I'm the principal case officer. You're my only assistant. We're it. Your experience, your radar, are part of the game we're going to play. Every detail has to be just right. If we're lucky, the rumors should bring a reaction later in the morning, or the afternoon."

"Let's pray. Then what?"

"When you've broadcast the news, come back here. Keep one of the envelopes on your desk, sealed, but with its sensitivity indicators in plain view. Make a perfect record of every person who calls or comes here asking for you or me. Note the time to the minute—I want to know exactly what they want and what their state of mind is—anxious, rushed, calm, that sort of thing. Even if someone only tries to get in touch with me, log the exact time each contact began and ended, by name and by content. Watch for people who try to see what's on your desk."

She nodded. "No problem. I've got good antennae."

"I know. That's why I asked for you. Even if I'm here, tell all my callers that I'm out but will get back to them as soon as I can. Be sure to ask them how they can be reached for the next day or so—get all the phone numbers you can, even of people they'll be visiting in other offices."

"Who do you think's involved?"

"That was next on my list. Tonight, if you will, write down any names that come to mind. Concentrate on people who spend most of their time in headquarters and are in a position to collect the data that's been leaking."

"That narrows the field," she said thoughtfully.

"I have a list, too. I'll give it to you in the morning, so it doesn't influence you when you make up your list tonight."

**Arlington, Virginia: Wayne's house—
1715 hours, 10 January**

Sam Wayne had been a mole for fifteen years. He even knew that the KGB cryptonym for his operation was SVYET (light), and the aptness of it was not lost on him: His "take" shed light, for the KGB, on all of CIA's Soviet operations.

Sam got a huge kick out of the fact that he was shafting his CIA colleagues, that he could strike daily blows for the cause he believed in implicitly—world communism under the USSR.

Sam had gone to Harvard during the Great Depression. The stock market crash caused him no economic hardship; nor was Sam moved by the suffering of others less fortunate. He was, however, angered by the failure of the system, the easy comfort he'd known all his life. He blamed free enterprise, and gravitated to the far left. He was courted by members of the Communist party on campus but shied away from their overt rebellion. After graduation, he was unable to get a decent job, his harshly negative attitude assuring that his prediction of unemployment would come true. He lived for some months on the generosity of his widowed mother, a wealthy Bostonian social climber whom he despised as well as exploited. Eventually, he found work as a journalist, and met officials of Amtorg, the Soviet trading corporation in New York.

One of them recruited him as a low-level disinformation agent for the NKVD, as the KGB was then called. Sam performed a series of mundane tasks for the NKVD, mainly planting articles favorable to the USSR in U.S. news media. He thought the work uninspiring, but it developed in him a liking for covert action and a loyalty to the NKVD. From the time of his recruitment by the NKVD, Sam downplayed his leftist leanings.

After undistinguished service in the U.S. Army in World War II, he spent two years in Moscow for his newspaper. What he saw in Moscow made him contemptuous of the Soviet Union's lack of economic progress but a firm admirer of the rigid central planning and the disciplined conformity of the USSR.

Sam worked hard in Moscow, learning Russian and being trained by the KGB, then called the MGB. His MGB handlers fed him newsworthy stories, usually critical of the Soviet system, for his newspaper so he could look good and devote more time to his training as a Soviet agent. They coached him to act the part of a man who went to Moscow ready to try to find some good in the Soviet system and came away a determined enemy of communism. Sam Wayne learned his lessons well, returning to the U.S. a first-class KGB spy and a darling of the right.

By now he thought of himself as one of the elite of world communism, twisting the tail of the hated free enterprise system and its proponents. With KGB guidance and subtle assists from their assets, he maneuvered himself into the Washington scene as a news reporter. There, he was spotted by a CIA officer in the Russia division, cleared, recruited, and hailed into the clandestine services as "one of our best career trainees, a man with all the right credentials: fluent Russian, a tour in Moscow, a realistic hostility to the Soviet system, and a fine reporter."

Despite a CIA medical hold on him, which meant he could never serve overseas, Sam had risen in the clandestine services and was now a senior officer in the Russia division. He was highly intelligent, an outstanding and tough-minded operational planner. He could be, and frequently was, witty and charming, although under it he was a sarcastic, dour cynic, a recluse by nature, his marriage his only safe haven in a hostile world.

He had recruited his wife, Sonya, for the KGB shortly after their marriage, playing on her Russian antecedents. Her parents had emigrated from the Ukraine to New York in the early 1900s. Sonya, too, was in the Russia division, a very senior intelligence analyst. The contrast between the tall, red-haired, lanky Sam and his short, rotound, black-haired wife was almost ludicrous. But nobody laughed, because they both had exceptional memories, excellent minds, and were workaholics. Because they never went overseas they constituted a corporate memory, a historical reference service that was invaluable to Russia division.

It was also invaluable to the KGB—and the KGB paid them well for it.

Russia division chief Jack Mason, a gentleman, was truly fond of Sam and Sonya. He treated them like his family, and trusted them.

The third member of the SVYET team was a tough-talking, hard-drinking case officer named Alec Besansky, whose Russian parents had also come to the U.S. in the early 1900s. He worked in the counterespionage (CE) staff. After Sam had recruited him for the KGB, Alec managed to get a medical hold placed on himself so that the unsuspecting CIA didn't send him overseas again. His red face, unruly brown hair, bloodshot eyes, and lumbering gait were as well known a fixture in the corridors of the Russia division as they were in his own CE staff.

Sonya often came to Sam's office during the day. Their CIA work didn't bring them together, but they were, after all, man and wife. Alec Besansky was not a frequent visitor to Sam's office: They had no professional reasons requiring direct contact. Alec often visited the Wayne house, but even then he was not at ease talking shop. He thought it unwise to discuss things openly, even in Sam's house. He much preferred the system of drops that they used for most of their clandestine communications. His counterespionage (CE) mind was always alert.

This evening, Sam had an announcement to make. "The conductor's going on leave," he told Sonya and Alec. "A temporary man will replace him. Probably some equally dimwitted knuckle dragger." Sonya and Alec bobbed their heads, listening patiently while Sam railed about the conductor going on leave. Sam was the only one who met him, and they had no basis to argue.

Sam was always sarcastic about their KGB case officers, whether or not they were competent. Boris Kuznetsov, now their conductor for seven years, was competent, a fact Sam refused to admit. Sam was irritated by any changes in his handling, and the notion that Boris needed a rest was ridiculous. "After all," he often said, "we're the ones who do all the work and take all the risks."

"I expect the replacement'll be okay, Sam." Sonya tried to calm her waspish husband. Alec smiled his support, anxious—as always—to get the business portion of the meeting over.

But Sam had become so sure of his ability to run rings around the agency that the risks had become slight in his mind. Fifteen years of success had him thinking his team was invincible.

"Listen," he said. "I'm to meet with this new man the night of the fourteenth. So let's get as much stuff together as we can . . . show him what we can do."

"Numbers game, eh?" Alec grunted cynically. His world vision consisted of innumerable self-serving lackeys producing results for others, others being those in power, with money. His motivation was essentially financial, his goal to be one of those others.

"Call it what you like, Alec," said Sam. "If we shine, we get more money and more satisfaction. The replacement will probably claim credit, piss on the conductor, and recommend we get a raise because we've done so well under his direction."

Washington, D.C.: foreign-service lounge—1730 hours, 10 January

Mark had taken the agency bus down to the State Department to check the foreign-service lounge for messages and mail. The lounge is mainly operated as an informal meeting place, answering service, mail room, message board, and office for foreign-service officers temporarily in Washington. To Mark, the relatively plush, comfortable suite on the first floor of the State Department main building, was always a step up in comfort compared to the austerity of the CIA headquarters.

There was only one item being held for him in the foreign-service lounge: a thin envelope with the return address of a store in Georgetown. He opened the note, expecting a bill.

The contents were a complete surprise: "My good friend, I too am in Washington and wish to see you. I will wait for your call. Pyotr."

The phone number in the note was a private, not a Soviet Embassy, number. The stamp, Mark noticed, had been cancelled that afternoon in downtown D.C.

Mark left the lounge, went to a public phone several blocks away from the building, and dialed the number.

Langley, Virginia: Mark's office—0800 hours, 11 January

Clara Brunswick was already at her desk in the outer office when Mark walked in. He closed the door to the corridor, sat next to her desk.

"Good morning, Clara. Did any names come to mind?"

"Eight," she said, giving him a folded paper. "I know it has to be done, but I hated it. I've known them all for years."

"I know," said Mark, glancing at it. "Traitors act just like other people. That's how they operate." He pulled out his list and put it next to hers. "I had seven on my list. Four of them are on both our lists. Ready to distribute the rumors?"

"Anytime. Now?"

Mark nodded. Clara's face was pale as she set off to lay down the bait.

Mark took an elevator to the basement and jogged on the indoor running track for half an hour. It helped calm him, and he felt better when he had showered, dressed, and gone back to his office. Clara was back at her desk.

"Everything went okay?"

"Yes, Mark. I dropped the rumor with some of the division's prize gossips. I wore my harassed look and everyone sympathized with me . . . a double workload, you know. I don't think anyone will be suspicious."

"Let's hope for a quick reaction."

"It may take all day."

"I hope not," said Mark. "Every minute's going to be an hour long." He grinned, shrugged, went into his office and shut the door so visitors couldn't see whether he was in.

The office layout, plus Clara's long experience in the Russia division, were parts of the trap.

Mark closed the venetian blinds so he couldn't be seen

from any of the windows across the courtyard. It was, anyway, better to read than to look at the sterile scene outside: a bit of winter sky and a cold courtyard that was off limits—flagstones, gray stone chips, uninspiring bushes, and hibernating trees—down onto which hundreds of windows like his looked through the building's light-gray stone walls.

The waiting began.

Langley, Virginia: Sam Wayne's Office—1630 hours, 11 January

It was late afternoon before Sam Wayne heard the rumor. He called Sonya and Alec at once. They were in his office, door closed, in minutes.

"Twice in twenty-four hours, Sam! Why?" Alec was irritated.

"I've a good reason," Sam said. He told them what he'd heard at a water fountain.

"Good grief," said Sonya. "This came out of nowhere!"

Alec was more explicit. "Shit! Sam, what do we do?"

Sam seemed confident. "We've no idea if there's anything to this other than wishful thinking. I'll bet that of the hundreds of KGB officers in Washington, ten or so are deliberately making defection noises at any one time. Some are bound to make it even more attractive by mentioning moles and stuff. But we must find out if this is real. Sonya, keep your ears open for clues as to what Cameron's on to. The Soviet is someone he knew earlier, otherwise they wouldn't have brought a station chief home."

"This could be a trap," said Alec, his CE mind at work.

"I thought of that," replied Sam. "We've got to be very careful, but we've also got to find out if it's true. The worst thing we can do is sit on our hands."

He looked at Besansky. "You know Cameron?"

"Yup." Alec nodded. "Not as well as you two do."

"We can't do it, Alec," said Sonya. "He'd tumble right away. He knows what our jobs are. He doesn't know yours, does he?"

"No, that's true. I could fool him, I'm sure."

"Good," said Sam. "Get next to him. Tease it out of him. Don't be obvious, just normal curiosity. And don't act nervous. By the law of averages this isn't a real case, and anyway, don't forget that defectors almost always balk at the last moment."

"I'll do it tomorrow," said Alec. "Too late today. I need time to think out my approach."

"Clara Brunswick has been assigned to help him," said Wayne. "That may be a start for you."

"I know her well," exclaimed Alec. "She should be a pushover."

**Washington, D.C.: a Georgetown inn—
1930 hours, 11 January**

Pyotr was seated in an unobtrusive corner of the dining room. He had shaken off an FBI spot surveillance an hour ago, then walked to the restaurant despite heavy rain.

"Hello, Mark. Good of you to join me for dinner."

"Evening, Pyotr. A very pleasant surprise to find that you've come to Washington, too. You said nothing before I left." They shook hands warmly.

"I didn't know myself, Mark, then I got a message ordering me here to help at a conference. They're shorthanded." He smiled, not really expecting Mark to believe the KGB was shorthanded in Washington.

"Come on, Pyotr," said Mark. "You can tell me why you're here. You know I won't tell anyone." They both laughed.

"You're here to receive a promotion, Mark?"

"Just between us, Pyotr, they're asking me to be secretary of state, but I'm refusing. All work, no play."

Pyotr burst out laughing. "Mark Cameron," he said. "I'll bet if you were really asked to take that job, you would. Or are you happy where you are?"

Mark smiled at Pyotr's obvious fishing expedition. "I'm supremely unhappy, Pyotr, that I'm not ambassador to Paris. Now, that's a job with a glittering social scene, lots of ways to enjoy yourself, and lots of ways to be useful." Mark paused. "Look, Pyotr. We don't know each other as old friends do, but we've quickly achieved a rather unusual degree of mutual liking, maybe real friendship. We both know what we do for our governments, so that can be left unsaid. Each of us is interested in whether the other could be persuaded to come over to his system. You wonder if you could recruit me, right?"

Pyotr's mouth fell open, and he stared at Mark. Before he could say anything, Mark went on.

"And I wonder if I can recruit you for our side. It's normal, isn't it?"

"Yes, but . . ." Pyotr was shocked by Mark's bluntness.

"If we're good at our jobs, neither will ever know what the other thinks about such a proposition. So we don't have to discuss it, do we?" He smiled to take the edge off.

Pyotr knew he couldn't report this to Moscow Center. He responded quickly, "Mark, you're very direct. I like that. And I agree, we should never discuss it."

"But," said Mark, "if you ever need a friend to talk to about anything, no matter how sensitive, how personal, I'll be there. Someone 'outside' your group, objective and discreet, with whom you can let down your hair."

There was a long silence, during which Mark wondered what was going on inside his head. Pyotr, in fact, was still struggling with a shock he'd been delivered the afternoon of the tenth, after his arrival in Washington. The KGB *rezident,* unaware that Pyotr had been exposed with Anna Iosevna by SVYET, had assigned him to replace Boris Kuznetsov as the mole's case officer while Pyotr was on TDY in Washington. "I'm giving you two cases, Petrov," the major general had said. "Keep you busy and on your operational toes, and it'll help stretch the FBI a bit further. Just make sure they don't keep up with you."

Pyotr realized that the *rezident* knew nothing about his affair with Anna Iosevna and the SVYET report of it. Embarrassed, he decided not to tell him, to go ahead with the assignment and make the best of it. He hoped he'd be able to handle SVYET by dead drops after the first meeting, not have to meet him face to face more than once. Once was going to be bad enough.

Meanwhile, here was Mark—the man he was supposed to recruit, the one person he wanted to discuss all his problems with and couldn't—bluntly offering a wailing wall. It was impossible, anyway. Mark would report it to CIA, and SVYET would send it to Moscow Center—and his goose would be cooked. Pyotr saw no practical way to assuage his fury.

"Thank you, Mark. I'll take that in the best sense: a friend on whose shoulder I can cry, if I ever need to." He paused, and the next words were almost involuntary: "My problems are mundane, common ones that revolve around people, not the institutions they serve . . . or warp."

The last two words were said very quietly, almost to himself, in Russian slang, but Mark caught it, realized that once again Pyotr's problems were almost bursting out of him.

Mark switched to the abstract: "People really are more important than institutions. If you turn it around the other way and the people exist to serve the state—or more likely, to serve those who control the state—then you have a pretty dreary society. But perhaps you look at it differently?"

Pyotr was in a rough place. He saw it Mark's way, and he was sick of acting a part he increasingly detested. But it would be too risky to reply that he agreed, then have to remove Mark's report of it from the SVYET take. Given SVYET's amazing memory, Boris Kuznetsov would certainly find out about it when he came back from home leave. He took refuge in the familiar Party line, disgusted with himself as he did it.

"Mark, you probably know our system as well as I do. Although you and I may have the same long-term aspirations, our leaders see things differently. Ours in the USSR are more radical, in theory, given Lenin's notion that the state will wither away one day. Meanwhile, our ruling group must keep control so that we can better reach that objective."

"And what if that goes on forever? Or at least through your lifetime? You won't feel cheated?"

"No, I accept the fact that it may take longer than we would like, but we'll get there." He had lied, but he knew SVYET was going to love his words—they would hear them shortly when the mole put a report of the meeting in the next drop.

Sensing they had reached the end of the conversation for

the time being, Mark changed the subject. The rest of their meal was spent talking about Washington's restaurants, monuments, buildings, and parks. Mark made Pyotr as comfortable as he could, avoiding any more provocation. They parted at nine-thirty, agreeing to meet in a week: same time and place.

Pyotr left the inn as content as he could be, given his problems. He had made no comments that would be offensive to Moscow Center. His own report could safely differ with Mark's on the question of whether or not Cameron had subtly expressed unhappiness with the U.S. system. And above all, he had enjoyed Mark's company. It suddenly struck Pyotr that he was putting his own happiness above the requirements of the KGB. He felt no guilt about it: He had crossed a bridge, and felt better.

Arlington, Virginia: Wayne's house—2200 hours, 11 January

As he got ready for bed, Sam Wayne thought about how he'd beaten the CIA polygraph operator in the only lie detector test he'd taken, a year after he'd joined the Company.

The KGB had kept Sam on the payroll after he left Moscow but didn't use him again for operations until he was recruited by the CIA. When Sam joined the Agency, they still waited. There was no doubt of his loyalty to the KGB; it was a matter of protecting him during his first couple of years, until his Moscow tour was above suspicion. Boris's predecessor had told him that before Sam went to work for the CIA, one liquid evening in a safe apartment: "There will be people who ask if you were recruited by us in Moscow. It's a logical question, no matter what your reputation. We'll only meet twice a year for the time being, while you dig in on the highest ground you can get to inside the clandestine services. Meanwhile, here's how you can beat the polygraph . . ."

The promise made to him by the AMTORG official who first recruited Sam was repeated several times, until it was deeply engraved: "When we finally throw out those capitalist swine and install a Marxist-Leninist paradise in the U.S., you, Sam Wayne, will have earned a top-level cabinet job in Washington!" It was heady stuff, and Sam was ready to do anything to earn it.

When Sam's time came to take the lie-detector test, he was ready. He took the medication his KGB handler had given him, and to the routine question "Are you now, or have you ever been, a member of any organization dedicated to the violent overthrow of the U.S. government?" his response had been an emphatic, "No, of course not!" Several times the young polygraph operater had protested that Wayne had moved. He should sit still, make no noise, stir no muscles. "Just answer yes or no, but stay quite still." He would repeat the question.

Wayne apologized, said he would do better. And he did. The drugs worked well enough, and when the polygraph operator asked if the very slight increases in Sam's blood pressure, breathing pace, heart rate, and palm perspiration were anger at the question, not guilt, Sam replied emphatically, "The question really pisses me off. I'm still angry about it." His vital signs weren't nearly as marked as when he'd taken the test questions up front, before the drugs worked. The operator, anxious to get rid of this irritating man with the anticommunist reputation, recorded it as "no reaction" and went on to the set of questions about homosexuality.

Sam smiled as he got into bed. It had happened so long ago, his first real victory after joining the Agency. But he was still proud of it.

Pulling up the blankets, Sonya whispered, "Who will replace Boris these weeks?"

"He just gave me a physical description and told me that the man will occupy Boris's apartment in the Baleen building, and drive his car. I've got the recognition signal, so I'll know he's the right man."

"Why does Boris take home leave in winter?"

"It's on the Black Sea, so I guess it's not too cold. He has no children, so school isn't a problem. There was a plush dacha available, so he took it."

He yawned and drifted off. Tomorrow was time enough to think about Cameron's so-called hot case. Sam had disciplined himself to sleep regardless of his worries.

Langley, Virginia: Mark's office—
0955 hours, 12 January

Mark sat at this desk, waiting. Yesterday's lack of a reaction had been bad enough. Was it to be the same thing today?

He tried to read the material in his in box: reports from other stations, intelligence estimates, documents marked for special interest by the division front office—but even the incoming special indicator cables from the field were of little interest. The waiting made it difficult to concentrate. He listened to the clock on the wall tick away and his nervousness mounted.

What was the mole doing right now? What was he thinking at this moment? How did he report to the KGB, and how often? How did they give him instructions? How sophisticated was their communications system with him? What kind of man was he? How cool and calculating was he? How would he try to pierce the protective shield that he now thought surrounded this special BRASS case of Cameron's?

The mole was surely bright, confident, unscrupulous. What had impelled him to treason? Had he been cajoled—unwillingly—or trapped into getting ever more deeply involved with the KGB, until he was unable to withdraw from their grasp? Was it a lark or a cause worth his life or was it only money? Probably the cause, not money, linked to a promise of power.

The phone's buzzer brought him abruptly back to reality. It was Clara, speaking in a faint voice on the office intercom:

"Mark, may I come in?"

"Of course, Clara."

She closed the connecting door carefully, showed him her log: "Take a look at this, Mark!"

The morning log already had eight entries:

1. 12 Jan—0845 hrs. Betty called re lunch tomorrow. (Betty's my friend. She asked no questions.)
2. 12 Jan—0851 hrs. Boris Prochnik called to remind you that you're to play tennis this evening at 6:30. He

said: "No need to disturb him." (Asked no questions.)

3. 12 Jan—0856 hrs. Regular courier with mail. (No questions.)
4. 12 Jan—0902 hrs. Office of training called. "Will Mr. Cameron lecture to career trainees at the Farm January 16? Subject: Operating conditions in central Africa." Told them you may not have time, due hot case. "We'll call back tomorrow." Clara: "May I have your name and number?" Voice: "I'm Mrs. Taggart, Wendy Taggart. Extension 0158." (She asked no questions.)
5. 12 Jan—0905 hrs. Clara called office of director of security: "Mr. Cameron wants to speak to the director." Voice: "I'll tell Mr.Tye." (Voice asked no questions.)
6. 12 Jan—0925 hrs. Regular courier arrived with mail. (No questions.)
7. 12 Jan—0946 hrs. Womans' voice, probably a secretary: "This right number for Mr. Cameron?" Clara: "Yes, can I help?" Woman: "Mr. Tye, director of security, is returning Mr. Cameron's call." Clara: "He's not available right now. I'm his assistant, Clara Brunswick. I placed the call. Can I help?" Woman: "I'll put him on." A few seconds later, man's voice: "Hello, Clara? This is Holborne Tye, security. What can I do for you?" Clara: "We need to know whether there's a Wendy Taggart in the office of training, and what she does." Tye: "This for Mark's case?" Clara: "Yes, sir, it is." Tye, after brief delay: "Wendy Taggart does indeed work there, and she makes appointments for speakers." Clara: "Thanks very much, Mr. Tye." (He asked no other questions.)
8. 12 Jan—0950 hrs. Alec Besansky dropped in "to see what's going on." Sat beside my desk, chatted about the weather. Tried covertly to see what I was typing. Clara: "Do you want to see Mark? I can tell him you stopped by. Right now he's tied up on a hot case." Alec: "No, not if it disturbs him. I just wanted to kick

around a few ideas. I'll come back when he's not so busy. What's this hot case?" Clara: "I can't tell you. He'd have to do that himself. You want me to set something up?" Alec: "I'll call him, okay. Don't bother him. It's not a big deal." (Alec seemed somewhat nervous. He left at 9:54.)

Mark read the log quickly, pointed to the Besansky entry. "Strange sort of conversation. I've met Besansky. Overage in grade, if my memory's right. Is he still on the CE staff?"

Clara said, "Yes. He's over here a lot, though, visiting people in the Russia division. Usually talking with the more junior case officers. From what I've seen, the older case officers don't take him too seriously. They think he's a big gossiper."

"Juniors, eh? And a gossip? Interesting. Was he different than usual today?"

"Yes. He wanted something and yet didn't want it to be apparent. That's not unusual for him, but he was a bit uptight. His conversation was strained, and in the end not really logical. Why drop over, then abort? Normally I'd have thought nothing of it, but now I'm looking . . ."

"Good for you, Clara. Now, let's see if your instincts are right. How would you call his secretary, find out where he's gone, and be sure she thinks nothing of it?"

"He shares a secretary with three other case officers. He keeps trying to seduce her, so she's not too fond of him. They don't talk much. He and his office mates play touch football. One of the mail rooms organizes it, but I don't know which. I'd fake a call about touch football."

"Do it quickly, sweetie! It's just five minutes since Besansky had left. We might still be lucky."

She dialed Besansky's extension.

A girl answered: "Extension five five four two. Can I help you?"

Clara put on a passable Southern accent. "This is the mail room. Is Mr. Besansky there?"

The girl replied nonchalantly, "No, he's not, but I expect him back soon. Anything I can do?"

"Thanks, no. Do you know where he went?"

"Well, he went to see Sonya Wayne, I think. And then he was going to 'visit along the corridor,' he said. He'll be back shortly, I imagine. Anything urgent?"

"Naw." Clara laughed to emphasize that it was trivial. "The boys are thinkin' of scratchin' up a touch football game . . . need all the victims they can get. I'll call back if it goes anywhere . . ." She entered Sonya Wayne's name in her log.

"Now," said Mark. "Call the team and invite them to a meeting at eleven o'clock in the DDO's conference room. We've got enough of a hint to warrant quick action."

"I wonder if they can all come on such short notice."

"Look at it this way, Clara. They're all aware this may happen, and they've got an hour to change their schedules."

Clara grinned. "Things happen when the DCI's interested."

Mark used his authority from the director to get the personnel, security, and medical files on Besansky and the Waynes brought to him by special courier. The files on the three made a stack almost a foot high, and took the hour to read.

Langley, Virginia: DDO conference room—1100 hours, 12 January

The team met in the DDO's large conference room, doors locked to ensure privacy. The five team members were all senior to Mark, but for the purposes of the hunt they had been instructed by the DCI to help him. Their contributions would be vital to his success.

It was a mixed and powerful group, able to turn the place upside down if that were needed to make the plan a success. And equally capable of stopping it in its tracks if they didn't like the way it was going.

Mark's presentation was carefully structured.

"As you all know, we put out bait, set up a watch, and waited for the mole to show interest. If he heard the rumors, as I was sure he would, he had to try to find out who the Soviet is. Or he would send a subagent to find out for him. And that's what I think he did. Using a subagent must have seemed safer to the mole, but I think it was his undoing."

Welcome news. There was a rustle of interest.

"Clara keeps a log of everyone who calls me or tries to see me or visits the office. We got nothing the first day, then a possible hit about an hour ago. Here's a copy of her log." Mark handed each team member a copy. "There are two pages for January eleventh, one for this morning. Only one entry is of interest, the one circled in red. The last entry, right after it, was made after Besansky left."

He waited a moment while they read it.

"Besansky!" John Giotto, chief of the counterespionage staff, was paler than usual. "Alec Besansky, on my staff and Sam and Sonya Wayne. Son of a bitch!"

"Besansky and I barely know each other. His work wouldn't cause him to seek me out, and although they've known each other for years, he's not really a friend of Clara's, so his visit—as well as his attitude during it—rang bells. The slimmest of hints, but that's all the mole will give us."

Giotto coughed, his thin frame hunching with the effort. "You're right. Alec Besansky's working on the Fourth International in the Middle East. He's got no particular reason to spend a lot of time in the corridors or see people outside his professional interest. He may know Sonya Wayne socially, however. They've been around here for years."

They nodded. Frank Wales, the DDO, motioned Mark to go on.

"He knows her better than that," said Mark. "I'll explain it right away. I realized that we had thin evidence so far, so I spent the time—since this log entry and now—reading the files on the three persons. When I read their files, I didn't expect to find anything much. Certainly no clues as to whether or not any of them could be the mole. But as it turns out, I did find something. Something so seemingly mundane that it would have meant nothing unless I'd been grasping for any straw." He grinned at them.

"I found it in Wayne's medical file. Before I get to it, you should know that in the Russia division it's a known fact that Sam Wayne has never gone overseas for a tour because he had a medical hold. He has a weak heart. He often alludes to his weak heart to explain why he's never served overseas—apologetically—and of course, we sympathize."

Desmond Ward, assistant DDO, commented, "He's made the point to me several times at lunch. He'd so much like an overseas tour, but . . ."

"Right, so I called the medical office and discovered that they have no record of a heart problem. The head doctor, who knows Sam quite well, not only told me there was no sign of a heart problem, but he looked up the EKGs in Wayne's record and confirmed it. There have been EKGs on Wayne's annual physical since his last promotion. No trace of a weak heart, nor has he ever mentioned it to a medic. So I assume Wayne has been resisting overseas duty so that he can be in headquarters all the time. That's what a mole would want to do. Our system is such that the medical files are almost never read by the operations people, so his weak-heart story was never checked. He has been able to serve in headquarters continually for the past fifteen years without suspicion."

Frank Wales said, "I would have really wondered, had I known he had no real medical hold. I accepted his story that he had one."

"Was that wise of him, Frank?" Peter Dallas, chief legal counsel, had a point.

"I'm sure he calculated it, Peter," said Wales. "When Wayne was hired, the medical staff was small and their files were a mess. He could have established the myth then with almost no risk. When EKGs became routine, the myth was already established and could only be exploded if someone in operations who knew him got approval to see his medical file and knew what to look for. That would only happen if we were suspicious of his story, but there was no reason to be."

"What else did you find in the files?" Holborne Tye, director of security, asked.

"Just one item, in Besansky's original PHS. He listed one Sonya Besanskaya as a cousin, and as a character reference. She was then already working as a secretary in the Russia division. She's since become Mrs. Sam Wayne. The unusual thing is that, according to Clara, they never told anyone in our division of their relationship, and that's not the pattern."

"Normally I'd not pay much attention to that," commented the DDO. "But in this case it's a clincher. What next, Mark?"

Mark replied, "First, put surveillance on them. Then we feed them a nugget, a piece of hard information that scares them even more, but not enough to make them run. It must make their leader—let's assume Wayne, because he spent two years in Moscow—call for an emergency meeting with his KGB handler, hopefully in a makeshift location. Third, we must have audio and visual surveillance on the meeting, with photos and tapes for legal evidence. We shouldn't disturb the meeting. The participants mustn't know we're covering them. We wait until Wayne is back under our control and we've all had a chance to see and judge the evidence. Then we arrest him, charge him, interrogate him and, hopefully, turn them around and work them against the KGB, of course. Eventually, perhaps we can use the mole to recruit his KGB case officer, although that looks remote right now."

The DDO nodded his assent and the other four agreed. It was a logical plan.

"What kind of a jolt do you want to give Wayne, Mark? And what if he can communicate with his case officer fully and quickly without a physical meeting?" Tye was certain that a KGB mole in the CIA would have some very sophisticated communications equipment, the best the KGB could concoct.

"Good point, Holborne," replied Mark. "But I think he'll want to meet his case officer face to face, to see if he can sniff out whether or not he's the defector. As to the jolt, I want to give Besansky a hint that the defector has promised to tell me who the mole is, in one week, on January nineteenth. That gives Wayne time to meet his case officer and try to identify the defector. I suspect Wayne has guts and he'll try to save the operation rather than cut and run."

"I agree," said Giotto with a thin smile of approval. "I'd face the man myself, try to figure out if he's the defector. A good operational nose might tell me. I'd go armed too, in case he is."

"You think he might kill the Soviet?" Dallas asked.

"He'd see no choice," Mark said. "A vital operation at stake, plus his team's freedom, maybe their lives."

"I think we'd better get on with it," said the DDO, closing the meeting. "John, would you and Holborne work out the surveillance details with Mark?"

Langley, Virginia: Mark's office—
1330 hours, 12 January

Mark got back to his office after lunch, to find Clara's log with three new entries. Two were of no interest. The third made him whistle:

> 16. 12 Jan—1304 hours. Besansky came back! He wanted to know if Mr. Cameron would meet with him this afternoon to help him identify Fourth-International activists in or near Bwagania. (Note: He seemed unusually anxious, very nervous. He asked nothing else.)

Mark decided to feed his jolt to Wayne through Besansky, immediately. Besansky was running scared and might crack if pressured properly. He dialed, and Besansky answered on the first ring.

Mark made his voice flat, cold: "Alec Besansky? Mark Cameron returning your call."

Besansky was effusive. "Oh, Mark. Thanks so much for calling me back. Thank you. I just have a request to make about the KGB and the Fourth International—you know, the Trotsky boys. . ." His voice trailed off. He sounded a bit frazzled, not like the experienced case officer his record portrayed.

Mark waited, saying nothing, forcing Besansky to keep talking.

"Hello? Hello? You there? I wondered, Mark, if you have any insights into KGB contacts with them in Africa. My boss is anxious to know."

"Africa's in your field, eh?"

"Er, yes. I mean, it's for a special report. John Giotto's interested." Mark knew this, at least, wasn't true. He'd got him.

"What's your deadline?"

"Right away. Can you spare the time . . . perhaps coffee?

The main cafeteria . . . maybe at two o'clock this afternoon?" He was really pushing. Mark stretched out the time deliberately. "All right, Alec. But I can't do it until later. See you there at four-thirty."

It gave Alec time to sweat and Mark time to refine the lure. It had to be perfect. If he goofed, the mole and his group would run for the border.

Mark called Giotto. "John, you didn't tell Besansky to look for KGB Fourth International contacts in Africa?"

"Absolutely not, why?"

"Besansky just told me you did. I wanted to be sure."

"That's it!"

"Right, John. I meet him at four-thirty in the main cafeteria. Can you start surveillance right away on all three? My guess is Wayne will ask for an emergency meeting tonight."

"The bastards. We've already set up the surveillance, in case you were right."

To Clara, Mark said, "Please get me the DCI on the phone and you stay on the line. Can you stay late this evening?"

"I'll stay all night if you'll include me."

"That's a deal, Clara." Then the director's familiar voice was on the line.

"Yes, Mark?"

"Mr. Director, we've got three almost certain candidates. I plan to throw out my heavy bait this afternoon. I need your blessing to entrap three American citizens, all staffers, with bait that may cause one or more deaths. You asked me to keep you advised."

"Do what's necessary, Mark. If anyone is hurt, that's the price of stopping treason. Just be sure no one's killed or hurt uselessly. Good hunting."

Mark got to the cafeteria at four forty-five. Alec Besansky was seated near the west windows, fingers drumming on the table. Mark watched him as he threaded his way through the tables. Besansky's body showed signs of considerable stress. Now sure he wasn't taking on an innocent man, Mark was intent on increasing that stress to the point of near explosion, where Besansky would make a mistake.

At a distance of six feet, Mark hailed him loudly, to rattle him even more: "Hello, Alec. I'm late. A problem that couldn't wait."

Alec jumped, then stood up quickly, smiling. The hand he offered in greeting was clammy. Mark searched his face. Tension and worry lines, but they're routine with many clandestine-services officers. The skin was oily, but he was not perspiring. The mouth was compressed, the left thumb nail was chewed, and Mark's gaze caused Alec to break eye contact and motion Mark to sit.

"Alec, you asked for this meeting. I can't see how I could help, having been in Africa for only just over four months. You'd better have a good reason. I'm a busy man." It was brutal, but it worked. Besansky's face twitched.

"Sorry, Mark. I know it's a long shot. Just thought you might be able to help." He was almost pleading.

Mark sat still, staring at Besansky. He said nothing, nor did he take his eyes from Besansky's. He could feel the man's tension rise. The adam's apple bobbed. The tongue licked over the lips. The fingers drummed. A twitch crept into the corner of the right eye. Besansky broke eye contact for the second time, rubbing both cheeks with hands that were now shaking.

"You know where I'm stationed?"

"Yes, Mark. Bwagania. It's remote, and there were no Soviets stationed there until a few months ago. I know it's unlikely, but I thought with your tremendous nose for business perhaps you'd already run into something that might help me." Alec was biting his thumbnail now, apparently unaware of his outward signs of stress.

Mark was irritated by the flattery. "I've neither seen nor heard anything about the Fourth International in central Africa. It's that simple."

By now Besansky's whole bearing was a plea for help. It was time to drop the bait.

"I do, however, have a new source who might be able to help." Mark chose his words carefully. Alec licked his lips, leaning forward, the nail forgotten, wildly eager for something substantive he could take back to Wayne, something that might save Sam's team and get him a pat on the back.

"A new source?"

"Yes. Someone very close to the KGB. He's beginning to come across with some interesting stuff. He wants to come over to us, you see, and he's giving us bits and pieces. Testing to see how we'll treat him. I'm scheduled to meet him soon. In fact, just one week from today. I'll put it to him. If anyone I'm dealing with knows the answer, he will."

Besansky was dumbfounded. He'd never expected to get this far with Mark. It was success beyond his wildest expectations. The look of relief was clear across his face as he struggled not to appear too interested.

"Sounds like a hell of a good source. Is he in Bwagania? Are you going back that soon?"

"No, he's here. He's done time in Africa, however, which is why I think maybe he can help your project." Mark leaned forward. "I'm not supposed to tell anyone this, but I'm glad of a neutral subject to query him on. We've been dancing around on one subject too long."

"What's that?" A blunt question, but a logical one. Mark responded by dropping the rest of his bait.

"A mole. This guy claims there's a mole right here in the clandestine services. We've all heard those stories before, but something tells me this guy may really know what he's talking about."

Besansky went gray. "Jesus Christ . . ." His delight at snaking the truth out of Mark turned into a wave of fear that swept up from his feet to the top of his head. He tried his best not to show his shock, but it was too much for him. The terror was easy to read, so Mark broke eye contact and went on:

"Promise me, Alec, this is for your ears only," Mark said innocently.

"Of course, Mark. Does he really have that kind of access?" Is he a KGB officer, was Besansky's real question.

"He has very good access, Alec. Perhaps an inside track. That's all I can say for now. More in a few days, but not for the moment."

"Thanks a lot, Mark. I'll call in a few days to find out what more your source says. He sounds fascinating."

Then he was gone, fists clenching and unclenching as he wound his way through the tables.

Their meeting had taken fifteen minutes.

Mark phoned John Giotto from the nearest office.

"John? It's done. I'll bet my life he's on the way to Wayne's office right now. Is everything laid on?"

"Right on, Mark. Come to my office."

Langley, Virginia: Giotto's CP—1705 hours, 12 January

John Giotto had a CP (command post) in an office next to his own. When Mark got there, he found two of the team seated with John: Holborne Tye and Peter Dallas. The project was obviously of great interest to them.

"We've got their phones tapped," Giotto said, "at the building switchboard, tied in to these tape recorders." He motioned toward three tape recorders, complete with dial recorders, in a wall array. "As more lines are tapped—such as their home phones—we'll bring more equipment on line."

As he waved and spoke, Mark was as always intrigued by the way Giotto managed to make his offices darker and more sinister than the others in the building. Dim lights, dark brown furniture, thick curtains, and John's own air of mystery gave the effect.

"Can we hear them off the phones as well as on them?"

"Yes, Mark," said Tye. "My boys worked a little magic with the phone system. Don't ask me what they did."

Besansky had apparently stopped somewhere, as he wasn't yet in Wayne's office on the fifth floor now.

"Had to make a pit stop, I'll bet," said Mark. "He looked as if he needed one badly."

"He'll need more than that," grunted Tye, "when we get to him."

Two of the transmitters carried faint noises of doors banging and footsteps, but they recorded no activity in those rooms. The third, however, was clearly in an occupied room. A typewriter tapped away in a room not far away. The occupant of the bugged room coughed and turned a page. You could almost visualize him sitting at his desk.

Mark asked, "Who?"

Peter Dallas replied in a whisper: "Sam Wayne." Just then there was a knock on the door, and Wayne's voice: "Yes?"

A moment of rustling, then a whisper: ". . . must talk to you . . . urgent . . . urgent . . ."

"I don't think there's anything to worry about, Alec. Not this soon." Wayne was trying to calm him.

Besansky whispered again. The key words came through clearly. ". . . they know the orchestra exists . . . identify us in . . . matter of days . . . served somewhere in Africa . . ."

Wayne replied, his voice carrying better, the whole sentence clear: "I don't know if this temporary conductor served in Africa, but there's no need to panic . . . just take it easy and I'll find out what I can."

". . . hardly any time . . . meeting in a week, maybe sooner."

Apparently, both men had decided on the spot that Mark's source was a KGB staffer. Wayne's voice and words accepted the bait as authentic, not part of a trap. The ploy had worked.

"I'm not supposed to meet him until the fourteenth, but that's too long to wait. I'd better call for an emergency meeting. Meanwhile just relax, Alec. Nothing worse than you running around looking like a scared rabbit. It's too soon for anything to happen to us. We've got a couple of days, maybe a week, from what you say. Go back to your office, or go home and have a drink. I'll talk to you tomorrow."

They could hear Besansky walk out and close the door. Then the dial recorder next to the tape recorder that was linked to Wayne's phone began to tick as it counted the pulses of the number Wayne was dialing.

Holborne Tye walked over and watched the thin tape. He copied the number of pulses and made a quiet phone call to start a quick trace on the number. Then he returned to his seat. Instinctively, the men leaned forward to hear Wayne's call better.

"Hello? This is Sam Wade. I have a bad toothache. Can you give me an appointment tonight, say at eight o'clock? Maybe at your suburban office? Thank you."

The other person was a woman with a Southern accent. All she said was "I'll ask the doctor and we'll call you back."

"I would expect him to leave the building now," Mark

commented. "He'll probably go home, and he'll get a weapon. Maybe he's got one in his car. But before he leaves the headquarters building, he'll want to take something for his KGB conductor to read—maybe some reports he hasn't had time to copy."

Dallas asked why he'd stop to take some reports with him. And why that phony name close to his own?

Mark explained: "The phony name resembles his in case anyone in CIA hears him, but it meets the needs of the accommodation phone. As for the reports, you can tell a lot from the way an intelligence officer acts when he gets a hot report, one he knows is really good. My guess is that Wayne will take an exceptionally good report with him. If the Soviet has defection on his mind rather than business, there may be signs of it—disinterest in a report that should have him jumping up and down. That's what Wayne'll be looking for."

"A long shot, Mark. Is it worth it?"

"Peter, there's so little to go on in a case like this. Wayne will be frantically looking for the tiniest of clues, for any little sign that his temporary case officer can be trusted—or not trusted. His life may depend on it. His KGB case officer's life *will* depend on it. So Wayne will use every trick he can, no matter how long a shot."

"Yes, I see. Certainly a Soviet thinking of defecting should be very much on edge . . . Wayne will count on that."

"Exactly," Giotto interjected. "Defection is an act of such trauma that it shakes those who do it—even those who seriously contemplate it—right down to their socks. No matter what the impetus for defection, it is an act of betrayal, of treason. Often the most traumatic part of it is the defector's thought that he has betrayed his KGB colleagues . . . which is in fact true. Most defectors, even before making the final decision to cut the cord, go through mental anguish that is so strong that it has to show in one way or another, in private if not in public."

A safe drawer slammed shut in Wayne's office. The noise of it was sharp enough on the loudspeakers in the CP that it stopped their conversation.

Dallas, not used to listening to the take from audio operations, put his finger to his lips and shook his head to warn the others. They smiled, realizing that he thought Wayne could hear them.

Tye said, louder than normal, "Peter, this equipment only transmits in one direction, from Wayne's office to the CP here. He can't hear you."

Dallas grinned at himself and tapped his head.

Mark asked Giotto and Tye if their surveillance units were in place and ready.

"Yes," Tye replied for Giotto too, looking at his watch. "They've all reported from their stations."

It was already five forty-five. The trap was ready and the hunt was on.

Langley, Virginia: Wayne's office—1745 hours, 12 January

As if he'd seen Giotto look at his watch and taken the cue, Sam Wayne slammed another safe drawer shut, twirled the dial, and left his office.

Tye pressed a button and a closed-circuit TV showed Wayne, carrying a briefcase, heels clacking on the hard floor as if they were shod with steel plates, passing a guard as he left the building. The guard glanced at his pass but didn't look at the briefcase.

Another TV camera showed Wayne walking across the parking lot and getting into his car. The microphone in the car came to life, and they heard the engine start.

"We've got a homing limpet under the car, and the cameras will tell us which exit he uses," said Tye. "We've got bugs and phone taps in the Wayne house and the Besansky apartment, plus a bug in Besansky's car and a limpet under it. We'll get good coverage."

Arlington, Virginia: Wayne's house—1808 hours, 12 January

The combination of limpet, microphones, and hot telephone taps gave the listeners a clear audio picture of Wayne driving home, parking and locking his car, and entering his house. He stopped at the door, probably to take off his coat.

"Hello, Sonya! Where are you?" His voice boomed out.

"Here, Sam. In the kitchen. Where else?" There was a nagging tone in her voice, although she ended with a giggle.

He ignored it. "We've got a real problem, Sonya. There's no doubt someone is about to defect, and he's going to squeal about us in a few days. We've almost no time. I believe the man's right here in town, and he could even be our conductor—the replacement. Alec got all this from the defector's case officer, Cameron. I've called for an emergency meeting with the replacement tonight at nine."

Her voice was shaking: "Oh! Oh, Sam! I never thought . . . what do we do?"

"One thing we start with is calm. We've always known the risk. Control yourself, it's the only way to survive. Stay calm and think straight. Now, I'm going to start on my way. You go over and get hold of Alec. Don't use the phones anymore. Tell him to get ready to leave. Then go down to American Airlines and book three tickets to Mexico, first flight tomorrow, using our emergency names. Then come back here and pack. We'll take a couple of suitcases, no more. Abandon everything else. The funny passports and money are in my safe. You remember the combination?"

"Yes, Sam."

But she was shaky, so he told her, "Twenty-four, forty-seven, nineteen. Clean it out."

The listeners looked at each other in delight. The safe combination handed to them on a plate!

Wayne walked into his study and turned on his Coda-Phone. They could hear an accented male voice: "This is Dr. Smith, Mr. Wade, your dentist, calling at six o'clock. I can see you at nine o'clock. At the suburban rail stable. Until then . . ." A soft click.

Mark nodded vigorously to the others: "That's Petrov's voice. I'd know it anywhere. If Wayne finds out Petrov's from Bwagania, he'll surely kill him tonight."

As if prompted, they could hear Wayne open a drawer and then the sounds of a handgun being loaded.

They heard Sonya stammer. "Why . . . that?"

"Sonya, if the new conductor is the defector, I've a good

chance of sniffing it out tonight. If he is, I'll kill him—the bastard."

"Good hunting, my dear." Her voice was still shaky. Then the front door slammed and he was gone.

Tye reached for a phone, his crisp voice like knife.

"Phil Link? Get a lock-and-key man and put a little team together. When she leaves the house, your guys go in. Watch out for booby traps; these people are serious. Open the safe—we have the combination: Photograph the passports, replace what money you can with marked notes, the kind with tracer chemicals on them. Photograph all the classified documents and anything else that might convict them in court. Install some more switchable bugs. Do anything else you think necessary . . . we don't know where we're going from here, so just use your head."

Mark commented, "Well, we know when they'll meet—nine o'clock. But where? What did he mean by suburban rail stable?"

"Don't worry, Mark. Tye and his gumshoes won't lose him." Giotto grinned at Tye. John rarely gave out compliments, even backhanded ones. But Tye was too busy to reply. He had the phone in hand again.

". . . get hold of the FBI and ask them to make a 'special' tonight on Petrov, Colonel Pyotr A. He's staying in Boris Kuznetsov's apartment and using his car, according to our info. His license is DPL-9612, a black Ford sedan usually driven by Kuznetsov. He'll probably go to Kuznetsov's Baleen apartment before he sets off for the meeting. That's b-a-l-e-e-n, in Bethesda . . . just over the District line. A great big apartment house . . . they'll know. Tell everyone Wayne is armed and ready to kill people."

Washington, D.C.: the Soviet Embassy—1810 hours, 12 January

Pyotr Petrov, walking back after calling Wayne from a public telephone five blocks from the embassy, was checked into the building by an FBI static surveillance across 16th Street, behind shaded windows. Seconds later, one of the FBI surveillants picked up a winking phone: "Yes?"

"Joe," came a tired voice from the field office. "Start a special on number six twenty-three, will you. It's a request from across the river." That meant the CIA. Joe snorted. Another special, and they were stretched too thin already. But he passed the word, and the FBI was ready for Pyotr when, thirty minutes later, his DPL-9612 appeared from the embassy garage.

Pyotr drove north on 16th Street and went around Scott Circle seven times. Seven times the FBI cars followed him around the circle, and Pyotr said to himself: So, they've picked on me tonight. I hope it's coincidence.

He drove north again and ducked into a one-way alley. The FBI cars, following standard orders for a special, let him go after a halfhearted box search. Now sure they were only doing a routine spot check, Pyotr congratulated himself on being free. He turned northwest, toward Bethesda.

Bethesda, Maryland: the Baleen Apartments—1924 hours, 12 January

Pyotr parked in Kuznetsov's space under the Baleen and jogged to the elevator. This damn emergency meeting was on a short fuse. He'd had to rush to prepare the documents and money for it, then there was the damn rush hour. He'd have to push things a little to get there on time, certain he was still clean.

Within three minutes he was in the sixteenth-floor apartment, enjoying a long, hot shower. By then a homing limpet was clinging to the underside of his Ford, already beeping silently. The agent who'd slapped it under the car did it with the skill of years of surveillance work. Then he unlocked the car, using a tool he'd fashioned himself when he was still in his teens. He installed a battery-operated transmitter in the car, hidden in the upholstery. It was switchable, its signal scrambled.

The job was done in five minutes. Pyotr's car was a rolling transmitter.

Rockville, Maryland: The Madisson bar—
1938 hours, 12 January

Sam Wayne sat in the Madisson bar nursing a vodka tonic. He'd been there a few minutes, but it seemed like an hour. He had chosen his seat so he could view the entire parking lot and, beyond it, the Rockville Pike with its whizzing traffic.

Sure by now that nobody was following him, he was strangely reluctant to go on to the meeting site. He had never killed a man before. If the replacement was about to defect, he must be executed at once. But Sam wondered how it would feel to pull the trigger.

Suddenly, as if the thought had become unimportant, he chugged down his drink and set off. He pulled on his white silk gloves. They would insulate him from the act of murder.

Langley, Virginia: Giotto's CP—
1942 hours, 12 January

Petrov was still in Kuznetsov's Baleen apartment, and Wayne had just been reported driving northwest on the Rockville Pike, having left the bar. The homing device indicated he was in no hurry.

Tye had a whispered conversation with Giotto, then made a call to his people: "Bill, get some rooms ready in the secure holding area, please. We'll have two clients. They may be violent. Be ready for two separate hostile interrogations. Then, Bill, have the two vans start northwest on the Rockville Pike. We'll probably be doing business in that area."

Mark asked him, "Where's the secure holding area?"

"In the District, Mark. We'll have to let Petrov go sooner rather than later . . . he'll scream diplomatic immunity. The holding area is next to a D.C. police precinct station, and we can shove him over to them if he won't defect. If he opts to defect but to stay in the KGB for a while, we'll keep him under wraps."

"Suppose Wayne knows it, or can guess at it?"

"Depends on circumstances tonight. If it goes our way,

neither will know the other has been arrested. But if Wayne takes a crack at Petrov, we'll have to intervene and then they'll both know. We don't want a dead Soviet on our hands, plus a live mole with a murder charge over his head."

Bethesda, Maryland: the Baleen Apartments—
2005 hours, 12 January

Pyotr appeared in the garage of the Baleen, moving rapidly. As he got into the car and started it, the hidden transmitter came to life. The homing device under the car showed a fast entry into River Road, bound northwest, and minutes later he turned north on the Capital Beltway. Five minutes after that, he took the right exit at Connecticut Avenue, but stayed in the right lane and was quickly back on the capital Beltway, this time heading back the way he'd come.

Langley, Virginia: Giotto's CP—
2015 hours, 12 January

The red light on the CP wall map showed Petrov's car doubling back as far as River Road, where again he reversed direction and moved over into the left lane of the Beltway, traveling fast.

"Cleaning himself," said Giotto.

As soon as the wall map lights showed that Petrov's car was exiting the Beltway onto 270 West, while Wayne's car was moving slowly northwest along the Rockville Pike, Mark jumped up, excited:

"Of course, they're both headed for it! I'll bet anything the meeting site is at the Iron Horse, off Route 270, past Gaithersburg!"

"Iron Horse? Never heard of it. Why do you think that, Mark?" Peter Dallas looked intrigued.

"Because it's a former stable that's been moved there from a farm. There's an old steam locomotive on an abandoned siding behind it. People pay to climb around the locomotive. They've made the stables into a truck stop—the kind of place with rough customers but damn good food. Remember,

Petrov said on the phone, 'at the surburban rail stable.' I suspect it's a vey thin code for this emergency meeting site. Holborne, how about one of the vans going there right away, on the off chance I'm right?"

"Okay, Mark," said Tye. "No harm in that. It'll be somewhere in that area anyway, I think. How long is it since you were there?"

"A couple of years," said Mark. "I go there sometimes when I'm home on leave. Why do you ask?"

"Do you remember what the ashtrays are like?"

"Oh, I get it. The heavy glass kind that don't break, if my memory's right."

"Good, very good." Tye talked into his phone, then said, "The vans are on their way."

"I'm off too, gents," said Mark. "This is my party."

"Want some help?" asked Giotto.

"Just a car. Can anyone lend me one?"

"Basement space one sixty-eight," said Tye. "I'll tell the boys you're coming down. They'll lend you a driver. Be careful with it, it's a beauty. Fully equipped."

"Want a weapon?" asked Giotto.

"No thanks," replied Mark. "I've got my stinkpot." He showed them his plastic DO powder bottle.

"What's that?" asked Dallas.

"DO powder—like Mace, only stronger," said Tye. "When he squeezes it, a thin stream shoots out a long way. Very good stuff."

"I hope you're insured," called Dallas after Mark.

Montgomery County, Maryland: CIA car—2025 hours, 12 January

Tye's car was right for the job, the driver more than adequate. He turned the car north along the George Washington Parkway, crossed the Cabin John Bridge, and headed out 270 West without getting below 80 MPH.

The car's radio kept up a running commentary. The two target cars were still on converging courses, heading for the Gaithersburg area.

Mark sat back, listening, thinking about the Iron Horse, remembering the horse brass, the rough unpainted wooden booths and tables, the noisy clientele, long bar, the huge plate dinners and imaginative sandwiches. It seemed an unlikely place for an emergency meeting, which was probably why the KGB had selected it. Its customers came for the food and to meet friends, not to see or be seen by strangers. The noise level guaranteed that you could talk without being overheard.

But even in those conditions, a good microphone on a table between two people can pick up conversations. The trick was to get it there, unnoticed, concealed.

He hoped the vans would get there before Pyotr and Sam.

Gaithersburg, Maryland: the Iron Horse—2045 hours, 12 January

Van number 1, marked PETE'S PLUMBING SERVICE, rolled into the parking lot and stopped facing the Iron Horse. The driver stayed in his seat, behind tinted glass, invisible from outside. He had a clear view of the front of the restaurant.

Behind him, two men sat hunched over their equipment in the body of the van, radio transceivers linking them to Giotto's CP at headquarters and to the van's stock of "quick fix" battery-powered bugs concealed in ashtrays, cigar boxes, briefcases, and books.

The radio told them that Sam's car had pulled over and stopped for a few minutes a mile south of the Iron Horse, perhaps to watch traffic roll by, perhaps to change license plates. Then it started up again, this time heading across toward Route 270. Pyotr's car had gone past the exit for the Iron Horse, but left 270 at the Bureau of Standards turnoff. It stopped for four minutes, then started off again, and was now headed back on 270 toward the Iron Horse.

The Iron Horse was becoming a strong possibility as the meeting site. The van driver turned his head and said: "This looks like the place. Go!"

His command galvanized a group of four into action. Two men, Uzi submachine guns holstered under their coats, jumped from the van's rear door and disappeared among the parked trucks. They positioned themselves so they could see the front of the restaurant and the diners inside, but so they were concealed by truck hoods. They kept their hand radios turned down low.

A man and a woman followed them out, closed the van door, trotted over to the Iron Horse, and went in. The four were part of a superbly trained surveillance and security team known as the Gang. Tough, ready for anything, honed to a fine edge, their job was to watch unseen, listen, photograph, and intervene if ordered to.

The man and woman chose a booth in the far right corner. There were eight booths between theirs and the door, two of them occupied. A long counter, almost the length of the room, was separated from the booths by a wide aisle. The diners, seated in booths and at the counter, drinking and talking, paid no attention to the newcomers as they walked to their booth and sat down.

The man and woman had miniature radio transceivers hidden under their clothing—a hearing aid for listening and a mike, taped out of sight against the throat, for transmitting. Their .38 detective special revolvers were handy but concealed. The woman had a bugged glass ashtray in her handbag. Her radio brought the news that Petrov and Wayne, in their cars, were closing rapidly on the restaurant.

She told the busy waitress who brought water glasses that they'd like to think before ordering: "Give us a few minutes, okay?"

The first contingent of the Gang was in place, ready.

Gaithersburg, Maryland: the Iron Horse—2047 hours, 12 January

Van number 2, marked CENTENNIAL CARPET CLEANING, pulled into the restaurant parking lot and stopped off to one side, obliquely facing the front of the building.

The driver reported by radio, "Vehicle number two on site." Inside the van, four more armed members of the Gang waited, in reserve, for the action to begin. They wore black sneakers, black jeans, dark jackets.

Mark had the driver of Tye's car drop him next to the PETE'S PLUMBING SERVICE van, then park between two trucks and stay in the car watching the Iron Horse, on call, shielded by the darkly tinted windshield and windows.

The van driver, waiting for Mark to arrive, opened the passenger door and let him in. "Howdy," he said casually. "I'm Dave. I'm really a captain of industry, but I'm lending the Company a hand tonight."

Mark laughed and shook his hand: "A wag, eh? Good to work with you."

Dave radioed the CP: "Cameron's in van number one, now. Everybody's in position."

The Iron Horse parking lot: DIPL-9612—2053 hours, 12 January

Pyotr made his final approach to the restaurant along Route 270 confident no one was following him. He was humming a Russian folk song as he turned into the parking lot. He circled the lot once, checking the forty-odd trucks and the smaller vehicles, noting with approval the lack of lights in the parking lot.

The two outside Gang members, alerted that he had arrived, watched from among the trucks, moving out of sight when his headlights swept near them.

Satisfied he was still clean, Pyotr parked facing the Iron Horse. He switched off the engine and waited silently, watching in the rearview mirror for the car that Kuznetsov had described to come through the parking lot entrance.

Pyotr had come early, to see if Wayne was dragging a tail. If so, he would abort the meeting and leave.

The Iron Horse—2054 hours, 12 January

At their table in the restaurant, the man and woman Gang members heard Dave clearly on their radios, his voice thin, sounding almost disinterested: "DIPL-9612 now has Maryland license plate PRD-29972. He must have switched plates at that last stop. He parked on site at eight fifty-four, driver only, Caucasian male . . . sitting in car."

The woman, seated facing the door, checked the booths, noted that there were still two vacant ones. One was near theirs, one next to the entrance door. "Let's force them into our booth, Chris. You take the next one, I'll take the one by the door."

Her companion nodded. "He's waiting outside for the other guy. Better hold off until the last minute, Katie."

The Iron Horse parking lot—2056 hours, 12 January

Pyotr stopped humming. Wayne's car was entering the lot, and as he spotted Kuznetsov's familiar black sedan, he said, "There you are, in Boris's car, using his dummy plates, you bastard."

Mark laughed, said to Dave: "He hates his KGB handlers. That may be useful in the interrogation."

Sam parked well away from Petrov's car. He, too, had changed license plates.

"Second target here," radioed Dave. "New plate, Maryland DFD 10706." Then he asked Mark, "You want Petrov to survive?"

"I want both of them alive. Alive and well enough to talk."

"Okay," replied Dave, and pressed his transmit button: "Listen, gang, everyone stays alive tonight. Second subject has arrived. He's parking well away from Petrov, in the far left corner of the parking lot, facing the lot exit . . . locking car now . . . walking over to Petrov's car."

Then they could hear Sam over Pyotr's car bug: "Excuse me," as Pyotr rolled down the window. "Is this the cover of your book?"

"Yes, it is. May I see the other side of it?"

"It's blank," said Sam, winding up the elaborate recognition patter.

"My name's Boris also," said Petrov. "Easier that way."

"Mine's Smith," said Sam Wayne in a flat voice. "Sam Smith. Let's go inside. It's cold out here."

As they walked toward the restaurant, their backs to PETE'S

PLUMBING SERVICE, a Gang member among the trucks took a telephoto picture of Pyotr and Sam, giving a description of Pyotr as he did so.

"He's disguised," said Mark, smiling. "I expected that."

The Iron Horse—2059 hours, 12 January

The woman Gang member, Katie, put the bugged ashtray on the table and the restaurant's ashtray into her handbag in exchange. The man, Chris, replaced their menus in the rack under the window. Then Katie and Chris picked up their water glasses, wiped the rings of water off the table, and left their booth.

Chris occupied the nearest empty booth and sat down, head buried in the menu, facing back toward the corner booth they'd just left.

Katie continued past him and sat down in the empty booth next to the door, also facing the corner her back to the door. She put the ashtray she'd collected from the corner booth on her table and took a menu from the rack under the window.

Now only the corner booth was vacant.

A busy waitress hurried by and grinned: "Didn't like that guy, eh?"

"Nor the booth," Katie answered. "Too dark. I'll order now, please."

"Be right back," said the waitress.

Wayne and Petrov walked in at that moment, looked around, saw nothing suspicious, and started for the corner booth.

Katie whispered a running description of the scene for the other Gang members, the vans, and Giotto's CP. She did it as if reading to herself from the menu:

"Both targets walking toward corner booth, Wayne leading . . . no apparent suspicion we're here . . . the steamed Chesapeake oysters look interesting . . . they're taking off their coats, about to sit down . . . aha, they exchanged identical newspapers as they sat . . . professionally done, but old Eagle Eye spotted it . . . they say boiled newspaper goes well with Maryland crab cakes . . . or should I order the bluefish?"

One of the Gang radioed from the parking lot: "I got a photo of that exchange. Order the crab cakes, Eagle Eye, but I'll have my newspaper fried."

In the van, Dave whispered: "Cut the chatter, Gang." Mark laughed and settled back to listen to Sam and Pyotr. Their voices came out clearly over the background noise as the glass ashtray did its job, its electronics hidden by a trick of optics.

"Shitty place for a meeting," Sam commented. "I thought it was risky when Boris told me about it."

"Let's make it short," Pyotr suggested.

"Suits me." Wayne looked at Pyotr carefully. "The disguise is okay, I suppose," he went on, disagreeably. "But using the same damn car as Boris is dumb."

"Not dumb, Sam. Just a calculated risk. You gave me no time. Anyway, I changed the plates, as you saw. Now, it's your kopek. What's the problem?" He felt Sam's critical gaze and wondered if he was always this nasty or if something special was eating at him. Boris had warned him, but still, he didn't expect this much hostility.

"I came across a real find today, that's what. I have it with me. It's two documents. One is a new study of mainland China's armed forces. Top secret. A report that'll make you look great. The other's the RMD of the CIA Rome station, plus a summary of all their assets. It's top secret too, a really hot item. But the reason for my call isn't the documents. I'll give it to you orally." He watched Pyotr closely for signs of stress, of lack of interest in the take.

There was some stress, and there was interest in the take. Nothing unusual. Was the man the defector and a good actor, or was he straight?

"Good," said Pyotr. "What's the oral matter?"

"I'll get to it in a minute," said Sam. He changed to the weather as their waitress came. They ordered sandwiches and ale, and she left.

Wayne watched Pyotr and planned his next gambit. He had to find out right now—up front—if this *was* the defector.

The waitress brought the two ales. Sam drank slowly, staring at Pyotr.

The Soviet, uncomfortably aware of Sam's silent stare, sipped his ale and looked wistfully around the lively room, watching the truckers joke with each other and the waitresses. "These people have a good time here, don't they?" he said awkwardly, wishing he could share their mood. "Noisy, but they're happy."

Then he looked back at Wayne. He was beginning to hate him. This was the man who'd passed on the photos and tapes to Moscow Center.

"A barrel of monkeys," grumbled Sam. "Some of these truck drivers have drunk too much." Then he stared straight into Pyotr's eyes. "This isn't your first overseas post, is it?"

The question brought the response Sam wanted easier than he's imagined. Far easier.

"No. I've served overseas five times, counting my present post. Boris probably told you. I've been sent here hurriedly to replace him while he's on leave. I've come from Bwagania."

For Sam, this revelation was cataclysmic. Suddenly, like a crash of thunder, it was all crystal clear. This man, without his mustache, cheek pads and eyeglasses, was Pyotr Petrov. So Mark Cameron was in the process of recruiting this wretched KGB officer. Within days, maybe hours, he would be telling Cameron who the mole was.

Sam Wayne had trained himself as carefully as an Olympic athlete to excel, not physically but emotionally, to hide his feelings no matter what, to exercise iron discipline. Now he did his best to cover his reaction to Pyotr's revelation, the fear and the fury that were shaking him all over. By a simulated attack of coughing, he was able to move his body, shift his arms and feet—using the movement and the spasms to cover the shock and regain control.

As his fit of coughing subsided, Sam wiped his nose, swore, scratched his head, and said, grumpily: "Sorry, the beer must have gone down the wrong way."

It seemed to have worked, for Pyotr showed no awareness. It was a costly struggle for Wayne, and the tension came out in snarling sarcasm. He couldn't tell this traitor that he knew he was about to defect. But he could make his last meal uncomfortable.

"Bwagania, eh?" Sam's voice was heavy and angry. "So you're the famous lover, Colonel Petrov? What a surprise to have you as my temporary contact. The Center is having a joke at my expense, eh? Sending me a second-rate man like you."

"The assignment was made here in Washington, not by the Center. I'd rather not be here either. But it's a fact. They expect us to interract as professionals, not make judgments about each other." Pyotr could feel the hostility between them rise another notch, like the mounting hum of an imminent short circuit.

"Professional, my arse," Sam spat the words. "I didn't know they still tolerate cretins like you." As he said it, Sam was already planning the execution of Petrov. The bullet would make a small entry hole in the hair behind his head, and a large exit wound in the face. The silencer would make the act unheard. The fact that the gun was unregistered—a gift from the KGB—would keep him unconnected with the murder. He would be out of the parking lot long before anyone would look into the black sedan, which would probably not be until morning . . .

The KGB would congratulate him, raise his pay, when they understood why he'd killed the traitor.

Pyotr had in fact noticed Sam's reaction. Why was it so strong, so overdone? What was going on across the table? He tried to calm the storm.

"We have to get along for a few weeks, Sam. Let's try to make it comfortable even if we don't like each other. I certainly didn't appreciate your sending those photos and tapes to the Center. I have no idea why they sent me to handle you. It was a mistake . . . I didn't know it was to happen until yesterday. But still, they expect us to work together while Boris is gone. We must try."

"I don't have to do anything, Petrov. I can give you nothing, no reports at all, while you're here. That'll make you look like a jerk at the Center."

Pyotr let it pass. "You must have something hot tonight,

Sam. What's the emergency, or do you plan to withhold that from us?" Just then the waitress came, bringing their sandwiches. Sam replied with some innocuous words about the weather for her benefit.

". . . and for once the forecast was correct. It rained for three days straight. All the sewers overflowed . . ."

She drew out of range. But the ashtray stayed there.

Pyotr tried again: "What's tonight's take, Sam?"

"It's in the newspaper. Read it later, if you can read. You'll have plenty of time for it."

The Iron Horse parking lot: van number one—2121 hours, 12 January

Wayne's ugly, furious tone was unmistakable over the radio of PETE'S PLUMBING. Mark pressed his transmit button:

"Listen, gang! Wayne knows now he's facing a defector. He'll try to kill Petrov, this evening, probably in the parking lot. He can't let Petrov get away, knowing he's going to sing to us in a week or less. Be sure that when they get outside, Wayne has no—repeat, *no*—chance to kill Petrov. Don't crowd them, but nail them both as soon as they get near each other. We want them both alive. Both! Lose the vans if you have to, but no lives."

The Iron Horse—2122 hours, 12 January

Pyotr, trying to save something of the battered relationship, said, "There's a bonus of ten thousand in the newspaper, Sam. I hope it'll put you in a better mood. And what about your oral report—the reason for this meeting?"

Sam looked at him and hissed, "A tip! A lousy little tip . . . for a whole year's work. That's all I'm worth? And you want my thanks for the tip. Well, you can tell them, Petrov, that they're not only stupid for sending you to handle me, but they're cheap as hell. That's only a couple of months' salary. My take is worth millions each week. The chairman ought to clean house while there's still time, before his committee gets away from him!"

"Come on, Sam. It's only a token. You do this for the cause, not the money."

Furious, Sam said, "I'm leaving, Petrov. I'm sick of this. I don't give a shit what you do."

He slammed a dollar bill on the table. "There's *your* tip." Then he caught himself. He had to entice Petrov to talk outside.

"I'll give you the oral report, but that's the end. From now on, we have contact by drop only." He got up. "I'll give it to you outside, at your car, where I don't have to look at you. I'll stop my car next to yours. Be there inside five minutes."

It was nine twenty-three.

Pyotr nodded, unable to say anything. He'd blown the relationship. Moscow Center would crucify him.

The Iron Horse parking lot: van number one—2124 hours, 12 January

Mark pressed his transmit button: "I want Petrov to know Wayne wants to kill him, but don't let him succeed."

Two messages came in. From a male Gang member: "Wayne's outside the restaurant, heading for his car."

From Katie: "Waitress going to Petrov's booth."

The Iron Horse—2125 hours, 12 January

The waitress said to Pyotr: "He's gone? You haven't finished your sandwiches. Weren't they good?"

"They're just fine, miss, but he's in a lot of pain. He had minor surgery yesterday. I'll go out after him."

He paid her in cash. She said, "Thanks, mister. He looked as if he were hurting."

Pyotr walked out quickly, carrying the newspaper Wayne had given him, paying no attention to the other diners, wondering about Sam's oral report. Something about it was making Wayne act very strangely.

But he still had no inkling of what was to come.

Inside the restaurant, Dave collected the bugged ashtray and radioed a warning: "Petrov's leaving now."

**The Iron Horse parking lot: van number one—
2126 hours, 12 January**

In PETE'S PLUMBING, Dave looked over at Mark: "The Gang's used to my voice. Shall I take it from here?"

"Go ahead. Remember the guidelines."

The driver locked his transmit button down: "Van number two, start up and prepare to move toward Petrov's car. Nobody leaves the van yet. Watch Wayne's car. You two inside Iron Horse, come out the back way, move over toward Petrov, but keep out of sight around the building corner. You guys among the trucks, keep down but move over toward Petrov. That's where the action will be."

**The Iron Horse parking lot: Wayne's car—
2127 hours, 12 January**

Sam was breathing quickly now, hyperventilating, his heart racing. He watched Pyotr walk toward his car and said: "Your last walk, you treasonous bastard."

Sam started his car, breathing the single word, "Kill," over and over, to set his mind on what he had to do. "Kill, kill, kill . . ."

He began his move, the car rolling slowly, first among the trucks until, in the more open area in front of the restaurant, he gave it the gas.

He could see Pyotr standing beside his car, opening the door . . . "Kill, kill, kill . . ."

**The Iron Horse parking lot: van number one—
2128 hours, 12 January**

"Okay, van number two, bail out your passengers and ram," said Dave calmly. "Everybody on foot, close in on the Petrov car on the double. Everyone in the vans, buckle up . . . use shoulder harnesses."

The foot surveillants raced across the lot, silent in their sneakers, hard to see in their dark clothes.

Dave headed van number one to the left, toward Pyotr's car, moving fast. Neither van used its lights.

The driver of Tye's car came out running, his Uzi ready.

Sam braked his car to a skidding, squealing stop alongside Pyotr's. The Soviet looked at Wayne, saw the electric window rolling down, the dark metal gun barrel coming up, and sat there for a split second, mouth open . . .

The drive of van number two timed his move perfectly. He rammed the rear of Sam's car just as it stopped, from behind and the right side: The van's reinforced bumper bit into Sam's right real wheel, exploding the tire. The impact jerked the car in a half spin around its heavy front end. The doors burst open. Sam was thrown violently back in his seat, then forward against the dash, his head cracking the windshield, his gun discharging. The silenced gun made only a *whump* sound, but the heavy slug slammed into the hood of a truck on the other side of Pyotr's car.

Pyotr doubled over in his seat and slid to the passenger side, away from Wayne. He opened the door and rolled out onto the ground.

Four Gang members jumped into Sam's car as it burst open.

From the backseat a man grabbed Sam's jaw, jerking his head back against the seat.

On the driver's side the second man, diving in, grabbed Sam's gun with one hand, gave his wrist a vicious karate chop with the other, and wrenched the gun out of his hand. Sam's trigger finger held momentarily and the gun fired another round, this time into the dashboard, before his grip was broken.

A third man, from the backseat, taped Sam's mouth and held his nose, cutting off his breath.

The fourth man grabbed his trouser cuffs and taped his ankles together.

They pulled his head down onto the driver's seat, his feet out of the passenger door, and manhandled him out of the car.

The Gang stood him up, handcuffed his wrists behind his back, tore the tape from his mouth, pushed him violently from one man to another, kicked him in the balls "by accident," and threw him into PETE'S PLUMBING. He hit the steel floor with a loud thump, skidding to a stop at the feet of the audio team.

An audio man yelled, "Watch the equipment, shithead," and grabbed Sam by the hair, twisted it in an iron grip, and banged his head on the corner of his worktable.

Sam, blinded by blood streaming from his forehead, stunned by the violence of the ramming and the Gang's roughness, lay on the steel floor, gasping in agony.

It was nine thirty-one.

The Gang had jerked Pyotr to his feet to watch. By now he'd seen what Mark wanted him to see: Wayne's gun, the ramming, the roughing up.

They let him watch Wayne projected into PETE'S PLUMBING, then they rushed him into CENTENNIAL CARPET CLEANING. His feet didn't touch the ground on the way, and he made no sound or protest.

Colonel Pyotr A. Petrov was paralyzed with shock.

Langley, Virginia: Giotto's CP—
2132 hours, 12 January

After the rush of reports from Gaithersburg, the silence seemed strange. Static crackled and the listeners relaxed, smiling at each other.

By radio from Tye's car, Mark's voice broke the quiet: "Well, gents, we'd better meet downtown and do the hard part. Clara's in my office, waiting to help. She'd love to join you."

"You guys get her and go," said the DDO. "I'll brief the director. Good luck."

As Tye, Dallas, and Clara got into Giotto's car in the underground garage, John said, "You sure you want to come, Peter? We may have to be rude." He grinned.

"That's why I'm coming," replied the lawyer coolly. "It also has to be legal."

"The things this republic does to hamstring itself," grumbled Tye. "No wonder people like Wayne laugh at us."

Washington, D.C.: van number two— 2148 hours, 12 January

They were halfway to Washington before Pyotr began to complain. He harangued his captors:

"I'm a diplomat, with full diplomatic immunity. You can't arrest me or hold me. You must let me go. This will cause a very grave incident between our two countries. Maybe a break in diplomatic relations. I am an innocent Soviet diplomat having dinner . . ." He went on and on.

One of the men said, "That was an attempt to murder you. We're protecting you pending investigation. That's it."

Then all five men simply stared at Petrov. It unnerved him, as they wanted it to.

PETE'S PLUMBING was a mile behind CENTENNIAL CARPETS. Wayne sat on the hard floor, his handcuffed arms hurting. He cursed as the cramped position got to him, realizing that it was part of the softening up before his interrogation. He had been told how it was done, and he dreaded it.

Five miles ahead of the lead van, Mark relaxed in Tye's car as it neared downtown D.C. There were two tough minds to break tonight. He had game-planned both scenarios a dozen times, assessing the chances of turning Sam as only one in three. A death sentence was so remote as to be no real lever against him. He rated the possibility of doubling Pyotr at two in three, almost a probability, if it was done skillfully.

Then he took a moment to visualize Linda—her smile, her hand on his shoulder.

Washington, D.C.: secure holding area— 2155 hours, 12 January

The secure holding area was a large, three-story red-brick Georgian house in Foggy Bottom, not far from the Watergate office-apartment complex, next door to a D.C. police precinct station.

The formal, pillared entrance looked like many other Georgian houses in Washington, but inside, the front hall had been modified so that with a few quick changes of furniture and screens, it resembled a police station's receiving area. A high counter faced the door, and long wooden benches lined the left front and side walls. On the right a corridor led toward the back, where, out of sight, a control room was located between two windowless interrogation rooms. Next to one of them was a comfortably furnished living room.

Upstairs there was a guest room and a full suite in which the caretakers lived: a retired U.S. Marine Corps officer and his wife.

Giotto, Tye, Dallas, and Clara Brunswick were already in the control room when Mark got there. The control room had one-way mirrors, loudspeakers, and microphones for observation and monitoring of the interrogation rooms. Phones let the observers comment instantly to the interrogators. There was a button for each room, to flash a small red warning light to catch the interrogator's attention. Speakers in the control room relayed the take from the bugs in the Wayne and Besansky houses. Clara Brunswick sat at a small table, ready to type out any statements.

"We've agreed," Giotto told Mark, "that Holborne and Peter will work the control room at first. Petrov will be nagged by a 'cop' for a while, to get him ready for you. We'll let Wayne sweat alone for a bit, then you and I'll start on him. You play tough guy, okay?"

"Sure," Mark agreed. "Then I 'rescue' Petrov?"

"Yes. I can play tough for you."

"Be careful." Dallas smiled bitterly. "Our laws protect the traitor at least as much as the nation. It's got to be legal, or Wayne could go scot-free. And don't forget Petrov's diplomatic immunity."

Secure holding area—2201 hours, 12 January

The two vans arrived separately, to ensure that the two men had no chance even to see each other. One of the Gang drove Petrov's car and parked it nearby. Pyotr was led into the phony precinct house, a hood over his head until he got inside, so he couldn't see or be seen. He was booked by a uniformed "sergeant," searched by a "detective," and the top-secret documents from Wayne were laid out in full view on a table and photographed. Pyotr, too, was photographed and then fingerprinted, as he loudly claimed diplomatic immunity.

"Sorry, sir," the man posing as a desk sergeant said. "Attempted murder, you know. Routine has to be respected." The searching and identification went on. Then Pyotr was in an interrogation room, and flinched as he recognized what it was. A cold room with three chairs, one small table. Gray walls and door. Spotlights recessed into the ceiling, focused on the center chair—his. He deliberately sat in the wrong chair and waited, shivering, anxious, and angry, his diplomatic immunity ignored by his captors.

PETE'S PLUMBING arrived shortly after CENTENNIAL CARPETS, and Wayne, also hooded, was frog-marched into the receiving area. The cut on his forehead was treated. He was relieved of the KGB money, the contents of his pockets were inventoried, and then the contents and he were photographed by the 'police'—security men with stony expressions.

Then he was marched into the other interrogation room and told to sit in the spotlighted chair. He obeyed sullenly, resigned to a thoroughly hostile inquisition.

There would be threats, maybe abuse, because the interrogators would be his CIA colleagues, angry and disgusted. It would be a chilling experience. But at least the law would be respected. It would protect him from violence, he told himself. From torture, the thought of which terrified him. His rights were as good as theirs. He ground his teeth, hating them.

Secure holding area: Pyotr's room—2210 hours, 12 January

They had let Pyotr and Wayne wait for what seemed like an eternity. It was, in fact, only a few minutes. Both men fidgeted and looked about anxiously, alone, tension rising, knowing they were being watched, knowing what was to happen next.

Pyotr was seething with hatred for the mole, who had insulted and sneered at him, then cost him his career by trying to murder him. There was no doubt in Pyotr's mind that he would be PNG'd—expelled from the U.S.—and blamed by Moscow for the wreck of SVYET, one of the KGB's best Washington operations in years. They would blame him for agreeing to meet hurriedly, without a protective KGB counter surveillance, without a system of warnings, and driving with diplomatic plates almost to the meeting site. They would castigate him for causing, then not sensing, the mole's lethal anger. They would now become suspicious of his claim to be close to recruiting Mark. They would think it possible that Mark had somehow engineered this evening's scenario.

Pyotr would be fired from the KGB, expelled from the Party. At best, he would become officially a nonperson—living on the charity of the Lapins. At worst, the chairman would invoke that treason charge and he would be jailed, maybe executed. Against that, his stark and cold interrogation room looked almost warm and cozy.

Secure holding area: Wayne's room—2211 hours

Mark and Giotto came in together but placed their chairs on each side of Wayne so he had to strain to look from one to the other. The cold of the room, spotlight on his face, handcuffs tight behind his back were old but effective interrogation tools.

"As of tomorrow, Wayne," Giotto said without emotion, his cold voice like a dry hinge closing slowly, "Moscow Center will understand you've been a double, working for us, for ten years. They'll never trust you again."

Wayne was silent, but he was listening.

Mark smiled at Wayne, but his voice was thick with anger. "We're telling Petrov, before he goes back to his embassy, that you were our man, that the emergency meeting was a fake you were running for us as a provocation. That the two 'hot' documents you gave him tonight were disinformation. That we regret our pressure drove you around the bend, made you try to kill him. The *rezident* will believe Petrov."

John gave Wayne a pitying grin. "The Center won't know which parts of your take for all those years to believe, which to distrust. Now they'll even suspect a lot of the material they were able to check on—did we arrange the confirmation, or was it real? In the end you'll have cost the KGB far more than you helped it. I'm sorry for you—you screwed your own side."

"You won't get much sleep while you wait for the court to sentence you," Mark snarled. "Or for the KGB to knock you off in the meantime. You, above all, should know how they do that. They can reach right into our jails."

Wayne stared at Mark, trying to sneer. He didn't know the KGB did that, but he believed it. He said nothing.

"The more you tell us, the less likely it is you'll be executed, you and your wife and Besansky. If you tell it all, you'll not even go to jail as long as you cooperate. Refusal to cooperate at all is almost certainly a death sentence." Dallas warned John, by making the red light behind Wayne blink softly, not to go too far.

"The courts will probably give Sonya a jail term, Wayne." Mark smiled wolfishly. "That's to our advantage, because if you don't cooperate, I'll see that she pays for you. You'll never know when or where, in jail or out, she'll be cut into little pieces and fed to the sharks." Mark ignored Dallas's red light, finished by shouting: "If we can get to her before the other inmates polish her off!"

Wayne was emotionally dependent on Sonya, his one Achilles heel. The threat was petrifying.

"Your regular conductor, Boris Kuznetsov, has been our agent for years, Wayne. You've really been suckered." John shook his head, looking sympathetic. It was a believable lie.

As his world tumbled, Wayne overlooked that they would have known about Boris because Petrov had used his apartment and his car. Sam believed Boris had betrayed him. He felt hunted down, with nowhere to turn. But he wasn't about to cave in if he could help it.

"Your problem," he said sarcastically, "is that I believe in what I'm doing. Communism is the wave of the future, of strength. It'll pass you jerks by. Anyway, if you kill her, you're no better than the people you despise because of what you suppose they do."

Mark was visibly furious, voice shaking. "You bastard, you think you can frighten us off with our own ethics. Well, maybe you can frighten our system into letting you get away with it, but you can't frighten me. Or hundreds like me. We'll get you, using your own KGB's tactics, and if it has to be through Sonya, so be it. Try me!"

Peter Dallas's insistent red light had no effect on Mark. But Mark's unexpected venom, his willingness to go beyond the law, were both fearsome and believable to Wayne. He turned to John. "You wouldn't let him?"

Giotto earned his own red light. "Free country, Wayne. We can order him not to, but we can't guarantee it!"

Wayne's face went gray as he directly faced the promise of violence against Sonya. The deck was stacked too high.

"Perhaps we'd only cripple her—eyes and tongue gone. Hard to spy if you can't see or talk." Mark looked fierce, but he hated saying it. Yuk, he thought. I've even disgusted myself.

It did the job. Sam Wayne suddenly folded. "Okay. You guys have all the cards. I'll work with you—as long as Sonya and Alec don't know about it and you leave her alone."

"No tricks, Wayne," said Giotto. "We've got Boris to check on you, and some other neat tricks, thank God."

"We'll be back in a while, Wayne," said Mark. "You can dictate a confession by just talking into the wall mikes. Then you can phone Sonya and tell her to stop worrying. Tell her that your conductor said they'd nailed a would-be defector yesterday and sent him home."

Wayne began to talk to the walls as they left the room. Breaking him had taken twelve minutes.

Secure holding area: Petrov's room—2224 hours

Mark and Giotto joined Tye and Dallas in the control room. The speakers relaying audio from the Wayne and Besansky homes brought in background noise, no voices. Dallas was listening carefully to Wayne's statement. Tye, watching

Petrov, said, "He's not budging. This stage has reached a dead end. You'd better go in, Mark."

Pyotr had been badgered for a quarter-hour by a persistent man who kept asking the same questions: "What is your real name? When and where were you born? What is your KGB assignment? Why did you commit espionage against the U.S.? Why did your agent try to kill you? Did you provoke him? Did he do it in self-defense?"

To all the questions, he only replied: "I am a Soviet diplomat with full immunity. I demand to be released immediately, or there will be a diplomatic incident."

The badgering had prepared Pyotr for Mark's entrance. He almost shouted his relief.

"Mark! Tell this man I'm a Soviet diplomat and must be released!"

The man, a security officer posing as a police investigator, said to Mark, "Attempted murder case, sir. We have to have his statement."

Mark smiled at Pyotr, turned toward the investigator. "Perhaps I can talk with him privately, find out what you need to know without any fuss."

"Be my guest," said the man, and left the room.

"In a mess, eh, Pyotr?" Mark was grinning. "Anytime you've been involved in a murder attempt, just call your friendly CIA contact."

"Mark, that's not funny. I am a Soviet diplomat . . ."

Mark interrupted: "As a KGB case officer buying classified information from a CIA officer, you broke our law and you violated the Vienna Convention. Your conversation with him was taped. They have the top-secret documents he gave you, the money you paid him. They photographed the exchange, and they have witnesses. For that, Pyotr, you can be declared PNG and expelled from the U.S. That's all that could happen to you if this were a normal case." He paused, smiling to convey his sympathy.

Pyotr said nothing, but his eyes showed he was listening.

"But also you were involved in an attempted murder. You must provide your full statement, by law. There's another difficulty: You're accredited to Bwagania, not to the United States. I don't believe you have immunity here."

It got him talking, which was the point. "I will only give my statement in the presence of a Soviet Embassy official, Mark. When will he get here?"

"Only if the authorities tell your embassy that you're here. But before we get to that, have you considered how the Agency knew when and where you were going to meet your agent?"

"All I know is I was starting my car after eating at the restaurant when this stranger tried to kill me . . ."

Mark shook his head, grimacing. "Come on, Pyotr, we know he's your agent. He's been ours too, for ten years. Only we get the real story from him. And from Boris Kuznetsov. Anyway, Sam wouldn't try to kill you. Was it the other way around? Did you try to kill an American citizen? Perhaps you didn't trust him?"

The triple shock took Pyotr's breath away. Kuznetsov and Wayne CIA agents, both doubles? Yet it was possible. Just about anything is, in the field of espionage. Then the accusation that he'd tried to kill the mole. The situation was even graver than he'd thought. Would the CIA convince the police *he* was guilty, not Wayne? Pyotr didn't know what the men in the vans had seen, or might invent.

He also found himself alarmed by the thought that he might be losing Mark's respect—and a friendship that had become important.

"Have you talked to the men in the vans, Mark? They'll tell you it was Wayne who tried to kill me." As he said it, Pyotr realized he'd fallen into a trap.

Mark smiled. "If you didn't know Sam, how did you know his name was Wayne? And how did you have copies of CIA documents on you that have his initials on them?" Sam's initials weren't there, but the trick was to move Pyotr along the road to admitting he knew Wayne.

"It's ten-thirty, Mark. I should be back at the embassy soon. They'll start to wonder."

"When?"

"Eleven."

"I'm in the business too, Pyotr. Midnight, at the earliest. Anyway, nothing happens until you've given your statement."

To his own surprise, Pyotr wanted to help Mark. He gave ground briefly. "You won't doctor it so that I look like a killer?"

"No, Pyotr. We're not in Moscow. The men in the van have to say what they saw. They won't be told what to say."

Pyotr wriggled again. "I met the man earlier this evening, in a bar. We agreed to have dinner. When he learned I was a Soviet, he tried to kill me. That's all."

Mark's disgust and irritation was real now. "You were meeting your agent—remember? The police know that. Your statement has to make sense so that they can release you. Diplomatic immunity—which you don't seem to have here—would only protect you if you tell the real story. Attempted murder's very serious. Don't play games with me."

"I can't admit to you, even if it seems obvious, that we were having a case officer-agent meeting. Officially, I deny that we're anything but casual acquaintances. You know that."

Mark was making progress. He switched to Russian: "Look, I'm trying to help you, Pyotr. Just tell me privately why he tried to murder you. Perhaps I can settle this without a statement."

Pyotr sensed a ploy, but he was furiously angry at Wayne. His fury, and the sudden change to Russian, brought his guard down. He felt as if his mouth had its own momentum, gobbling up his thoughts and voicing them. His words tumbled out: "He first tried to get rid of me in Bwagania. He sent Moscow copies of your photos and tapes of me and Anna."

With that, Pyotr had crossed the first bridge. Now, Mark had something to get his teeth into. He said, "We already knew that from Wayne, before you got pissed and threw your drink at the ceiling. Wayne tells us you're known as an incompetent lush, a disgrace to the KGB."

"I hate Wayne more than I've ever hated anyone." Pyotr clenched his fists and ground his teeth.

Mark tried to turn Pyotr's detestation of the mole in the

right direction. "He was just doing his job. The KGB called the tune." It worked.

"That bastard Ossilenko, he and Wayne . . ."

"Amen. A pair of shits. Tell you what I'll do," said Mark. "I'll accept your statement, with no admission of your real relationship with Wayne, on the condition you agree to have a personal, private chat with me now about your future."

Pyotr knew exactly what Mark had in mind: an invitation to defect.

All his anger and frustration at Moscow Center boiled up. Still, he said, "I know what you're up to and I won't accept it."

Mark came back at him anyway: "Shall we start?"

Pyotr shook his head. "I have to think."

"All right. I've got to leave you for a moment anyway. Someone else wants a word with you. Then I'll be back."

Secure holding area: control room—2237 hours

In the control room, Mark said, "You want to pressure him a bit, John?"

As Giotto headed for Petrov's room, the speakers brought in the dial tone of the Wayne home telephone. He stopped to listen.

Sonya, ignoring Sam's orders, dialed Besansky's number, her voice loud and clear in the control room. "Alec, it's getting on toward eleven and no call from Sam. Why don't you come over here with your stuff. We may have to take off in a hurry." Her voice was stiff with anxiety.

"Easy, Sonya." But his voice was shaking. "Let's give it another fifteen minutes. Then I'll come over if he hasn't called. Don't panic."

Dallas looked through the one-way mirror at Wayne. "He's finished talking. How's the summary coming along, Clara?"

"Just typing the last few words," she said. "This is fascinating."

"Stick with Cameron." Dallas laughed. "He'll get you a mole a month."

"Me in Africa? No thank you."

"I'll take it in, John," said Mark to Giotto. "I'll have him phone Sonya as soon as he's signed it. He can sign the full version later."

"Better give him a strong warning about two-timing us, Mark," Dallas grunted.

"I thought you'd never ask." Mark grinned.

Secure holding area: Wayne's room—2239 hours

"Sign here, Wayne. Then call home. Use this phone; it's hooked up. Sonya and Besansky are getting ready to run for it." Mark handed him the one-page summary confession.

Wayne skimmed it, signed it, reached for the phone.

"No tricks," said Mark, signing as a witness. "If you screw with us, Wayne, we'll ask for the death penalty for all three of you. We'll know if you play games. Not only from Boris. Giotto's just opened a new window into Moscow Center, one they'll never suspect in a thousand years."

Wayne looked at him coldly. The threats sounded empty, experience told him. But then again they just could be true. His secret resolve—confess, cooperate, and live to screw them another day—was a razor blade with two edges. He dialed his number.

"Hello, Sonya. Relax. They found the spy and shipped him home already. I'm going to have a few more drinks with my friend. He's okay. Go to bed. Goodnight."

"Not bad, Wayne," said Mark. "But just in case, we'll be watching you and listening to you twenty-four hours a day. Don't try to leave the D.C. area, and don't forget—if you play games with us, we'll tell the KGB you've been doubled for years. They have nasty ways of getting even, as you know."

"You won't have a bug in our bedroom?"

"When you have trouble getting it up, Wayne, just remember how you earned that bug." Mark laughed at him.

The steel bindings around Sam Wayne were imaginary, but they felt cold as they bit deeper into his skin.

Secure holding area: Pyotr's room—
2239 hours, 12 January

"Mark likes you too much to mention this, Petrov, but I don't suffer from that emotion." Giotto smiled his most menacing smile. "If you go back, we'll get word to Moscow Center."

"What word?"

"That you discussed defection."

"But I haven't."

"You've already talked about Wayne and Ossilenko. That's a start. They'll fry you for that."

"They'll laugh at you."

"They'll believe our messenger. He's one of your people. Not only that. He'll tell them that you threatened Wayne because of the photos and tapes of you and Anna Iosevna. You had it in for him. He lost his temper. You screwed up a superb operation. They'll believe it."

"They'll never believe it."

"You know they will."

Pyotr said nothing.

"The real issue," continued Giotto, "is whether you want to go on in an organization that's going to cut your throat, in a system you despise."

"I love my country, and the system works well."

"Bullshit, Pyotr. You don't believe that."

"I certainly do. When is the man from my embassy coming?"

"All right, Pyotr. You belong in there, and no amount of personal risk will stop you from going back."

Pyotr waved his hand and bowed, a motion that eloquently said, Yes, you got it.

Giotto shook his head. "Why would any sane man choose prison, possibly death, certainly disgrace, over freedom in a country where he can say and do just about anything he wants?"

Pyotr just smiled. There was no way to decipher his expression. Giotto pressed on: "Your life in the Soviet system's been pretty good, Pyotr. All the privileges, just like tsarist nobles. But all that's going to be lost, Pyotr. Your family too, they'll probably turn away from you. You'll be an outcast, if in fact you survive. No job, no career . . ."

"You don't know that. You're just guessing."

"No, Pyotr. Ossilenko'll see to it that you're crucified. And they'll have every reason to shoot you down, which—with your lousy record—won't be hard. You're on probation, right?" Giotto was guessing.

"Yes, that's right." Pyotr looked somber. He was listening more carefully now. This man knew a lot.

"On the one hand you go back to one of the harshest, least forgiving societies in the world, and you end up like a grease spot on the floor. You can't even influence events, so you'll be doomed to watch that system continue trying its best to destroy itself and the West—if they let you live to see it. On the other hand we offer you a new life, a job consulting with us, freedom, a chance to really influence things. Is there any basis for going back?"

Pyotr said nothing. The unwelcome argument was a replica of the unwanted debate going on inside him. He felt like a bear in a trap: steel teeth around his neck, steel teeth around his ankles, pulling him apart.

"I must think."

Giotto left the room.

Secure holding area: Pyotr's room—2245 hours

"Come with me, please." Mark led Pyotr through the door into the sitting room. It was warm, well furnished, and there was a small bar. Pyotr, drink in hand as he sat in an armchair, felt relaxed by the contrast between the interrogation room and this plush salon. That was the point, and they both knew it.

He looked at Mark with a grin: "I can say it for you, Mark. Your friend just coached me."

"Go ahead," said Mark in Russian. "You may be able to convince yourself better than I could."

"Behind me, a broken career, almost certain disgrace, punishment, shame, perhaps prison. Without question, my in-laws will try to remove me from the family . . . divorce will be proposed. I'll be a nonperson."

"A bleak picture. Anna Iosevna, perhaps?"

"No. She'll hang on to Ossilenko."

"Ossilenko? She's like that?"

"Yes, like that."

"Why bother, then?"

"I love her."

"Yes, I see." There was genuine understanding in Mark's eyes, and Pyotr could see it. Where did the official in Mark stop, the human begin?

"In front of me," Pyotr went on, "a mountain of goodies from the CIA: salary, security, U.S. citizenship, a job, a house, a pension, new friends . . . why not?"

"There's another option, surely?"

"Yes, Mark. I stay in place, work with you in Gitabwanga, against them."

"How would you feel about that?"

"I like you. I respect you. You like me and respect me. Our friendship's become important to me. But . . ."

They had reached the critical point. Pyotr had laid out the case neatly. The outcome hinged on what Mark would say in the next few minutes.

"Exactly, Mother Russia."

Pyotr nodded, his eyes closed.

Mark sat quietly thinking. The turning of Sam Wayne, accomplished quickly by a barrage of threats, was tarnished by definition. The likelihood it would stick indefinitely was slender. Recruitment of Pyotr, however, although it could perhaps be forced, would be infinitely more valuable if Pyotr could be induced to make his own free choice between loyalty and liberty, between life among known predators or among the unknown.

Only one thing was now certain: The more Pyotr talked, the better the chances he'd defect.

"You're quite sure your career is ruined? That Moscow Center will blame you?"

"They won't blame me for inheriting a couple of doubles. Some heads may roll for that, but not mine."

"Ossilenko's, maybe?"

"If I can help it roll, yes."

"What will they blame you for?"

"The obvious—my talk about recruiting you was hogwash. I couldn't handle Boris's agent, and he tried to kill me. I've been arrested, blown wide open. It'll be a media field day as well as a diplomatic incident."

"You could gloss over it, make them concentrate on the fact that you uncovered two doubles."

"No. They'll interrogate me. It will make this look like a picnic."

"Drugs?"

"Among many other things."

"Does going back make sense, then?"

Pyotr had spent an hour wondering about that. The faces of his antagonists passed in an imaginary parade: Ossilenko, the chairman, Lapin, waiting to jump on him . . . the disappointment of Raspatov. Then there was Olga, whose fury he would have to face daily if he didn't go to jail. Aleksandra, growing up the daughter of a failure. But he said, "Loyalty is a strong habit. You should know that."

"Pyotr, would it help if I offer you more than my personal friendship, if I guarantee to you that I'll always be available no matter what? A brother, if you will . . ."

"And Aleksandra?"

"Of course. Would she come with you?"

"I don't know. I wouldn't want to ask her to face that for a while. She's too young."

"Makes a strong case for staying in place . . ."

Pyotr was silent for a full minute. "You'd have done well in the KGB." He meant it as a compliment.

"No way. I don't have the stomach for state repression."

"Mark, no speeches, okay? I said it as your friend."

"All right, no polemics. But I'd like you to hear me out, without emotion, just as if this were a business discussion about someone else."

"You know where I start, Mark?"

"I can guess. How our country looks to you: America is a mess, a sick society. It's the world's headquarters for violent crime, drugs, poverty, bigotry; you name it, we got it. Why would you choose that?"

"Right. Why run from one problem to another?"

"Well, we could arrange your resettlement in any country of your choice—the UK, France, Australia, Canada, Brazil, whatever. But here we can better ensure your safety and a meaningful job. And here in the U.S., with all our problems, Aleksandra would grow up in a society where the welfare of the people is the purpose of government, not a privilege to be handed out to the chosen few."

"Very eloquent, my friend. Compelling. Bring her here to rot in the soup of America's excesses. She needs guidance, not license."

"She's at the top; she'll do well in either country. But there's your future as well as hers. Both of you should be happy."

"The pursuit of happiness, eh? Is that sensible, while Moscow tries to bury you?"

"If you were Party secretary-general, would you try to destroy the West? Or try to preserve it?"

Pyotr's face showed signs of fatigue. "You've got a point, Mark. Personally, I'd preserve the West so that we could slowly make up a society that has the best of both worlds. But I'm not the secretary-general. I've no choice but to follow my instructions. Unless they change, we'll bury you if we can."

Pyotr had crossed another invisible line: Again he'd revealed profound disagreement with his government. Now he had to be pulled across the final line delicately, without affront to his sensibilities.

"But you do have a choice. That's just the point, my good friend. Don't let habit tell you what to do." He smiled, touched Pyotr's arm. "Make up your own mind. Do what you think is right, not what your government wants. No matter what your decision is, even if I don't like it, I'll applaud you for making it yourself."

Mark's warmth and his unexpected reply impressed Pyotr. "I always make my own decisions. Spell it out for me."

"I speak for the director, Pyotr. In exchange for your complete cooperation—which will include a year of working for us while you stay inside the KGB—we'll issue you U.S. citizenship under the DCI's annual quota 'for services rendered.' While you stay in the KGB, we'll make sure Sam Wayne doesn't change his mind and sing to Moscow about tonight. When eventually you surface, you'll have a job as a CIA consultant, a house and car here in the Washington area, and a bodyguard. After a year you'll be free to terminate your contract, leave the U.S., and resettle anywhere you think it's safe."

Pyotr nodded. For some reason he was enjoying the game. The concept intrigued him.

"The dangerous part's while you're still in the KGB, inside the embassy in Gitabwanga," said Mark. "I'll work with you to make that as safe as possible." He looked into Pyotr's eyes. "Unless, of course, there's another mole and he somehow learns what you're doing."

"There isn't. The *rezident* here would have hinted . . ." He stopped abruptly.

"Thank you, Pyotr. That was a very valuable piece of information." Mark smiled. "I believe you crossed the line with that, don't you?"

Pyotr thought about it for a while. Moscow Center would execute him for admitting there wasn't another mole. He had indeed crossed the final line, and it was much easier, much less wrenching, than he'd expected. He felt as if a sack of grain had been lifted off his chest, a sack that had been there many years. He simply nodded, without words.

It was eleven o'clock.

Mark shook his hand, poured them another drink. "Welcome to the Company. Now we have work to do. We have forty-five minutes to find out a few things from you, get a credible package ready for you to take back to the *rezidentura,* and decide what the 'emergency meeting' Wayne called for was about."

"The *rezident* and the Center will buy anything reasonable."

"Good. Now, Pyotr, please identify your agents in Bwagania and those you know about elsewhere: names, addresses, what they do for the KGB, in order of their operational importance to the KGB, a quick summary. Use this notepad. Then list all operations against the U.S. you can think of and who's running them. If there's any time left, start listing KGB staff officers by true name and aliases. We can pick up from there when we meet next."

"Okay, when will that be?"

"The evening of the fourteenth. Why not, you're supposed to be recruiting me? And you've got the night off. Tell them Wayne's being sent to a training center for a week. That's the reason he called for the emergency meeting—he couldn't make it the fourteenth."

"That's the kind of thing Wayne would do. You'll help me with the phony recruitment of you?"

"We'll make you look good, but I'm not going to pretend I'm really interested. You know that. I'll slowly tease you without shutting the door . . ."

"So we can drag it out?"

"For a year, Pyotr. A full year—the term of your agreement with us." He got up. "I'll be back shortly."

"I'm starting now," said Pyotr, picking up a pen, grinning. It had U.S. GOVERNMENT imprinted on it.

Secure holding area: control room—2310 hours, 12 January

Mark walked into the control room to find four people sitting fascinated, their body language showing disgust. They were watching and listening as Wayne dictated his summary damage report to the walls of his interrogation room, head down, fatigue dominant, depression evident in his halting voice.

Clara looked up at Mark, smiled, and said: "You did well, you and Mr. Giotto. You know, Mark, I've rarely hated a human, but I hate this man." She pointed her chin at Sam.

"You'll get a front-row seat at the guillotine, if it comes to that. You've got the package for Petrov to take back with him, the stuff Wayne is supposed to have given him?"

"Mr. Giotto has it."

"Good. We can give it to Petrov now. At least we control this affair. It's a nice feeling."

Langley, Virginia: the director's office— 1130 hours, 13 January

Jane, the DCI's executive secretary, went through her routine as deliberately as ever. She looked over the top of a document and smiled her recognition. She finished the document, faced it down on her desk, and picked up her phone. Her quiet voice had the impersonal, indecipherable quality of someone chewing ice. There was no way to tell if she knew about last night's action. Three minutes later, the light came on and she nodded toward the inner door.

The director was standing in front of the picture windows when Mark came in. He turned abruptly and came across the room, hand outstretched. "Well done, Mark! Very well done. I never thought three days ago it could be done so fast and so well. It's not often everything works our way."

"Thank you, sir. We were lucky, that's all."

"That's the kind of luck you make for yourself, Mark. The kind of luck I'd like to think we train our officers to achieve. Well, young man, I've already lifted that two-year promotion freeze on you." He smiled, blue smoke billowing up. "You're also welcome in my office any time business brings you this way. In other words, Mr. Cameron, your exile is over. You have, almost alone, rehabilitated your career."

"Mr. Director, you've no idea what that means to me. It's wonderful to be on the move again."

"When do you go back to Bwagania, Mark? And by the way, how's Linda doing?"

"I go back in three weeks, sir. We need the time to let some of the specialists help me debrief Petrov while he's supposed to be working on his recruitment effort against me. It's a neat situation, where the KGB expects him to spend maximum time with me when he's not working on SVYET."

The DCI laughed. "And Linda?"

"I want to marry her. I think she'll agree."

"I feel like cupid, Mark. I told her to keep an eye on you, help you. I'd no idea she'd do it this well."

Mark couldn't resist it. "Do all your agents marry their targets, Mr. Director?"

The eyes twinkled, the smoke ballooned. "How long will Petrov stay here?"

"A month or so, until Kuznetsov gets back. Then I expect him back in Bwagania. He'll give me all the scoop on Red Snow Two, and help me think up ways to torment Ossilenko."

"Ossilenko recruitable?"

"Most unlikely, sir. But we can always dream. Petrov doesn't absolutely rule it out."

"Some of our most valuable defectors have been assessed before the fact as absolutely unrecruitable, then to our surprise they've suddenly come across and told us they had to put on an act to survive."

"I know, sir. That's one of the things that keeps the odds reasonable."

"I haven't had a chance to keep up with this since last night. What about that SOB Sam Wayne?"

"He played it straight with Sonya last night. He phoned her at midnight, gave her the story we concocted: He got a bit drunk with Petrov, was hit by a truck while driving home, and ended up in the hospital 'for observation.' He's a Reserve colonel, so we got him in a military hospital, under control. The cover is he's not badly hurt, but there may be nerve damage. She visited him early this morning, and she's at work now, apparently without suspicion. Right now he's sitting up in a private room, writing a history of SVYET and a damage report. John Giotto's busy planning what we'll pass the KGB through Wayne the next few weeks."

"Wayne knows nothing about Petrov's defection. Won't he assume Petrov will tell the KGB that SVYET's washed up?"

"Normally, yes. But we've instructed him to tell Petrov he's only nominally under our control, that in reality he's a triple—a double who's been redoubled. Complicated, but it should hold water for a while. Petrov thinks it will."

"What about Kuznetsov? He won't buy that, surely? He'll turn it against Petrov, for not reporting their arrest."

"We told Wayne to say nothing about it to Kuznetsov. He thinks Kuznetsov's our man. Anyway, Wayne'll be wired at all his meetings with Soviets. We'll know if he disobeys us."

"I hope you can keep it all straight, Mark. Wayne's a

slender reed. Don't let the KGB catch Petrov and knock him off."

"He's safe as long as Wayne's controllable."

"What's your rating of the odds on that?"

"Fifty-fifty, sir. Depends how much he believes our threats. I think we scared him shitless."

The DCI smiled. "Keep him that way. Give my regards to Linda."

Washington, D.C.: The Ocean Club— 2030 hours, 14 January

"Mark, I laugh every time I think of all the expensive dinners we're going to have at KGB expense." He looked around the plush restaurant, tables far apart and waiters at a discreet distance. "The food's terrific here."

"Our debriefings aren't wearing you down too much?"

"It's a grind, every afternoon, but not too bad."

"How are things at the office?"

"The *rezident*'s delighted with my report of the meeting with Wayne. I told him all went well and the take was good."

"He doesn't see it?"

"Only after the Center works it over. Ossilenko's orders. The *rezident*'s also pleased we're seeing so much of each other. You're showing more signs of disaffection with the Company, you know. You almost look recruitable."

"Keep it up, drag it out. You've got a good imagination."

Pyotr grinned. "I do. Talking about imagination, the Center bought the emergency-meeting story. They're anxious to know what the DDO's special assignment for Wayne is."

"You can tell them it was a routine visit to the Farm, just a conflict with your scheduled meeting tonight."

"Luck of the game, I'll tell them. SVYET didn't know me, so he overreacted. How does it go from here with SVYET? You haven't told Wayne I'm with the Company now?"

"God, no! Here's the story with Wayne. Initially, he thought we would tell you that we'd doubled him years ago. Yesterday, after he started to cooperate, we told him that we hadn't told you that—that it was only a gimmick to get him to cooperate. Remember, he doesn't know how much you saw in the parking lot. We've told him you were questioned by the police and released right away. You didn't see him try to kill you. You went home from the Iron Horse, not to the *rezidentura*. You don't know what to report until you've got Wayne's story. He's going to tell you, via dead drop, that he was picked up, doubled, but is in fact a triple still working for you."

"He thinks I'll buy that?"

"It doesn't matter, really. The only purpose of this is to keep SVYET going for a while, even after Kuznetsov gets back. And, of course, to protect you."

Pyotr had a wry grin. "Then Kuznetsov isn't . . ."

". . . our man? No. Sorry, friend. All's fair in this game."

Pyotr shook his head. "Wayne's a thin wire to hang a heavy operation on."

"I know, but there's no choice unless we wrap up SVYET now, which we don't want to do for obvious reasons. We just have to control him. That's a certainty."

"Can you have him insist on dead drops only from now on, no direct meetings? I don't want to meet the swine again."

"We wondered about that. Will Kuznetsov buy it?"

"I think he'd be delighted. Let's work on it. Or else just let him have an accident before he talks to Kuznetsov."

"Nyet. You're in a different camp now."

Langley, Virginia: Mark's office—1630 hours, 23 January

Mark had read the letter a dozen times since it arrived the day before in a pouch from Gitabwanga. It was dated January 14. The words seemed like her hand on his shoulder, her cheek against his:

> ". . . miss you more than a letter can tell, and can't wait for you to come home. I've tried to manage as well as you do, my love, but the station needs its real boss. I need you too, so come back as soon as you can. I've cabled bringing you up to date on what's happened since you left. It's official and so it

> can't convey the full flavor of such things as the king's postmortem on the Red Snow affair, Paul Passatu and his bright, amusing face as he talks to me (and tries to seduce me in his own silly way—without a hope of success), and François' wit as he describes how he was almost canned but was able to show it was a fake document ploy engineered by General O. I love you, my darling, and can't wait to get a cable announcing your ETA.

Linda's cabled sitrep was well written, and Mark was pleased with the way she summarized her message: a long step forward in becoming a working case officer.

The cable covered the king's postmortem:

> PRESENT IN BASEMENT COMMAND POST: KING, M'BOUYÉ, PASSATU, DE LA MAISON, TAKAHASHI. KING PLANS SPECIAL JUNE ELECTION OF NEW PRIME MINISTER. NO MENTION OF HEIR TO REPLACE M'TAGA, OR WHO ENGINEERED ATTEMPT ON KING, OR WHO KILLED HIS SON AND SCHACHT ALTHOUGH EVERYONE PRESENT AWARE SICILIAN'S ROLE (SEE PASSATU REPORT BELOW). KING DOWNPLAYING EVENTS TO REDUCE POLITICAL TEMPERATURE.

Then re François:

> DE LA MAISON BACK FROM PARIS WHERE NARROWLY ESCAPED BEING VICTIM OF KGB ATTEMPT HAVE HIM REMOVED FOR DISLOYALTY. LIAISON RESUMED NORMALLY.

On Paul Passatu:

> HAVE CONTINUED TRAINING HIM IN OBSERVATION, REPORTING, PHOTOGRAPHY, COUNTERSURVEILLANCE. AN EAGER STUDENT SHAPING UP WELL AS LONG-TERM AGENT. REPORTING CONTINUES EXCELLENT, INCLUDING DETAILS SICILIAN MURDER OF M'TAGA AND SCHACHT AT KING'S REQUEST.

On Prince Kalanga, she had welcome news:

ON KING'S OKAY, INTERIOR MINISTER HAD KALANGA ARRESTED ON CHARGES POLITICAL AGITATION. UNDER INDEFINITE HOUSE ARREST WHICH FITTING FOR HIM.

Re Ossilenko, she was brief:

OSSILENKO UNDER LOCKSTEP SURVEILLANCE BY BWAGANIAN SÛRETÉ. KEEPING HEAD WELL DOWN. ANNA FREQUENT VISITOR HIS HOTEL. APARTMENT UNUSED.

The cabled then related her handling of various other operational situations, all with minimum fuss. It ended with a standard comment:

DETAILS ABOVE BY DISPATCH ASAP.

His cabled reply read:

TRAP SUCCESSFUL. CAMERON ETA GITA 0630 8 FEB. WELL DONE TAKAHASHI.

Washington, D.C.: CIA safehouse—1900 hours, 6 February

"This is my last evening here," said Mark. "I go back to Gita tomorrow."

"I'll miss you," said Pyotr. "We've done a lot of work and had a lot of fun together. I like the specialists who've worked here with us, but it won't be the same."

"Not for me, either. I'll be impatient until you get back to Bwagania."

"You going via Paris or Dakar?"

"Dakar. It's quicker. Linda's waiting for me."

"I understand. I went over to the *rezidentura* this evening, as you know, and was lucky. I've got some new stuff to give you. More names of KGB and GRU assets in the U.S., with addresses and cover organizations. I'm digging them up slowly but surely." He handed Mark a single sheet of paper.

"I have to memorize them, you know, then write it out before I meet you people."

"I know. Nice work, Pyotr. The specialists will go over it in the morning—I'll give it to them before I leave. Please, don't take any unnecessary risks." Mark was continually amazed by Pyotr's instant transformation from an antagonist to a remarkably good CIA asset.

Pyotr laughed. "Okay, no risks. But you must focus on a serious danger to the U.S. I'll give the specialists a status report on the *rezidentura*'s efforts to recruit agents on Capitol Hill—a heavily funded priority KGB effort to acquire influence in the U.S. Congress as well as collect prime intelligence. You'll find it fascinating. It's a priority project, and they intend to recruit at the top as well as among the staffers. They're deadly serious, and they're good at it."

"We know about it," replied Mark. "But your details will be vital. Anything else before we go out and dine?"

"Another dinner courtesy of the KGB. Yes, the Center has approved my suggestion that I visit Paris en route back to Gitabwanga. They didn't question it. I'll get as much as I can while I'm there, on KGB operations in and from France. I know the *rezident* well, and he'll gossip enough to make it worth the trip."

"Good," said Mark. "By the way, Linda advises that Colonel de la Maison is back in Gitabwanga. Apparently, SSR learned of the closeness of his liaison with me, and they almost canned him."

"Ossilenko did that, Mark. I forgot to tell you. Based on your reports of that liaison, which SVYET sent in, Ossilenko dreamed up a disinformation operation and popped the package into SSR channels in Brussels. I'll give you all the details on how it was done as soon as I have them. Meanwhile, you should know that my man Yegorov photographed your lunch with de la Maison and the shots were doctored in Moscow Center. That was part of the disinformation package."

"Luckily, de la Maison figured it out and convinced SSR it was a fake. What does that mean for Ossilenko?"

"Certainly not a commendation, Mark. It may be a problem to him even though he's the chairman's cousin. When disinformation operations start going wrong, the author has to pay a penalty. In this case, I suspect he'll only be chewed out and they'll let him make up for it by making Red Snow Two work. But now that I'm working with you, we can make Ossilenko look like a cretin and ruin his career."

"Or if your theory is right and we might eventually work him into such a state that we can defect him, we should be careful how much we damage him first, and in what way. What do you think?"

"Why not try? The damnedest patriots have defected before." He laughed. "You just got me."

"Whichever way it goes, we both owe that bastard one, so let's get even."

Gitabwanga: Bwaga Airport—0700 hours, 8 February

"Welcome home, my darling." Linda was there to meet Mark, her face rosy in the early light, golden hair ruffled by the cool morning breeze, body hard against his.

He whispered in her ear, "Will you marry me, my love? I'm rehabilitated now. No need to be ashamed of me any more."

"Silly man, I've never been ashamed of you. And you never needed rehabilitating. I love you, and yes, by all means I'll marry you."

Georgetown, D.C.: a Catholic church—2317 hours, 25 February

Sam Wayne had been tickled by the irony of it when Boris Kuznetsov had selected a Catholic church as one of their meeting sites. It was actually quite a good site. It was dark inside, even in daytime. At night it was difficult to distinguish the features of people ten feet away.

The church was open twenty-four hours a day and almost certain to be deserted shortly before midnight. The pews were arranged so that small objects could be left in a book rack, picked up by Boris without physically being near him. Or they could sit, one diagonally in front of the other, heads bowed, whispers unheard over the faint hiss of traffic outside.

They had met here once before, a year ago, disguised. Sam had crowed to Boris about how they were using an asset—a symbol—of the opiate of the people to advance the cause of atheism. There had been nobody else in the church, and Sam had explained the architecture, the stained glass, candles, pews, altar, and organ pipes to his stolid conductor, larding his explanations with cynical comments about the place. Surprisingly, Boris had been quite interested, staring up at the massive pillars that disappeared into the darkness overhead, the windows showing their colors against the dim lights outside, the sinister-looking confessionals, and the great brass cross that dominated the altar.

Tonight, however, Sam was in no mood to revisit irony. He hated his agreement with the CIA to be its double. He hated Boris for being their man, for his treachery, which had revealed his own. He hated it that neither could admit it to the other. It was bitterly cold, and he hated the cold. He had always hated the Agency, and now he'd come to hate the KGB, recently personified by Colonel Petrov—"that despicable man with the morals of a stoat." He hated having to lie to Sonya for the first time. She had been the only person he had never lied to since he was a very small boy. She'd sensed something was wrong and she'd badgered him about it, and he'd hated that, too.

On his way to the church, Sam had suddenly realized that he was full of hateful anger, but above all he hated himself. That last insight had almost choked him with its portent.

Boris was precisely on time, his grin seeming not to be friendly but inane and treacherous. They sat together, and before any words passed, Sam—trembling all over—pulled out a revolver. Boris started back, his eyes blinking rapidly with surprise and alarm.

Sam stared at Boris, raised the muzzle of the gun and, without a word, pulled the trigger. The single explosion echoed off the walls and stone floor of the old church.

Gitabwanga: Mark's house—2230 hours, 26 February

"I've news for you," said Pyotr. He had dined with Mark and Linda, and now M'Pishi had gone home. "That SOB Ossilenko has decided he's an expert on Bwagania. He's going to come back quite often, he told me, to see that things are just the way he would want them. He's playing into our hands."

"Let's drink to that," said Mark. "To the rapid and complete Pyotrification of Ossilenko!"

"Oh no," said Pyotr as Linda winced and stuck out her tongue at Mark. They toasted the idea anyway.

"Now," said Mark. "We've learned something that will interest you."

"What's that?" asked Pyotr.

"What is the greatest gift you could receive just now?"

"Anna Iosevna back in my arms, free of Ossilenko."

"The second greatest?"

"That Sam Wayne will disappear."

"How would he do that?"

"An accident. I suggested that. You're thinking of it?"

"No. What sort of an accident would you think of?"

"He chokes on a fish bone?"

"Better?"

"A snakebite, and he dies in agony?"

"No, Pyotr. He wanted his good friend Boris to share the moment. He committed suicide yesterday, in—of all things—a Georgetown church, during an operational meeting with Boris."

"I'll be damned," exclaimed Pyotr. "There is, after all, a God."

Glossary

Access agent An agent used primarily to gain access to a target; for example, a Bwaganian national recruited for the purpose of exploiting his access to a KGB officer.

Accommodation address An address to which mail is sent to be held for, or forwarded to, a third party. An accommodation address may be provided by a person unwitting of the real nature of its function, or it may be provided by a witting asset. An *accommodation number* is a telephone number belonging to an apparently uninvolved party. Messages from a KGB officer are, for example, taken by that party (or an answering machine) and relayed to his agent.

ADDO Assistant deputy director for operations. He is also deputy chief of the U.S. Clandestine Services.

Agent A person peforming tasks or otherwise working under the control of an intelligence or security organization, usually clandestinely and outside the organization's official offices. There are all sorts of agents, such as staff agents, career agents, contract agents, support agents, disinformation agents, sleeper agents, and of course the good old reliable information agents.

Aka Also known as. For example if James Smith uses the alias John Doe, the record would show: James Smith, aka John Doe.

Assessment In espionage, the word *assessment* takes on a special meaning. It refers to the process of evaluating or assessing the character—including motivation, honesty, value, and recruitability—of a potential agent.

Asset A person whom an intelligence service can count on to peform specific tasks. An asset can be anything from a fully recruited agent to a casual informant. The term is sometimes used loosely to refer to inanimate objects the service can count on, such as safehouses, listening posts, and so on.

Audio installation A single bug or set of microphones installed secretly in a target room or rooms, connected to a hostile listening post by radio or wires. It can be either permanent or temporary.

Audio take The product of an audio operation such as a hidden microphone. The take is usually in the form of audio tapes. It is sometimes in the form of movie or video coverage.

Audio technician A technician specializing in setting up audio installations. Such technicians often work under hazardous and difficult conditions, inside hostile target buildings or apartments.

Bio Biographical information.

Bird The target of a surveillance operation.

Brass May refer to spent cartridges or shells, or to senior officers. Leaving brass at the site where a gun has been fired tells trained observers how many rounds of what caliber have been used by what kind of weapon, and can lead to identification of the particular weapon.

Brief A request for intelligence from one office to another. See also Requirement.

Brush contact Contact, usually between a case officer and his agent, that involves passing documents, words, or objects during the brief time when the two brush past each other. Successful brush contacts must occur on the basis of two preset watches that are completely accurate, or some outside signal such as the chimes of a church clock.

Bug A hidden microphone used in an audio installation.

CA See Covert action.

Cable traffic The flow of cables to and from an installation. For example, a field case officer may remark that "there's been a lot of cable traffic from HQS today."

Carbon A chemically inpregnated sheet of paper that is positioned on top of a seemingly innocuous letter. When the writer lightly pencils his secret message, the slight pressure on the carbon deposits an invisible message on the underlying letter. That message can be made visible only if it is developed with the right substance.

Chef de poste French term for chief of station.

CI/CE Counterintelligence and counterespionage.

Clear text The uncoded text of a message.

C/O Case officer: an intelligence officer assigned to run cases. In headquarters he or she may simply handle the paperwork for a case. In the field, a case officer spots, assesses, develops, and recruits agents and then trains and runs them. Running agents includes securely meeting, briefing, and motivating them, directing and receiving their reporting, and sending it on.

COB CIA chief of base. See COS below.

Cold pitch A recruitment pitch made without previous development of (perhaps even without previous contact with) the target.

COMINT Communications intelligence: efforts to read another organization's encoded communications.

Comintern The Third or Communist International, formed in 1919 by Lenin and Trotsky as the international recruiting and propaganda organ of the Soviet Communist Party. It was officially abolished by Stalin in 1943, although Moscow continues to perform its functions. The "First International" was Karl Marx's 1864 London meeting of the International Workingmen's Association; the second was the 1889 Social Democratic Second International in Paris. Trotsky's Fourth International has lasted from 1930 until today as a faction bitterly and actively hostile to Stalin and his successors. With Trotsky's rehabilitation now in its initial phase, the remnants of his faction may lose some of their incentive.

Commo Communications, usually categorized as staff communications (communications between headquarters and field posts, for example) or agent communications (communications between a service and its agents).

Compromised Describes an agent or an activity that has become known to, and perhaps come under the control of, an unauthorized or hostile service.

COS The most common abbreviation for the CIA chief of station in any country. The station is usually in the capital city and the COS is known by that city, not the country (e.g., COS Gitabwanga, not COS Bwagania). In larger countries there may be CIA bases (each with a COB, or chief of base) in cities other than the capital. The COB also takes the name of the city, not the country (e.g., COB Palladia).

Country team The section heads in a U.S. embassy whose functions directly support the ambassador's substantive responsibilities. The country team usually includes the Deputy Chief of Mission (DCM), the heads of the political, economic, and commercial sections, the senior military attaché, the CIA station chief, the U.S. Information Service (USIS) and Agency for International Development (AID) chiefs, and the chief administrative officer.

Cover Physical, documentary, or oral means of misrepresenting the sponsor of a person, organization, or operation. Thus, a CIA building may be disguised as a Department of Defense building; a KGB officer may assume the cover of an Austrian businessman; a GRU operation may be conducted as if it were a commercial business unconnected with espionage. The use of cover is almost synonymous with clandestine activity.

Covert action (CA) Any clandestine activity (as distinct from the gathering of intelligence or CI/CE information) undertaken to influence events or people, when the sponsoring service and usually its government are deliberately either not identified or misidentified.

CP Command post.

CPSU Communist Party of the Soviet Union.

Cryptonym Code name given to an asset such as an agent, a safehouse, or an entire operation. A cryptonym differs from a pseudonym or an alias in that it is usually not a full name (such as John P. Doe); it is more likely to be a single word that doesn't necessarily make sense (such as EBTPATSY).

CS U.S. Clandestine Services: the covert personnel and organs within the CIA Directorate of Operations.

Cutout A person, address, or telephone used to break the line of communications between an agent and his or her sponsors. An accommodation address is a cutout. So is a telephone (perhaps unmanned) that accepts a message and retransmits it to another party.

Danger signal Any sign that warns an agent or his case officer that a meeting, or the servicing of a drop, must be aborted—usually because the agent or the drop has been compromised.

DCI The director of central intelligence.

DDO The CIA's deputy director of operations, who is also chief of the U.S. Clandestine Services.

Deep cover Nonofficial cover (such as business, academic, media, or student cover), in contrast to official cover (such as cover using diplomatic, consular or military activities operated openly by a government).

Defection in place Defecting (or being recruited) but remaining in place for a specific or unspecified period of time. A KGB officer who defects in place will remain in the KGB, not appearing to have defected, until he has met his commitment to the service that recruited him or it is no longer safe to stay in place.

Developmental A potential agent or other asset being developed (and usually assessed) prior to recruitment or employment.

Dial recorder An automatic device used to identify and record the phone numbers dialed out by a telephone that is bugged. Dial recorders are usually located in an LP, beside the tape recorders that log and record a target's phone conversations.

Disinformation False or misleading intelligence fed by one service to another.

Double agent An agent or subagent who has been turned around and now works for another service against his former one; usually referred to as "a double" by case officers.

Doubling The act of conversion of an agent into a double secretly working against his apparent, unwitting sponsor.

Drop A person, place, vehicle, or other means by which an object (reports, materials, and so on, usually in a container or envelope) can be securely conveyed between agents and/or their sponsors. In a *live drop,* the act of movement conceals and effects the transmission of the object; an example is a magnetic limpet containing reports, stuck to the underside of a car. The person who put it there and the one who removes it may be in different countries, and the driver may not know he or she has conveyed the reports. A *dead drop* is usually a concealment in which one person stores a package for later recovery by another. A hole in a tree is a simple example of a dead drop.

ELINT Electronic intelligence.

Entry team A team, usually made up of technicians and field case officers, that enters a target installation, surreptitiously or in disguise, in order to case it or to make a clandestine audio or photographic installation.

Fabricator An asset who fabricates or makes up his reports, usually because he lacks the access he claims to have. A fabricator normally works on his own behalf, often claiming to be affiliated with another service or a dissident organization.

False flag A recruitment attempt in which the pitch appears to have been made by a sponsor other than the real one. An example is a KGB recruitment in which the KGB recruiter represents himself as working for the CIA.

FCP The French Communist Party.

FNU First name unknown.

Fourth International The Trotskyite communist international organization, still active today.

FYI For your information.

Garble A garbled or unintelligible word or passage in a cable.

GRU Glavnoye Razvedyvatelnoye Upravlenie: The Soviet military intelligence organization.

HC "Honorable correspondent," a French term for person—not a paid agent—who provides intelligence, voluntarily or for money, but is usually controlled only through his or her loyalty to France.

HQS Headquarters.

Hrs. Hours. Field case officers using a twenty-four-hour clock will, for example, write midnight as "2400 hrs."

HUMINT A somewhat ungracious abbreviation for intelligence acquired through the use of human assets.

IA Intelligence assistant: the title of a CIA employee who is senior to a secretary, but junior to a case officer.

Illegal A term used by the KGB to denote a staff employee of the KGB who serves overseas under deep cover, usually for a long period and posing as a citizen of a country other than the USSR.

Intel Intelligence. The two main categories are *positive* or *foreign intelligence* (information about another country's economic problems, for example) and *operational intelligence* (information about another service or a protective system or country conditions that allows you to operate in that milieu and so acquire positive intelligence or conduct covert action).

KGB Komitet Gosudarstvennoy Bezopasnosti: the Soviet Committee for State Security. The KGB is the successor to the various Soviet state security organs that began with Felix Dzerzhinsky's infamous, bloodthirsty Cheka in 1917.

Legend A cover story: a biography invented to cover an agent or case officer so that he or she appears to be someone else. A legend must be backed up by appropriate documents, such as passport, identity card, driver's license, snapshots of loved ones, letters, the right laundry labels, and *pocket litter* (bus or theater tickets, for example) supporting the legend.

LNU Last name unknown.

Lock and pick tech A technician specializing in picking locks. Such a tech often accompanies an audio-installation entry team.

LP Listening post: a safe area used to accept and tape signals from a bugged area or device. An LP can be a vehicle or a room in a building. In one famous case, the Berlin Tunnel was dug to hide extensive listening equipment.

Make To identify a hostile activity or agent. A "bird" who spots a tail following him or her has made the surveillant.

Mattress mice A pejorative term used by field case officers to describe headquarters types who try to protect their jobs by inventing unnecessary bureaucracy. Parkinson's Law is the operative form for mattress mice. They can destroy an operation by nibbling at it from underneath. They usually have no concept of the damage they cause, since their only goal is "honorable" retirement.

Mole A penetration agent working for a hostile sponsor inside an unwitting intelligence service.

NMI No middle initial. An index card referring to an unknown agent in one operation read "LNU/FNU/NMI."

OP Observation post: a safe position from which to observe someone or something, whether or not photography is used.

OPS Operations. Most field personnel use this abbreviation.

PCS Permanent change of station: official reassignment of personnel from one station to another or posting for a tour of duty (usually two or three years).

Penetration A person who is employed by one service while secretly working for another service. A mole and double agents are examples of penetrations. A penetration operation employs one or more agents as penetrations.

Piston agent An agent or subagent who switches loyalty, usually for financial reasons, from one service to another and back again. An example is pistoning between the CIA and the KGB.

Pitch A recruitment spiel. Often a case officer will refer to "making the pitch" when discussing a recruitment attempt. The pitch is usually discussed in detail beforehand, often with prior concurrence of the service's head office. The pitch is the actual act of asking a person to become an asset of a service or organization.

PNG Persona non grata: a person expelled from a foreign country. A KGB officer found to be engaged in espionage activities while under diplomatic cover in New York, for example, could be declared PNG by the U.S. government. Alternatives to PNG would be to let the agent continue his or her activities while under covert surveillance, or to try to recruit the agent to stay in place and work for the United States.

Poly Polygraph or lie detector. Most case officers believe that persons can be conditioned to beat the poly. Compulsive or pathological liars are usually able to beat it.

Poste The French term for an overseas or foreign station.

Pseudonym An alias issued by the head office of a service to refer discreetly to an agent or contact. Case officers often refer to their agents only by pseudonym.

Requirement A request for intelligence information from one office to an individual or another office.

Rezident The KGB chief in a country, equivalent to the CIA station chief or the British SIS station commander.

Rezidentura A KGB station or post, usually in a foreign country.

Safehouse A house, apartment, or area controlled by a service or its assets, where secure operational activities can take place.

SIS The British Secret Intelligence Service.

Smoker A fabricator, perhaps better known in the trade as a BS artist. He blows up smoke, not facts.

Spotter A person who spots likely agents or assets. The process of recruiting an agent usually begins with spotting. The sequence is often this: spot, assess, develop, clear (get HQS approval), recruit, train, manage (exploit), motivate (a continuing process), turn over (to another officer when one goes home), and eventually terminate the relationship when the agent is no longer useful or is unable to function.

Staffer An officer or agent who is employed on the staff of a service, as opposed to a contract agent, for example. Thus a *staff agent* is a staff officer under nonofficial cover, whereas a *contract agent* is an independent contractor also under nonofficial cover. A *contract employee* is an independent contractor who works under official cover, usually in an office supervised by staffers.

Stakeout A person or persons who watch another person or a place, usually trying not to be seen doing so. A stakeout is often posted as a guard to give warning.

Surveillant Someone covertly watching another person or installation, whether from a fixed location such as an apartment (*fixed surveillance*) or on foot or from a vehicle (*mobile surveillance*).

SW Secret writing.

Switchable bug A microphone or set of microphones that can be switched on or off from a remote location. A switchable bug may have, for example, one hundred hours of active transmitting time in its batteries, and as much as three thousand hours of active listening time (waiting to be turned on).

Tail A surveillant engaged in following a "bird" or target on foot or in a vehicle.

Take The product of a technical or human intelligence or counterintelligence operation.

Tap A telephone tap.

Target A person, activity, or installation that is the object of a surveillance, recruitment, or other operational effort.

TDY Temporary duty: usually a short official visit to a location far enough away from the traveler's normal duty station to require a hotel or temporary housing.

Trace Biographical information about a person. A case officer usually requests traces from his home office or other field stations on all the contacts he makes. Traces are often called name traces.

"Heavens!" I exclaimed. "That the time?" I left them beaming at each other. A hit!

Exit Lovejoy. I'd keep his loan, my fee for effecting a lonely hearts intro. Fair's fair.

The street was abuzz with police. I watched from the corner among a small crowd. The factory was being boarded up. Cloaked folk stood gazing.

"It's no victory," somebody said close to my elbow.

"I know," I said.

"It will simply move on, Lovejoy. More legions of slave children, different guises."

"I know that, too."

"Mrs. Sweet tells me there were five in Great Britain."

"And the rest." I always sound bitter, wish I knew why. I do try to sound lighthearted and chirpy. I've never yet seen me smile in a photo. I wonder what it is.

"They are introducing legislation—"

"Shut it, love." When law steps in, truth flies out the window.

I watched as the police loaded up the furniture, much partly completed, some hardly started.

"What will you do, Lovejoy? Now Katta and Mr. Chave have got engaged?"

That made me turn and look. She tried to give me a hankie, silly cow. You can always trust a woman to be stupid. "I've already got one, ta. Engaged?" I thought she meant hired.

"To be married, Lovejoy." She was near to a smile. "Katta asked me to give you this."

Hotel notepaper.

Dear Lovejoy,

Timeo Danaos et dona ferentes! My betrothed and I shall expect you at our wedding. Do bring a guest, darling.

Love from your new neighbor,
Katta

What had happened to the accent? That's women for you. Me and Lysette strolled off. No good checking on the police now they'd finally got weaving.

"Mrs. Sweet wishes to see you, Lovejoy, tonight. She'll call at your hotel."

"She does?"

"It will take several sessions, I think, from the way she spoke. She has a massive inventory of antiques she wants you to check, before Miss Chevalier arrives tomorrow."

"Miss who?"

"Miss Chevalier. Monsieur Pascal told me there's a way to reduce the criminal charges against you, if you cooperate with the authorities—here, Switzerland, Great Britain."

"Meaning cooperate with Lorela Chevalier?" I'd saved her firm, her reputation, her antiques, her job. . . . She'd tried to phone me at the hotel a thousand times. I'd finally left the receiver off the hook while Katta—er, swallowed my pride.

"I think so, Lovejoy. And Mercy Mallock will be with you soon. She faxed the hotel."

"Mercy?" I brightened. "What's she say?"

"Her letter is too long, too personal, and impertinently presumptuous. You must have nothing more to do with her."

We turned into the street gale, par for Paris. This was starting to look sour. I mean, Katta'd served, as it were, her purpose in detoxifying my soul with her unique brand of adventurous love. But Lilian Sweet was a different proposition. Back in East Anglia I'd not last an hour if word got about that a SAPAR hunter had decided to cottage up with me. And Lilian had proved her determination more than somewhat. I'd not shake her off in a trice.

Lorela Chevalier, on the other hand, had definite possibilities. Lovely, attractive, feminine as a flower. But with the giant responsibility of her great Repository? And willing to offer heaven-knows-what for me to replace old Leon? To live with the glorious Lorela, in utter affluence, comfort, warmth, wealth, surrounded by the densest collection of perfect antiques the world could assemble? I'd die of ecstasy in a week.

No paradise for the likes of me.

"Are you going to the hotel, Lovejoy?" I'd stopped at the square where me and Gobbie'd met. And Lysette.

"Well, aye." I felt uncomfortable. I'd nearly said I'd nowhere else to go.

"Miss Danglass is waiting there, Lovejoy." Lysette was standing close. The wind whipped our coats about us.

"Jodie Danglass?"

"Yes. She's been waiting awhile. She said she has urgent offers from a Big John Sheehan, about some glass replicas he wants you to market for him. He's asking after some Carolean mica playing cards he bought from a young widow. It's rather complex, Lovejoy." Sherry Bavington, the bitch. She must have come calling, nicked the micas from my ever-open cottage. I'd strangle the thieving cow, after I got a lock for the door.

"Aye, it would be complex all right." With Big John Sheehan it was never easy, cheap, or straightforward. Sending Jodie to France was his way of saying to the trade that he had nothing to do with the child labor—not that anybody'd ever believe he had. "She mention which? The Portland vases?"

Lysette's eyes were pure, that ultra blue you get in Greek paintings.

"Lovejoy. I don't think you should become involved in something new, not just yet. Not with Monsieur Pascal's team still investigating." Pause. "Do you?"

"No," I tried, cleared my throat. "No," I said, firmer.

"Darling, I have an idea." She smoothed my lapel. I hardly felt her hand. "Paris can become rather crowded. Would you like to stay somewhere else? Only for a short while, not too long."

"Stay?"

"Yes. Rest, read, have time to visit interesting museums." She smiled, quite casual. The wind swooshed her hair across her face. She scraped it aside with a reproving tut. "Some antique shops aren't quite played out. That sort of thing."

"What about Pascal and Lilian, the rest?"

"Need we tell them where we were going, darling? I think not."

"We'd never make it."

She smiled. "Oh, yes we would, Lovejoy."

"You're not an antiques hunter too?" It was a joke but came out despairing. What had I thought, those epochs ago? That too many people were paid but loving eyes.

"Not yet." Her reply started out serious, emerged as a joke. I felt her smile.

"Let me think." I stood there. She slipped her arm into mine, and we sat on the curved bench beneath the tree. "Hang on," I said. She'd put her arm round my shoulders, pulled my head gently down onto her shoulder. It was the wrong way round. I'm the masterful all-caring protective provider. She was the weaker vessel. "If Jodie Danglass is here from home, and Lorela Chevalier is offering—"

"Shhh," she went. Her fingertips pressed my cheek, turning me to her. She touched her mouth on mine, very soft.

Applause sounded. The cafe windows were crowded, grinning faces and salutations everywhere. She broke away, scarlet.

"Look," I said. "How about we try that, then? Might as well, eh?"

Took me less than ten minutes to talk her into it. One thing, I'd not lost the knack of persuasion.